Nb

0.95

Wind of Change at Castle Rising

By the same author:

Shadows Over Castle Rising
War Comes to Castle Rising
The Lormes of Castle Rising

Wind of Change at Castle Rising

FANNY CRADOCK

E. P. Dutton   New York

First American edition published 1979 by
E. P. Dutton, a Division of Elsevier-Dutton
Publishing Co., Inc., New York

For information contact: E.P. Dutton, 2 Park Avenue,
New York, N.Y. 10016

Library of Congress Catalog Card Number: 79-54780
ISBN: 0-525-23468-3

10 9 8 7 6 5 4 3 2 1

To Alison with Love

Contents

The Family from 1907, descending

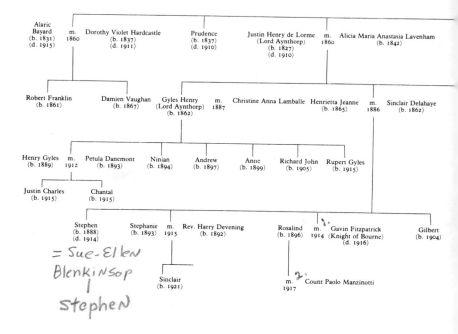

= Sue-Ellen
Blenkinsop
|
Stephen

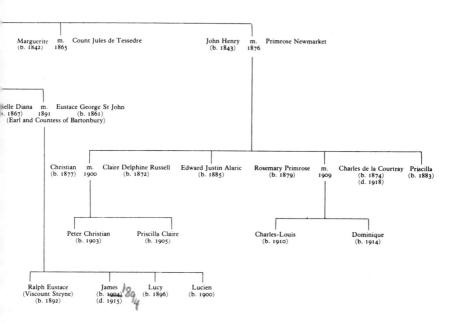

Marguerite   m.   Count Jules de Tessedre
(b. 1842)   1865

John Henry   m.   Primrose Newmarket
(b. 1843)   1876

ielle Diana   m.   Eustace George St John
». 1867)   1891   (b. 1861)
(Earl and Countess of Bartonbury)

Christian   m.   Claire Delphine Russell
(b. 1877)   1900   (b. 1872)

Edward Justin Alaric
(b. 1885)

Rosemary Primrose   m.   Charles de la Courtray   Priscilla
(b. 1879)   1909   (b. 1874)   (b. 1883)
                          (d. 1918)

Peter Christian
(b. 1903)

Priscilla Claire
(b. 1905)

Charles-Louis
(b. 1910)

Dominique
(b. 1914)

Ralph Eustace
(Viscount Steyne)
(b. 1892)

James
(b. 1904)
(d. 1915)

Lucy
(b. 1896)

Lucien
(b. 1900)

Author's Foreword

I began Book 1 in 1966. The name I gave to the Lorme castle just walked into my mind. I wrote just over 25,000 words and then set it aside owing to other commitments.

Many months later our friend Miss Alison Leach, who had been our personal assistant for many years, came down to see us and announced, 'I suppose you know there *is* a Castle Rising in Norfolk!' She showed us a little guide book which she had found in which it was mentioned. We subsequently discovered it marked on a modern map, just above North Wootton and a few miles from King's Lynn; but as it is no longer inhabited and is, in fact, a ruin, I decided to retain the name since it had by now become inseparable from my thinking on this book. In the original MS I had sited my Castle Rising on the edge of the Blakeney Marshes because of the Viking Funeral.[1] The original Castle Rising then turned out to be only twenty-six miles from Blakeney!

When I resumed work on Book 1 in the winter of 1972–3 I decided to help myself to my own family history from 1064 in Normandy to the 1800s in England. By then I was in possession of some ancient family data which took me into Essex on numerous explorations which were relevant to records showing that a certain Sir Gilbert de Pêche, Bart. – a Norman – settled in this country in the eleventh century. The records stated 'Pêche was the name of a considerable family who owned many manors hereabouts'. So I resited my Castle Rising on an eminence above one of these.

I then discovered that the dictionary definition of *péché* is 'sin, trespass, transgression'; if, however, this is made plural – *les péchés capitaux* – it becomes in translation 'the deadly sins'. Small wonder then that Sir Gilbert de Pêche is

[1] See Book 1, *The Lormes of Castle Rising*.

recorded as 'sometimes called *"Peccatum"* meaning sin in abstract "for he was a verie naughtie fellowe"'!

This settled for me – as any reader who fights his way through these books will appreciate – that from then onwards I would plagiarise certain aspects of my own family for certain Lorme characteristics. Later I gave the Lormes the Pêche crest, an astrolabe,[2] and the arms of our Norman ancestor Sir Gilbert. In fact, the earlier Lorme 'runts' are Pêche 'runts'; but those who come after the 1800s are entirely my own creation and bear no relation whatsoever to any person or persons either living or dead.

FANNY CRADOCK

[2] An old instrument for taking altitudes.

CHAPTER I

An Addition to the Family

The reactions to Sawby's announcement were so slight that even he was shocked. He was, despite his experience, quite unable to understand that they were all beyond registering any more emotions after what they had just endured over the birth of Petula's twins and the death of their pompous and gargantuan Bishop Alaric.

Sawby had opened the doors of the Blue Drawing Room with the utmost reluctance. Once inside he stood waiting miserably for Christine to observe him. Eventually,

'Yes Sawby?' she enquired.

The man heard himself saying mechanically, 'There are callers, my lady.'

'Oh not today!' she exclaimed. 'For us?'

'No my lady,' even to himself Sawby's voice sounded wooden, 'they asked for his lordship, my lady.'

Before Gyles could respond Priscilla's almost shrill expostulation jarred out, 'Who in the world would call today of all days!' It jolted them from a fragment of their apathy while the butler experienced the curious sensation of being two people, one speaking and one listening in acute discomfort.

'I think they are newly arrived from abroad, Miss,' he answered Priscilla, adding with a slight turn of his body towards Gyles, 'They wish to see you my lord. I have shown them into the Library.'

'Well who the devil are they?' Gyles' dormant irritation flared.

Again Sawby took and observed himself taking one deep breath. Then the explanation emerged.

'They are, my lord,' he managed, wondering why his lips both looked and felt so stiff, 'A Mr Silas Blenkinsop and his daughter my lord whom the gentleman named as Mrs Stephen Delahaye.'

Henrietta Delahaye's hands soared and clasped together like trembling butterflies. 'Oh Sinclair,' she breathed moving the butterflies shakingly towards her husband's shoulders.

The Dowager, predictably, merely exclaimed, '*Tiens!*' which forced from the little Countess Marguerite a sound midway between a chuckle and a snort. The rest froze in their seats as though Sawby had held Medusa's head out for them to look upon.

The head of the family removed his monocle, drew a handkerchief from his sleeve, polished assiduously, replaced both monocle and handkerchief, the while maintaining an awesome silence. The eyes of the family were like those of hungry terriers awaiting sustenance as they watched.

'I ... see,' Gyles said softly and inaccurately, temper soaring. 'Well then what the devil are you waiting for man? Show them in immediately and announce them to us, go man go. Since when have you kept members of my family waiting in the Library?'

The little Countess and the Dowager exchanged glances. A glint sparked in the eyes of both these two 'Old Naughties' as, like hounds reacting to the huntsman's horn they metaphorically feathered their tails, picking up the unmistakable scent of excitement and intrigue on which they perennially depended as the breath of life to the pair of them. This time the Dowager said very softly '*Merde alors*' which no one thought she knew. She added to Lady Constance at her side, 'So it all begins again. Have I not always prophesied we had not heard the last of Stephen? Ehu! might this not be the prelude to *damnosa hereditas* once again?'

Came the little Countess's muted whisper, 'Do you suppose she really is his widow or his *irrégulière*, Alicia?'

Constance rose with a hasty, 'Not now my darlings,' then glancing at Christine she murmured, 'If you will excuse me, I really should...' But Gyles' raised hand stayed her.

'Please stay Constance,' his voice had a rasp to it which was unfamiliar. 'After so much this is only one more example of this Family's capacity to pile Pelion upon Ossa.'

Constance nodded slightly, obeyed and – 'Mrs Stephen Delahaye,' said Sawby from the opened doors. 'Mr Silas Blenkinsop.'[1]

The men rose. The women remained seated. In the doorway stood two very nervous people, one a fair young girl,

[1] See Book 3, *War Comes to Castle Rising*.

simply but perfectly turned out and swathed in sables, her hands in a sable muff, a wide hat sweeping up from a face which every woman in the room realised was as lovely as any of theirs now or in the fading past. The other, the Dowager, blinked for an instant, *was* the incarnation of Mr Samuel Pickwick dressed by Savile Row and wearing wide-rimmed glasses. Said he in a strong American accent, 'I really do apologise for this unwarranted intrusion....' One hand stroked the Pickwickian stomach as if to reassure himself, 'I had thought this might be the better way, but now I am filled with doubts. May I please present my little girl?' He pronounced it 'gurrl' then added, 'and might I please be informed as to whom I have the honour to address?'

Sawby vanished unnoticed.

Gyles stepped forward, hand outstretched. 'I am Gyles Aynthorp,' he introduced himself. 'Let me present you to my mother the Dowager, my Aunt the Countess Tessedre ...' Gyles continued formally, painfully around the entire gathering while the little 'gurrl' with a smile fixed resolutely, let her eyes roam around until she saw the stick beside Sinclair and Henrietta with those fluttering hands clasped but tremulous. Then control snapped and she was across the Aubusson and beside her mother-in-law, the sweeping hat snatched off and thrown down, her curly head between Henrietta's arms as, 'Oh my dear, such a shock ... so welcome though ... you are so lovely.... why did Stephen never tell...?'

The room heard her answer, 'We never told Daddy either...'

The father stood sturdy in his correct clothes, foursquare and bowing; Mr Pickwick in solemn mood, ceremonious, out of his depth; but holding himself together despite the, to him, alien and lofty company.

Once the catalogue had been read Silas Blenkinsop moved and began, 'Honoured to meet you ma'am,' bending over his generous stomach, kissing above hands and not contacting them which every woman observed with growing approval.

Christine's eyes warmed to him, accepting, 'Here is no confidence trickster. This is authentic, honest, even if unfamiliar,' her mind adding like a silent wail *'oh that dreadful boy!'* meaning of course the dead Stephen.

Beside her stood Henry who shook hands when his turn came, and when the sturdy American had completed the round Gyles heard his wife saying in her soft voice, 'This must have called for a great deal of courage Mr Blenkinsop but pray why have you left it so long? I must suppose you realise that we know nothing...'

The 'gurrl' now sat with one hand in Sinclair's, the other in Henrietta's, looking from one to the other with brimming eyes.

'Well now,' her father replied slowly, 'that is what needs a very great deal of explanation.'

The few trite words and the girl's instinctive gesture had already stilled any doubts that these were Stephen Delahaye's unknown widow and her father come to introduce themselves.

The Dowager spoke. 'Gyles my dear,' she said, her voice bland but revealing to the initiated that she was already scheming, 'pray pull the bell since you are nearest. I feel sure Mr Blenkinson and er...' she hesitated deliberately for the 'gurrl' to supply 'Sue-Ellen ma'am if you please.'

The superbly coiffed white head inclined graciously, 'And Sue-Ellen – thank you my dear – must surely be in need of some refreshment.'

Suddenly speech erupted among them. When Sawby came in he absorbed the changed atmospherc as if he were one of those pieces of blotting paper which he ensured were inserted daily in the blotters of every guest room, boudoir and dressing room. He noted the sudden warmth in the atmosphere as he took the order for, 'Fresh tea please Sawby,' from Christine 'and Mr Blenkinsop would like a whisky and soda.'

The doors closed on the butler who was seeking to frame his description of the change to his wife Pansy – Appleby to the staff – belowstairs. He decided on 'social thaw set in' while behind the closed doors...

'Well now,' Mr Blenkinsop was saying slowly, 'I won't deny to your ladyship that such would be very welcome but,' his brow creased. 'Is it the thing at this time of day in the presence of ladies I would like to know?'

'Quite the thing I do assure you,' said Gyles smilingly. He was unbending fast. Nor did he fail to observe with pleasure how naturally the American switched himself over to small talk while the footwomen brought in the tea equipage and tray with tantalus and pony glasses saying with a semblance of perfect ease, and only sweating slightly, 'Young Stephen talked once about your Castle but I never imagined such magnificence, it must be the finest Castle in all Britain.'

For the first time they flinched at the distasteful use of the word 'Britain', anathema to English, Scots and Welsh alike and only used across what Mr Blenkinsop would later call 'the herring pond'. Making a mental note to prime Sue-Ellen, Henry smiled with approval and encouragement as he sat silently fascinated by this 'top-hole old boy' whom he decided had 'bags of guts' and was a 'sterling feller' as with the girl, a 'peach' whom he felt assured would 'hit it off absolutely with my Petula'.

Gyles was saying smoothly, 'It is by no means the finest I can assure you, nor indeed the largest, or the most famous though I cannot deny it is the oldest of them all. You must see Herstmonceux ... Castle Howard in Yorkshire ... the Royal Castles ... perhaps I may have the pleasure of showin' some of them to you and, er, Sue-Ellen.'

'Well now,' Silas Blenkinsop said regretfully, 'I guess such a pleasure will have to wait a while, although I am conscious of the honour you do me. You see I am a man of business. I manufacture aeroplanes. I also am strongly inclined to the view that old Uncle Sam will be joining in this terrible war before very long, which makes my aeroplanes mightily important business. Right now I have deliveries to make to the Old Country.' He broke off to accept the whisky, remained silent concerning the absence of ice, just held the glass untasted until the doors closed behind the servants. Then raising it slightly he said going rather red in the face, 'Thank you for receiving me and my little gurrl so kindly. Now, if you will permit me I will endeavour to give you a satisfactory explanation.'

Belowstairs the servants fretted and speculated until Sawby withdrew the seniors to the Steward's Room and sent the rest scurrying about their business, indicating with a nod that Mrs Parsons the cook, Monsieur André the chef, Pansy his wife and Mrs Pearce the housekeeper withdraw with him. Behind closed doors he then divulged both what he knew and what he conjectured while above stairs in the drawing room the Family and the two startling visitors remained closeted for an extremely long time while, quietly, and without any visible emotion in his strong unfamiliar speaking voice Silas Blenkinsop explained himself, his daughter and his situation.

When his tale was told and the Family had done what they could to assimilate and at least digest in part the startling facts, Gyles promptly invited Sue-Ellen and her father to stay with them but Mr Blenkinsop would not hear of it.

'You have been very kind,' he told them resolutely, 'and you have taught me that your British self-control is not a legend after all. Even so, no man in his wits would foist two strangers on such a family as yours when there is a bereavement, as you so generously brought yourselves to explain to me. We have no business here at this time. My car is outside. My chauffeur will carry us back to Claridges within two hours. There we shall stay, if you will kindly overlook my blundering way of putting it, until your obsequies are ended and you have had time to digest all that you have been told.'

Both slightly dazed and considerably impressed they all urged him unsuccessfully. He remained adamant, his eyes flickering from Christine, to the Dowager, to the tiny Marguerite, to Henrietta Delahaye. 'Sue-Ellen and I have a morsel or two to digest ourselves ma'am,' a smile creased his round face expansively. 'You are a mighty powerful family to have come upon so suddenly. If we take our leave now we will gladly come back when you are ready for us. I reckon on being here for a month anyway for I do not have a berth before that and therefore we will stay at Claridges where I have no doubt we can fill our time with sightseeing and then come back to you in better shape.'

He would not be persuaded. In short, he dominated the entire episode while his Sue-Ellen sat between her in-laws chattering happily about her baby, Stephen's posthumous son; but at one penetrating glance from her father she was on her feet at once as Christine took the floor.

She crossed to the girl, took both her hands and said, 'From now onwards my dear you must think of this as your home and we as the other side of yours and your son's family. Will you now please tell us if he has been christened?'

Sue-Ellen nodded, finding speech difficult, then she managed, 'He was christened Stephen, Sinclair, Gyles, I hope Lord Aynthorp will not be displeased.' Gaining control she went on speaking rather fast now, 'If you will really let me, Lady Aynthorp, I would dearly love to come and visit with you for a while after my father has returned home. If you and my mother-in-law wish it I will bring the baby with me. Daddy has gotten me an English Nanny if that would not be an inconvenience?' She looked startled at the ripple of laughter this invoked.

Christine explained. 'It would be delightful; but let me justify this amusement. It would also be dramatic and we will welcome all three. You see we have a very old English Nanny who has been in this family since she was a child and in such families as ours these old women are frequently more autocratic than we, so we shall have to put our heads together when the time comes to practise a little diplomacy.'

Christine's explanation brought out for the first time two ravishing dimples, 'It sounds like my old Mammy only more so,' she agreed causing the watching Dowager to decide, 'That gel's a beauty, Meg and I must take her in hand. We'll give her some "form", after which we can sit back and watch the young men clamour.' Simultaneously her sister-in-law was deciding, 'That one will not remain a widow for long, now who around here needs some new blood . . . ?'

In the midst of all the drama, all the stress, the old family ebullience was surging in these two rightly named 'Old Naughties' who saw at once, in the new situation, the promise of endless scheming pleasure. They watched approvingly as Christine bent forward and kissed Sue-Ellen saying, 'You must learn to call me Aunt Christine my dear, and remember you do not visit us. You must learn to accept that you have merely come to your second home, please make it soon for I fear my sister and brother-in-law will find it hard to contain themselves in patience until they hold their first grandson in their arms.' She put up one slim hand to Sue-Ellen's cheek. 'You look such a child to be both a widow and a mother. At least you may be assured of a warm welcome from all of us. And if you find our ways strange at first we all hope you will become used to us very fast.'

So saying, under a benison of approving glances, Christine tucked one arm resolutely through Sue-Ellen's sables adding, 'Now no goodbyes, just as we say in France *à bientôt*, and we will prepare rooms for you so as to be ready whenever you decide to come.'

The father and daughter murmured their '*bientôts*', Mr Blenkinsop with an execrable accent but determined to copy as best he might. Then Christine led Sue-Ellen across the hall followed by Gyles and Silas Blenkinsop.

Sawby, hovering behind, was just permitted to follow down the steps and open the door of the large hired Daimler motor drawn up on the gravel below. The chauffeur came running from the servants' entrance where Mrs Parsons regaled him with beer and sandwiches, but it was Gyles who handed Sue-Ellen in and shook Mr Blenkinsop warmly by the hand. Sawby from the farther door arranged rugs over knees. Then Gyles asked casually, 'Do you shoot sir? For if you do we could give you some fair sport. The birds are hopelessly overstocked with not enough guns to bring them down.'

'Indeed I do,' the rubicund face lit up eagerly, 'but not I guess quite up to your mark. You will need to instruct me.'

'Gladly,' Gyles assured him, 'though I reserve my doubts as to the necessity. By the by, there is absolutely no need to go off to Purdy's for guns, we have ample here and would be delighted if you chose to use them.'

The shrewd old eyes were warm in the bespectacled face, 'I guess I owe you a great debt of gratitood,' his American was becoming more pronounced as the strain told. 'I thought you British were said to be cold and withdrawn.'

'Ah,' replied Gyles, 'but then you see we are not exactly British, having sustained our French inclinations, inheritance and way of life, besides, of course, our blood and the French are said to be more, er, outgoing and emotional so perhaps that will account for what you have found in us.'

To Sue-Ellen, round-eyed and now radiant he added, 'And you, young lady, must also come out with the guns in line with Lorme tradition. All the Lorme women shoot and I feel assured you will take to it readily.'

Sue-Ellen looked at him straightforwardly. 'I must admit Lord Aynthorp,' she said daringly, 'I prefer looking after animals to killing them; but for the pot it is alright especially in time of war do you not think?'

Slightly startled Gyles concurred, adding, 'I have a fiend of a son,' he confided, 'who is obsessed by animals, and I may add insect life too; so much so he has plotted to deceive me with a secret menagerie which I must pretend I have never discovered. With him I feel sure you will find a strong alliance. Dear me, I can see shoals ahead!'

For an instant she looked dismayed, but the twinkle reassured her.

Meanwhile the chauffeur waited, stiff-backed and Sawby stood blank-faced and amazed. Abruptly Silas Blenkinsop's hand shot out, only the glint of gold betrayed his intention. Sawby murmured an astonished, 'Thank you, sir,' and there was a slight clinking sound.

'Until next time then,' Silas said hurriedly to Gyles, thankful to have crossed the tipping hurdle successfully. The last word lay with Gyles.

'And the first of many I hope,' said he. Then he stood back, Sawby closed the door and the two Blenkinsops vanished down the drive bend, two pairs of hands flapping at the opened windows.

Gyles remained standing long after the car had slid from view. When he turned and mounted the wide stone steps very slowly and Sawby closed the great door behind them. Immediately, Gyles swung off to the long corridor which led to the chapel path and pushing open the ancient door went in to the candle-lit Norman Sanctuary where his uncle lay in state.

Marguerite was at the altar arranging flowers. She turned at the sound of his footsteps, called to him softly, 'Well Gyles here's a pretty kettle of fish! Will we never have done with dramas in this family?'

Gyles halted, taking in the tranquillity, the plumes of gold from the thick candles in their sconces, the scent of the hot-house flowers, the catafalque with the heavy velvet folds falling from the coffin as they had done when his father's body lay where Alaric de Lorme lay now. Then he answered. 'I think,' he said thoughtfully, 'that this is one drama we may come to welcome in the years to come. New blood Meg, alien blood maybe, but good blood, lusty, and I imagine wholly steadfast. It almost makes me wish the rapscallion had lived. I am inclined to think that lovely gel might have redeemed him after all.'

Throughout the Castle, groups were discussing the 'callers'. Belowstairs, the dissection was resumed over tea for Mrs Parsons and Mrs Peace; *tisanes,* for Chef André and the sour-faced Mademoiselle Palliser, the Dowager's strongly disliked personal maid; and coffee for the Sawbys, with Sawby as the star performer since he only had experienced both the original arrival and the changed climate at departure. These older members of the domestic hierarchy indulged themselved with toothsome snippets of past scandals concerning the late Stephen Delahaye – typical Lorme runt in a far longer succession of runts to Lorme litters than any of them had even conjectured. Rogues and renegades generally turned up with predictable regularity down the great line of Lorme generations which came from Normandy in ten sixty-four to sow their French wild oats on English soil thereby causing both financial depletions and social perils to the Family which otherwise set standards of the utmost probity.

In their private suite of rooms the two Delahayes sat counting their new blessings before a blazing log fire. Fate had dealt viciously with both of them but now seemed to be smiling, and they revelled in it. Behind them lay Sinclair's stroke, brought on by their Rosalind's peccadilloes – unfinished business this – with Rosalind bolted from her Irish Knight and fled to Italy where she must now remain 'for the duration.'[1] Sinclair was almost wholly recovered from that. Henrietta too was, as the servants phrased it, 'a changed woman' since her third delinquent child, Stephanie, breaking all runt records for such offspring, had brought to the family their first experience of public scandal by her suffragette activities. Then, by his heroic death and subsequent posthumous decoration, Stephen had eradicated all the bitterness of his scandalous past and was now ennobled in their minds – if in no others – by his obliteration. Finally came this afternoon's benison of a grandson, by a beautiful girl.

The third debate was between Henry de Lorme, Gyles' eldest son and his cousin Ralph, recently become Lord Steyne on the succession of his father Eustace to the title.[2] Ralph was a casualty of this war. He had sustained a brain injury during the carnage of the first great German thrust to the Belgian coast. That was when Eustace his father, turning, as it were overnight from a dilettante and rather a bore, had elected to ride roughshod through the corridors of power, obtain a private ambulance and plunge into the holocaust to bring his son to England, narrowly avoiding killing the entire rescue party by his endeavours. Now Ralph was recovered and merely convalescing in the Castle wing which the Family had transformed into a Convalescent Home for Officers under the care of Lady Constance and the Family's Dr Jamieson. Ralph was now innured to the fact he would not fight again. The next best thing, a military instruction post, had been obtained for him, and in the meantime he had become, as his cousin irreverently described him 'a toss pot for all our problems and complications'.

Now the copper-headed heir was recounting the afternoon's events to the still bandaged, fair-headed Ralph. Both were ensconced in a corner of the convalescents' Rest Room, sufficiently removed from the chess players and the armchair strategists not to be overheard.

When Henry had finished speaking Ralph said abruptly, 'Bloody, sodding liar!'

'Who me?' Henry sounded shocked. 'I say old chap . . .'

'No, not you you idiot, Stephen.'

'Why so?' Henry's indignation changed to curiosity.

'Well now,' Ralph laced his hands behind his bandaged head, 'I'll tell you. Up to now I've played *bouche fermé* with a lot of the episode; but none of it matters any more.

'I ran into the blighter in an *estaminet* in the August of last year – Christ! It seems a lifetime ago now – and we had scarcely settled down with our beers when Stephen swaggered in, RFC kit, gold Asprey cigarette case an' all, lookin' mighty pleased with himself. He seemed in no way put out at meetin' me. He called for bubbly, flirted with the girl who brought it, even had the flamin' gall to ask after the Family and gave a long report on the events he had experienced since he vanished with poor Uncle Sinclair's money. He claimed he was workin' but frankly admitted he had an ulterior motive in this. He disclosed it too, completely unembarrassed. If I can recall his words he said there was "a girl involved", yes that's it, he told me she was "pretty as a picture and her father is a millionaire". So I asked him point blank if he intended marrying for money. He simply smiled and said "Of course", but after he had explained how he came to join the RFC he definitely stated that he and the girl were only officially engaged. Tell you the truth the whole scene made me sick.'

'Right,' Henry scowled at his hands a moment. 'I suppose that you realise one thing which has not come to light old chap – the money? No one has an inkling the nice old boy is a millionaire. What a lark eh? Do you think it's true? I mean Stephen was a perfect master of embroiderin' to suit whatever end he had in mind at any given time, so one is naturally suspicious.'

'Somehow,' Ralph deliberated, 'I think not. I felt and still feel he was so sure of himself and so very well aware that he was up against a tough character in the old boy, that he would never have worked to get engaged let alone secretly married if he hadn't known full well that a fortune went with the lady.'

'Oh Gawd,' Henry muttered. Instinctively one hand shot to his head and rumpled it into the customary disorder. This drew Ralph's disapproving gaze. 'You know,' he said severely, 'it's time you stopped that shockin' habit Henry. After all you are no longer a boy. You're a married man and a father and it's high time you behaved sensibly.'

Henry grinned. 'It ain't a matter of growin' up,' he defended himself, 'my old man still hauls out his monocle and polishes it when he's bayed. Give or take a bit we've all got mannerisms, so why start pickin' on me?'

Ralph unbent sufficiently to grin. 'Well try, anyway,' he urged, 'it ain't dignified. Now what was I sayin'? Oh yes, for my part I shall believe your Mr Blenkinsop is a real millionaire if and when he tells me so himself...'

'I'll tell you this,' Henry cut him short, 'if that old American gent who looks like Mr Pickwick says it is so then it most certainly will be. He's a stout feller even if he is a bloomin' Yank.' Which coming from Henry could only be deemed effusive. He fell silent then brooding for a moment. Taking a different tack he said rather regretfully, 'It's a bloody shame old Stephen had to die. I mean, marryin' a beauty with a million or two ain't bad for anyone and this beauty's no ordinary gal, believe you me she's *strong*; I dunno quite how to put it but I have the feelin' she could have coped, made somethin' out of Stephen...' he paused again, adding with a typical *non sequitur*, 'Wonder how his little basket is comin' along.'

This promptly led the serious Ralph to deliver himself of a homily on the wickedness of frivolity on such a subject and the absolute vital necessity of 'keepin' your flamin' mouth shut now and forever on that subject'.

The homily fell on stony ground. Henry had already shot

off at another mental tangent, and was wondering how long it would be before he could discuss it all with his Petula. He speculated for quite a while before saying abruptly, 'I'm goin' out there too, just as soon as Pet is fit enough. I'll tell her then. I must. I have to talk it out with someone. In the meantime can it be you? And will you agree if I don't say anything more about Stephen's basket to keep your mouth shut on what I tell you?'

Ralph surveyed his cousin indignantly. 'You know,' he pronounced, 'there are times when I find you positively immoral. Anyway *your* haverings are safe with me although you will have to wait a bit, you lucky beggar.' After which they fell to talking about the war.

Perhaps the most mischievous discussion was conducted in another private suite belonging to the Dowager, the tiny indomitable Alicia Aynthorp whose marriage to the late Lord Aynthorp had been so tumultuously flawless that his departure left her only half a person, merely marking time until she could pass on, rejoin her Justin and begin to live fully once again in whatever sphere of existence awaited her.

Time and again, in her own productive days Alicia Aynthorp had repeated to her children and her Nanny, the beloved Victorian saw, 'Satan finds mischief for idle hands to do' serenely unaware that Satan was also actively engaged in finding healing mischief for herself and her sister-in-law, two Machiavellian old gentlewomen whose purpose in life was gone beyond their present reach and who, with their unquenchable vitality, sought to assuage loneliness by doing what the servants in general and Plum, the highly privileged old coachman in particular described as 'have a finger in every pie'.

They not only prodded those pies, they stirred them round; scheming, plotting, wangling, and frequently driving Gyles Aynthorp over the edge of self control with their often costly, sometimes perilous and almost invariably successful machinations.

Even now after the horrors of Petula's *accouchement* and the shock of finding Alaric dead in his chapel stall while interceding with his Maker for Petula's recovery, they could still rally, still conjure up a sparkle and still embark with relish on a fresh onslaught against the family's much needed peace of mind.

They now sat, tiny slippers discarded, *peignoirs* foaming about their small elegant persons, swathed in froths of lace and flounces, gracefully disposed on two *chaises longues*, sipping at their *tisanes* and unashamedly plotting yet again.

'Imagine,' sighed Marguerite happily, 'when this dreadful war is over – provided we can keep her here – how such a little beauty will draw the eligibles!'

'I am,' concurred the Dowager with relish. 'It reminds me of what my father said once about oak-eggar moths.'

'Now Alicia, what in the world have whateveritis moths got to do with Sue-Ellen?' Marguerite eyed her sister-in-law with sudden asperity.

'I will explain if only you will pay attention Meg. Papa said – I can remember it as if it were yesterday – that when female oak-eggar moths were in season or whatever it is that happens to 'em when they want to procreate, the male oak-eggar moths home in on them from as far as three hundred miles away. Now do you understand? I believe that *if* we take the gel in hand, groom her to our ways and customs, help the dear pretty child in every possible way to achieve her manifest potentials, she will be just like one of Papa's oak-eggar moths to our young eligibles.' She ended her explanation on a note of triumph.

Marguerite giggled delighted. Of course,' she agreed, 'it is inevitable.'

The Dowager began drumming her fingers on the buhl table top at her elbow. 'This is once when Hetty will have to present one of her own family herself,' she declared emphatically. 'What fun we shall have! But, if what she wore today is any criteria – those sables were superb – she has a natural flair and natural good taste when it comes to clothes. That part will be easy. I would say it is evident she has a very proper sense of what a gel of quality should wear. I wonder who are her antecedents. Mark my words there is good blood there. Even that nice rubicund old man behaved impeccably, except in comin' here at all without first announcin' himself.'

'Well anyway,' Marguerite rose to replenish her cup, 'it would have been much duller if he had decided not to come at all. I thought it went extremely well; but doesn't he look like Mr Pickwick? The likeness is really remarkable. Now where shall we begin?' She sat down again and leaned towards her sister-in-law. 'Should you imagine it would be a wise move to make some excuse to pop up to town so that we can see them both before they return here? I think we need to know what, er, financial backin' they have. And I for one have not the faintest idea as to the amount of money needed to make aeroplanes. Nasty dangerous things.'

'Of course,' the Dowager agreed abstractedly her mind clearly on other matters. 'Naturally she will marry again, but we must both be very careful she does not fix herself on anyone unsuitable. I believe she might do extremely well – after our grooming.'

'Strawberry leaves?' Marguerite speculated dreamily.

'Why not, but is there not also the possibility we might make a match for her inside the family? A little new blood would be wise I fancy . . .'

The hatching and matching continued. It overran the hour at which the Countess was due to play chess with a convalescent. It overran the time when the Dowager distributed fresh books and magazines to the wounded young men. When the dressing gong sounded their eyes met guiltily. Then Palliser scratched at the door and came in to enquire, 'Have I permission to dress you my lady?' So their ploy was temporarily suspended.

The Family came back to unpleasant realities the next morning, finding themselves entangled with the complexities of interring a Bishop, inserting announcements in *The Times*, the *Morning Post*, in writing letters, allotting rooms to visiting family and arranging the inevitable memorial service. Reluctantly they put '*l'affaire* Blenkinsop' – Christine's label – into limbo whilst the disposal of Alaric's colossal remains was brought to a suitable conclusion.

Back went the family into mourning, out came the black veils and down came the prelates, who sat overlong with the port and Gyles, Henry, Sinclair and Ralph. On the morning after their arrival the black-plumed horses and sombre hearse were peered at through the drawn blinds at every window. Out came the senior servants in decent black garments, the few remaining men and the land girls, lady gardeners, poultrywomen, and other female ex-suffragette replacements with black bands over their arms forming a guard with the village folk. They lined the entire length of the drive and ran right to the lychgate of the little Norman chapel. Nor was this the end of the matter. Though, as was traditional and they considered only civilised, the women of the family stayed behind those drawn blinds both for the funeral service and the interment; all the leading Lormes of both sexes attended the memorial service in the Abbey. The cars were mustered. The black was assumed. The cars moved off, followed by matching, small streams from neighbouring estates. All converged to hear a more youthful prelate extol the great virtues of the greedy and sancti-monious Alaric. For this the Abbey was decently filled since he had great connections.

Only Henry, chafing at the essential but dreary hypocrisy of it all, and naughtily glancing about him at the assembled company, suddenly spotted the foul-mouthed old Duke of Barton and Sale, who had recently broken a leg, struggling up the aisle. Henry slipped hastily from his pew to assist the gallant old bawdy. In so doing he spotted, right at the back, black-garbed like them all, that unmistakable Pickwickian face and the flower-like one beside it, the unrelieved black making Sue-Ellen's youthful beauty 'stunning' as he after-wards explained to Petula.

Meeting his eyes for a fleeting moment Silas Blenkinsop put one black gloved finger to his lips, shook his head, clearly saying to Henry 'pay no attention to us', and Henry nodded in confirmation, smiling warmly. Then he hastily composed his features and tried not to hear the pithy expletives which erupted from the Duke as he permitted Henry to haul him to his pew.

Henry then bided his time until his father was safely back in his shabby old study after dinner, made his excuses and slipped away to put his copper head around the door and ask, 'Spare me a moment sir?'

Gyles looked up. 'Of course, come in. I was just thinkin' how the older ranks are thinnin',' Gyles said wistfully. 'Come and cheer me up. Sometimes I find this war intoler-able without the dubious benefit of extra family losses.'

'I'll tell you somethin' to cheer you then.' Henry sank into one of the worn leather chairs immediately facing his father across the old refectory table whose cross-bar generations of booted and spurred cavaliers had worn to a shard. 'Do you know who came to the Abbey today sir, quite uninvited?'

'No?' Gyles raised an eyebrow. 'Tell me.'

Henry reported what he had seen and saw Gyles' eyes warm to the little tale.

'I managed to have a quiet word with them afterwards,' Henry added, 'but they wished, no insisted on slippin' away. Actually the old boy asked me to tell you he'd wait a further week and then telephone. I think he is rarin' to show off his grandson y'know.'

Gyles was filling and tamping his pipe. Henry waited until the match flared and the pipe was drawing satisfactorily then heard his father say, 'I liked him – unreservedly. You know your rumbustuous grandfather disliked all Americans. He was always eruptin' at their alleged ways and antecedents. He said America was founded on rogue Irishmen and the sweepin's of the malcontents of Europe. I never argued. It simply didn't pay to cross swords with yer grandfather, but I had my reservations. I go along with him a hundred per cent over the Irish part. They're a dangerous race and their influence has never been sound anywhere – except in battle. They live to fight; thrive on skulduggery, revel in brawls; but I'll stake my life old Blenkinsop stems from good stock. I'm lookin' forward to meetin' him again. So if he does not telephone me within the week I will telephone him. The gel's a beauty too and seemin'ly nice with it. Extraordinary isn't it that after all that young devil's deceits and cheatin's he picks on two fine people and then up and dies before he can be moulded by 'em?'

After this illuminating speech Gyles puffed at his pipe. Father and son sat relaxed until Gyles rose. 'I promised yer mother I'd turn in early tonight, she's been under a terrible strain, I wonder if it's too late to drop in on Petula before-hand!'

'No,' said Henry. 'She's readin'. She's gettin' on like a house on fire, let's go together.'

As they moved out into the corridor with Diana the Borzoi bitch as ever following at Gyles' heels, Gyles said again, 'Yes I really thought old Blenkinsop behaved rather well. I believe I may very much enjoy his future company.'

But fate had not yet done with the Lormes. It seemed to them afterwards when they reflected upon the whole sequence of events as if once again, as had happened so many times down the centuries, once fate drove the knife in she turned the blade and would not be satisfied until she had driven it in to the hilt.

Precisely five days later Gyles received the anticipated telephone call. Silas Blenkinsop explained with massive regret that he had just received a cable from his factories. He was wanted urgently in Texas and his return could not be delayed. He added that by a stroke of good fortune, and after pulling more than several strings he had obtained a berth on a much smaller ship and was due to embark in the morning; but he assured Gyles he would be back 'just as soon as I can put matters to rights and get a passage'. In the meantime, with some diffidence he asked if he could 'presoom' upon their kind offer and entrust Sue-Ellen, his grandson and nurse to them while he was away.

There was a good deal of apologising on the one hand and assurances from Gyles on the other until eventually it was agreed that Gyles would drive up and conduct the trio to the 'second home'.

At length Gyles replaced the receiver and sat staring sombrely across the room. Once again unease assailed him. Once more, as had happened on that afternoon when he climbed the great staircase at the precise moment that Stephen and his aircraft were blown to pieces, premonition, like a stab between the shoulder blades pierced him. Later in the afternoon Sue-Ellen rang. She explained that little Stephen had a slight cold. So in these circumstances could she stay on at Claridges for a spell as the nurse was fussing at moving the boy before the cold was 'quite gone'? To this Gyles naturally agreed, and in turn Sue-Ellen rang off having promised to telephone each day to report on baby Stephen's cold. She assured Gyles she was perfectly comfortable, thoroughly enjoying London even in these wartime conditions. She also remembered to send special messages to her in-laws and to the other women of the family.

Still Gyles was restless. His temper shortened, there were a couple of typical Justin Aynthorp outbursts, until the family, sensing that there was something amiss dealt with him warily for the ensuing three days. Two days followed of serene reports as to the baby Stephen's improved condition, then on the third a demented, unrecognisable voice choked down the telephone the news that the ship which carried Silas Blenkinsop had been torpedoed and sunk with all hands.

When Sue-Ellen was eventually collected by Gyles and

Henrietta and brought back to Castle Rising she came as not only a widow but also as an orphaned millionairess. This was the way in which, at last, Stephen's son arrived at his grandparents' home in the summer of 1915.

CHAPTER 2

A Very Shabby Household

Londoners danced and sang in the streets, waved flags, turned barrel organs and embraced each other in excited frenzy on the night of November 11, 1918. The surviving members of what Henry had christened disrespectfully 'the old gang' sat around the wide chimney piece in the Library assessing the breaches which the war had made in their defences. Talk was intermittent, very quiet, as if, at long last even for them, the holocaust had like a monstrous succubus drained them of their ebullience. Even the Dowager leaned against the back of her chair, for once unable to sustain her habitual ram-rod posture.

It was evening, so they were all turned out impeccably through the attentions of their maids and valets; yet there was about them now a worn look which had never manifested itself before. For all their privilege the acute observer could perceive in them the first faint markings of deprivation. It emanated like an aura and swirled around them. It was no more than a mist but it declared itself in the grey at Gyles' temples and a fading of his famous copper hair. It displayed itself again in the veins on his long hands, clasped now about a brandy balloon into whose depths he stared sombrely. It was manifest too in Sinclair's perpetually bent shoulders. These, as with a man who has suffered from arthritis and recovered, remained as if the joints refused to accept resuscitation and therefore stayed defensively crouched against past pain. On Henrietta, sitting at his side as always, it showed in the fine lines which fretted the corners of her mouth. They were even more deeply drawn in the faces of both the Dowager and the little Countess who suddenly appeared to have lost all but the unquenchable beauty of their eyes and the classic shapes of their jawlines, below which the skin had shrunk and loosened. In both their faces, past beauties as they now were, there seemed just an inkling that presently fine noses and fine chins would begin to nutcracker upon each other. John Henry's deprivation was displayed by his over-leanness repeated in his Primrose's appearance. They both seemed to be entering upon that unkindly state which heralds old age with a sudden boniness of ankle, wrist and shoulder- blade which no amount of well-cut tailoring nor subtle draping can conceal. Not that they made any effort at concealment. All of them had been far too involved to observe themselves properly for a long time now. Perhaps the greatest proclamation that none had emerged unscathed was in the familiarity of the clothes they wore. They had worn them for longer than ever before in their lives and for Lormes collectively, to lose elegance and their contemporaneous hold on fashion was to be sunk to unprecedented depths.

It was explicable. For John and Prudence the death of their nephew George had been like the death of a son. He had spent so many of his brief span of years at the Castle. Fate had not let them go at this sacrifice for Christian, their eldest son, was missing too, so that Claire and the two children Peter and Priscilla were on the rack, ravaged by fears for his safety. Nor had this made up their personal tally, which they knew with weary resignation was as nothing to their friends, one of whom had said in this room not a week ago, 'They are all gone Prim, husband, two brothers, four sons, and so many cousins that there are scarcely any men left in the family. There is no future now for any of us and I fear so much for our girls. We have left England's finest on the soil of France and there will be few of their stature now for future marriages.'

Primrose sighed, staring into the peacock flames. Worse than all the uncertainties: dear, charming French Charles de la Coutray, their daughter Rosemary's young husband had been killed during the last day's fighting.

How much the weight of Sinclair's bent shoulders was the result of Stephen's death was debatable since by dying as he did, Stephen had brought his parents back to life by giving them back their pride in him. Certainly the disastrous Gavin Fitz-Patrick, Knight of Bourne had been heavily responsible by persuading their beautiful, silly Rosalind to run away with him – at least he married her – but this was done because he was confident that with the beauty went a large parcel of Lorme wealth with which he could restore his crumbling Irish estates and restock his stables. He had discovered too late, to his bitterness, that even in the old drawbridge days no portcullis could exclude him more absolutely from a farthing of Lorme money or the possibility of ever re-entering Castle Rising than Gyles' letter of rejection. Finding himself saddled with the girl and nothing else he ran riot, ill-used her viciously and ultimately left her sick, pregnant and alone when finally, in a great upsurge of frustration he bolted, choosing war as the better part and losing his life in the endeavour.

While the free world exulted in its hard gained freedom the Lormes stared at the past and found the future intimidating in the extreme.

Sheer petulance had lain its mark on Gabrielle, Countess of Bartonbury's beauty, turning down the corners of her mouth and making her eyes resentful. She had an overwhelming personal grudge against this war which had caused her such bitter disappointment. In her opinion it had 'spoiled everything', made a mockery of her new inheritance, her new position and above all of her new opportunities.

With the women of England, the fragile, cosseted women of privilege having turned their backs abruptly on everything Gabrielle considered made life worth living; to devote themselves instead to rolling bandages, staffing convalescent homes, wrapping parcels, working on menial tasks and launching appeals, and with her Eustace – that once compliant, attentive, conventional husband gone, in her opinion, stark raving mad as well[1] – it had been an unbelievably boring war for her and one against which she now nurtured a tremendous personal grudge. Not for her the starchy uniforms, the tiresome headdresses of VADs which seemed the only pictures the fashionable world condescended to publish currently, starting with that awful one of Princess Mary. Not for her those utterly boring committees which had become the only direct route to the Royal Ladies. But then, she thought resentfully, what else could be expected of a gruff, bearded sailor monarch who ordered the sealing of his wine cellars until the war was won, thus evincing a monarchical austerity worthy of a Trappist monk and not the son of the most exciting, amusing, gay Monarch who ever held glittering court where these two 'fuddy duddies' now reigned. She was supremely

[1] See Book 3, *War Comes to Castle Rising.*

indifferent to the fact that they had come to the throne un-
wanted and unwelcome, due in part to the preceding
Clarence engagement and the subsequent transference of
Princess May's hand to Prince George's to sour the opinion
of their subjects; yet despite all this they were now more
strongly enthroned both in monarchical fact and in love and
admiration than anyone had ever imagined would be possible.

Gabrielle was only interested in quality as represented by
the frivols of the eighteenth century. She was at this moment
in a seethe of petulance as her mind slid from the theme of
monarchs to the ever present irritant – her husband. *Why*
should Eustace have changed overnight from a pleasantly
vacuous and compliant escort to a madman who charged
about the battlefields of France messing about with
bloodied, muddied men and putting his life in daily risk by
so doing? It was not fair to her. She wriggled with barely-
suppressed fury, shooting off again at a further tangential
thought to soliloquise upon her 'tarsome' son Lucien. She
began to wish she had never decided on this flying visit to the
Castle. She had done so merely because of 'that wretched
boy', now coming up to manhood, and who was to her also
quite incomprehensible, unnatural and unreachable. Who
ever heard of a Bartonbury refusing to go to public school?
And furthermore, wangling, finagling and plotting his sly
way so as to stay mouldering in this now gloomy
mausoleum; and was he not now practising further evasions
to avoid going up to Oxford?

'He shall go,' she said furiously and aloud causing all their
faces to turn to her in some bewilderment.

'What did you say dear?' asked Henrietta, shaken from
her own frightened thoughts as to whether Stephanie and
her young clergyman husband had survived their service
with Eustace's private ambulance team. Even as she spoke
her lips had been performing yet another voiceless prayer
for their safety.

'Oh nothing,' Gabrielle shrugged irritably, 'I need a drink
Gyles please.' She made as if to move but Gyles stretched
out for her glass and replenished it with her favourite
Benedictine. The Dowager watched thoughtfully. No one
so far had ever succeeded in drawing the wool over her old
eyes, and a gleam of contempt sparked in them now for
Gabrielle who to her was wholly meritricious. Totally unaware of her mother's assessment she sipped the liqueur and

began enraging herself still further over her daughter Lucy. There she was, the proven belle of her season; offered for by half a dozen glitteringly eligible *parties*, refusing them all, coming back here and seeming content to keep the Home's books, slaving away at dreary ledgers when she was not closeted with Lucien in the music room or careering God knows where about the countryside in her car with that scarred chauffeuse who gave Gabrielle the shivers. Lucy had been equally sly over renting that London house and then had gone off to live there with that Miss Poole as a chaperon. She at least should have known better. Abnormal that's what they were this brother and sister. What indeed had happened to this entire family? Thus she speculated, staring at her dangling slipper, silk-stocking clad *legs crossed*, defiantly displaying too much ankle in the 'Coco' Chanel frock which one of her cousins had smuggled in a diplomatic bag from a Paris besieged in those last awful months of the winter of 1917.

In Gabrielle's view the Family were now sunk into a morass of good works, wearing dreary old clothes while Paris absolutely bristled with scandal, gossip and current fashions. Coco Chanel alone was creating simply divine new clothes and employing three hundred workers despite Big Bertha's long-range cannon which thundered out nightly during '*le bombing*'.

Gabrielle had conveniently forgotten the 'dull bits' in Clarice's recent letters. The bits which told of the British Army being outflanked, turned about face and sent galloping back through Pontoise, Lyons, Nevers to Malines with the French Light Horse and Dragoons flung in too late and both failing to reach the British across the fourteen mile gap forced apart by the Boche; while Clémenceau threw out Pétain, replaced him with Foch and all the French reserves were flung into the second *Chemin des Dames* battle; or that this resulted in seven hundred cannon lost and eighty thousand prisoners taken. It was still only dreadfully boring stuff to Gabrielle. She looked up abruptly. 'How soon Gyles do you suppose I could get to Paris?' Her voice sounded shrill.

Gyles misinterpreting her, imagined she was anxious for Eustace and replied kindly, 'I do not know but I could most certainly make enquiries for you my dear. You should be in a **very** strong position. Though I must warn you, they are dreadfully short of food, heat, of almost everything.'

'Pfui,' exclaimed Gabrielle. 'Please put out feelers for me Gyles, I would be immensely grateful.' Her spirits lifted instantly as she picked up a magazine and began leafing through it. While, '*Escape, escape,*' she rejoiced, thinking as she turned the pages, 'If Coco can chop off her hair then so can I. It might make me look younger too and that would put a cat among the pigeons with this family.'

Gyles lapsed into worrying about his own concerns. With so many of the estate men gone he sought a way to muster his resources so that when at last, as they now knew would happen, Henry would be released from his prison camp and repatriated. He and his son must then have a clear campaign mapped out for beginning the weary work of restoration and rehabilitation. As if this sparked off a sudden telepathic link with Christine, Gyles looked up to see her watching him; her *petit point* idle in her grey silk lap, her hands folded over it.

'When,' she asked, 'do you think Henry will be freed my love?'

Gyles rose slowly, 'I am going to London tomorrow. I will badger and irritate every big-wig of my acquaintance in an effort to find out something. At the moment,' his lean face creased into a wry smile, 'all of us in like case can only answer you in the context of the Browning story "Only God knows".' As he and Diana left the room he smiled to himself, warmed by Christine's expression and the realisation that she at least, among them all stayed as young as ever – despite what had happened to Henry – that had been their worst day, when Sawby brought in the dreaded yellow envelope. Gyles ripped it open and read the curt statement, 'Regret to inform you 2nd Lieutenant Henry Gyles de Lorme has been posted missing'.

Those few words brought the Castle to its knees. They turned the Dowager's face to grey ice in which only the eyes burned ... dry.

It had at length driven Gyles out on to the old saddle back, where he had walked on that black night in nineteen-twelve when premonitions of impending war had touched him so powerfully.[1] This time Gyles sought strength from the land he held in trust ... *but for whom?* he anguished as he strode. If Henry were gone, would it then be Ninian, who even now

[1] Book 2, *Shadows over Castle Rising.*

was in the fighting line, this second son, already Lieut.
Colonel Ninian de Lorme DSO, MC. If Ninian went too?
then what? – Andrew? – a nice enough chap, he at least safely
within the castle walls tonight; but he would never replace
Henry. Gyles wrestled with his own devils as he had always
done, solitary, wearing himself down physically until he was
able to return with some semblance of external calm. He
slipped back undetected through the old garden door which
Henry had used to display himself and his Petula in all their
finery to Plum on the night of his now legendary
engagement and his ball.[1] There abruply Gyles reached and
halted in that long, slightly damp-smelling passageway. He
had known when Stephen went, and yet he had been reading
The Times in tranquillity when Sawby came in with this
telegram. Could the tremendous bond between himself and
his eldest son really be so loosened by separation that if
Henry had met his death violently in battle he, Gyles, would
have felt nothing? His head came up again. He found the
proposition wholly false; and then again he stopped short,
suddenly certain, completely and unassailably certain that
Henry was not dead. He had gone out into the grounds each
night, patrolling in his turn as did all the men now. Yet he
had not seen so much as a shadow of that hound whose
appearance heralded the death of a de Lormes. Nor had that
familiar rasping bay sounded at any time since Henry had
left for France.

Gyles reached his rooms unseen. Here, unaided, by
choice, he bathed, changed, brushed his hair and noted for
the first time the silver at his temples; but all the time his
confidence grew until there remained no further room for
doubt. Going downstairs again to comfort Christine he
realised that he could not, dared not make any reference to
the hound to his wife lest her feminine imagination cause her
to think she heard or felt something of its presence. As ever
he accepted wryly, he must keep all to himself; pull them
together, sustain his stricken mother and the suddenly
shrunken little Marguerite and solace as best he might the
lost little girl his daughter-in-law Petula seemed to have
become.

She had turned instinctively to the newest member of the
family. Sue-Ellen was there to meet her, clasping the hands
stretched out to her, silently confirming her understanding

[1] Book I, *The Lormes of Castle Rising.*

through her own painful knowledge of what had brought this family to their knees. Sue-Ellen *knew*. She had travelled this way herself; but for her it had been a journey without any hope. Thus the two young women drew close, one to another, until Petula called for her if Sue-Ellen was absent for a moment.

'Sue-Ellen, where are you? Has anyone seen Sue-Ellen?' and 'Where has Mrs Stephen gone?' was the cry to whatever servant she encountered. That telegram bound them together as nothing else could have done, welding a rapport between them that was ultimately to link them as closely in the years ahead as the Dowager and the little Countess. 'There were few bonds,' Petula reflected when she was calmer, 'more close than those forged by shared sorrow.'

If Petula rode, then Sue-Ellen rode with her, handed into the saddle by Plum, seen off by his anxious old eyes as he stood bent and bandy in the doorway of his stable sanctum until they were swallowed up by the home park trees. He was there when they came back to give them a hand down, to mutter to them as if they were mares at their grooming, 'There now, steady as we go, that's the ticket my pretties,' until at length Pet cracked and flung herself weeping into the coachman's arms.

'He'm alright my liddle love,' Plum soothed hoarsely. 'He'm special. Like I've always said.' The painful tears trickling down his own furrowed cheeks giving the lie to his spoken assurances. He let her cry herself out against his old coat, producing one of his infamous red bandana handkerchiefs with which to wipe her cheeks. Then he gripped her chin, grunted 'That's the ticket, now give Plum a nice smile lovey,' as if she were a small girl who had fallen and grazed her knees.

One day at her request he took her out in the dog cart, drawn by the stout and lethargic cob whom Richard in a sudden burst of misplaced erudition insisted on christening 'Rozinante'. They were halted at the level crossing to let the train pass through on its way between Upper and Lower Aynthorp stations. The sun was making a spectacular exit, sheeting the sky with crimson and gold. Plum turned to her, saw the hopeless tears sparkling on her lashes, sought desperately for consolation and only achieved, 'There, there, don't cry my liddle love, look at the pretty train!'

But Henry had not joined Stephen. After his training,

after embarkation, with only four months divided between the trenches and behind the lines, he went out on a scouting party with his sergeant and two corporals; they stepped into an ambush, were surrounded and captured and that was the end of Henry's war.

Understandably, on this long-dreamed-of Armistice night Petula's thoughts were of Henry who had not seen either his 'hair' – Plum's name which inevitably stuck – or his twin daughter Chantal since the pair were beginning to toddle. Petula had naturally taken great pains to ensure that 'Daddy' was kept very much in the forefront of their minds. This old Nanny pooh-poohed, declaring roundly that it was 'a waste of time till they was older' – and rocking even more vehemently than usual.

Yet, when Petula rushed straight to the nursery after being told that it was 'all over', gathered her pair into her arms and explained to them that 'Daddy is coming home!' she was rewarded by 'Will he bing pesents?' from her round-eyed Justin Gyles and a reiterated chant from Chantal, as the pair wriggled out of her arms and began marching round the nursery chanting, 'Daddy comin' home ...' until Nanny declared her 'pore head was liable to split', which Nanny Rose privately decided would be a very good thing.

Sitting recalling this in the Library, wondering for the hundredth time 'when will he come?' Petula caught Gyles' eyes on her, smiled and asked wistfully, 'When Uncle Gyles?'

He needed no explanation. 'I do not know my dear, but as I said I will beard the mighty in the mornin' startin' with the General. He might be able to tell us something.'

Predictably the Dowager brightened. 'What a celebration that will be!' she exclaimed with a touch of her old sparkle. 'Do you not suppose we must have to have a celebration dinner?'

'No Mama,' Gyles answered quickly, 'I imagine Henry will prefer a very muted welcome. I may as well confess now that the danger has passed that I have feared and dreaded that young devil would try escapin'. That was his chief peril after bein' captured. I am reasonably sure he *tried*, for this provides the most logical reason for his transference from one camp to another. I did manage to learn from a thoroughly informed source that the second one was far more severely guarded. I think Henry must have made an attempt and by the grace of God did not get shot in the back for his pains ...'

'That is what I feared too,' Petula confirmed.

Immediately the sparkle in the Dowager's old eyes at the prospect of a celebration after so much austerity – by her standards – was replaced by an ominous glint which Gyles had little difficulty in interpreting. 'Now Mama,' he said severely, 'we shall pull no strings, if you please. You will not go careerin' off to London on some spurious pretext in order to suborn old *beaux* on Henry's behalf. I will not have it! My eldest son does not require any special privileges. We will have no more of those capers and this time, Mama, *I mean what I say*. Priority in such matters goes automatically to the wounded and to those whose health has been impaired. No son of mine is crashin' that kind of queue so let us have that clearly understood between us.'

'*Tiens,*' said the Dowager, for once considerably damped.

Gyles went on, 'I also imagine that a feller who has been incarcerated for close on two years will be sufficiently sustained by the knowledge that freedom is within his certain grasp to contain himself in reasonable patience, and, when he does come home,' Gyles was becoming magisterial, 'I am confident he will wish to be alone with his wife and children; besides being given time to reorient himself. Borgia Orgies can come later.'

Stung by this last, 'What a disgustin' way of referrin' to a dinner party to celebrate the return of your eldest son and heir!' the Dowager snapped. 'I know, my dear Gyles, that I permit you excessive licence; but *droite de seigneur* can be extended too far. I even permit more from you than ever I did with your father; but this is in excess of vulgarity. Borgia Orgy indeed!' and she began fanning herself at a great rate, straight-backed once more and thoroughly revitalised.

Happily a cough in the doorway diverted their attention.

'Yes Sawby?' Gyles still sounded incensed.

'It is already past nine-thirty my lord,' his voice tinged with disapproval, 'the village folk and tenants are already half way to the Hill so I thought perhaps I should advise your lordship.'

'Good Gad of course!' Gyles leaped up. 'We had completely forgotten. Has Plum brought the dog-cart for the Dowager, the Countess and Mr Delahaye?'

'It is waiting below my lord. I have also informed the rest of the family; then the servants are ready to follow behind.'

This blew the fog of introspection away effectively. They all streamed out to the great hall where commotion flowered as the young ones came thumping down the staircase, vastly excited by the lateness of the hour and their own participation. All were chattering like rooks. Behind them came the maids and valets holding outdoor wraps, while from below-stairs the footwomen hurried with hot water bottles and rugs.

In the midst of the *mêlée* Petula stood as if suddenly entranced with pleasure in this little ceremony of achievement, murmuring, half to herself, 'It has come at last. Oh, if only Henry were here!'

Gyles shrugging into his extended Inverness grunted, 'Probably is in spirit, let us just be thankful he is safe. Now come along we're keepin' everyone waitin',' using gruffness to hide his own emotion. He then took it out on Sawby demanding, 'Have you a Guernsey under that thin coat and if not pray why not?'

There was such a remarkable echo of the late Justin Aynthorp's familiar irascibility that the Dowager started, turned and met the butler's eyes. The unlikely pair exchanged a gleam of recognition and amusement. Sawby merely answered, 'Yes my lord,' holding out the 'thin' coat to disclose the knitted garment underneath.

In the general uproar Diana was encircling herself and barking. Maids were kneeling, button hooks in hands to fasten over-boots, to hand gloves, and to fold scarves close under furs. Only Lucien stood detached, wishing fervently that Lucy were there with him and thinking other very secret thoughts which he struggled to suppress. Sue-Ellen at his side asked softly, 'What are we doing? Please Lucien why are we all going at this hour into the freezing cold? No one has explained and I would dearly love to understand?'

'I'll tell you on the way,' promised Lucien, taking her arm. 'Come, let's not wait for the others.'

They were forced to step back halfway up the hill as a carriage appeared smelling almost overpoweringly of mildew and camphor as did the coachman's rusty old caped coat. Out popped the face of the formidable Duchess of Barton and Sale to shout at them, 'Good evenin' to yer, couldn't miss this, ain't it all splendid?' before she was borne on upwards.

Sue-Ellen chuckled. 'You couldn't find her anywhere but in Britain, er, England,' she corrected herself hurriedly.

Thoroughly relaxed, Lucien confided, 'Richard took a grass snake in his shirt to Pet's wedding. It got away in the chapel, crawled into the old gel's muff and squirmed out across her ankle while the wedding pictures were taken. There was an awful scene. She fainted, and when she came round and realised what had happened she loosed such a volley of oaths, as you just should have heard!'

So they came to the summit, giggling companionably to where Gyles stood with Christine a pace behind him chatting to friends. The wind had strengthened slightly. It ruffled Gyles' hair. It blew out the skirts of his unfastened Inverness, making him look of another age as he stood one arm outstretched to take the long flaming brand which Sawbridge had lit for him.

'So,' thought the young American, 'his ancestors might have stood for some pagan ritual ... well ... this is a pagan ritual too!' reason reminded her.

During that long climb Lucien told her the two tales of Puck's Hill upon whose summit they stood now together. For the first part, he explained how from time immemorial the villagers had clung to the belief that the labyrinthine earth corridors and chambers beneath their feet were inhabited by the Little People and ruled over by Puck who annually led them out by night on All Hallows' Eve to wreak their mischief upon any miscreants in the surrounding villages. Then Lucien went on to explain how during the Napoleonic wars, brands had been piled upon hill peaks throughout the land to be lit when warning came of impending invasion. He ended, 'And when none came the bonfires were lit in celebration of victory. Since then we have always lit a bonfire on Christmas Eve in times of peace as token of our thankfulness. When we were at war we just carried more brands to lay upon the pile as symbols of our confidence that we would win. Then as before when each war was won we did what we are doing tonight. It is part of the Lorme tradition.'

With shining eyes Sue-Ellen glanced around her at the swaying, massed figures, black in the darkness, forming a dense ring around the un-lit fire. She saw Gyles take a step forward, and as a great cheer went up saw him bend to thrust his flaming brand deep into the tunnel Sawbridge had made through the centre, lined with paraffin-soaked wood shavings. The flame bit. A dozen smaller flames flickered, gained in strength, leaped upwards, forcing a great plume of smoke into the sky, as gold, blue and tawny-orange the flames intensified and the Armistice bonfire began to roar in triumph. The crowd stayed back as the heat intensified and Gyles, suppressing a sudden desire to shout as he drove in his brand, 'For England and St George', stepped back, embarrassed, to hear Petula's voice saying to her father above the uproar, 'Saved once again Daddy from the power of the dog.'

Gyles listened intently for Sir Charles' reply. He was caught, too, in the drama of the moment, totally involved. Sir Charles' wife Constance at his side, his daughter and both Gyles and Christine heard his reply. 'I think my dear that we have all come within the power of the dog and since you mention it I may as well add that tonight I should be without fears, even without anxieties if I could possibly think otherwise. For I fear that the end is not even in sight. I am certain that it will all come again within our lifetimes and therefore the tag for this whole, unspeakable affair is for me at any rate "unfinished business".'

CHAPTER 3

A Land Fit for Heroes

While his wife, his father and this great company of family and friends stood beside the blazing beacon on Puck's Hill, the future heir to Castle Rising sat with his feet on an iron stove in a hut in a prison camp, warming his hands around a mug of thin cocoa and smoking his last cigarette. Henry was in very thoughtful mood. The general consensus of opinion was that the Camp Commandant had behaved with commendable dignity.

He addressed them all in his ugly, clipped English. He told them that hostilities had ceased and announced that as transport became available they would be sent home. He added a rider which Henry decided 'comin' from a Hun', showed a distinct touch of humour.

'Gentlemen,' said the harsh voice, 'technically you are free; but for practical considerations I advise that break camp you do not. Due to matters which are now beyond our control the fatherland is not reliable for anyone in the British uniform. I suggest it would be foolish to take unnecessary risks at this late hour.'

This caused a slight ripple of amusement. It also promoted a great deal of discussion, and soon the compound was filled with small groups of men standing about inside the barbed wire assessing the practicality of 'makin' a dash for it'.

A Scots Colonel effectively damped down the eager ones. Moving from group to group he stressed, 'Not one per cent of you speaks German. As far as I can make out the population is starving and this area is filled with deserters who will not be fussy about defending themselves. My advice is to stay inside this barbed wire for at least forty-eight hours while I see what further information I can obtain. We'd need pack horses anyway to carry our food with us. This last enormous influx of food parcels just might be turned to advantage.'

They waited. Forty-eight hours later the senior officers went to the Commandant's office and returned with the news that there were trains available – of a kind. There were even engine drivers to man them, but there were no engines with which to pull them, or at least there were none that the Commandant could obtain. They likewise reported that the food shortage in the area was acute. Then they called for volunteers. Having made their selection a party marched off to the nearest village and its railway station – a mere hamlet – but one blessed with a few sidings. Here they ran the station master to earth, a once stout man now dwindled and as Henry said, appraising him, 'all over pleats and no grub to fill 'em out poor sod'.

The bargain was struck in just under four hours with the help of a packet of Brooke Bond's tea and a couple of food parcels to implement it. When the first of these was opened out for the man's inspection his eyes bulged. Thereafter the bargaining commenced between the one bilingual member of the prison camp – an ex-language master at Dulwich – and the drooling station master. More men were produced and at length the agreement was formulated. The Germans would keep the two parcels as a token of good faith. They would undertake to present themselves with two carts at the prison camp that evening. The carts would then be loaded with the prisoners' bundles which would then proceed under British escort to the railway station. If and when the promised engine materialised the Germans' parcels would be handed over. When the schoolmaster came to the matter of marks the haggling intensified. Finally a price was agreed and the party returned to await the arrival of the promised carts. As they left so the ravenous Germans attacked the two parcels, while the schoolmaster observed thoughtfully, 'Though what the hell I would have answered if that old cormorant had asked me where our parcels would otherwise be disposed, I shudder to think. I should have been up a creek without a paddle!'

When the carts were eventually loaded a guard was mounted over them comprising equal numbers of villagers and camp inmates. In the morning fifty per cent of the prisoners marched ahead and fifty per cent in the rear to discover, when they reached the station, than an engine really had been produced. It swarmed with men. Its appearance was damping in the extreme. As the two colonels agreed it looked as though it had seen stout service during the Crimean War.

Henry's recollections of that journey were of men packed into dirty carriages from which the seating had been ripped for firewood and of men plastered over the battered roofs, lighting little fires, brewing up on their cold perches. As train after train lumbered past them going the other way, similarly over-loaded with defeated, retreating enemy of both sides waving to each other and shouting friendly insults. The creaking train worked its way with many halts and innumerable delays across the defeated country until the engine gave one last enormous and asthmatic belch. Some of its ironmongery clattered and ground alarmingly. Then it died on them.

They made a whip round for any remaining foodstuff. They calculated how long was left before they reached the frontier and by bribery, with bundles of almost worthless marks they eventually conjured up a replacement engine. As this was coupled on a cheer went up. Then slowly, very slowly they began to move again. They wheezed to the Swiss border after five days in their clothes; without washing, without latrines, and with officers and other ranks sharing the foul duty of 'muckin' out' the shell of a carriage which served them as a latrine until at last they tumbled out into the arms of the Swiss Red Cross on the other, Swiss side of the frontier.

Stretched out full length in a huge white bath for the first time in two years, enveloped in scented steam, scrubbed until his skin hurt Henry looked down at his naked person, decided he was 'thin as a bloody rail', and finally accepted that, impossibly, unbelievably, incredibly ... he ran out of adjectives, but he would be home for Christmas!

Step by very gradual step he completed the journey; hour by hour their communal spirits lightened until shouting and grinning they poured down the gangplank onto English soil at Dover where willing hands proffered sandwiches, tea and cigarettes; and a grizzled veteran with three rows of medals on his chest handed over train vouchers and English money. Henry then found himself clinging onto the tail of a lorry bucketing towards Dover station.

He flung himself out, worked his way to the ticket collector's tiny hutch and begged permission to use the telephone. Waiting in a twitch of impatience, cap on the back of his head as he sought to rumple his hair and only succeeded in scratching it he heard a familiar voice saying with measured stateliness, 'Castle Rising, good morning, this is the butler speaking.'

'Mornin' Sawby,' Henry's voice sounded slightly hoarse, 'This is Mr Henry, Sawby, yes Mr Henry . . . I'm at Dover. I've just landed. . . . Is anyone about yet . . . ?'

Sawby's voice came back, less stately by far. 'Oh no, Mr Henry, sir, it is very early you know. Only Mrs Henry has come down and she has gone riding with Mrs Stephen.'

The 'Mrs Stephen' jolted him a bit, but 'Never mind,' he said not realising he was shouting. 'Tell 'em I've got to report to the War House and I must just get some togs, m'tailor has a suit waitin' and I'm practically in rags.'

Back came the voice, slightly raised, 'Mr Henry I could send a man up with fresh clothes, Pine would come I know. He could be at your club by the time you reached London.'

'No thanks all the same, I'll cope,' Henry was still shouting, 'but Sawby . . .'

'Yes Mr Henry?'

'Er, give 'em all my love will you?'

He was refused permission to pay. He glanced at the station clock, ejaculated, 'God's boots,' and raced for the platform where a train stood waiting. He flapped his voucher at the ticket collector, and flung himself into the corridor as the whistle went. Behind, faintly he heard the old ticket collector shouting after him, 'Good luck son!' which made his day.

For sentiment's sake on arrival at Victoria he hailed a solitary hansom, told the old dodderer on the box, 'Guards Club please cabby,' and leaned forward sniffing the musty odour of damp leather, inhaling with rapture great gasps of London air, a composite of smoke, soot and fog. As he passed a top-loaded brewer's dray, the two dray-horses elected that precise moment to relieve themselves. As he phrased it later to his young brother Andrew, 'The blighters let down the number two tanks right on cue!'

Henry immediately loosed such a shout of laughter that the old cabby peered down anxiously and had to be reassured. Then, having reached his destination, Henry wrenched at his tie and endeavoured to straighten his cap as he paid the man off. With assumed nonchalance but actually feeling 'starkers' Henry entered his club, bade the doorman a cheerful, 'Good mornin' George, trust you've been keepin' well,' as if he had only been absent for a week and immediately set about obtaining a room for the night.

This mission accomplished he hurried out again into the pale December sunshine. There were too many men in hospital blue! He flung them salutes in acknowledgement of their own as he went by, smiling every time until both jaw and arm began to ache then he turned thankfully into Burlington Street where the crowds were thinner. The suit he had fitted just before going to France was waiting for him in Savile Row. It was as he said to the distressed fitter, 'A trifle on the loose side but I'll have to wear it, I'll bring it back later if I don't fill out, but I expect I shall. I'll cut off now and get a shirt and a few other things and be back within the hour, then you can burn this lot.' He reassumed his tunic reluctantly, rushed off and two hours later descended once more into Savile Row with a brand new bowler tipped well down over his Norman nose, a perfectly rolled umbrella in one gloved hand. Soon he had a handful of extra guineas in his pocket, shamelessly and easily borrowed from his tailor.

He began to hum. Reaction might follow later but this was all pure gold like the money in his pocket. He shopped, he slipped into Scotts where he sank a pint of their best Bollinger and downed three dozen oysters, after which he tucked into some prime blue Stilton and paid the reckoning feeling both a trifle tipsy and excessively inflated. Nevertheless he set off again to complete his 'shoppin''. Walking down Bond Street his progress was halted abruptly by a collecting box, thrust at him. He pulled up short and stared.

'Spare a copper for an old sojer sir,' he heard. The words penetrated. Sudden rage engulfed him. He struggled to pull some coins from his pocket, to drive them through the slot and 'You do it!' he urged helplessly and then drew his hand back as if it had been stung exclaiming 'Oh Christ, you can't!' as he saw the empty sleeve pinned across the man's chest. He grabbed the box and patiently, head bent, struggling to regain composure, he rammed the money in. Finally, 'Where did you get yours?' he asked, handing back the box.

'Wipers sir, first push.'

'And you can't get a decent job?'

'No sir. It seems there ain't much call for one-armed valets sir, nor one-legged grooms neither like Bert 'ere.'

He went through the sorry group and Henry had a word with each of them. Finally he asked, 'Are you here every day?'

'Yessir,' they chorused, 'then evening times we does the theatre queues. On Sundays we work the Park at Speakers Corner.'

So this is what it had come to already! He strode on down Bond Street his thoughts chaotic, the one-armed, the one-legged, the blind, standing in the gutter singing for coppers. With dreadful clarity the famous words came hammering back at him, the stentorian call to arms to protect this island home of theirs and make it 'a land fit for heroes to live in'. Such a pledge, never to be forgotten, nor forgiven either, effectively turned the gold of Henry's first day at home to dross. He brooded, even while he shopped. Next morning he hired a car, took the wheel and wound through the familiar streets ... Aldgate ... the Commercial Road where the lean stalls were almost obscured by the endless queues ... down through Stratford ... Bow ... and up the hill through Leytonstone into open country beyond. While the chauffeur sat silent, arms folded across his chest Henry began to wonder what the full cost would be and what, if anything, had been gained for the price not only of the million pitiful dead but also for the almost more pitiful living. Would that bill ever be met? He came to the crux of the matter as he touched the fringes of Epping Forest where long-dead kings of England had hunted boar and stag. Would anything ever be the same again? The wheels spun, the engine sang softly and the car raced on while the questions piled up in his mind like the spilliken bodies piled on the battlefields of France. Had he come back to a new England of cripples and poverty; of unmarried girls whose prospective husbands either lay dead or else filled those tragic hospitals for incurables which were even now coming into being to house their useless complements of hulks or at best to equip the limbless with makeshift artificial limbs?

This was when, for the first time, something of Henry's father's prescience touched him coldly, laying a cold hand on his shoulder while an inner voice warned him that yes, indeed, nothing would ever be the same again. It told him that he had returned to an alien world, in which alien values would oust the old true ones as, like some hideous army, evil forces set to work burrowing at the foundations of all that he and his kind had held to be both priceless and indestructible until, at length the burrowing would bring this country down to ruin and disaster.

He braked as the gates came into view. He opened the driving door, said to the impassive chauffeur, 'I want to stretch m'y legs. Give me about ten minutes and then take this crate up to the Castle.' Then he turned into the outer fringes of the Park and struck out diagonally so that he might see the great façade of his home spread out reassuringly before him.

There were fallen timbers littering the ground where no fallen timbers had ever been before. Here and there whole trees had come down to lie where they fell. As he reached the fringes of the inner west drive, he saw that weeds ran where he had never seen one before.

At last, he came within view of his objective. It showed him that one of the gargoyles had fallen and had not been replaced. Even here! he thought, despairingly, as one hand instinctively went to his head and he rumpled it in a gesture of utter defeatism. Were they so short of labour? What the devil had happened since he had last seen his inheritance?

He was so shocked that anything, even a world war, should bring about neglect to Castle Rising through any cause or for any reason that he entirely forgot the hired car and chauffeur, forgot his parcels, forgot everything except his urgent need to see Plum before seeing anyone else. He swung to the right, dropping back again into the concealing trees and began working his way round through the pleasure gardens. Even here he noted there were weeds in the paths, the topiary had not been clipped, nor were the verges of the lake cut back and trimmed into their customary winter order.

At length he reached the stables, via Richard's much increased menagerie and the door Peak had cut into the back of the stables. There he paused, hearing Plum's voice apostrophising some luckless female stablehand. Despite his thoughts this drew a grin from him as he stepped into view. Plum came out brushing his hands together and flinging a last valedictory order over his shoulder. He saw Henry, gave a great snort and rushed to thump his shoulder, wring his hand and thump again in an orgy of pent-up thankfulness.

'Here, Hi,' protested his victim, 'easy there Plum, rein it, this is m'y best civvie suit and I'm not the man I was, whoa' you old sod.'

Plum chose to be nasty, seizing this guise as a cover for his emotion. 'Sod is it!' he shouted wrathfully, 'well then, orl I kin say is war ain't improved you Mister 'Enry – sir.'

Henry relaxed visibly at this contact which shrieked 'No Change!' and reassurance. 'Well you haven't changed either,' he said fondly, grasping the old man's hand. 'Can I come in and talk? I haven't even seen m'y wife yet nor m'children either.'

'Children is it,' groused Plum, 'be'aving like a chile yerself! Sneakin' up 'ere, givin' me the twitters, will you never learn no manners?' He turned and walked towards his fusty lair with Henry following. The man was, as usual, Henry's immediate tonic for Plum at least stood token of the sound, the solid and unchanged. The old coachman indicated a stool. 'Set you dahn there,' he ordered, 'ain't got no lardy cake for yer though, we're short 'ere, terrible short and make no mistake abart it. Things is terrible tight in the village and we don't bother 'is lordship 'ee's got enough on 'is plate orlready. We're bloody short-'anded too, not that the wimmen don't work. They're allus a workin' but no woman born can do a man's work on the land in the same time as wot 'ee would.'

Plum put him in the picture, talking, glowering, and all the while noting every detail of his cherished future master's appearance, the bony wrists, the none-too-healthy colour, the overall extreme thinness and suddenly he broke off to enquire, 'Ow old are yer now?'

'Twenty-nine,' said Henry promptly, adding, 'I feel it today too.'

'We all feels our age 'ere now,' Plum said sourly.

'Well never mind,' Henry brushed this aside, 'have some of those suffragette women gone already? I walked up through the Park and round. I didn't feel I could face the family yet. Tell you the truth I came here first, you ought to be flattered you old curmudgeon.'

Plum's face softened. 'Well that I am,' he said grudgingly.

'Plum the place is so shabby!'

'Ar,' Plum nodded, picking up the earlier query. 'No none

of 'em's gorn yet but they jest couldn't do it all and now I suppose they'll 'ave ter go, so as ter make room for our returning menfolk.' He added after a pause and quick, sidelong glance, 'At least wot's lef' of 'em.'

Gradually he gave Henry the tally, itemising the losses with pungent appendages of his own.

'Rose rules the roost in that danged nursery now and not afore her time,' he began, 'nah! Nanny ain't dead, that old termagant 'ull see us all out she will; but she's proper parst it now. She just rocks and eats, at least that's wot Mrs Parsons tole me. Ole guzzle guts,' he added malevolently for he had always detested the old woman. 'Then o' corse yer third footman Richard you know abart, like wot you do abart our lovely Mr George.' He paused here for a violent blow with his usual soiled bandana then resumed, 'Edward and George 'as come through; but my groom Perry copped it on the Somme and me faverit stable boy, remember 'im, young Will wot 'as always chewin' and wanted ter be a jockey? Well I jest 'ope they 'ave jockeys where 'ee's gorn!'

Henry leaned forward, his head in his hands listening as the old voice rambled on.

'Then o' course there was the 'orrible time wen we lorst our Monsewer Charles de la Coutty summink, wot married Miss Rosemary in France an' then there was this larst 'orrible suspense with Colonel Christian ... missing two months! But 'ee's through, though 'ow bad 'ee's wounded we don't know 'ee ain't been delivered back to England 'ee is in 'orspital somewheres, I aint 'eard nothing more.'

Henry had turned a stricken face when Plum named Charles de la Coutray, but said nothing. Plum rambled on.

'Then we lorst annuver yard boy, young Alfred. We only 'eard recent like and Flead the under-gardner lorst a leg, an' Gillings the thatcher as was drafted to fight them dratted Turks – they did 'im in at Gally-Polly.'

Henry frowned, then the light dawned. 'Oh, Gallipoli, that's where Rupert Brooke died.'

'Friend of yourn?' asked Plum without interest. He resumed his dolorous report, 'Old Perkins the blacksmith at Lower Aynthorp 'ee's lorst three sons, *three sons*! Gawd 'elp 'im. There's an 'ouse of sorrer ef you want one! 'Is lordship is puttin' up a Memorial and a Roll of Honour in Upper Aynthorp church where that nice young sky pilot of Miss Stephanie's is a goin' ter be the noo vicar.'

'Then they're both safe!' Henry exclaimed thankfully.

'Ar, but they ain't back yet, but Lord Bartonbury is and from all accounts 'ee's fine, and yer brother Andrew's 'ome, 'ee got wot 'ee called a "Blighty" and come back to convalesce in our 'ome, 'ee wos still there when Armistice come so 'ee's alright too but wot abart Mr Ninian I don't know. They say that wen Mr James went 'ee became a changed man. I 'eard tell as 'ow he spent his time at the front atryin' ter get killed, so o'course 'ee never got a scratch. Got made Colonel instead. Imagine a Colonel, your younger bruvver!'

Plum fell silent. He sat, hands on corduroy knees staring through the opened stable door. When he transferred his gaze to Henry, he spoke in an entirely different one.

'Nar listen son, and pay attention ter yer ole Plum. You carn't never make a nomelet wivart breakin' eggs. Nor can you run a war wivart killin' men. That's life that is and no amount of frettin' is ever goin' ter change it. Wot we all got ter do now is respec' them wot's gorne and do wot we can fer the livin', we gotter make life better fer them as comes back to live it art with their pore 'eads filled with filth and 'orrers.'

Henry shook his head as if someone had struck it. Softly he said, 'Thanks Plum old chap, thanks a lot. I won't forget. I promise. Respect the fallen and ease life for those who come back. Why old chap that's the job m'y father and I have to do from now on isn't it?'

'Yers,' said Plum sniffing, 'yers that's it,' saying which he seized his nose in his noisome bandana and wrung it as if it were the prime cause of all their troubles. When he had stuffed the rag back into a bulging pocket he summed up. 'More classy said, but wot I meant just the same.' Then he added, 'Ow long you goin' ter spend along er me? You bin 'ere a time orlready.'

'Christ yes!' Henry started up. 'Give my love to Mrs P. Tell her I'll be down to see her before bedtime. I told that poor wretched chauffeur to wait ten minutes and then bring up the car.'

'Then cut along do,' Plum advised, fishing out his gunmetal treasure. 'They'll be goin' mad at the Castle.'

The Lormes had not exactly lost their reason, but when the car came up and the chauffeur had waited a further ten minutes he climbed the steps, pulled the bell and enquired of Sawby, who opened it, 'Excuse me, but is Mr de Lorme with you? He told me to bring the car up; but that's forty minutes ago and ...'

Sawby repeated 'Mr Lorme did you say?' somewhat magisterially.

'Yes, that's him.'

'Raikes,' said Sawby over his shoulder, 'pray inform the family Mr Henry's come. If I know anything he's gone to see Plum first. . . .'

As Henry dashed into view round the shrubbery where he and Petula had run on the afternoon of the Costume Ball the family were massing at the top of the steps with the staff crowding in behind them. With a quick intake of breath he looked up and then he was up those steps two at a time and enmeshed.

There was a huge teddy bear for Justin. A blue-eyed, flaxen-haired doll for Chantal. This, when you pulled the string said 'Mama' and 'Papa'.

'Gain!' commanded Chantal enchanted with this thing nearly as big as herself. Henry obediently pulled and pulled again, while Petula hung over the back of the big armchair in their sitting room, content to watch the light in Henry's eyes as he played with his twins.

'Where Papa been?' demanded Chantal, pushing the doll at her mother and winding her fingers around Henry's coat buttons.

'Playin' soldiers for the King,' he told her solemnly.

'Then slute!' cried Justin laying aside his Teddy, 'C'mon Papa, slute.'

'Ain't got a cap on,' Henry objected, 'Can't salute without a cap.'

'Me get one for you.' Justin pushed himself off his father's knee, stuffing both fists into his lean stomach. The he slid down and trotted off to burrow in a drawer. He came back brandishing his garden hat – a scarlet fisher cap with a long tassel.

Henry shouted with laughter, assumed the cap, flung his son a smart salute and promptly Justin copied him.

'No limp,' Henry said softly in an aside to Petula.

'Special shoes,' she whispered back. 'We saw someone, tell you later, they just have to be re-made every three months. I can promise you my darling we have cherished him.'

'Has he been in the saddle yet?' Henry asked over the top of his son's curly copper head.

'Since he was two. We got him a cob – shaped like a barrel, by his third birthday he was screaming to ride Morning Star.'

Their eyes met, 'Oh Pet,' he said weakly, 'it's almost too much.'

She bent over and kissed him. Chantal burrowed between them crying, 'Kiss *me* Papa kiss *me*.'

Henry hugged her close, buried his face into her neck and blew hard. She shrieked with pleasure and inevitably, 'Gain,' she ordered, 'gain Papa.'

Thus Henry purged his 'hiatus' as he called it and Petula wore stars in her eyes which brought a sparkle back to the Dowager's and to the little Countess's until Henry was as his father put it, 'In a fair way to bein' ruined by the pack of 'em.'

Then Rose came in, and cueing her husband, Petula exclaimed, 'Here's Nanny Rose to bath these two imps. Come on children it's bath time.'

'*Nanny* Rose?' murmured Henry questioningly as the twins were led away babbling about their new toys and demanding, 'Papa barf me, Papa barf me.'

'Yes,' Petula explained when the door closed behind them, 'Nanny's spent. It was a tussle to de-throne her but your mother managed it and now she sleeps most of the time. I think's she's slipping away.'

Henry digested this, then his mind wandered, 'Have to call that bear Edward,' he decided. 'You must give Justin my book. I wonder what's happened to it. Pet have you found Edward the Red Teddy Bear?'

She nodded. 'But if you teach that boy to sit on buns like Edward's elephant friend ...' she threatened.

The rest of her sentence was drowned as he caught her in his arms. 'I will,' he promised, 'but not in the drawin' room and not in front of Nanny, nor,' he reflected,' in front of Nanny Rose either, c'mon let's go and "barf" 'em.'

Petula let herself be led away, knowing full well that her husband would have no peace until he had seen his son's foot and knowing also that when he had that would be an end of the matter. In the event Justin chose to be what Rose called a Very Naughty Boy. He was docile and beautiful when lowered into the big hip bath before the fire; but when he was settled in the warm soapy water with his fat little legs stuck out and his celluloid ducks floating round him, he just waited until both parents were bending over and then he smacked the water hard with both hands drenching them both from top to toe.

That night after the quiet dinner which Gyles had decreed and after Henry's visits to Mrs Plum and the household below stairs; as the stable clock chimed two through the half-opened window he lay in the big bed where Petula had nearly died and abruptly fell asleep against her shoulder while she stared out across his rumpled head remembering....

How she had sat on the window seat in this room in the last days before the twin's terrible entrance into the world and how she had dreamed of sons: the heir, a soldier like Christian, then an explorer, and a famous horseman ... many sons whose wives and children would in the fullness of time come to live within the pattern of this still very French household, it's Castle run like an old French château.

She knew now and had known since she was well enough to be told that there would only be one son and with him and the daughter she had never envisaged having she was well content. She had come to terms with the fact that she would never conceive again. Her two would never be lonely. She knew that, too, for other members of the family were already bringing their sons and daughters to the Lorme nurseries to grow in concert with their cousins as she had grown with Lormes from the time she was a baby. She breathed a small prayer for the health and safety of her twins, in the serenity which had come to her from the moment she had felt Henry's arms around her once more. She lay awake for a long time making plans for their future, a completely contented young wife who asked no more out of life than did her mother-in-law – her husband, her home. Before she slept her last thought, carrying her over the threshold of sleep was of their forthcoming Christmas and the ushering in of the New Year *together*. News had come from Eustace Bartonbury, that Stephanie and her Harry were through unharmed, and on their way back to England. Petula was a little puzzled as to why, after risking the trip to Paris, Gabrielle was staying there and not accompanying her husband home. However – she was becoming very sleepy now – doubtless there was a reason. And there was good reason too, for this to be a very muted Festive Season by the grandiloquent standards of the late Lord Aynthorp, her beloved 'Grumpy'. Thinking of him, she crossed the threshold into sleep.

When Christmas came they were all together again, admittedly with their ranks thinned, but gathered once more, as their line had done for centuries behind the benevolent protection of the stone gargoyles. Those gargoyles had seen Gyles and Henry return across the roofs from Charles Danements's manor house after Henry's bachelor dinner party on the eve of his wedding, with both the lord of Castle Rising and his heir indisputably in their cups.

It was just another manifestation of the Lormes' persistent 'Frenchiness' as the County called it. In every great French château aunts and uncles, ancient and often impoverished relicts, cousins, younger brothers and sisters and their progeny clustered under the one roof, living their lives out often in amity, sometimes in solitude, never questioning the right of any relative to château-protection and hospitality. The wealthy supported the impecunious, not with the slightest patronage or manifestation of virtue; but merely from an in-bred *esprit-de-corps* which surmounted all other inequalities with grace and without question.

Thus, among the Lormes, Sinclair Delahaye and his Henrietta, daughter of the late Justin, and his surviving widow Alicia, the Dowager, scarcely remembered their lack of funds. Shopping was invariably a matter of credit, with bills sent automatically to Gyles. Travelling brought a chauffeur-driven car to the door to convey them to train or boat, while tickets automatically appeared on the writing desks of their private quarters and quarterly bank statements confirmed that their current accounts were being replenished regularly. Thus it became hard to remember dependence rather than hard to remind themselves of its fact. The demands of state, country or, as in the late Bishop Alaric's case, occupation, brought about temporary absenteeism, but the certainty of their return to security was always and had always been underwritten by the reigning head of the Castle.

It was one of their 'lulls', as they were always called in this extraordinary family; brief periods when no high dramas cut across the tenor of their days, when no one revealed any shattering transgressions and their personal barometers all registered 'Set Fair'. Even Gyles, with Henry home to share in the endless discussions on the future of the Convalescent Home, the estate, the museum and the problems of staffing and management, began to feel they might after all 'come about' without any justification for his fears of shipwreck.

There was pain of course in the revival of the Invitation Meet on Boxing Day with the ranks thinned so heartrendingly of younger men. Henry, skylarking with Andrew, was haunted by James's wraith from 'Gone away' to the last kill. For Primrose it was her nephew George whose spirit hovered throughout; while for Rosemary, defiantly mounted and riding with the rest, it was more in the hope of breaking her neck than having a good run that she took her fences so recklessly. There were gaps in all the assembled families. The Alleyns from Birdbrook Place had lost two sons; the Lawleys another, the Keighleys from Setchall Abbey their eldest daughter, who had literally vanished when her ambulance was blown up in Compiègne. So the tally ran through Crawleys and Cavendishes, Devenues and Balmers, all of whom had seen their children go; and would now wait in vain for them to return to the lands they should have inherited. There was not a single family in that great turn out who had come through unscathed; but they rallied. They spoke of their dead as they rode with the living and at the end of the day they trotted or drove back to great houses which could never be as great again in the years which lay ahead.

As Lawrence Binyon wrote, so these families confirmed poignantly, 'At the going down of the sun and in the morning we shall remember them.' They remembered and they manifested their pride by speaking of them often, with outward serenity.

This gave Gyles Aynthorp a problem with which he wrestled unsuccessfully as Pine dressed him for dinner on Christmas night. It almost reconciled him to breaking with tradition on the grounds of compassion for his womenfolk; but at length found himself unable to do so. As a result Chef André's superb dinner was as sawdust in his mouth and he drank deep, which Christine did not fail to observe, absolving him because she knew the cause.

When 'the King' had been drunk Gyles rose with reluctance to give the toast 'Absent Friends' and in so doing glanced towards Rosemary and Sue-Ellen, the lonely ones; but they rose with the rest, drinking with composure.

Only one member of the Family was, as Nanny would have described it, 'in all his states'. Damp-handed, restless, keyed to fever-pitch, Lucien among them all had absolutely no involvement in the proceedings, neither caring nor feeling one way or the other, just existing in an agony of suspense. When the family spoke of his forthcoming birthday he kept his eyes well down, saying nothing but seeking every possible opportunity to absent himself or, failing this, to remain unobserved if possible.

Lucy swept down on Christmas morning. She and Elizabeth drove down in the Darracq with her gifts, for it was not yet time for them to learn what car she now drove in London. She greeted her father charmingly, presenting herself as usual as the exquisitely-mannered girl they had always known, aware even so that this cut no ice with any of them any more for that first flight of hers had stripped the scales from their eyes.

As she drove down she was back in thought to that day when she announced, at the very last moment, when her bags were packed into the car and Elizabeth was waiting, 'I am going away Aunt Christine. I have rented a house in London you see. I have decided that I prefer to live alone.' As her relatives gazed at her incredulously and Christine attempted to speak, she interrupted a trifle breathlessly, 'No please let me finish Aunt, I have also engaged the services of the inestimable Miss Poole whom you all admire and respect. She will live with me as my permanent companion. I first broached this to her when she was here for that brief period when she acted as interim governess when the others went back to their own countries because of the war. I also have Elizabeth as you already know so I am ensured against the slightest breath of scandal. My house is furnished and ready for me. I am taking Violet as my personal maid because she too wishes to leave here and Miss Poole has engaged a domestic staff to wait on me. It will always give me great pleasure if you will come and see me. With Arlington House closed I can provide an excellent *pied-à-terre* for whomever needs to spend a night in London.' She paused for breath but hastily resumed, lest they should cut her down before all was made quite plain to them. 'I decided to do exactly this a very long time ago, when Granny died and left me sufficient money for my independence. I know you would wish it otherwise; but as I am of age I have at last won through to a freedom of choice. I would so very much prefer you to wish me well now, rather than that this should cause conflict between us, because it is too late and I must go.'

Small, pale, trembling slightly, hands gripped together, she had them on the ropes. That sweet, gentle little Lucy should plot, plan, scheme and execute such a massive and shattering deceit and carry it through to the point of no return without anyone having even an inkling of what was happening, left them bereft of words.

Henrietta made a feeble attempt. She opened her mouth. She gasped out, 'But Lucy how could you!' At which Lucy just gave a little shrug but did not answer.

The Dowager quoted softly from Virgil, '*Virisque adquirit eundo . . .*' but Christine, with hard, bright eyes and all her qualms justified by this revelation, set down her table napkin, glanced round the table and then spoke.

'I for one,' said she, 'accept every word you have said, my dear Lucy.' Her voice was glacial. 'I have no doubt whatever that you will be happier away from us. You have never been really happy here have you?'

Lucy was equal even to this. 'No,' she agreed, 'you see none of you have ever understood – ' she paused, poised on the edge of peril, reshaped her words and concluded, 'that I am a very solitary person and that this is how I wish to live. It has always been my preference.'

Christine was becoming angered beyond endurance. To Gyles' horror he saw his gentle wife struggling with a purely female emotion, saw her impotence against the armour of this young girl's determination. Watching this conflict, he also saw his wife struggling as she struck back with the only weapon left to her.

'And what of Lucien?' she queried harshly, 'are you content to leave him?'

Lucy stiffened. She lifted her head and met Christine's eyes. 'Yes Aunt Christine, we are both quite content,' she said steadily.

Eustace, home for a few days as Lucy had known he would

be, was the one to break the awful silence which followed his daughter's last words. 'It seems,' he said, his voice kindly but his face very sad, 'that I have been a poor father to you my dear to bring you to such a step. I ask your pardon. I know only too well the stubborn streak which persists in all our family. I know too how this lies hidden until suddenly we discover there is something we just must do. In a way, little Lucy, I understand it all. Is it not exactly what I did myself when I decided to drive an ambulance team in France? And frankly, my child, I regard myself as a better man for that experience. I only hope with all my heart that you will say the same when you look back on this step you have chosen to take. So let us now put an end to this – er – somewhat painful confrontation and above all let me wish you well.'

It was so unexpected and yet so perfectly in character that it nearly brought her down. Constance made a little helpless gesture. The hot colour flooded Christine's cheeks as she took to herself Eustace's implied reproach. Then suddenly, impetuously, Lucy did something she had never done before. She ran to Eustace of her own volition. She let him put his arms around her and, laying her fresh young cheek against his scarred one, she said, 'Thank you dear Papa, thank you very, very much.'

Eustace patted her shoulders. 'Please Papa,' she then asked him, 'please come and see us before you go to Yorkshire.' She pulled back then, disclosing the calling card she clutched. She pressed it on him, 'Here is my address and my telephone number Papa, come soon, but now I think you will agree it is better that I go.' She drew herself away. She looked across at Christine as if hoping her Aunt would soften; but there was no change in the flushed, alien face, so she turned back with another little shrug. 'Then thank you all at least for not trying to stop me and, well, goodbye everyone.' And so saying she turned and ran from the room without a backward glance.

Christine drew a deep breath. 'She has planned this down to the very last detail,' she said harshly, 'she has always intended to leave us. Oh, Gyles, what in the world will become of her!'

'Why nothing of course,' snapped the Dowager. 'Pray do not lose all sense of proportion over this affair Christine. It is not the end of the world. Nor has the gel gone off with a man, or in any other way compromised herself. Consider I pray you the circumstances of this departure. She is one and twenty now. She is undoubtedly chaperoned in such a way as to ensure no breath of scandal. With the ways of the world as they are today any gel of means and social prominence can set up her own establishment without causing a ripple on the surface of the increasin'ly grubby duck pond of modern society.'

'It is not that at all 'Licia,' the Countess weighed in, for once taking a different line, 'what has shaken us all so profoundly is the deceit. Frankly that appalls me. I might as well add I think we are all considerably piqued. We are unaccustomed to dislike. It pains us.'

Christine took up the theme, 'There I entirely agree, but when one thinks what has been involved, why the gel should've been a man, not a pretty little female! Such plottin' and plannin', such dissemblin' and so many untruths! You know Mama do you not,' she looked accusingly at the Dowager, 'we set the seal upon this day's work the moment we gave Lucy permission to buy that wretched car!'

The rift could not be sustained. It was not in any of their natures for this to happen. Curiosity would have overcome it, without any other factor being considered. *They had to know what was going on.* As the little Marguerite declared, in what was an unanswerable defence for just wanting to know, 'There is more in this than meets the eye! Alicia and I will go. We will then see for ourselves. We owe as much to Eustace and Gabrielle. Lucy cannot be abandoned like some excommunicated trollop.'

When Eustace ventured to point out that he too was going, Marguerite cried him down.

'What will you see I would like to know?' she demanded rhetorically, 'Lucy can draw the wool over your eyes, you're too kind and besides you're only a man!' This last delivered with such triumphant scorn that Eustace merely smiled and nodded.

'If, as we suspect, there is something else afoot then only a woman will find it out. No *we* will pay her a friendly little call. She has always admired that charmin' little papier mâché tray of mine, I shall take it to her as a house warmin' gift.'

All through this drama Gyles had sat quietly. Now he rose, white with anger. 'Watch that tray Mama,' he said direfully, 'it's got John the Baptist's head on it!' Then he strode from the room.

Despite this, the first approach was made. Lucy had anticipated it, so was well prepared.

When they were settled back in the Royce afterwards, the Dowager declared, 'That was a mare's-nest, Meg. She's done what she said she was goin' to do and there's an end of the matter. Now we can all relax.'

When Eustace came back from his visit, he too expressed his pleasure in his daughter's good taste. He also informed Gyles that he would appreciate the tutor Sissingham taking Lucien to see his sister for a short while each time he went to London to work in museums and picture gallerys. This brooked no argument and Lucien ceased to look like a zombi. No one had any inkling of the calendar which he had made for the year 1918. This he kept in a locked drawer, the key always hanging from a thin ribbon around his neck. Every night he went to bed he crossed off another day which brought him nearer to the one ringed round at the end of December when he would at last be eighteen years old.

Somehow the time passed. Now the car was once more approaching Lower Aynthorp village on this cold Christmas morning. Lucy forced her thoughts away towards other channels so that by the time they reached the Castle she would be armed for her encounter.

She and Lucien had already engaged a first nucleus of workroom girls. They had been working for two months on the designs which they and Piers had selected for the first collection. In between the girls made the clothes which Lucien had designed for his sister's Christmas visit. They were totally unfamiliar to her relations, as the trio had intended they should be.

Lucy's slim ankles showed above little bronze shoes with big buckles on them. She wore a redingote closely moulded, opening out over a narrow, slightly hobbled skirt, from which it was plain to see that the wearer had disposed of tight lacing. Over this ensemble she had flung a loosely draped chinchilla wrap, Piers' Christmas present. On her head perched a very small tricorn tipped at a bewitching angle at 'rehearsal' and by Lucien. When the Dowager appraised this she pronounced on the instant '*très coquette*' and 'charmin''.

Claire was quite bowled over as Lucy and Lucien had intended she should be. As Lucy shrugged back the chinchilla and took a small glass of madeira from her Uncle Gyles, Claire exclaimed enviously, 'My dear what an absolutely deevy ensemble! Is this the new line? You simply must tell me where you get your clothes, I'm in rags.'

Lucy dimpled, replied, 'Let me arrange to have a card sent to you for their new collection. I will keep it all a secret until then,' and the pair moved closer to each other the better to entangle themselves in the complexities of fashion chatter.

'Do look Tante Marguerite,' Claire was clearly overcome with envy, 'this is the arrow-slim line I told you was just beginning in Italy; but nothing anywhere near so chic and positively revolutionary as this.' Which drew Lucy into the circle marvellously.

Then Sawby appeared with her huge pyramid of Christmas presents – carried by Raikes – and enquired of her little visiting ladyship, 'Would you like these arranged around the tree? Or should you prefer...'

'Around the tree thank you Sawby,' said Lucy carelessly. Then remembering something she added, 'Please look among them for two boxes which have your name on them Sawby. Those are for you all if you would be so kind as to open them and distribute the contents among you.' All of which was further calculated to enhance the minx's stature and thus make the going easier. No sooner had the door closed than it was flung open by Lucien who rushed into his sister's outstretched arms.

'Tch, tch!' exclaimed Primrose, 'Really Lucien you are gettin' such a big boy now you must stop these transports, actin' as if you were a baby.'

Down came the mutinous look as Lucien stood with one arm around Lucy's waist. He turned his instantly flushed face, 'Oh but I couldn't Aunt Prim. Surely I can kiss my own sister whatever age I am?' He had grown so tall that he had to bend low to whisper to her, 'Which is *my* parcel? I want to look at the outside anyway, Lucy-Lou just show me, I promise not to touch.'

'Then go with Sawby darling,' she gave him a little

indulgent push, 'but promise not to try and open anything and *hurry back.*'

The Dowager was watching attentively. She had been doing a great deal of this kind of watching recently whenever the brother and sister were together, though for once in her life she elected to keep her deductions to herself. Between herself and the little Countess a shared policy of 'the least said the soonest mended' had been agreed. It was also implicit to them both that no amount of interference would change anything. Even so, curiosity had led to reflection, reflection to speculation and deduction until she saw fairly clearly what lay ahead. She went so far on one occasion to admit to the little Marguerite, 'I have fancied myself as a schemer all my life. I have also had a fairly high opinion of my powers; but play Canute I will not! The role is too depressing besides bein' rooted in failure which is not at all to my taste.' After this she dropped the subject, returned her attention to the game of chess they were playing at the time, made her move and crying out, '"Checkmate" I fancy', indicated that after contemplating defeat her confidence was in some part restored by this small triumph.

Lucy's parcels caused another stir. The family and their friends were still in the era of shiny white paper wrapping decorated with transfers and tinsel. The Castle's 'travelling man' who came annually in November had this year laid out in the parcels' room, exactly similar merchandise which he had brought before the war – except that the quality had deteriorated slightly. There were still pads of cut and pleated papers for stretching out across the nursery and the servants' quarters, the same paper, narrow ribbons and transfers. There were still 'snowstorms' in small glass domes, silver fairies, sugar mice, fat peppermint humbugs and twisted miniature walking sticks in striped candy.

Lucy's parcels were wrapped in gold and tied with wide silver bows or in reversed colours gold on silver. The former were hung with silver labels while silver butterflies perched in the gold ribbons, and vice versa. These formed another topic for delighted comment.

Lucien had refused to have a single ostrich feather boa in his first collection. Instead, after frowning at the plethora which erupted from huge cardboard boxes brought by his 'travelling men' he exclaimed suddenly, 'Tulle! that's what we'll **have**, tulle boas! all ruched and all absolutely without those tarsome tassels which always dangle in the teacups in the drawing room at the Castle.'

So tulle boas were made by the workroom and some were set aside for Claire, Petula, Rosemary, Constance and Primrose. Rosemary's was in palest mauve, the colour she was expected to assume presently to replace her 'weeds'. There were bedjackets for the older women – lacy foamy affairs with pleated sleeves and satin ribbons. Lucien had taken great pains over the design for his Aunt Christine's present. He eventually drew a pattern which the embroidcress repeated down the length of a white satin stole in white bugle beads, pearls and crystals on white duchesse satin. Christine could not repress a cry of astonishment and pleasure at this lovely thing. Whilst these presents were in train Piers undertook to comb the antique shops for 'clever things'. He produced a pair of eighteenth-century duelling pistols and had them transformed into table lamps for Gyles Aynthorp's office. 'The lighting's shocking in there,' he explained. He found a magnificent first edition Jorrocks for John, a splendid brocaded dressing gown for Sinclair, and produced pairs of correctly monogrammed, thick cream silk pyjamas with fat matching frogs for Henry, Andrew, his own brother Ralph and young Charles Danement. Charles' father received an illustrated, limited-edition volume of *The Manor Houses of England* and so it went. Lucy's presents were a huge success. Lucien's own private present, given to him secretly and again found by Piers, was a set of twelve volumes of *La Mode de Paris* which he had seen in a Sotheby's catalogue.

The day went off extremely well. In the morning, Lucy pleaded a pressing engagement and was gone as the first arrivals for the Invitation Meet were trotting up the drive. She left in her wake an astonished, grudgingly admiring gossip of relations and a strained, over-excited Lucien.

There was a last hurried meeting between brother and sister in the laundry room where they hugged each other, whispered little consolations and finally separated on the words, 'Only five days, my darling, and then you will be free.' This enabled Lucien to stand on the steps and wave to her as the car slid away. All the family remarked later with complacence how well Lucien seemed to have settled down.

Christine went so far as to say to Gyles that night, 'I must own I am favourably impressed. The girl seems to have come on remarkably. Perhaps it was all for the best. Particularly so as that precious pair seem to have accepted separation like two normal people.'

Gyles only grunted, but as he was hock deep in estate papers, and exhausted after a hard day's hunting it was possible he did not give his wife's observations his fullest attention.

In the meantime 'the lull' continued. On the twenty-seventh they had an informal shoot. There was the best muster of guns for four years and an astonishing number of pheasants were brought down. After guests had been supplied, several brace set aside for the household, and one brace filched by Plum, the rest were bagged up and despatched on the night train to supply Monsieur Ritz's clièntele. The Family turned their attention to preparations for New Year's Eve.

CHAPTER 4

A Very Light Encounter

Sue-Ellen and Richard were mucking out the various pens, runs and houses of his menagerie under the critical scrutiny of Plum. That worthy, seated as usual on an upturned bucket, alternately explored some cavity in his teeth with an unlovely thumb and apostrophised the workers.

Soon after breakfast Gyles, Henry, Petula and her father had trotted off on horseback for a preliminary survey of the home farms and cottages, prior to setting in train some very necessary repairs. They did not intend returning until nightfall so were well-equipped by Chef André with flasks, thermos and sandwich boxes containing the famous Lorme sandwiches. They were also resigned to accepting sundry additional offers of sustenance; having no doubt that assorted country specialities would be urged upon them by the tenants and their womenfolk.

As the small party moved off, Henry sighed, 'Heigh ho for Cowslip Wine and Ginger Lump! not forgettin' slabs of cold plum puddin'; I always end up after these forays belchin' like a chimney.'

'Henry!' exclaimed his wife, scandalised, 'pray spare us your revolting similies.'

As their mounts disappeared between the trees, a battered Swift two-seater with a canvas tonneau-cover drew up at the Danement's Manor House. Young Charles Danement eased himself out cautiously from a welter of shabby baggage, went to the door and pulled the bell. Then he stood waiting and whistling softly, 'Rolling home, rolling home by the light of the silvery moon...'

He had forgotten that his stepmother and father were still based at the Castle, where they had decided to remain until Constance had re-engaged a full complement of staff for their own home. This had clearly not happened yet, as witness the strange couple who confronted the impatient Charles at last through the opened doorway.

It was a depressively anti-climatic homecoming. After a short parley Charles climbed back into his car, well-damped by his reception.

It was little better when he slowed to a standstill below the Castle steps. This time Sawby opened the great door, unbent so far as to smile broadly and beam a 'Welcome home Mr Charles,' adding regretfully, 'Sir Charles is out riding with his lordship, Mrs Petula and Mr Henry, and her ladyship has driven across the country to return one of our convalescents to his home.'

'Oh blast!' young Charles looked so crestfallen that Sawby suggested, 'But Master Richard is down by the stables with Plumstead sir. Mrs Stephen is there too. The Countess is expected to return from the village shortly.'

Vastly put out already, thoroughly at a loss to understand whom Sawby meant by 'Mrs Stephen' as his father had omitted to explain her in any of his letters, Charles grunted, 'Mrs Stephen? which ladyship? Oh never mind, I'll find out later.' Saying which he wandered off again down the steps and after a moment's hesitation turned off in the general direction of the stables.

As he reached the opened door at the back which provided access to the 'menagerie' he saw a ravishingly pretty girl, fair curls escaping from a rakish black velvet cap, a smut on one cheek, busily engaged in scraping matted straw and droppings from the old greylag's nest and piling the stuff into an already brimming wheelbarrow; as Richard came from behind the kennels with an armful of fresh hay.

This domestic scene halted the newcomer effectively. He stared at the dishevelled beauty in mixed wonder and admiration, deducing that this must be the mysterious 'Mrs Stephen'.

Plum removed the exploratory thumb from his mouth. 'Tell you smmink – madam,' he vouchsafed, 'ter look at yer no one would credit you was wot you is and a lady besides ter see yer now, workin' with them pesky hanimals. Its contra-dickkery that's wot it is.'

'Oh no it ain't – er isn't,' Sue-Ellen corrected herself hastily, finding as Petula did that Plum's English was contagious. 'It's fun and I enjoy it. I'm happiest with animals,' she paused to tuck in an escaping curl. Richard pushed past her with the hay and began talking softly to the invisible greylag who had withdrawn to a dim corner in dudgeon at such unwelcome intrusions.

'I'll tell you a secret if you like,' Sue-Ellen volunteered.

'Yers, do that,' Plum answered with relish, 'tell us then, I like secrets I does.'

Sue-Ellen hesitated, then, 'I am going to buy some really interesting, er, big animals.'

'OhmiGawd!' ejaculated the startled coachman, 'wot sort then?'

Sue-Ellen elected to tease. 'Just a lion or two,' she told him airily, 'some tigers, an elephant, some deer and a small pack of wolves because they are such friendly creatures.'

Plum's face was so comical, his alarm so intense that Charles creased with laughter. Richard dumped the hay and came back to the wheelbarrow.

Then Plum gave tongue. 'You pesky female,' he erupted, quite beside himself, 'lions is it! tigers! an' hellyfunts! Well I can tell yer now it ain't me as will be goin' within a mile er them 'orrible critters and that's a fac'. I never 'eard such a thing in all me days.' He broke off and looked at the pair of them malevolently. 'Anyways it won't 'appen. 'Is lordship 'ull giver yer the rightabout 'ee will. Blimey! 'ee'l blow up like wot 'is dear dead lordship used ter do.'

Richard gave battle instantly. 'Oh no, he won't,' he shouted, 'he'll be ever so pleased because it will be an added attraction when we re-open the museum to visitors and *you* will be their keeper and you'll have to lead the elephant about like a mahout *and* groom the lions and tigers!'

Plum soared from his bucket, 'I'll 'ave you know,' he shouted back – although they were within a yard of one another – 'you sinful young warmint,' his face was crimson now, 'I'm 'ead coachman 'ere and I'll 'ave you understand, thet's for 'osses not wild hanimals. Jest you get that inter yer 'ead. Ef there's any more talk of wild beasties I'll be off ter tell her old leddyship that's wat I'll do...'

Charles decided it was time to make his presence known. So, shouting himself, he stepped out crying, 'Plum old chap, how very good to see you!' seizing the old man's hand and pumping it up and down.

Plum tried to sustain his wrath; but the sight of young Charles, cap at a scandalous angle, brown eyes sparkling with pleasure and the aftermath of mirth, he capitulated.

'Well now, an' 'oo 'ave we 'ere eh? Welcome 'ome Mr

Charles I'm right glad ter see yer,' then, seeing a possible advantage he added, 'it's 'igh time I 'ad someone 'ere as can 'andle young warmints like these wot is chasin' me inter an early grave.'

Charles turned, 'Hello,' he said to the boy, 'I think you must be Richard, but you're so surprisingly tall I ...'

'Yes I'm Richard,' the boy instinctively straddled as if to steady himself for a sudden onslaught. Still, he extended a grubby paw and Charles took it. 'You're young Charles aren't you?' he asked. 'I think I remember you.' At which point, Lorme that he was he remembered his graces. Waving towards Sue-Ellen who was watching interestedly he said, 'This is Sue-Ellen, Sue-Ellen this is Charles Danement Sir Charles' son, er, Mrs Stephen Delahaye our new American cousin.'

'Only by marriage,' Sue-Ellen smiled. Charles flung her a salute, uncapped and took the extended hand which had a wisp of rather messy straw adhering to it. As he did so he heard the vision say, 'You were Stephen's special friend weren't you? He often spoke of you and the scrapes you got in together.' Charles' head spun. 'You see,' Sue-Ellen ran on, 'Stephen was my late husband; you did not know he had been killed?'

Charles managed a nod; while continuing to stare as she ran on.

'Of course you did not know we were married, indeed no one knew, not even my father ... until after Stephen was dead.'

'F ... f ... fancy keeping you a secret,' Charles managed, his nervousness causing him to stutter. 'I must apologise for this intrusion; but Plum's an old friend and I've turned up three days early and there was no one at the Manor. Then when I went to the Castle Sawby told me they were all out, ridin' and things so I came down here. Tell you the truth I was fed up.'

'Well don't apologise,' said Sue-Ellen sympathetically. 'Here, take a bucket. Now that you're here we might just as well stop work for a few minutes.' She handed him his bucket, slid another under her slim behind and Richard just squatted on the cobbles.

'I was telling Plum,' she resumed wickedly, 'about the proposed zoo. Not a conventional one, but just a few very special animals to begin with. Then if people show an interest and are willing to pay extra to see them I can always add more.'

'I see,' said Charles limply. 'Might I just ask why you want a zoo?'

'Well now,' she linked her hands around her knees and stared at him gravely, 'my baby son doesn't really occupy enough of my time and I adore animals. Besides it seems such a practical addition to the museum and I've got the money just lying idle; and anyway Richard and I are potty about animals. He worries about them when he's away whereas now I'm here I look after them for him, and save Plum the responsibility.' The last remark tagged on with hasty diplomacy.

Still struggling under the impact of this unexpected encounter Charles murmured, 'I see,' then, turning to Richard, he enquired, 'Are you at the School already?'

'Oh no, I'm still prepping 'till the summer term, then I believe I go into Elmfield, at least that's what father said.'

'My house,' Charles nodded, 'you couldn't do better.'

'Well that's consoling anyway.'

The ice cracked during this exchange. Sue-Ellen and Plum exchanged glances, his still fairly wrathful, hers appealing. She attempted to apply balm. 'Come about Plum do,' she urged, 'we were only trying to pull your leg. I'm going to find a team of trained men to look after the new animals, I promise you I will, so do stop glowering at me. Your face is enough to sour cream!'

'Ar mebbe,' he grudged, 'but,' speaking to Charles and jerking a thumb towards the offender, ''er wants ter bring us lions and tigers and hellyfunts and 'tarnation wolves ter chew us all ter pieces.'

'Oh no they won't,' Richard contested, 'that's just ignorance. Wolves are really domestic animals and they never attack humans.'

'Eh?' even Charles looked startled.

'Oh yes,' assured this extraordinary boy, 'I'll tell you all about them later if you like. It's all in a book I read written by a man who went to live among them.'

'Never mind about that now Ricky,' Sue-Ellen interrupted them, 'I've just had an absolutely topping idea.'

'Then the Lord 'ave mercy on us!' muttered Plum.

'No Plum listen, wouldn't it be much more unusual and kind of distinguished if we had a *white* zoo?'

'White?' Charles repeated, 'all white?'

'Yes,' she warmed to her theme, 'say a white elephant, some white tigers, I remember your sister talking about one belonging to some Maharajah she stayed with before she was married.'

'That's right,' Charles confirmed, 'so she did.'

'And,' Sue-Ellen ran on excitedly, 'we could have white deer, white egrets and white owls – I saw a picture of a most beautiful one in a book.'

'There aren't any white lions,' said Richard flushed with excitement, 'but there are white Polar bears; and a North American mountain goat that's as furry as a bear; white deer; the Sacred White Cow of India . . .'

Abruptly Plum lowered his defences to mutter, 'You could 'ave some of the Duchess of Barton and Sale's white peacocks, they'd make a norrible din though, like our own common ones does.'

'Yes, gorgeous,' agreed Sue-Ellen, 'and it's a lovely sound. Now what else can we think of?'

'Snow geese,' Richard prompted, 'and a snow leopard, pity though there aren't any white lynx.'

'Aren't lynx the most vicious of all the cats?' queried Charles.

'Possibly,' Richard brushed aside such trivia, 'there are white camels too. Oh Sue-Ellen, what an absolutely spiffing idea! Let's make a list and then we'll go and see father. At least,' caution intervened abruptly, '*you* can see him. It should be more, er, diplomatic.'

'That will be a scene worth witnessing,' said Charles with some relish. At which point, dimly, they heard the warning gong for luncheon.

'Oh lor!' exclaimed Richard, 'what a nuisance, now we must go and get cleaned up. You're staying to luncheon of course? I say, do I call you cousin Charles, sir?'

'Don't sir me,' said Charles rising, 'cousin will do very well, though no one knows I'm here, so I don't know about luncheon . . .' he sounded wistful.

'Of course you'll stay,' Richard decided.

'Should I?' Charles turned to Sue-Ellen.

'Yes,' she confirmed, 'besides there's jugged hare, I know because Chef André told me when I was in the kitchens this morning and Aunt Christine would be most disappointed if you didn't come.' She held out a hand, 'We shall have to hurry though or I'll be late changing. See you this afternoon Plum.'

'Ar,' Plum nodded absently. He had food for thought and now found he was in a hurry himself if only to share the latest Castle news with Mrs Plum whose own dinner would doubtless be awaiting the return of her spouse. He tidied away the buckets, muttering to himself, 'Cost a mort er money, but then she's got bushels accordin' to wot they all say ... ar ... well then ... ooo ever 'eard of a white zoo? That'll set the tongues a waggin' I'll be bound!' and so ruminating he shouted some instructions to his 'lads', and set off to plod home through the park as usual.

Charles followed behind the other two also ruminating, '"Aunt Christine" she said ... made free of the kitchens ... not even scared of his flamin' lordship ... and whom can I ask I wonder?' Then as he ran up the steps behind them, deciding 'the little Countess would know all,' he resolved 'I'll pay her a call this afternoon.' He surrendered his cap to Spurling, attempted to straighten his tunic and picked a last wisp of hay from his jacket preparatory to being announced.

His welcome amply compensated for earlier frustrations. Stephanie appeared with her Harry to whom he took an instant liking. By the time they went into luncheon his personal barometer had done an abrupt volte face, enabling him to do full justice to the *Râble de lièvre*, the Stilton and the Prince Albert pudding which followed.

The future vicar of Lower Aynthorp also disclosed during the meal that he and his wife had spent the morning with the retiring incumbent. They were both brimming with plans for their villages. Stephanie declared with the utmost satisfaction that now she would be able to achieve her ambition to form a proper branch of what she called her 'Women's Institute' and also start both a Girl Guide Company and a Brownie pack. Not to be outdone her Harry announced he would become the future Scoutmaster of his own Boy Scouts and Stephanie chattered him down with proposals for 'WI' lectures, competitions, needlework displays and a revival of tuition in making the county's traditional 'straw dollies' at which Plum excelled. 'He can teach those women,' she exulted.

Charles sat marvelling at the metamorphosis and indeed

the marriage of what he thought of privately as 'this unlikely lass.' He was equally fascinated by the startling change in Eustace Bartonbury who had walked in just after they sat down to luncheon.

When the women left the room, Charles moved up to sit beside him and after a little initial prompting, sat listening absorbedly to stories about Eustace's ambulance unit and their exploits in France. He also won Eustace's approval by the pertinent question. 'What will happen to your chaps now sir? Have they all got jobs? There's so many fellers comin' home with no work to welcome them.'

Eustace smiled, 'No indeed, that is the great tragedy; but in this case it is no problem. I shall absorb them into my estate. We've had terrible losses in Yorkshire. Ralph's comin' up with me next week to make all the necessary arrangements and also to overhaul and reorganise almost everythin'. It's all had to go by the board durin' the war though I do have an agent who has to some extent held things together – the poor chap was turned down by his medical board so stayed on right through – which was a blessin' for us though of course the poor feller was pretty put out himself, as you can imagine.'

When they eventually left the dining room to the hovering footwomen, Charles managed to excuse himself. Taking the staircase three at a time he headed straight for the little Countess's private quarters. Here, for the price of drinking a cup of 'disgustin' gnat's water' as he later described Marguerite de Tessedre's *'tisane'* to Henry, he extracted the full story of Sue-Ellen's induction into the family circle. This gave him more food for thought besides bringing back his depression. It was one thing, he pointed out to himself as he headed back towards the stables, to enjoy the company of a 'charmin' gel' but quite different to discover that she was immensely rich. However, the quartet spent a companionable afternoon among the animals and by the time dinner was served and Charles united with his own family at last, Richard and Sue-Ellen cornered him to display their first 'List of White Animals Suitable for a Zoo', a title writ large in Richard's schoolboy hand.

It was Sue-Ellen's intention to tackle Gyles Aynthorp immediately after dinner. In the event Henry reached him first. There, ensconced in one of the familiar old leather armchairs with Diana sprawling across his father's feet and all the old maps and papers surrounding them, Henry broached the subject which was uppermost in his mind at the moment.

The familiarity of his father's old office did much to diminish the gap made by his time in France and the prison camp. The room was thick with memories. Here he had tackled Gyles all those years ago when Petula Danement, as she was then, had turned him down for the third time. Henry looked around him now, as he sprawled before the leaping fire. He recalled how after that third 'turn down' he had spent the night wrestling with the problem and come face to face with the inescapable fact that if anything happened to his father, he the heir, would know absolutely nothing of the responsibilities which he would inherit with the title. He grinned slightly as he remembered, too, those three abortive attempts to turn the door handle and how at last, sweating, he had got himself inside only to find that 'the old man' made it all very easy for him. The formidable parent in fact met his son more than half-way.

Well, he was now twenty-nine, admittedly a trifle rusty on how affairs had gone since he had declared his intention of throwing up his 'cushy' job and getting to France to 'see some action'. He had already got him a son to carry on the line, should anything happen to him. As it transpired he saw nothing like the scrapping his father had experienced during the Boer War; but at least he could now hold up his head when other men spoke of war and now he was keener than ever before to resume his place at Gyles' side helping to pull the estate round again.

Gyles opened the conversation by observing quietly, 'I wanted to chat things over with you to learn, first of all, if you agree with me that our first priority must be to sort out our staff and estate worker problems. We have a double duty as I see it, both to the ones who joined up and to the ones who have worked here for us so splendidly – making a valiant effort to keep pace.'

'Of course,' Henry agreed absently. Up went his hand to rumple his head into disorder which caused Gyles to smile, knowing only too well what the gesture denoted.

'What is your problem?' he asked quietly.

Henry grinned, 'Transparent as ever ain't I?'

Gyles nodded. 'You've somethin' on yer mind. Let's deal with it first, then we'll revert.'

Henry stared thoughtfully into the fire. Then he sighed, and plunged into an account of his meeting with the disabled men in Bond Street.

'At first,' he acknowledged, 'I was boilin' with rage that things could have come to such a pass so soon after all that carnage. Then I went to see Plum and he put me in the picture over our personal losses. When he had done so he lectured me – you know his way, Sir. He said, in effect, that it was no use lookin' back because this made confusion more confounded. He told me bluntly that our job was with the living, to make things as good as we could for the ones who came back to us and I immediately thought of those three men standin' singin' in the gutter.'

His father's eyes were very warm as he listened. 'Did you manage to discover what your three did before the war?'

Henry nodded, 'Two of them only. The one-armed chap was a valet, the peg-legged feller was a groom but I don't know what the blind feller was. They're all workin' men y'know.'

'If we are goin' to re-open the museum,' Gyles mused, 'old Crotchley's past it and wants to retire, we shall need a custodian. Someone to man the turnstyle, take the money. Did you manage to find out whether any of the three were married?'

Henry shook his head.

'Well if the one-armed feller had a wife she could form part of the museum's cleanin' women's team and when he's not ticket collectin' he could be in charge of the heatin' system, given we provide a boy to do the stokin'. That would take care of your one-arm. There are also quarters for a custodian as you know and old Crotchley is goin' to live with his married daughter, so they could move in straight away. Then the peg-legged feller could help Plum, not with muckin' out stables, but there are the cars to clean, harness to take care of – you know young Willy's gone?'

Again Henry nodded.

'Well it would ease both Plum and Grantham, or indeed Simpkins when he returns and I don't doubt Mrs Simpkins would be able to take a lodger if the chap is unmarried. Both Simpkins' children are now in service, so that might prove a solution to number two. As for the blind chap he would have to get trained and I'd be willin' to foot that bill. We could send him to St Dunstan's Hospital to have him taught how to do basket work and mat makin'. Your mother was only complainin' this mornin' that Mrs Peace had come to her with a list of urgent replacements as long as your arm – wait a bit,' Gyles jumped up. 'I have it here somewhere on my desk.' He crossed to the refectory table, rifled through some papers and brought one back to the fireside. 'You see, she wants door mats, matting for staff corridors belowstairs and for the dairy and laundry rooms. It all costs money. We would be far better if we had a man on the strength to make it all, besides, we need game bags for market, not to mention the baskets we use for the hothouse fruits we supply to old Ritz; there would be a savin' in this too with more than enough to keep one man busy I should say.' Gyles looked up, 'Why don't you and I drive up to town in the mornin'?' he asked, 'there's nothin' happenin' here. We could see your chaps, get the details from them and if all turns out as we hope we could then set the wheels in motion. Put it down as our first joint contribution to the peace effort eh?'

Henry smiled gratefully. 'Thanks a lot sir. I think they're pretty decent chaps but y'know all this makes me see the size of the problem we've got here with our own lot. Placin' chaps elsewhere who have been disabled, findin' jobs for the women, workin' out just how many of the old lot will want their jobs back. I may as well admit it that there's a restlessness around which is new to you and me. Some of 'em may not want to go back to their old way of life, long hours, little pay and I've heard murmurings of unease belowstairs.'

'My dear chap,' Gyles acknowledged, 'wages will never go back to what they were. Prices have risen too much already. We have to be prepared to pay more to people who want shorter hours. There's a chit on there which your Pet worked out for me: staff wages. It says all there is to say eloquently enough. The seventy members of our indoor and outdoor staff alone, discountin' their traditional perquisites, cost us over a thousand pounds a year in 1914. That is now the staggerin' sum of a little under three thousand. I spent ten thou' on modern mechanised farm implements, after shellin' out close on half a million when yer grandfather died. Materials are costin' double too. Why, the stuff we used to patch up cottages, barns and sheds alone cost a small fortune and now we've a thorough overhaul to do as you saw today. On top of that there's this new employment tax at two shilling's a month for every man and woman workin' for us. A small item you may think but these things add up. The majority of the thatch is in a scandalous condition too. We've always had our own man. They've been Gillings at it for four hundred years and now the last one's gone and everyone tells me I must expect to pay double for a replacement besides havin' a stranger in a traditional post which has always been held by a man recognised as the finest thatcher in the county.

'Times have changed and we must learn to change with them...' He paused and added, 'Or go under, which is unthinkable. Y'r mother tells me Mrs Peace's requirements in replacements of household items is gargantuan, rangin' from table linen to staff uniforms. Besides which, havin' outfitted all these excellent women they must now go and we must re-equip, so the whole thing begins all over again. As you know free cottages go to all chauffeurs, gardeners and other married estate workers; and free coal and light. Oil's up, coal's up and goin' over to electricity for them would set us back a pretty penny; but it will have to come. Timber's scarce, too, for we haven't had the labour to contend. I added more farm machinery in seventeen. I had to; result of U-boat deprivations. Land went under the plough for wheat when heavy restrictions on imports plus our losses resulted in a drop of from five to three million tons. There are strong rumours that the ban will be lifted now which would mean abundant wheat flowin' in again from abroad. This will bring heavy losses to our farmers on top of all they've have to endure already. They'll have to turn the ploughed fields over to grazin', buy more cattle and sheep and revert to dairy farmin', but they haven't got the capital to lay out, so you know on whom that burden will fall!'

'Of course,' Henry agreed, 'money's always been forth-comin"from us in times of hardship in the past. I don't doubt you will regard this as a precedent to be continued, sir?'

'Naturally,' Gyles reached out for a ledger and passed it across. 'When you've time, glance through that. It records all our sales for the past few years of game, hothouse fruits, flowers and vegetables.'

At Henry's surprised expression Gyles explained, 'You see, in 1916, Petula very wisely pointed out that there was a vast potential market for flowers with so many men in hospital and so many people wantin' to bunch 'em. Obvious really. So we did what we could in this direction too and judgin' from the figures in here we are more than justified to continuin', even in expandin'.' He added, 'What your mother said before all this shemozzle began, just after your grandfather died in fact, was that my main interest must be in the careful husbanding of our resources so as to be sure no man should stand at risk of losing his employment. To cut down on staff now would be shameful. As it is, the papers are full of stuff about emigration. Newfoundland is being exalted as a land of promise for some of our present unemployed. The Irish are floodin' into America; the Scots are goin' to Canada and New Zealand as are our own people. While we have the basic wherewithal to create profitable employment, and so long as it pays its way, our future policy must be staff expansion rather than staff decimation as I am sure you will agree?'

Henry nodded, studying the figures intently, noted the steadily rising graph in the sales of hothouse fruits, luxury vegetables, and even in game despite the lack of guns and the absence of regular, organised shoots. The flowers he saw were beginning to become important. 'Who opened up these flower contacts?' he enquired interestedly. 'We supply quite a string of hotels now I see.' Gyles told him the score.

Marguerite de Tessedre numbered among her cronies old Lady Norrington of Roding-Aynthorp whose gardens were, before the war, considered to be among the finest in the British Isles. When she found herself devoid of menfolk; with sons, nephews and grandsons fighting; brothers and cousins and finally her own husband based in London and working at either the Admiralty or the War Office, she gave a luncheon party at the Carlton, insisting that all the flowers were to be sent from her own glass houses for the decoration of the private room she reserved. Obsequious managers received her when she called on the morning of the luncheon. They were profuse in their praise of the 'exquisite, rare blooms' and, as she had anticipated, they eventually became bold enough to tell her ladyship that such blooms and foliage were becoming very hard to find. From this enterprise her ladyship's intention developed. It was only a short step further for her to say graciously that such information both surprised and pleased her. She was herself in a quandary, having been offered through the Lady

Constance Cummins the pick of her ex-suffragette girls –
ones chosen for their skill in the more eclectic forms of
gardening. Now she felt it incumbent upon her to place
these girls elsewhere as she was loth to put them out of
employment; but with no entertaining and half the rooms
shrouded in dust sheets what else could she do.

The rest automatically followed. A respectful submission
was made and accepted. Thereafter a bi-weekly despatch of
floristry flowed from her houses to meet the Carlton's needs.
Within months demand exceeded supply. Other hotels and
restaurants addressed themselves to her ladyship who
promptly passed them on to her dear friend Marguerite,
pointing out she too might sell from Castle Rising.
Sawbridge then found himself supplied with two more lady
gardeners who, with two of their younger colleagues, hastily
co-opted, took over the tending, cutting, bunching and
despatching of their bi-weekly deliveries. By this time
transportation became an acute problem. At the onset the
new vans drove to London. Later they went to Upper
Aynthorp Station. Thence the flowers travelled on the slow
night train which reached Liverpool Street at dawn. Here
the various hotel vans collected their spoils and bore them
off.

Then came requests for wedding flowers. Marguerite de
Tessedre acquired two more girls and commandeered a shed
adjacent to the hounds' kennels which were no longer in use
as the hounds were gone to the Duke of Barton and Sale's
kennels for the duration. Here she instructed in the art of
bouquet and spray making and found herself a stimulating
interest in so doing and a secret audience of one – Pansy
Appelby – who sneaked down whenever an opportunity
presented itself to watch and learn.

Henry listened, fascinated. 'You'll have to build them a
place of their own,' he mused, 'I think we should consult the
Trusloves sir. It might be better for us to turn all these
activities into a small company, call it Aynthorp Enterprises
or some such name. After all, I've bin thinkin' that if we
have to turn from wartime wheat to peacetime dairy farmin'
it might be a plan to sell our own butter, cream and eggs.
There was another thing hammerin' at the back of my mind!
Blow me if I haven't forgotten what it was.' Automatically
he rumpled his head, which clearly proved helpful for, 'Got
it!' he then exclaimed. 'Yes, I was walkin' down Burlington

Street when I saw in a florist's window one of those ticket things which they stick up to describe the merchandise in glowing terms. This was a large ornamental bowl filled with plants and flowers, all tied up with fancy ribbons. The ticker read – I don't remember the exact words but somethin' about "Latest Trend, Charmin' and Fashionable Gift". *Tante* Marguerite does what she calls "arrangements" better than anyone I know. Perhaps we might even open up a place of our own. It's the comin' thing sir, aristocratic tradespeople. Lady This's hat shop; the Duchess of That's flower shop. We might even end up with a what d'you call it, yes, market garden of our own and grow our own supplies.'

Gyles stood up, knocked out his pipe and with scarcely a pause took up the theme, 'This would be the solution to employin' all the women whom the men will otherwise make redundant; always supposin' they want their jobs back again.'

'Exactly, but – er the expenditure?'

'Pshaw,' said his father with more than a touch of the old Justin in his rebuttal, 'I'm always tellin' yer mother yer can't make omelettes without breakin' eggs – I wonder though if *Tante* Marguerite is up to it? We shall have to talk it out with her.'

It was eventually agreed between them that they would pay a visit to the lawyer's while in London on the following day. If the Trusloves considered Henry's proposals at all practical then they would sound out the little Countess. 'Anyway,' as Henry said, rising, stretching and speaking through a tremendous yawn, 'I believe old Sawby has a pretty touch with flower arrangements too. I seem to remember pickin' up a bit of belowstairs gossip, somethin' about his thinkin' himself every whit as good as *Tante* Marguerite if only he had the chance; but you know how jealously she hangs on to doin' them all herself.'

When Henry tumbled into bed beside his sleeping wife, his last waking thought was of the three ex-soldiers with their collecting box. He grinned contentedly and drifted into sleep in which his dreams gave him a mad sequence of Castle Rising as a giant shop and he in a striped butcher's apron 'sellin' things'.

CHAPTER 5

The Shape of Things to Come

Nanny Rose was acknowledged to be in charge now even by Old Nanny who just rocked away beside the fireguard and slid towards senility. From Nanny Rose's viewpoint, this was tantamount to adding one more baby, albeit a very old one, to her collection.

The young woman was one of those rare creatures who was born to become a second-hand mother to an endless succession of babies, without enduring what she considered the dubious delights of labour pains. Much as a dedicated *pâtissier* finds unceasing pleasure in the scents which envelop him, of vanilla and freshly baked breads, of spices and the pungencies of sweet almonds; so Nanny Rose delighted in the smells of airing nappies, Johnson and Johnson baby powder, warm soapy water and the flower-like sweetness of clean babies enveloped after baths in vast turkey towels. She would sniff delightedly as she tied herself into stiffly-starched aprons or fastened the strings of elaborately goffered pinafore frills, manifesting thereby the love for her way of life which is inherent in every gardener or indeed every compositor who revels in the smell of printer's ink.

Nanny Rose would never marry. She was one of a large family who had escaped from what she always called 'the marriage trap'; thus saving herself from the fate she saw made manifest in both her parents' and her own generation; the drudgery, the anxieties, the struggles to 'make ends meet', the aches and pains concomitant with excessive child-bearing, all winding up in sagging figures, dropped wombs and backache.

She was wont to dilate upon this subject for the benefit of her nursemaid Doris in whom she saw the echo of her earlier self, seeing the girl as a brand to be snatched from the burning, and indoctrinating her with all the zeal of a religious fanatic in pursuit of a convert.

The *leit motif* of evening sessions between the pair when work was done, babies all bedded, night-lights burning comfortingly beside cots and small beds was invariably the same. While they 'did the mending' and old Nanny dozed, occasionally waking with a jerk and snort, only to lapse back into slumber almost immediately, was 'It all depends upon your getting the Right Place and that's what we've both got here,' Nanny Rose declared.

Under her rule there was markedly less friction with belowstairs than when Nanny had held autocratic sway. Nanny Rose believed implicitly in a phrase she was wont to repeat either when turning a naked baby over on her lap to fasten nappies, or in all her dealing with the other servants. 'Gently does it,' she would murmur over and over again which resulted in greater harmony and far more 'perks', in the shape of little attentions voluntarily bestowed by the termagant Mrs Parsons and by the footwomen who supplied their trays. Gone were the shrieks of 'Wot's 'appened to my plum cake?' and 'Where's that dratted footman?' or the dubious welcome when the offender appeared, of 'You're late again!'

If Spurling climbed the many stairs to bring a tray of Mrs Parsons' 'fancies' with the statutory cocoa at nine o'clock, saying as she put down the tray, 'Mrs Parsons said she thought you might like these,' Rose would rise, exclaim pleasurably, 'There now, isn't that kind! Mrs Parsons really shouldn't trouble,' which of course was repeated by Spurling and much approved by 'the termagant'.

'Nice,' she would comment, 'brought up proper that one was, not like the old 'orrer',' which needed no further elucidation.

Even the children liked Nanny Rose. She was the one person who could subdue the extremely naughty Richard as he moved from stage to stage committing fresh mischiefs. His ingenuity grew with his stature. Rose had only to say, 'Oh my poor head, I do declare Master Richard you make my place a hard one, sometimes I think I shall have to give in my notice!' looking the while both pathetic and appealing, for Richard to apologise and undertake to mend his ways. He never did of course; but dramas were terminated more easily while nursery uproars were far more infrequent. Her one problem child out of the present batch was Rupert whose entry into life had been so perilous to his mama.

Whatever Richard had done at any stage, Rupert was worse. His temper was pure Lorme at its most demoniac, which Rose was able to recall was 'the spit image of 'is dead Lordship' and nothing could be more explicit than that. Rupert also *threw*. Once the point of no return had been reached, signalled always by an imperious stamp of one foot and the quick colour flooding to his face until both this and hair were of like colour, he would sweep anything and everything off table, shelf or cabinet screaming to the full extent of his not inconsiderable lungs and, as he learned to speak, dealing out invective while creating havoc. Thus, if they were at tea and he became enraged, bang! would go one foot on the underside of the table, and 'Rotten old tea, rotten old Nanny go-and-see-God . . . evvyfing' and over would go cakes, dishes, mugs with, if Nanny Rose was not quick enough to rise and haul him away kicking and screaming, one wild last tug at the cloth to dispose of any survivors from his initial onslaught.

As Nanny Rose confided to her underling during their evening cocoa sessions, 'What worries me most is the *violence* in such a little boy. It's not natural. If he's like this now I begin to wonder what will happen when he grows up. D'you know last time I wasn't quick enough and he actually grabbed the cake knife before I could stop him. It's frightening that's what it is.'

The pair resolved to remove cake knives from the nursery tea-table; but when the next explosion came Rupert clutched a fork with his pudgy hand and jammed it into Richard's thigh.

'Ouch! you little sod,' Richard yelled grabbing his crimson-faced little brother and thus toppling both their chairs, plus a plate of scones which Rupert managed to flail in transit. The pair wrestled and screamed in a welter of broken chair backs, smashed plate and scraps of buttery scones.

Nanny Rose managed to haul Richard off then she made an heroic dive and grabbed Rupert around his middle. She bore him off, limbs flailing like a windmill, deposited him in the nursery broom cupboard, banged the door, locked it and dropped the key into her starched apron pocket. 'And there you stay,' she shouted through the locked door, 'until you come to your senses you bad, naughty, wicked boy!' Through the stout door came the unbelievable retort, 'Shit on you!' which sent her back with scarlet cheeks to whisper the awful word to Doris.

Dishevelled, breathless, hastily straightening her cap and tucking in wisps of hair which had escaped during the struggle Nanny went in search of assistance. Doris and she then cleared up the mess, dropped the broken china into the wastepaper basket and swept up the crumbs with the hearth brush – the broom being incarcerated in the cupboard with the still yelling delinquent, while Doris calmed the rest of their charges as best she could.

Richard had already capitulated, apologised, consoled sagacious Nanny Rose who was wisely weeping into a large pocket handkerchief.

'I'm ever so sorry Nanny but the little sod jabbed me with a fork. He may be only three and a half but he's so strong . . .'

Nanny permitted herself to be consoled; but as she resumed her place at table and Raikes appeared with a fresh supply of scones she said firmly to her assistant, 'Leave him alone, let him quieten down proper. There's plenty of ventilation in that cupboard.'

'And brooms,' said Richard gloomily.

'Never mind,' Rose ruled, 'another half hour should do the trick.'

All through this performance the other children had watched fascinated, and even now as they resumed tea it was in silence so that they could listen to the thuds and yells still emanating from Rupert's prison. When at length silence came, Rose drew out the key and went to unlock the door. On the floor, bumbling contentedly, sat the erstwhile small fury. He had managed to smash two broom handles. The dustpan now lacked one altogether and had been jumped on until it looked more like a tin pancake than a housemaid's help. Now he was busily tugging the tufts of hair from a soft handbroom, having already completely denuded the long one.

He was put to cot in disgrace. The blinds were drawn down and securely fastened to a hook. The curtains were closed and, without benefit of night-light he was left to ponder on his wickedness. Nanny Rose then marched down the staircase in search of 'Mummy'.

Well conscious of the necessity for respecting protocol she first sought out Spurling and requested her to ask if her ladyship could spare a few moments. Spurling ran Christine down in the gun room with Gyles, obtained an assent and Rose went in. As she entered she heard her employer saying in a most unfamiliar voice, 'Well I shall not go Gyles,' and his lordship reply, 'If you do not my dear that really might set the tongues waggin',' then he broke off, coughed and Christine turned.

'Come along in Nanny,' she changed her voice immediately, 'his lordship is just going, aren't you, my dear?'

'I am,' Gyles answered, a trifle grimly Rose thought, adding from the doorway, 'but don't run away I shall not be long.' The girl stood aside, held open the door, closed it after him and at Christine's invitation 'took a seat' or rather sat perched on the rim of one.

'What can I do for you Nanny?' enquired Christine.

'Well my lady,' Rose looked at her, 'it's just Master Rupert again. He's had another tantrum. Of course he managed to break quite a lot of crocks before I could stop him, but not only that he actually stuck a fork into Master Richard.'

With a great effort Christine controlled her twitching lips. 'Did he – er – draw blood?'

'Oh yes, my lady. Then I put him in the broom cupboard to cool off and when I let him out he'd jumped on the dustpan, broken two broom handles and pulled all the hairs from two brooms as well. At least he'd nearly finished the second one when I let him out.'

The affair was discussed in depth. The list of breakages was accepted. 'I will give these to Mrs Peace,' Christine undertook, adding, 'but in the meantime I will discuss the matter with his lordship. Is the nursery otherwise manageable?'

'Oh yes, my lady, Master Richard is a handful; but I can always deal with him very satisfactorily. The rest are no trouble and come to that nor is Nanny, she just rocks and sleeps and eats.'

There was however one member of the brood whom young Nanny Rose failed to take into account in her report, chiefly due to the fact that he was Schoolroom and not Nursery. Yet old Nanny had trained Rose and inflicted on her many prophetic sessions, when she rocked and predicted according to the state of her corns which were as a crystal ball or a pack of Tarot cards to her in her clairvoyant moods.

Of course this young man, whom old Nanny detested and who reciprocated her feelings, had a remarkable talent for protective colouring. By its nature it went unremarked for this was the virtue of the gift. Thus he passed unnoticed by anyone except old Nanny from the nursery to the greater freedom of preparatory school and thence to Winchester. At thirteen and a half Gilbert Delahaye sat for his entrance examination. He was so amused by what he regarded as the pedestrian quality of the questions that he spent the first few minutes of his set time weighing up the advantages and disadvantages of achieving a high rating; decided that nothing but advantage could accrue from such an exercise and proceeded to hand in such excellent material that he was forthwith salvaged from the rubble of his own age group and placed among fifteen-year-olds from the onset.

His interest in and talent for any form of sporting activity was in exactly inverse ratio to his scholastic abilities. After sundry abortive attempts to make anything from such unpromising material, plus three pairs of broken spectacles without which he blundered about field, court and wicket like a drunken hen, and after due consideration of his astonishing prowess at desk or *viva voce*, he was carefully included out, thereby once more attaining precisely what he wished.

While he was engineering all this, quietly and unobtrusively as usual, he also weighed up his companions. Eighty per cent of them he rejected outright. From the remaining twenty he acquired one equally retiring character who was Jewish, undersized and myopic. This one had learned early that discretion was the better part of valour. The fact that he possessed an elder brother, half-way through his last but one term, tall, bulky and brilliant, weighed heavily in his advantage. Brinkman minor – the original second 'n' in his name had been conveniently jettisoned by their astute papa – was an undisputed 'wart' against whom the hearties might have formed a bullying squad, but this proportion was offset by the physical size of Brinkman Major who moved like a bulldozer, knew his own strength to a nicety (and despised it) but used it wherever and whenever necessary to ensure his own and his small brother's freedom to pursue their chosen paths without duress. Brinkman Major was regarded by his mentors as a mathematical genius. In the privacy of their common room his tutors expressed the view that where Brinkman Major blazed his impressive trail Brinkman Minor would almost certainly follow with young Delahaye giving clear indications of similar talent. Eventually the trio were left to their own devices which was precisely what they had intended from the outset.

They became as nearly one as their age differences permitted. They circumvented authority whenever possible and warded off any abortive attempts at ragging by some peculiarly nasty and unsporting combined efforts, invariably directed in moments of crisis to the more vulnerable parts of the male anatomy.

In direct contrast to their behaviour towards their companions, the Brinkmans displayed impeccable manners towards all adults, only singling out the games master, who was of course the reverse of an intellectual star, on whom to polish their sarcasms in the most polite phrases, which were none the less deadly and – to their dim-witted adversary – unanswerable.

They were unpopular. This furthered their desire to be left in peace, so pleased rather than disturbed them. When Gilbert's first term ended he returned to Castle Rising for the Easter holidays convinced that the two Brinkmans were essential to the furtherance of his own deep laid plans. These, as matters developed, necessitated their being invited to stay with him. There was much to discuss and as the war drew to its ending 'much' became a very great deal indeed.

Gilbert bided his time. He mentioned casually that he had two friends whom he would like to bring home. He indicated to his parents that he might like them to come for a visit 'later on'. Henrietta murmured, 'How nice dear,' and his father stammered, 'So glad dear boy. The, er, friends you make at, er, school are, er, so er, important in later life.' There the matter was left until Brinkman *père*, already knighted at some expense to himself, which he could very well afford, spent much more lavishly on charities until he at length found himself elevated to the peerage in the Birthday Honours of 1918.

During the summer holidays Gilbert furthered his plans by drawing the family's attention to his friends' father, now Lord Brinkman of Emscombe in Surrey. Oddly enough it was Gyles Aynthorp who set the seal of approval upon the proposed visit of the sons by remarking at the breakfast table, 'I've met the feller. Quiet enough, immensely powerful, a financier of considerable stature. Jewish of course, but then so are the Rothschilds and the Cassels. I see nothin' against the boys comin' provided of course it meets with Henrietta and Sinclair's approval.'

This battered couple, taking, as usual, the line of least resistance acceded without demur and in due course Christine wrote a pleasant letter to the new peeress in which she invited both Joseph and Lionel to spend Christmas at Castle Rising.

By the time Gyles Aynthorp was a very old man, the oncoming young had shown him the inevitability of what developed. He became in turn reflective, suspicious and ultimately convinced as the years progressed that it was all a natural, inverse development. Luxury, tradition and fastidious elegance provided a natural breeding ground for revolt for the always anarchistic young, needing only a climate of opportunity in which to burgeon. The seeds had lain dormant over the centuries, save for the Family's re-curring 'runts'. This was largely due to the rigidly main-tained limitations of the formative years of past youthful generations. Even so, the persistently delinquent strain persisted, confirming this anarchical tendency.

When the social barriers were lowered the climate became much more favourable for anarchy. Growth was stimulated. Then by the gradual removal of class barriers, until at schools and universities the 'have nots' won the freedom of education which had once been the almost exclusive right of the 'haves', the high born, the privileged; the inflow of the fanatical – made eloquent at last by education – increased until it dominated and Gyles' breed were subject to the intellectual increment of revolution. Now, all this lay dormant, so even Gyles' inherent intuitions failed him. All this had to wait for the progressive years and seasons before it emerged. By then it was far too late.

Large, pale seventeen-year-old Joe Brinkman drove himself and his brother down in a six-cylinder Napier tourer which his father had given him on his last birthday. Gilbert fidgeted from window to window until the car swung into view. Then he so far forgot himself as to race down ahead of the footwomen and Sawby, wrench open the door and run down the steps to welcome them. Stopping short beside the car door he said, 'Hello,' rather lamely, while trying to conceal the fact that he was out of breath.

The three climbed back to the entrance where Sawby now stood with the footwomen below, busying themselves with the boys' impedimenta. Joe – short for Joseph which he abhorred – carried two opulent bouquets which he subsequently proffered to Christine and to Gilbert's Mama. The Brinkmans were a quiet pair, somewhat dazzled by the setting but striving to conceal it. By the time they had been presented to the assembled members of the family and had been led '*en suite*' to luncheon in the breakfast room, Joe was unable to conceal his interest in his surroundings. He turned to the Dowager and murmured, 'I hope you do not mind my admiring your linenfold, Lady Alicia. It is magnificent.'

This broke the ice effectively. The Dowager launched herself into a spate of information concerning the linenfold. When luncheon ended the boys accepted Richard's invitation to 'come and have a look at the stables', and Gilbert went with them, albeit reluctantly while Sue-Ellen and Gyles smiled at each other conspiratorily. She had already bearded this lion who in response had roared as gently as any dove concerning her zoo proposals. He now led her away to resume the discussion while the rest of the family passed judgement on Gilbert's friends. The general consensus was that they were 'surprisin' considerin' their unprepossessin' appearance' – thus the Dowager; while Henrietta contributed rather primly, 'Well dear, some of us had to be behind the door when good looks were being distributed.' And Christine added as her mite, 'They have charmin' manners, you must show them round the Castle *Belle-mère*, if it would not tire you.'

As any suggestion of impending senility put the Dowager into a state of instant fury, a lively dispute ensued during which the young visitors sank into limbo.

'Stables is it,' the Dowager decided angrily, rising, stately and huffed as she excused herself on the Parthian grounds that she was in need of a little exercise and fancied she might walk to the village.

As the doors closed behind her, 'Well, you asked for it Aunt Christine,' said Petula laughing as she too prepared to leave them. 'I'll bet I know where she's really gone.'

'Where pray dear?' enquired Henrietta.

'Stables, come on Henry we'll follow and see the fun.'

The education of Sue-Ellen along the lines envisaged by the Dowager and the little Countess had made scant progress. They could do very little anyway until the girl's mourning period for her father ended. By the time that year had passed the war situation made progress even more difficult and by the time the Armistice came everyone was too involved. So Sue-Ellen pursued her chosen course.

Every six months her late papa's agent made the long trip from Texas to report, discuss and receive his instructions. Silas Blenkinsop had trained his daughter so well that by the time the war was over the girl had the reins of government firmly in her long narrow hands. In effect, and far ahead of her time, she just carried on and carried forward from where her father left off and it was she who wrote, in the January of 1919, advising Sam Greenbaum to come over as soon as possible. She wrote in her round, still rather girlish hand,

I have a strong instinct that the next development for us should be in the field of commercial aviation. Now that everyone has become accustomed to the fact that aircraft have come to stay, it is imperative that we maintain the lead my father established. This I am confident can best be done by turning our full attention to the production of comfortable, even luxurious passenger aeroplanes. I can already envisage the time when people will travel by air from the States to Europe as a matter of course. If we are to lead the way there is no time to be lost. My son is now close on five years old, so he can travel with me as I am reluctant, as you know, to leave him for any lengthy period. Nor do I wish to interfere with his education once he is old enough to go to boarding school. Therefore the time is ripe now for me to spend at least a year at the factories so that I can make decisions on the spot; but before that I would like you to come over here so that we can review the whole situation with Lord Aynthorp who is a very shrewd man, despite the extremely privileged position which he enjoys. I wish him to favour us with his opinions and suggestions from the onset. Then when you return you can instruct the Mobberlys to prepare the house for us and inform them now that we shall be bringing Stephen and an English nanny. In the meantime

I will draw up the necessary plans for the rooms which they will occupy.

Please alert the Mobberlys that the swimming pool must be thoroughly cleaned by experts. I also believe there is an improved form of pool heating now available. Please bring all the necessary brochures, pictures, diagrams and estimates with you so that I can authorise you to have this fixed by the time we come. My in-laws enjoy poor health, but I am hoping to persuade them to come too; though I am inclined to think they may take some persuading.

She wrote on, about the proposed building extensions and about the necessity for additional personnel. After filling a great many pages she ended on a characteristic note.

In the meantime I am engaged upon a very small project of my own over here as I have decided to make my permanent home in England. This again involves Lord Aynthorp who extends you a warm welcome as usual.

Dear Sam, as my father's oldest and closest friend I must close on a more personal note. Although I miss father dreadfully I may as well 'fess up as I used to do when I was a little girl. Lord Aynthorp has been so wonderful to me, so kindly and so understanding that I feel already I have found in him my greatest consolation. It is such an easing to me to take my problems to him that I cannot envisage ever leaving the Castle now. As everyone in this remarkable family seems to want me, this is what I intend.

Later on perhaps Stephen might go to Harvard, after he has had a spell at his father's old university. We can talk more about that when you come over. When you have had time to make the necessary arrangements please cable me your date of arrival and name to whom you wish to delegate during your absence which I promise will be as short as I can make it. I know how you fuss when you are away.

Your affectionate Sue-Ellen.

She sat for a while staring out over the grounds, then she picked up her letter, read it through again, left it on her desk for the footwoman to collect and hurried off to Gyles' office.

Reflecting on these things as she sat in Gyles' quiet office, she decided to force the issue. She began, 'I have something difficult to ask of you and I do not quite know where to begin. I am so conscious of the great deal you have done for me and the wonderful way in which you have welcomed me into your family – given me a home in fact – for my father's house in Texas can never be home to me again now that he is gone. I guess I was just a ship without a rudder when you brought me here. Now, as you know, I am myself again. I have greatly benefited by your advice, too, over my business affairs. Presently I shall have to go back to America to launch a whole new project; but my main interests lie here. I want my son to have an English education' – she had long ago learned never to say British – 'and indeed I have written to Sam telling him all this and that I want, if I may to have him come over and visit with me before I take my trip.'

Gyles cut in warmly, 'My dear, you must know by now that we all welcome you here. You *have* become part of this family and you have given immense pleasure and happiness to my sister and her husband. Indeed I would say, as would we all that you have done much to recompense them for ... er ... for ...'

'Stephen's behaviour,' Sue-Ellen said swiftly. 'I *know*, you know. One cannot be here among you all without having learned, shall we say a lot I only suspected before I came.'

'Exactly so,' Gyles instinctively took out his monocle and began to polish it. Then he said, 'Sam is welcome any time he cares to come, you must know that too, so what is it that you are wantin'? I'm sure you have only to ask.'

Sue-Ellen looked at him doubtfully. 'Well, no, you see Uncle Gyles it is a matter of your family pride and I would not care to propose the unacceptable.'

Gyles looked at her thoughtfully. 'I think my dear you had better explain although I have a suspicion I know already; but please go ahead and tell me in your own words.'

She still hesitated. 'Even if money comes into it?'

He nodded. 'Even that.'

So she began. She explained her own interest in caring for animals. She touched on the time she spent with Richard behind the stables, part of which she had told him already. Then she went on to outline her plan. 'Your mother has a phrase "Satan finds mischief for idle hands to do". I shall become ripe for mischief if I do not find myself a taxing occupation. If I ever marry again it will not be for a very long time. I am quite sure about that. I could travel of course but I want to stay here. Please can I have a zoo? It might be an added item of interest to the public when you open the museum again. The thing is that I have such a very great deal of money lying idle and I want you please to give me the land and in return let me buy the animals and employ proper keepers to take care of them. It's little enough compared with what you have done for me. I have it all worked out. I even have a list. You see I thought it would be of more interest to the public if I made it a white zoo?'

Gyles looked up from scrutinising his hands. 'A white zoo?' he repeated.

'Yes, all white animals. The range is wide as you can see from my list and as you charge admission to the museum so we could charge for entrance to the animal reservation. I think it would be altogether better to put the whole thing on a business footing, make the reservation pay for itself, if possible, go for a profit.' She made a helpless small gesture with her hands. 'I suppose it is my father's business training, but I really do believe you could look on this as being to my advantage, as an investment; with you putting in the land and me footing the cost of the animals as my capital investment. Then I could pay for staff and maintenance against the potential revenue. We could divide the takings between us fifty-fifty.'

Despite himself Gyles was interested. And when he asked, 'Have you the list?' stretched out his hand and took it from her, Sue-Ellen knew she had won.

Of course, he temporised. He even explained his policy, which he said differed greatly from his late father's in that where the late Justin Aynthorp had always taken his own line and thereafter presented any new decision to the Family as a *fait accompli*, he preferred to have the Family's consent before embarking on any new project. He ended by saying, more to himself than to this astonishing young woman, 'I would be certifiable if I did not know already that my Mama and *Tante* Marguerite will concur only too willingly. They must be discounted because such a ploy with all its complications is calculated to entrance them. You must have observed that already.'

They talked on after this for some time. Finally he rose, escorted her to the door, patted her shoulder and delivered his parting shot. 'Do not deceive yourself though my dear that you have hoodwinked me. Your fifty-fifty proposal is in line with the one chicken-one horse proposition; but I take your intention and find it charmin'. Let us leave it at that for the time being.'

The area behind the stables was filling up on this bright January afternoon. The Dowager was already ensconced in a rickety old chair covered with a carriage rug. Two cushions from the governess cart had been tucked behind her back by Plum and a second rug used to cover her knees. She was enjoying herself enormously. Richard was displaying his treasures to the two Brinkman boys. Then Nanny appeared with little Stephen who instantly began clamouring for a ride. A moment later Petula and Henry stepped out to join the group. No sooner had they exchanged greetings than a stable boy poked his head through the opened door announcing, 'Texas Ranger is already saddled Mr Plumstead.' Stephen promptly flung himself against the Dowager's rug-covered knees shouting, 'Come and see me ride "Bemmer",' which was the best he could achieve with the *Belle-mère* he had adopted for his personal form of address to his great-grandmother.

Obediently 'Bemmer' moved aside the rug and informed him gravely, 'Then you will have to pull me up,' at which moment a flushed and breathless Sue-Ellen ran towards them crying, 'We're going to get our white zoo. He only has to find out if it's alright with the family.' And then with a blatant relapse into her old speech, 'Oh gee am I excited! I'll tell the world I am!'

Richard swung round, eyes blazing, 'You mean you told father about my animals and he didn't go up in smoke?'

'Not at all,' Sue-Ellen rumpled his hair fondly, 'and he'll go shares with me and you'll have real wild animals at last, my love. As a matter of fact,' she added thoughtfully, 'it's only really dawned on me right now that the old devil knew all along.' She seized a bucket and inverted it beside the Dowager and Stephen who, with a disgusted look, turned away from his 'Bemmer' and let out a huge yowl.

'Oh, my darling,' his mother turned penitent, 'did I interrupt something?'

In between yowls Stephen managed, 'I was going riding. Bemmer was coming to see, now you spoiled everything.'

There was a hiatus as his mother swung him up onto her shoulder. 'Ride on Mummy,' she said placatingly. 'Come on we'll put you on Texas Ranger and when you have your ride you can show yourself to Bemmer, how's that?' The others watched as the pair vanished through the stable's back door.

As they reappeared, Richard said, 'I shall have to find out who is the best man to buy them from, it's very important we get the very best.'

As though she had not broken off, Sue-Ellen answered from the doorway, 'Relax son,' she said, still very American. 'Uncle Gyles knows someone. He says he's called Frank Buck, and we're going to meet him.'

Plum decided he had remained mum for long enough. ''Ere, 'ere,' he ordered, ''old 'ard a minnit your lady, er madam, did yer ask 'is lordship if we could 'ave keepers or are you just lumberin' me with a load wild beasties?'

Sue-Ellen laughed. 'No, cross my heart. I said keepers, truly I did.'

'Ar,' Plum's old face cleared wonderfully, 'and kin I 'ave the mannidgin' of 'em. Keep 'em in order like?' Suddenly he manifested an unsuspected jealousy. 'Arterall, I've 'ad the lookin' arter o' them pesky cripples ain't I?'

'Cripples,' shouted Richard instantly crimson with fury, 'they ain't cripples you old B—,' he broke off aghast, clapped one hand over his mouth and eyed his grandmother awefully over it.

'I have heard the word "bastard", Richard, before today,' she observed tranquilly. 'I would only beg leave to point out to you, my child, that with your manifold advantages of circumstance and education your use of such a word to express reproach shows a lamentable paucity of vocabulary.'

Petula and Henry giggled. Sue-Ellen, still not wholly accustomed to the Dowager's unpredictable attitudes just stared disbelievingly. 'Lamentable paucity of vocabulary!' she exclaimed. 'Oh gosh! that's one way of putting it.'

'Quite the best way I do assure you, my dear,' the Dowager remained unruffled, 'I recollect that the word is a favourite with Plum whom, if I am not wholly mistaken is wont to apply it with depressin' frequency to old Nanny, whom he detests.'

Plum collapsed, turned his head away and muttered, 'Shem a witch, that's wot!' To mask his confusion he gave Richard a shove, 'Now come young feller me lad,' he hectored, 'git yer hanimals cleaned up, don't jes stand there gawpin'.'

Sue-Ellen rushed on her fate joyously. 'What's more,' she babbled, 'I gave him a copy of my list. He took it without a murmur. He did say he would have to consult with the family first as that has always been his policy, which I understand. . . .' she began to falter.

'Was not my late husband's way,' the Dowager supplied blandly.

'Eer – yes,' Sue-Ellen admitted dreadfully embarrassed.

The Dowager was not to be ruffled it seemed. 'When he does ask our opinion my dear I shall tell him your proposal has my blessin' and I can vouch my sister-in-law Marguerite will concur with that.'

Sue-Ellen's eyes widened as she realised the enormity of the pit which she had dug for herself. Poised on the brink, she became tongue-tied, the more so as the Dowager's eyes now sparkled with amusement.

'I have the impression,' she observed to her riveted witnesses, 'that my son said as much to you and belittled the value of our support . . . ?' She made the words a question and then waited with great composure.

'Er . . . well . . . not . . . in so many . . . er . . . words,' Sue-Ellen faltered.

'Ha!' the Dowager cast the rug aside. 'So I was right! He did. Such brazen effrontery! You can take it from me, my dear, you *will* obtain family approval; but now I must leave you. Henry kindly help me out of this chair. I shall devote the rest of the afternoon to ensuring success for Sue-Ellen.'

Henry stepped forward, choking with suppressed laughter, 'Oh you old naughty – you're going vote catchin' aren't you?'

'Never mind what I am going to do,' said her ladyship briskly. 'You will see in due course, oh yes, you will see.' So saying, having gained her feet, she accepted her stick from her grandson and thumped off.

When she had gone, 'What now?' asked Petula tremulously.

Henry appropriated his grandmother's chair and stretched out his long legs. 'I fancy,' he predicted, 'I can plot the old harpy's course for us all. First a little social call on dear Sinclair and Henrietta. Then a casual, "Oh how surprisin' to find you here!" when she has trotted all over the Castle to root out Uncle John and Aunt Primrose. Then, I think, some trumped up excuse for getting at Mama, and finally a long conclave with *Tante* Meg. Oh it's as plain as Palliser's unlovely countenance m'father hasn't a dog's chance in hell!'

Sue-Ellen was still looking bewildered. 'You mean I shouldn't have told her, don't you? Oh dear, I am sorry, it just slipped out, I was so excited.'

'He means nothing of the sort,' Petula soothed, 'he only wants to point out that you did the one thing calculated to get her back up. Once she's roused, Grandmama is perfectly, deliciously ruthless. She will stop at nothing. She and Uncle Gyles adore each other; but the rivalry between them is stupendous. Surely you have noticed that life is one long, running battle between them? It was the same with Grumpy when he was alive.'

'We-el,' Sue-Ellen admitted, 'I had noticed something of what you say. What I would like to know is, *who usually wins*?'

Petula and Henry said simultaneously, '*Belle-mère* always wins. She has a finger in every pie.' They then turned to each other, shouted 'snap!' linked little fingers, Petula yelled 'Dryden', Henry retorted 'Pope', and Sue-Ellen sank back onto her bucket and looking utterly bewildered. 'I just do not understand a single word,' she complained, 'will someone please explain?'

They did so.

No one had even noticed, let alone commented on the disappearance of Gilbert and the two Brinkmans. They had just vanished as Sue-Ellen rushed out with the news. They were not in fact seen by the rest of the family until the following morning.

In the days when James and his cousin Ninian, who together were nicknamed 'The Inseparables', had been sixteen, an in between age which was neither young enough for the schoolroom nor old enough to be allowed to dine with the family; they had been given a small, indeterminate room which they promptly christened 'In Transit'. Here they enjoyed complete privacy, were waited upon at night by the youngest footman and were content to divide their attention between the food on their plates, the racing news and their form book. After a great deal of circuitous prompting by

Gilbert he had managed to convince Christine that it was she who had found a felicitous solution to coping with Gilbert and his friends by giving them the same rather characterless chamber. 'After all,' as she pointed out to Gyles, 'a fourteen-year-old host to a boy of his own age and another of seventeen constitutes a knotty problem with placements at formal dinners; besides being chronically boring for them poor dears.' Thus Christine assuaged any pangs of conscience she might otherwise have felt while the trio were delighted.

As Joe said, monitoring the pouring of a large sherry for him by Spurling, 'Now we can talk in peace and get something started at last.'

That, it transpired, was precisely what they did.

It all came to a head when Gilbert produced, with the soup, a cumpled copy of the *Morning Post and Telegraph,* folded at the personal column and with one item ringed round with red pencil. He handed it across to Joe.

'What's this?' he enquired laying down his soup spoon.

'SALE, of Government Surplus Stocks, Wednesday, January 1st next, 11A, Marine Sales Room, Dover.' He looked up to see Gilbert regarding him thoughtfully. 'Oh well then,' he said easily, 'we'll drive down together and see what's suitable, if anything.' While the footwoman was absent he propped his elbows on the table and spoke the words which put the last small piece of their current puzzle into place. 'I forgot to mention, I believe, that my father opened a banking account for me last birthday. He deposited five hundred pounds to start me off and promised to double any increase I could make in that sum before I was twenty-one.'

For some extraordinary reason Gilbert, who seldom smiled, promptly doubled up with laughter. When Raikes appeared with their fish she was astonished to see all three boys in like condition. Through the noise the footwoman thought she heard the curious observation,

'That'll cost him a pretty penny won't it? Ha, ha, ha, ha, ha!' The words of course were spoken by Joe.

CHAPTER 6

The Unchartered Freedom

Lucy awoke on the morning of Lucien's eighteenth birthday and stared thoughtfully at the ceiling which Piers had painted for her. Mr Silk, her King Charles Spaniel slept on at her feet. The fat little cherubs above her head seemed to be smiling this morning as if, for them too, this was to be a very special day.

Lucy lay for a while, suspended between the states of sleeping and waking, her forward mind still dormant, her thoughts flitting like the butterflies which fluttered in perpetual indecision around the painted ribbons held in the cherubs' dimpled fingers, now vanishing between the fluffy clouds of their painted heaven, now emerging to perch on the ribbon strands.

Dear Piers, she thought fondly, revelling in the delicious setting he and her brother had created for her, so much of it done surreptitiously in those stolen visits, covered only by Sissy's presence and by Sissy's devoted studies at the museums and art galleries at which Lucien was supposedly informing his devious mind. Now on this so long awaited day he was to become the secretary to their new company, holding not only his own given shares but Lucien's too until the boy should come of age in three years' time. It amused her to reflect on those return journeys which the pair had made to Castle Rising, Sissy instructing on what he had seen and learned and Lucien absorbing it all intently, his fair, curly head bent as he made little scribbled notes of his own while the train wobbled and shook.

Lucien knew only too well that he would not have succeeded in deceiving the wily old Dowager unless he had been briefed, and adequately informed when it came to yet another of those seemingly guileless interrogations to which his grandmother submitted him at irregular intervals. He knew also that he could never have borne any of it if the waiting years had not given him those precious 'gallery hours' when Sissy sweated away in a composite state of adoration, for Lucien and in terror – of the Dowager Lady Aynthorp.

Lucien lived for those hours when, in absolute dedication, the trio worked away on their house, planning, designing and directing the workmen they employed, engaged on the total ploy of getting all ready according to their united tastes in preparation for the day when Lucien would 'escape' and, as usual, Lucy would cover that deliberate and precipitate retreat for them both from the Castle and Lorme rule at last. They had fought and plotted, lied and deceived in order to win what they would win today; but Lucy would have been totally inhuman had she not felt some pangs of regret as she looked back over what they had done so pitilessly. However, as had always happened and always would; her acceptance of both the necessity and the inevitability of their actions hardened her against the Lormes who had tried so hard to keep her from her brother.

Protected as she had always been she could see no possible justification for the Lormes unremitting efforts to separate them from each other. Her concept of the links which had held them close from babyhood went no farther than 'it had to be'; for as yet life had not imposed upon her the demand that she face reality. She only knew that she and Lucien needed each other so completely and understood each other so exclusively that all her life, from the first moment she held her new-born brother in her arms, had been dedicated to his wishes, his desires, and his future, so that for her it was beyond questioning that the ends justified the means.

A wave of exultation swept her as she realised that at this moment Lucien was making his final preparations and that tonight – a huge wave of excitement flooded over her in a triumphant surge – *he would sleep here in their own home*, free, safe and inviolate at last. For, as she had always intended, she would play his last hand in the game for him if only because she had always known instinctively that he had not the strength to play it for himself. No matter, she had the strength for both of them. She had known this from the time he fled to her to sob out his griefs in her arms as a tiny boy. She had been ready then with the consolation he needed. She was ready now and, she promised herself, fully awake at last and very clear of thought – she would always be ready no matter what would endanger Lucien in the future.

As her mind became settled again she began a methodical check of the details for this last and first day.

She was going to Castle Rising to tell them at last exactly what had been going on since the day she obtained their permission to drive and buy her own motor – provided, of course, she chose a chauffeuse who was trustworthy enough and suitable to constitute adequate chaperonage for 'Careenin' around the countryside stirrin' up welters of dust and wreckin' the roses in the hedgerows besides puttin' up an obnoxious stench,' as Gyles Aynthorp described this exercise.

By making herself absolutely necessary to this chauffeuse, Lucy had gained her unswerving allegiance. With this accomplished she merely moved on towards the gaining of a far tougher objective: Miss Poole, with an 'e', as she always reminded potential employers of her services as social secretary *par excellence*. Christine Aynthorp had engaged her for the last London season of 1914; the Dowager had deemed her 'indispensable'.

The intervening years had been for Lucy a period of personal dedication to her own and her brother's cause. *They* intended he should at least go to the ''varsity'. Lucy determined to allow no more waste of time once Lucien reached his eighteenth birthday . When she was eighteen she had come into the little fortune left to her by her maternal grandmama – albeit only the interest would be hers until she was twenty-one – therefore she had worked out at once that by the time Lucien was able to inherit his equal share of that estate, she would have been mistress of her fortune for over a year. All her sights became focused upon Lucien's eighteenth birthday when, on the very day and not one hour later, they would share the home and run the fashion house as they had always intended. She knew beyond any doubt that with her brother's departure, with the faithful Sissy of course, his fortune would be out of Family control, and when she pointed this out, making it perfectly clear that Lucien wanted nothing else and that both had plotted towards it through the years, the battle would be won at last. She knew instinctively that neither her once rather futile but now rather splendid Papa, nor her shallow, lovely Mama would attempt any embargoes thereafter which could lead to scandal. All she had to do was to point out as kindly as possible that only scandal *could* result from their interfering any more. their *partie était pris*; and this, made known not just to their parents but to the entire family, her Aunt Christine and her Uncle Gyles in particular would make an end of the matter once and for all.

Then quite suddenly an alien thought arose, one which had never trespassed before. 'Perhaps,' she questioned, 'Lucien and I are a new kind of runt in the Family. Or, at least,' she amended hastily to herself, 'perhaps that is how *they* will see us which is really all for the best because runts spell scandal and scandal is unendurable to them all. Best of all they might find themselves forced to acquiesce publicly if all went well. . . .' On this Christian thought, the Lady Lucy flung back the silk sheets and foam of lace and ribbons which covered her and groped on the floor for her tiny feathered mules.

It had never occurred to this young girl that the fragile thing of beauty in which she slept alone was a bed for love, a bed designed for lovers' dalliance. It pleased her because she found it 'quite delicious'. When she lay back in it with the pale blue sheets folded back to disclose her monogram, and sat up in it in her chiffony nightdresses and marabout bed jackets, designed for her by Lucien, she merely derived added pleasure from studying her reflection in the oval looking glass overhead, around which the painted cherubs swung and flew. Above all it pleased her since, this transcending all other considerations, Lucien had shared in all of it until the day when it was completed and she was asked by him to dress herself in the first of the new nightgowns and climb up the low silver steps into the galleon bed so that he might study the final effect.

Had it been pointed out to her that it was a romantic bed, suited to both romance and passion she would very likely have riposted, 'Impossible, it isn't big enough for two my darling silly boy,' for that was Lucy.

She crossed to the silver and white coiffeuse, lifted the silver hair brushes with more cherubs embossed on them, which Piers had discovered in a disreputable shop in Chelsea, and began brushing her curls, eventually tying them with a pale blue ribbon. It reminded her as she did so that she had done precisely the same just before going down to the Music Room at the Castle for that first meeting with Piers.

All the emotion that stirred was the reflection that it had

been such a very long and difficult period between their first meeting and today when, as a trio, they stood poised upon the brink of achievement. She turned away and went back to the galleon. She climbed in, pushed Mr Silk down so that only his little face showed above the bedclothes and reached out to press the hidden bell button on her bedside table, which had once been a needlework box for a French Queen who went headless to her grave. On it now lay the pink jade heart which Piers had given her when he left Castle Rising. For one fleeting instant she wondered if perhaps at that time it had been symbolic of more than friendship; but she quickly shrugged that thought off too.

Waiting for Violet to bring her breakfast tray, Lucy tried to probe herself, seeking to find any void in the spread of her content with her chosen way of life, to be living as always at Lucien's shoulder, in his shadow, protecting, encouraging, adoring. She smiled at such a foolish fancy. Of course she could never want for more than the total fulfilment that would be hers when Lucien left Piers' flat and came walking through the door into their own home and into their shared career. By so doing she realised, he became Lucien of '*Lucy et Lucien, Haute Couture*', future darlings of the fashionable world, to which by reason of their birth and upbringing, they had complete *entrée* already.

Nothing clouded the serenity of Lucy's face which still retained that childlike look which she resented; yet she faced a scene with the Family in anticipation of which the staunchest of men might flinch. Inwardly she fluttered just a little, feeling the need to press her hands together for a moment as if drawing power from the contact palm to palm. Still nothing showed in her face which was as artlessly pretty as when she sat in the car in the Mall on the way to presentation at the Palace, with three feathers in her hair and admiring crowds flattening their faces at the windows. She had enjoyed every minute of the brilliant season. Dimples out and secrets neatly cached she turned heads and was besieged by admirers. Then in the small hours, sitting rubbing her aching feet against each other, she covered page after page to Lucien and posted them surreptitiously every morning. As she smiled reminiscently, Violet scratched on her door and coming in, her face just showing over the high held tray, she bade her new employer, 'Good morning, milady, it is a lovely day for Mr Lucien's birthday and please cook says shall she send the cake up for tea this afternoon or put it on Mr Lucien's present table?'

'On the present table, please,' Lucy bent forward for pillows to be slipped behind her. 'I may not be back in time for tea and then Mr Lucien might not care to cut it without me so let us be on the safe side in case he thought he might have been forgotten.'

'Oh, miss,' Violet sounded shocked, 'as if we could forget Mr Lucien, we're all ever so excited he is coming home.'

The girl could not have said anything more calculated to please and 'Bless you,' said Lucy, a trifle absently for she had seen the little cockaded note which decorated the tray. She snatched it up; only the Dowager and Lucien still folded cockaded notes.

This one was brief, saying only, 'Good morning lovely Lucy-Lou, unbelievably you will open and read this at the beginning of our so long dreamed for day. See you before you go to the Essex Dungeons. All our love, Lucien and Piers.'

Lucy smiled indulgently. Naughty Lucien, referring to Castle Rising as the dungeons, knowing full well that he only ever did this when he was in his most flaunting mood and when backed, no surrounded by his protectors, Piers, Lucy and Mr Sissingham, his erstwhile tutor. Sipping her chocolate, Lucy envisaged the stuttering 'Sissy' coming in through the white door with its brass knocker shaped like a hand, and its brass lion door handle, to begin his first day's work with the account for *Lucien et Lucy Couture*. Precious little work they would do today with her away! Breaking her croissant, Lucy then remembered that Sissy's long apologetic letter of resignation lay in the small dressing case Violet had packed for her to take with her. Beside it lay another 'Sissy missive' to the Dowager in which the young man did what he could to apologise and to thank her for all she had done for him over the years.

'We're sickeningly ungrateful,' Lucy said aloud, 'we're four black sheep!'

Violet peeped around the door where she was busy laying out Lucy's travelling clothes. 'Beg pardon, milady, did you call?'

Lucy shook her head. 'I was talking to myself,' she smiled, 'oh, and that reminds me, have you any message for your cousin Pansy?'

'Appelby, milady,' corrected Violet, 'oh, if you would milady, just my love and to let her know I am well and very happy and ask that she and the family is too.'

'It shall be done' – Lucy's mind was elsewhere – then, 'Tell me, Violet, did Miss Rosalind talk to herself when you maided us both for our first season?'

The maid's lips closed resolutely. She waited in silence. Eventually, 'It is no matter,' Lucy added carelessly, 'but I must confess I am curious that you will never speak of her.'

The girl's eyes were sorrowful. 'Then I will,' she said, sounding suddenly as if she had been running very fast up a great number of stairs. 'Miss Rosalind, er Madam Fitzpatrick as I understand she is called now, was very firm with me right from the beginning. She said, "I am a very private person and I do not allow anyone to discuss me at any time", so I suppose,' she hesitated then added, 'I have the habit milady that is all.'

Lucy looked wide-eyed over her cup. 'Soooo,' she marvelled, 'you knew what was going on. You kept her secret. Oh dear, what a tragedy! And now he is dead with few to regret it and she's a widow.'

Violet so far forgot herself as to shake her head. Grey eyes met brilliant blue ones and with remarkable courage Violet said, like an indictment, 'She just, er, escaped milady which was what she wanted to do.' Silently the girl added 'like me' but said no more.

'Quite right,' Lucy mused. 'I wanted to escape too and you came with me but as you will not discuss Rosalind with me, so you will never discuss me with anyone.'

'That is right my lady,' the girl stood firm. 'I never would have come if I had wanted to do different.'

As she hurried towards her bathroom with what must be, she already knew the only sunken bath of its kind in London, Lucy thought she had detected a faint note of reproach in the maid's voice. She decided to drop the matter, climbed into the scented water and lay back speculating on just how many of the occupants of Castle Rising really wanted to be there, more than anywhere else. Running over them in her mind she decided, 'All except perhaps the young convalescents who were longing to get home and that after all is not relevant.' So she began soaping herself and humming a little tune.

The little jewelled clock on her coiffeuse ticked away the

morning minutes rapidly. By the time she was ready the hands had reached nine thirty so, leaving her dressing case for Violet to take to the car, Lucy hurried to the lift and soared up one floor to her brother's private working world.

In four weeks they would show their first small collection. She had done what she could to iron out as many creases as possible in advance of Lucien's arrival. The mannequins as they were now called were already engaged, the champagne ordered, the invitations engraved and the list attached all ready for Lucien to go through so that they could then be posted. Blessed as she was by Miss Poole's efficiency and Miss Poole's almost unbridled enthusiasm for 'this amazing venture', as she privately termed it, Lucy found it all very uncomplicated. The only part she disliked was seeing the 'travelling men' – this thought a remainder from the Castle's name for the little man who travelled the great houses with Christmas, Easter and Hallowe'en decorations which he spread out for examination. Lucy found little differences between this character and the men who came to their house with patterns of silks and laces, with cards of buttons and buckles, with sample pieces of embroidery, tassels, cords, and such vital things as hooks and eyes, poppers – neither she nor Lucien could bear the term 'press studs' as used by the workroom girls – with sewing silks and 'No. 8 straws' as the long sewing needles were called, and with buckram and lino, muslin for *toiles* ribbons, and artfully shaped pads for supplying curves where curves were lacking. They also brought special sewing silks for something called 'sprats' heads' and varying lengths of whalebone, these last for which to their unending astonishment they found no sale whatever. This morning however Lucy decided to dismiss them all on the grounds that 'Mr Lucien will be here himself this afternoon if you can return then or later'. With pretty smiles, inwardly chafing slightly she dismissed them and went across to the bare, deal table under the wide uncurtained window where six girls sat at work. Another similar table, was set by the next pair of windows in readiness for the next contingent whom Miss Poole had already interviewed *in depth*, requesting that they return on the morning after Lucien's arrival with some example, no matter how modest, of work which they had done for themselves.

The big room – two knocked into one by this time – was dotted with 'stands', which was the name given to the canvas-covered torsos on adjustable pedestals which were dotted about, covered with gowns in varying stages of completion, or just with '*toiles*': the initial muslin patterns from which the cutters made up the materials given to them. Two very small elderly women with black velvet pads fastened by black elastic bands to their wrists drew pins from them and stuck them in their mouths as they worked away at a couple of the spectral 'stands' and another stood at a long ironing board, pressing open a seam. All round the room, above head level were bolts of materials, while pinned to the edge of the shelves were Lucien's completed sketches for ball and dinner frocks, for day and walking outfits, for mantles and cloaks, and one for a white wedding dress. Attached to each was a scrap of the fabric to be used, and each sketch like some gruesome religious painting was stuck about with arrows with notes instead of blood drops dripping from them.

Lucy passed through quickly, with a friendly nod for each girl and opened the door at the far end marked 'Office. Private' behind which lay the ex-tutor Mr Sissingham's domain.

She opened her *pochette* handbag, extracted a note, propped it against the inkstand and withdrew closing the door behind her. Sissy, she had decided must have a little word of welcome and good wishes to meet him when he entered for the first time.

Then she hurried towards the lift again and was carried to the ground floor. Here all was chaos still for until now and except that Piers' murals were long finished, this was their camouflage when callers came. Already the crystal chandeliers were in place, though swathed in linen bags. Already the soft velvet drapes were hung, though shrouded too in dust sheets to protect them from both dust and prying eyes. This morning the carpet layers were in and the sound of incessant tapping greeted her as she sped out closing the lift doors behind her. Men on scaffolds were arranging window drapes while men on ladders inserted electric light bulbs into wall lustres. A small army of men in white coats perched on planks overhead were applying the last and ninth coat of powder-pink paint to the woodwork. This had been a very special Piers' suggestion for, as he explained gravely to

Lucy and Lucien, 'It is no longer the sole prerogative of the *demi-mondaine* to use face powder. Women are *all* using *papier poudre* therefore if the paintwork echoes that complimentary shade it will flatter their reflections as nothing else could do half so well.' He decreed three coats of undercoat, two of flat paint and four of the shell finish to complete.

Picking her way carefully through men and ladders, keeping very clear of the walls, Lucy passed through the opened door and went down the four white steps to where, against the kerbstone, her motor awaited her. Standing sentinel beside it was Elizabeth with, on the end of the pale blue lead she held firmly in one gloved hand, Mr Silk who wibbled himself in ecstasy as Lucy appeared.

She scooped him up, scratched his poll, greeted Elizabeth and turned to climb in just as a wheezy old taxi lumbered around the corner, pulling up behind her car the door flying open before the old cabby could apply his brakes.

'That was a near thing!' shouted Lucien, flinging himself out, 'pay the cabby, Piers, there's a good chap, I say Lucy-Lou you look spiffing.' He rushed across the pavement, slowed to hug her carefully lest he spoil her finery and then held her at arm's length. 'We stopped the cab,' he told her, 'to buy you some violets they look so right against chincilla, oh dash, I've left them in the cab!'

His sister and the chauffeuse smiled indulgently.

'Oh no you haven't,' Piers called to them, pocketing his change and coming towards them, 'here, let me pin them on for you, Lucien left them on the seat.' He came up to her and pulling a long pin from the silver-wrapped stem of the posy first inverted it and then affixed it, stem uppermost and sunk into the softness of her chinchilla collar. He confided while so doing, 'Lucien is so excited he doesn't really know what he is doing. Come to that, nor do I,' he stepped back automatically to study the effect.

Then he nodded, satisfied, and held up one finger. 'Remember Miss, violets drink through their faces and not through their stems, so tell your maid when she unfastens them to put them face downwards in a shallow bowl of water. Then by morning they'll be new again.' He added, 'You look delicious,' and Lucy laughed happily.

'You look very elegant yourself,' she told him, made as ever to feel slightly uncomfortable by the blaze of his 'searchlight' eyes.

'Dress rehearsal,' he told her smilingly, 'we're both got up to kill in our present-our-first-collection-clothes. What do you say about your little brother, doesn't he look quite beautiful this morning?'

Standing on the pavement the trio were totally absorbed in one another.

'Lor,' thought Elizabeth, 'he really *is* beautiful. He should've been a girl, only he's too tall.' Lucien stood very straight, his topper and kid gloves in one hand, in all the splendour of his first morning coat, complete with grey waistcoat and with a white gardenia in his buttonhole.

Piers was saying, 'I have decided to paint him like that. If Mr Somerset Maugham can get onto the Line in those togs so can Lucien.' He walked around his subject while Lucien stood unmoving. 'What'll you call it Piers?' he asked curiously.

'The boy David I should think,' said his Jonathan cynically. 'Now enough of this rot. Lucy you'll be late back tonight if you don't go and that simply must not happen. Tonight is ours and utterly special so get going my pretty lass and do your lady of mercy act for us both.'

When they had installed her, patted Mr Silk and wished her well the car began to pull away, but Lucy heard Lucien asking again, 'Piers stop rotting, what will you call my portrait?' and the tart reply which came back, 'Boy Dressmaker if you're not good, now come along and make some pretty frocks while I bully the workmen.'

Lucy lay back against the grey upholstery and began rehearsing what she would say. She had already briefed Elizabeth, bidding her 'time the drive carefully if you please so as to be sure I arrive at the Castle either just as or just after Sawby has rung the gong for luncheon'. To herself she added, 'then I can postpone the scene until after they had fed and wined, which will be much easier.' She knew well enough that nothing would be said while the servants were in the room. The old, familiar phrase which she and Lucien had reduced to a little mocking chant of their own came back now – '*Paas, de-vant les dom-es-tiques, iques iques taisez vous mes enfants s'il vous plait, ait ait . . .*' was about to stand her in good stead. This chant was their particular way of warning one another if any of the Family were seen approaching when they were in private conclave.

What in fact Lucy experienced during that drive was really very similar to what any human creature experiences when they have nursed an inescapable grievance for a very long time, only to find that it is not a grievance any more because they have escaped from its bondage. The rigours of avoidance and secrecy were gone from her. She was her own person at last, secure, serene and absolutely devoid of fear because now they could not touch Lucien any more either. She had never experienced in her whole life such a lifting of spirit, such a glorious exhilaration as she did now. Behind her, rushing about his workrooms, his salon and his home, being cherished by his staff, solaced for her absence by his greatest friend Piers, was a completely safe Lucien at last, and because of this Lucy drifted into a little dream of content as the car sped towards her old home.

Not so the inmates of Castle Rising. Their lull had ended when, with Lucien's birthday parcels assembled beside the breakfast table, the Family had all come down to breakfast, even the Dowager eschewing her customary breakfast in bed to share the meal with 'the birthday boy'. However, one seat remained empty. Only when he had helped himself from the hot plates, said, 'Coffee please Sawby', in answer to the enquiry, 'What may I pour for you my lord?' and shaken open his *Times* did Gyles look out over the top like a scout reconnoitring across a fence and enquire mildly, 'Where, pray, is Lucien? Surely he has not overslept on his birthday.'

Sawby waited. He knew well enough that there were two absentees this morning and knowing, put his usual two and two together and found they made a most unpalatable four. Then it came. 'Sawby, have the goodness to enquire after Mr Lucien if you please. It is already . . .' out came the gold half-hunter, up went the case and, 'nine fifteen,' said the master of Castle Rising.

Sawby vanished, but not to seek out Lucien. Slowly, despondently he went belowstairs to where, through the opened doorway of the Stewards' Room he could see his fellow senior servants enjoying a tranquil post-breakfast cup of whatever beverage was their particular choice. He glanced away, well knowing Mrs Peace never came belowstairs at this hour. His wife whisked through on her way to the back door.

'Pansy, love, have you seen Mr Lucien this morning?' he asked softly.

Pansy turned, shook her head, 'Mr Pine passed me on the corridor, he said as Mr Lucien's bed had not been slept in nor Mr Sissingham's neither. Oh Arthur, are we in for trouble again?'

Sawby nodded, with a significant jerk of his head towards the opened Stewards' Room door, 'I must suppose so,' he murmured. 'I'll see Pine myself don't you worry your pretty head love.'

Worried as she was, she made him a little coquettish *moué* saying impatiently, 'Now Albert Sawby, don't talk about love when there's work to be done,' before hurrying away.

Sawby climbed back again to the ground floor, up the staircase and along to Gyles Aynthorp's dressing room where he found his quarry reading last night's evening paper and smoking a quiet cigarette. Sawby closed the door behind him.

'What's up with Mr Lucien and that tutor?' he demanded, 'his lordship has sent me to fetch 'em.'

Pine put down the paper and took a long pull at the cigarette. 'You'll have a problem,' he said gloomily, his long face seeming even longer than ever. 'If you ask me what I think it is that the male bird's left the nest and took young Spotty with 'im. There's no clothes left in neither room, nothing but bed linen and some rubbish in their wastepaper baskets. Come to think of it, I 'eard a car late larst night. Thought nothing of it there being a "hop" in the Music Room, I thought it was some laggard going 'ome.'

'I see,' Sawby sighed. 'Well we might've known really. With Lady Lucy gorne it was only to be expected. On his eighteenth birthday too, right on the dot and no time for a with your leave or by your leave! Well I must get back. I can tell you, Mr Pine, this is not going to be a very pleasant day.'

As they drew up at the foot of the steps Lucy saw, stepping out, handing Mr Silk to Elizabeth, arranging her furs, that the outward signs of war were already fast disappearing. She had not looked up on Christmas morning, but now she did, to the scaffolding across the area where the gargoyle had fallen, to the paint pots resting thereon with which the window frames were being 'touched up' and to the windows where someone had polished the glass until it shone as it had not done for four years.

Then, taking a deep breath, she mounted the steps and pulled the bell. They were just going through to luncheon so, shedding her furs, revealing a simple sheath-like dress of soft navy blue *charmeuse* with a wide bertha collar in white pleated silk and matching falls at her wrists, grasping her *pochette* resolutely, she greeted the processing members of the family and fell in with them. No questions were asked; she slid into the chair held out for her by Raikes, shook out her table napkin and dimpled a friendly smile at Sue-Ellen. Then she greeted Charles who exclaimed, 'I say Lucy you're looking simply ripping!' and tossed him back, 'Whatever are you doing here I thought you were still in the Fleet Air Arm?'

'I'm on leave,' he grinned, 'not de-mobbed, worst luck, that might take another month or so before it happens just because I want it now. If Pater is returnin' to the Manor there's a monumental task for all hands and I want to be on deck when the time comes.'

'I suppose,' the Dowager murmured resignedly to her, vis-à-vis Sir Charles, 'this nautical inelegance will dissipate itself in the fullness of time.' To her sister-in-law Marguerite she added even more softly, 'As long as he does not declare his urgent need to, now let me think, oh yes I have it "let down his Number 1 tank" I must suppose we should be grateful.' Thus the old indomitable proved again her astonishingly wide arc of information even on matters which have been deemed unsuitable for an old gentlewoman. It certainly entertained her opposite number for Marguerite collapsed with laughter which she wholly failed to conceal behind her table napkin.

'Mama,' observed Gyles drily, 'has committed another of her indiscretions. Pray Marguerite, may we not share it?'

'Oh no,' exclaimed the Countess, 'dear me no, now be quiet Gyles, ha ha ha,' which broke quite a lot of ice in a somewhat unexpected manner. Under their 'performance' Christine was becoming very angry. In the light of what had already passed, she was under no illusions as to the cause of Lucy's unexpected arrival. It was undoubtedly associated with Lucien's and indeed his tutor's equally unanticipated disappearance.

Only Eustace was undisturbed but he, surprising man,

newly come again from France had taken upon himself to telephone his daughter when she was already being driven through Epping Forest on her way to this luncheon. In the event Lucien had picked up the telephone, heard his father's voice and said delightedly, 'Oh Papa! where are you? When did you get home and are you alright?'

'I am perfectly intact,' Eustace Bartonbury assured his son, 'what I want to know now, my boy, is why you are there and not here?'

There was a pregnant pause, during which Eustace clearly heard some whispering. Eventually, 'What did you say Papa?' Lucien's voice came back.

'You know what I said,' replied his father equably, 'let me put it another way, when are you coming home?'

That was when Lucien lost his head. Having been caught wholly off his guard and by now very flustered he gave the game away. 'I *am* home,' his voice sounded defiant. 'I am not coming back Papa and nor is Sissy, please come up here and I will explain everything. Or better still please ask Lucy, it's what she's there for.'

'To explain?' Eustace pressed him.

'No, yes, oh Papa I can't do this please let me leave it to Lucy.'

Eustace put back the receiver and did some hard thinking.

He came back to the present with a jerk now to hear Lucy greeting Stephanie, saying something suitable and charming to her husband Harry. Staring down at his plate Eustace began marvelling that he had sired such an incomprehensible and devious pair. He was jolted out of his speculations by Ralph who was saying cheerfully, 'I say sir, now that you're home ought we to go up to Yorkshire to take another look round? Things were in such a fearful mess last time and I'm game to come with you as before if you agree.' Thus was Eustace hauled from his speculations while the rest simmered and seethed; while Gyles fumed and the footwomen placed covers, presented entrée dishes, and Sawby moved round the table pouring wines. They were all caught in the web of their own contriving but luncheon had to be served as it was always served.

It seemed to go on for an interminable time thought Lucy, chattering valiantly, although now with two bright spots on her cheeks and her eyes rather overbright. But at long last she caught her Aunt Christine's glacial glance, grasped her *pochette*, laid down her napkin, rose with the rest and made her way in turn into the hall. Here, murmuring, 'I must just run up and take off my hat I think the band is too tight,' she suited action to words, ran lightly up the stairs and took refuge with Nanny, Nanny Rose and the babies.

When a footwoman came in with the post luncheon tea-pot for the sustenance of the two Nannies and Doris, Lucy said lightly, 'Spurling, would you please let me know when the dining room empties?' and thus carefully contrived her return, just as Christine was pouring coffee for her men folk.

Once again Gyles grasped the nettle the very instant Sawby closed the door behind him. He said quite conversationally, 'Well Lucy, I must suppose that your visit concerns the sudden and unaccountable disappearance of Mr Sissingham and your brother?'

Young Charles, Ralph, Stephanie and her Harry quietly rose, made their excuses and vanished, Constance and her Charles followed.

Then Lucy lifted her head and Eustace watching her intently thought she did so with a distinct movement of defiance the like of which he had detected in his son's voice over the telephone.

'Yes, Uncle Gyles,' Lucy affirmed. 'I have come to explain.'

None of them would ever forget the scene which followed or rather the two scenes, for while Lucy's scene was the one which shattered them all, the one amongst themselves which followed after the small grey Darracq had been driven away was undoubtedly the more protracted.

CHAPTER 7

A Conference and a Prophecy

Eustace Bartonbury had watched his daughter closely throughout the protracted luncheon. His telephone conversation with Lucien that morning, combined with the obvious distress he perceived in his daughter, roused in him such a surge of compassion that he could no longer contain himself. To the astonishment of them all he made a direct appeal to her across the room.

'My dear child,' he said. 'Why do you not let me do this for you? I spoke to Lucien this morning. It was easy thereafter to deduce what was in the wind. But first let me make quite clear to you that *I accept what you and your brother have done* and I promise that I will do nothing to stand in your way.' Lucy stared at him wide-eyed, the rest forgotten, until suddenly the import of his words penetrated and radiance lit her brimming eyes.

'Oh Papa,' she said inadequately.

'Yes, my dear,' he nodded, 'and as your father will you give me permission to explain on your behalf now that you know I have no intention to oppose either of you?' He added, lapsing into French, *'j'apprecie ma p'tite que le coeur à ses raisons que la raison ne connait point.'*

Lucy's bewilderment was reflected in all their faces; but before any could intervene Eustace, with a slight inclusive gesture of his hands addressed them all, saying, 'Please do not any of you imagine that I have been party to my children's deceit. I only knew this morning and even then most of what I know stems from my own deductions. Nevertheless the fact is that Lucien and his tutor have gone from here and neither of them will return. They are at Lucy's house and there they intend to stay. So would it not be wiser for us all to accept this and let them go with our good wishes and without recriminations?'

Christine had taken up her embroidery and was stabbing the needle into the frame and withdrawing it as if it were a knife and the frame some victim whom she had stabbed.

With needle poised for another stab she cried out, 'Stealing from the Castle in the dead of night! A boy of eighteen and a penniless tutor, really Eustace, have you taken leave of your senses?'

Eustace shook his head. 'Far from it my dear, but sometimes it is wiser to bow to the inevitable is it not?'

'But this is not inevitable,' she cried again, 'the boy has three more years to wait before he comes of age!'

At this Eustace's eyes hardened, though he responded gently enough, 'Would you contest his right to go when his father has consented to it?'

She flushed at this. 'I would most certainly like to know what his mother has to say, my dear Eustace.'

'Then let me tell you.' He folded his hands and looked down at them. Very slowly the words came, 'Gabrielle told me when we met in Paris, and I quote her own words, "that boy is a dead bore and I am sick to death of him. He can do what he likes for all I care and so for that matter can you." I apologise for disclosing such intimate matters which I know you will agree is in excessively bad taste; *but you asked* Christine and I feel bound to warn you that intervention from Gabrielle is not within the bounds of possibility.'

The Dowager then spoke into the silence, raising her lorgnettes and levelling them at her son-in-law.

'Are we to understand Eustace that my grandson is not just engaged upon a naughty escapade; but that you, his father, have set the seal of your approval on his going from here for good?'

'That is so *Belle-mère*.'

'Then pray enlighten me further. Is this, er, departure approved by you on the grounds of greater suitability for your son?'

Eustace sighed. 'On the grounds that it is Lucien's wish so to do – no more. Only Lucy can confirm or deny that this is so.'

'I confirm it,' said Lucy swiftly, 'Lucien has fought hard enough and long enough for his freedom. Now, unless you are all prepared to become involved in a scandal, he is free and he and I intend that he shall remain so. I had never hoped that my father would support either of us; but this knowledge gives me the greatest happiness as I know it will Lucien too.'

'Free!' Christine exclaimed, 'what is all this nonsense

about freedom pray? Have we been gaolers? Is this castle a dungeon? And has that silly boy imagined himself a prisoner in our hands?'

The pattern of battle was changing now. Little Marguerite gave indication of it.

'I must confess,' she said thoughtfully, 'that all of us have from time to time felt somewhat out of our depth with Lucien ... such an unusual little boy ... so gifted ... most remarkable ... perhaps with Lucy things might be different for him ... even possibly easier and more comfortable.'

'*Tante* Marguerite!' Christine gave her embroidery a particularly violent jab, 'how could you say such a thing ... runnin' wild, without let or hindrance, what that boy needs is discipline.'

Gyles Aynthorp, silent witness so far, busy now examining with what seemed undue attention the silver ash upon his cigar tip, elected to participate at last.

'It must have required a somewhat adult measure of self-discipline to bring this off I imagine,' he observed drily. 'The average youngster of Lucien's age would have shown something ... given something away ... the self-control alone has been remarkable.'

'Yes, Uncle Gyles,' Lucy came in a trifle breathlessly, 'I would remind you that the self-control for both of us has been the result of the most rigorous self-discipline. If you please I would now like you to listen to me. I will tell you what none of you know which, if you will forgive the impertinence, gives the lie to Aunt Christine's insistence that Lucien needs discipline.'

Now she had them. Now they could scarcely wait as this threat or undertaking to reveal more was delivered. The Dowager dipped into her reticule and brought out her smelling salts which she sniffed at, delicately.

John laid a protective hand over Primrose's slender one as they sat side by side. Marguerite de Tessedre took a sip of her *tisane* and made a small moue indicating it was cold. Lucy took the floor.

'Without discipline,' said she, feeling the colour rising to her cheeks, 'how could we have managed what we have done in such absolute secrecy that you know nothing of it even now? Without control, planning, organisation – all adult qualities – how could you, *Tante* Marguerite, and you, *Grandmère*, have come to visit us and seen nothing? Indeed how could Lucien have returned here from his working visits to London with Mr Sissingham, and answered correctly your regular interrogations, if he had not disciplined himself to learn the answers from Sissy who visited those wretched museums and picture galleries on his behalf while Lucien worked with Piers and me? He did all that and besides, he, a silly boy, as Aunt Christine has called him, simultaneously kept our workrooms, yes, his and mine, supplied with detailed, meticulous designs for dresses which at this moment are reaching completion. They will be worn by professional mannequins *in our salon* at the presentation of our first collection in just over a month's time.

'We have formed a company called *Lucy et Lucien Haute Couture*, Mr Sissingham merely stands proxy for Lucien on the board, until he comes of age. Piers Fournes is a director too. Oh yes, Piers has worked with us throughout because he saw from the very beginning how great was Lucien's talent. Lucien has enormous talent you simply must appreciate. Yet this is only the beginning as you will see for yourselves if you accept these invitations,' she paused, drew from behind her *pochette* a large envelope and shook out the invitations it contained. 'I intended leaving them for all of you on the hall salver, but you may as well see them now. I do not for a moment suppose that any of you will come, yet if you do not I imagine the great world, which will be there in force, will begin asking very awkward questions. Just because Lucien is different and because all of you are so enmeshed with what you call "form", you have driven us both to take these admittedly deceitful measures to ensure Lucien's talent is seen and recognised.'

She broke off, attempted to speak again, cracked at last and with a choked, almost inaudible, 'Only Papa has shown us any understanding,' she turned and ran from the room.

No one made any attempt to follow her. It was doubtful if they could have done so had the wish been there. Even the embroidery needle was stilled at last. It lay where Christine had let it fall on the stiff silk of her dress. Then very faintly a sound reached them from outside, of a motor's engine starting. After it came the noise of tyres crunching on the gravelled drive. When these faded the silence seemed faintly shocking.

At length the Dowager rose and shook out her skirts.

'I am inclined to think, Gyles,' she said tartly, 'that we have brought this upon ourselves;' but whether the chill in her voice was for them, herself or Lucy and Lucien no one could be sure for she left the room and even Henry, expert as he was at 'door duty' failed to reach it in time to do more than close it behind his grandmother's back.

In the back of the Darracq, huddled into her chinchillas Lucy was crying.

When she rushed from the room Lucy found that in picking up her *pochette* she had also taken the invitations, so she dropped them on the salver after all as she ran to the great door, wrenched it open and fled down the steps to the waiting Elizabeth. She gave no thought to the conflicts those invitations would engender. One by one the silver-edged, engraved cards were drawn from their envelopes and read by their recipients. One by one they raised a ferment of dispute until it seemed that every private sitting room or boudoir became the scene of conferences during which of course, snippets were gleaned by maids and valets. These at length, largely as a result of Clair's indiscretion in propping hers upon the mantelshelf were pooled to yield an eventual, very clear picture of the lastest issue to be joined.

A copy appeared in the Servants' Hall, borne by the triumphant hand of houseparlourmaid Mason; snatched from her by Mrs Parsons crying, 'Give that 'ere this minnit Miss'; after which she carried it off triumphantly to the Stewards' Room, the door was kicked closed by Mrs Parsons' left buttoned boot and the senior servants attached themselves to this copy of that invitation like leeches, as they endeavoured to suck its import dry with speculation.

Had they been a gambling staff it was beyond dispute that a 'book' would have been opened on the instant and the odds figured to a nicety as to who would and who would not accept the invitation from 'that precious pair'; but they did not gamble, the limit of their excesses being a sixpence upon a Derby runner by the women, a shilling by the men. Also they were intensely loyal and once they had taken in the significance of this succulent tit-bit, which gave instant colour to the pathetic limitations of their drab lives, they accepted that this was a family matter and the Family was sacrosanct. Additionally, they felt a powerful sympathy for their employers and a strong resentment towards 'Mr

Lucien' and 'her little Ladyship' who had made it very plain that neither of *them* felt any such allegiance.

In short, the Castle zizzed like a hornets' nest. Little groups formed in passages and on landings as well as in boudoirs and bedrooms. These dissolved the instant a servant appeared, then re-formed again while the matter came to be the sole topic belowstairs. At length Sawby sent forth a fiat from his place at the top of the staff luncheon table.

'It is enough,' he told the double row of startled faces. 'You have all so far forgot yourselves as to carry on even at mealtimes with unceasing and impertinent speculations about your betters. I walk into the dining room and *they're* all at it too. Of course *they* stop immediately but one knows what's what and pre-cise-ly what's afoot and its unnerving. Even my own wife is at it all the time even when we walk to and fro from our cottage. Then Mr Plumstead buttonholes me and asks for "the latest about the you-know-what schemozzle". Even the Stewards' Room has become unbearable. *Now it will cease.* From this moment anyone mentioning the subject in any way concerning Mr Lucien and her little Ladyship will pay a penny to the swear box. If I find more than two pennies there tonight the fine will be doubled.' With scarcely any pause he ran on, 'Agnes there's a smut on your nose. How many times have I told you not to come to table until you have washed your face? No,' as the girl moved, 'not now, after Grace will do and now for what we are about to receive may the Lord make us truly thankful, Amen.' For this last, two rows of resentful heads bent and two rows of gloomy faces were lifted thereafter.

On the way back to their cottage that night Sawby confided to his wife Pansy, 'There's more important matters to speculate upon my girl, and that's a fact.'

Her voice came back through the darkness, 'Oh go on, Albert, tell.'

'Well,' Sawby was by now indulging himself, 'I may say, in all the days I've served in this Castle I never thought to say the words I am about to utter.'

Pansy shivered with delight. 'I don't believe it, that I don't.'

'Well it's true, Pine told me. He says his Lordship sleeps in his dressing room. There's a kind of iron curtain come down between them. According to Palliser who was told by

Pearson who confided in me, my lady is getting that thin she has a lot of extra work on her pore hands taking in her gowns.'

In this as usual Sawby was corrected. The pathetic truth was that Christine longed to make her peace with Gyles; but every time she made up her mind to try she was held back. She seemed to have become two people; one unchanged, loving and desperately lonely on her side of what Sawby had described so aptly as an iron curtain. *This* Christine knew well enough she need only make the slightest gesture to be in Gyles' arms again, to be comforted and forgiven; but twin in her was another, alien Christine whose every nerve twitched with anger and disgust against those two young people. Her very potent instinct insisted that no matter to what extent the Family found her behaviour deplorable it still remained that there was something rotten, decadent, *wrong* about this beautiful and gifted pair. They were motivated by something completely different from a mere precocious dedication to Lucien's talents.

The other Christine, the one they all knew and loved, had struggled against this frantically. She had fought to suppress her *alter ego*; but it was useless. There remained this frightening presage of the dark and decadent which she could neither banish nor understand. She had fought it in sleepless nights. She fought it now, sitting at her escritoire, pen in hand, trying to write her formal acceptance for herself and Gyles; but still that other self cried out in warning of the inexplicable, forcing upon her a darkness of spirit in which she could see nothing except the fear which had caused her to behave so inexcusably.

She forced herself to write, 'Lord and Lady Aynthorp have much pleasure in accepting the Honble Lucien and the Lady Lucy St John's kind invitation to their Reception on Wednesday January the twenty ninth. . .'

She wrote on, sick at heart. She inserted the folded sheet into its envelope. She affixed the penny stamp. Then she rose with immense reluctance and envelope in hand went to the door. In a sudden spurt of courage she ran down the great staircase, crossed the hall and hurried along the corridor to Gyles' old office. Then, as her sons had done before her she pulled up short, her hand outstretched to the doorhandle, courage seeping away, to step back in alarm as the handle turned, the door opened and Gyles stood there looking down at her.

'My dear,' he said, 'I was going over to the museum to see how the work was progressing. I hope I did not startle you. Come in, the museum can wait, I have been wanting to talk to you.'

Mutely Christine held out the evelope. He took it, glanced at the name upon it, held out his other hand to draw her in as she stammered, 'I've written it, I have accepted for us . . . oh Gyles, I am so very unhappy.'

He put a protective arm about her shaking shoulders. He led her to his old arm-chair, persuaded her to to sit, then took both trembling hands in his own, the letter tossed aside.

'Now why do you not just take your own time my love to tell me all about it?'

His gentleness defeated her and she began to cry. 'My poor darling,' he soothed, 'as Nanny would say you really are in all your states. Take my handkerchief to mop those tears while I get you a little drink.'

He poured her a thimbleful of brandy from his desk tantalus, held the glass to her lips and made her drink, his eyes deeply troubled, for he knew now that there was more to this than he had at first thought – a mere, feminine and completely understandable outcry against ingratitude and deceit.

In the end she did tell him. She tumbled the words out with her head against his shoulder and nothing she said dispelled the unease which grew with her admissions. When she had done, calmed to some extent in sheer relief at the telling, Gyles continued to hold her closely, staring out over her head, thinking furiously.

When he spoke again, he did so with extreme care, weighing his words and investing them with as much assurance as he could muster.

'It is very understandable,' he began, 'with our history you could hardly be expected to feel otherwise. When you consented to marry me you took on the burden of Lorme delinquencies which have persisted down the centuries. Indeed they were obscenely manifested in Edward Justin whose,' he hesitated, 'whose sexual predilections, forced him to leave England even, as we can all remember happened with the disastrous Stephen for wholly different reasons. We call them our "runts". We have learned to live with them, have come close to ruin on occasion because of them, for on each and every occasion we have retained our pride only by the most rigorous concealment of their misdemeanours. Such things take their toll. In the eradication of all traces of their acts we have of necessity grown fearful. We start at shadows, lest they presage another awful incident. We have in fact developed a vulnerability to the anticipation of fearful things because of the fearful things which have already occurred. I know exactly what you are experiencing. It is a shared *fear*,' he stressed the word particularly, 'but fear we must remember my love is man's greatest enemy. Fear brings us all down, transforms us, so that whereas without fear we are a compound of flesh and spirit fitting as closely together as a glove upon a hand; when fear comes the spirit shrinks to a terrified, minuscule thing, crouching inside what has become a huge dark cavern of imprisoning flesh. That is what has happened to you, you must believe me my darling. We have never spoken in detail concerning Edward Justin. It would ill-become Lorme menfolk and be an outrage to their women; but nevertheless you have a distasteful inkling and in the unusual, not to say obsessive bond which has persisted between Lucy and Lucien you have allowed this to people the corridors of your mind with fearful things. You will understand just how I know how far your frightened instincts have led you if I mention one other family to you – Lord Byron and his sister. Let me tell you something else.'

He had felt her calming as he talked on. Now he took both her shoulders and turned her slightly so that she was face to face with him and he could see that the sparks of fear in her still-beautiful eyes were diminishing. '*I took this road* concerning that disquieting pair, *with Henry*. We do not need to particularise, nor would I care to even to you, but we made your journey into fear. We discussed the matter in this very room and in the end we reached the same conclusion as I am convinced you will too when you have allowed your reason to dominate your fear.' He could see she was not convinced, but yet was weakening. 'Look at it this way, I stated in front of you all that we had no alternative to acceptance of this invitation, not for curiosity, not for fear; but rather for precaution – setting aside the social hubble-bubble which might arise among our friends if we did not put in an appearance. I too require confirmation of what both Henry and I decided is the truth. By absenting ourselves we surrender to the menaces of speculation and conjecture. By going, we see for ourselves.

'I am bound to admit,' he sought for a lighter vein now, 'that I am not anticipating a pleasurable experience; but I am assured we will all find it a salutary one which will dispel these "runtish" fears and leave us in some measure of peace to continue our own lives. We are a fairly formidable assembly, not without perception, nor wholly unsophisticated either. By the signs and portents which we shall be able to interpret between us we can I most truly believe dismiss this matter once and for all.'

Gyles knew that he had succeeded at last because Christine said suddenly, 'Eustace thinks all is well doesn't he?'

'He does. Moreover my dear *they are his children*. Think how we once misjudged Eustace, dismissing him as an ineffectual, harmless creature, and how he has grown in stature during this disastrous war, and by the way I understand his services are not to go unrecognized.'

'Really?' Christine actually smiled tremulously. 'Oh, that would be lovely and so well deserved. You know Gyles that is another cause for anxiety. I think that marriage is foundering.'

Thankfully Gyles grasped the straw thus extended, so that when the footwoman came to announce that tea was served Christine was able to dismiss her calmly, rise, straighten her gown, study her reflection in the wall glass and murmur ruefully, 'I look a wreck, I am so sorry Gyles, of course you are right and I am an evil-minded woman. . . .'

To the family's extreme satisfaction the pair strolled in to tea together, with Christine's hand inside her husband's arm. They were enveloped in an aura of harmony which declared beyond question that Sawby's iron curtain had been raised at last and all was well again.

Henry and Petula spent the afternoon behind the stables with Sue-Ellen and Plum. They felt in need of a little comic relief after the frigid luncheon atmosphere. No sooner had the trio settled on their usual upturned buckets, with Plum leaning against the lintel of the illicit rear door than young Charles Danement's head poked out, crying, 'Anyone at home?' Within moments of his settling on a bale of straw, Priscilla joined them.

Outrageous as always, Plum removed a wisp of hay from his mouth and enquired, 'Well one an all 'ows things progressin' abart yer latest schemozzle?'

Sue-Ellen's eyes widened apprehensively; Petula giggled. It fell to Henry to say automatically, 'Plum that is not a fitting question for you to ask,' his twinkle belying the rebuke.

'Never mind that,' Plum retorted, 'remember I'm spechul an' wots more Mrs Plumstead as scaped the bottom of the barrel and come up wiv' a lardy cake for whomsoever tells us. See.'

This defeated them and within moments they were in the thick of yet another post-mortem with their old coachman.

'We shall go,' said Henry flatly, 'my father would never permit us to stay away.'

Priscilla shook her head. 'Your mother will not go I promise you!'

Plum's eyes twinkled pleasurably.

'Go where?' asked Charles, coasting his straw bale nearer to Sue-Ellen.

'Lucy and Lucien's reception and first mannequin display,' Sue-Ellen explained. 'Oh gee, I reckon it will be a great disappointment to us all.'

'What!' exclaimed Henry, 'watchin' a lot of gels prancin' about in extraordinary clothes and meetin' all the old dowagers!'

Petula elected to become stately. 'I trust,' she said coldly, 'that you will not express those views before the family, besides which I want to go.'

It became patently clear they all wished to go.

'Tell you what,' Henry then reflected, 'I'll lay twenty to one we all go, any takers?'

Priscilla snapped, 'Done.'

Henry nodded, 'In fivers suit you?'

She did a rapid calculation, realised that her desire to buy some of the couple's clothes would have to go by the board if she lost, but would not back down.

'Certainly,' she agreed, 'in fivers then.'

'Bbbut that's five hundred pounds Priscilla, if you lose!' Sue-Ellen exclaimed.

'So it is,' Priscilla answered mockingly. 'I just hope Henry can raise the wind for a fiver when he loses.'

Sue-Ellen frowned. 'Well, I reckon I agree with Henry. Uncle Gyles is walking about looking very severe and Aunt Christine is not at all herself. On reflection I'll take another five hundred off you if you're game.'

'Well I'm not my pretty, sorry, you'll have to find another taker.'

'Me,' said Petula abruptly.

'Blimey!' said Plum vanishing like a jack in the box behind the door and reappearing with the lardy cake and a penknife, ''ere goes the gamblin' der Lormes! We'll 'ave the fambly skint afore long, now come along ladies and gents, gather rahnd and we'll 'ave a bit of mother's spechul.'

This little scene explained in full the delighted smile on Sue-Ellen's face when Gyles Aynthorp entered the White Drawing Room for tea with his wife on his arm, and the expression of consternation on Priscilla's face.

'Well now,' said Gyles settling himself and taking a cucumber sandwich from the tiered cake stand, 'as everyone is here this is as good a time as any to ask which of you have accepted Lucy and Lucien's invitation, other than ourselves of course?' He despatched the sandwich tranquilly while instant babble broke out. When this had subsided, leaving him in no doubt that everyone intended going he spoke again.

'I suggest then, as a week has already elapsed, that it had best be done quickly. To spur you on I would like to propose a visit to London also at your earliest convenience. Lucy was at some pains to remind us that the greater part of our acquaintance would be there so you will all require new frocks and furbelows, for which I shall be happy to pay the reckoning.' He turned to Christine with a smile, 'You will go too my love will you not?'

'Gladly,' she smiled, 'but it had better be tomorrow for already there is insufficient time. We shall have to prevail upon ... dear me I do not know nowadays ... I have quite lost touch ... Mr Reville perhaps? Or that new woman Lucille? I think I must telephone now if you will excuse me, dear.' She rose as she spoke. Marguerite rose too, 'Perhaps Paquin?' they heard her speculate as she too hurried from the room.

Gyles remained as the room emptied of his womenfolk, surrendering wryly to the unoriginal thought that no one could ever comprehend the workings of the female mind.

Henry hung back too until at length he and his father were alone. Then, 'Is somethin' worryin' you sir?' he ventured, one hand flying to his hair as usual.

Gyles looked up blankly, 'Eh? oh sorry, dear boy, I was thinkin'. Yer mother has been excessively disturbed by Lucy and Lucien's behaviour as you very probably realise. She has experienced some instinct, prescience, call it what you will, concernin' that precious pair.'

'Pair?' Henry queried. 'Not trio?'

'No,' said Gyles hastily, 'it's bad enough as it is. Could we have been wrong d'you imagine?'

Henry grinned, ruefully. 'How should I know sir, remember I've been away. Tell you the truth I've often wondered. I *think* we were on the wrong track. I had plenty of time to think, you will understand, and whenever I got off on that tack I always came back to' whadyoucall'em "that pretty pair". Is that why we're goin'?' he looked keenly at his parent.

'Partly,' Gyles answered abstractedly. 'Naturally it's part, er, social, we er, must be seen you understand.'

'Indeed yes,' Henry agreed enthusiastically, remembering his wager and the five hundred pounds. 'By the by, sir, there's no need for you to foot Pet's bill, I've er, had a pretty decent win.'

Gyles' abstraction vanished. 'Yer not gamblin'? are yer? It's in the blood y'know.'

'No sir, I'm not. It doesn't amuse me sufficiently. Just a very occasional flutter and I'm not misled by Lorme luck either. Look here, sir, all this is pure speculation, why don't we leave it until we've seen the lie of the land, then we can talk again. I'll undertake to keep a sharp look-out and so I'll dare swear will you!'

'And your mother,' Gyles said grimly, 'to say nothing of your grandmother and *Tante* Marguerite and Aunt Primrose. Perhaps we'd do better to let the thing lie fallow for the moment.'

'Well then,' Henry stood up. 'I need to stretch m' legs. I'd like to see how things are progressin' at the museum. Can you spare the time to come with me?'

This attempt to divert was rewarded by a smile. 'Takin' the old man's mind off his problems eh? Well, why not? I was settin' out when your mother came to my study. There is ample time before dinner.'

Delighted that his subterfuge had worked Henry followed his father from the room. They went into 'Clobber', the small railed room off the hall where rows of Guernseys, coats and ulsters hung with boots, shoes and galoshes standing in racked rows underneath and a dolorous old elephant's foot which sprouted shooting sticks and umbrellas. They made their selection, Gyles pulled a cap from the shelf, drew out a walking stick, then together they crossed the hall and struck out across the paddock.

'I had a letter this morning,' Gyles said suddenly, 'from those chaps of yours, enclosing their references. We'll take them on. That feller Dawson, the one-armed man, is married as I think you know. He sounds pathetically grateful, a touchin' letter in fact. He sent the blind chap's references too and gave me his colonel's name in case I might want to check with him. I sent a letter off to Pearson this mornin' with a donation of course, so as soon as I hear from him whatsisname Carter can begin his trainin' at St Dunstan's. On our way back we'll have a word with Plum but I don't anticipate any difficulty there either. Jimmy Porter the third lame feller wrote separately. He's sound enough too so with any luck we can have him down straight away. I was worried at first at breakin' up the band for the other two but Porter tells me they've found work as doormen at two small hotels in Kensington so it's all worked out very well. Old Crotchley was thankful when I told him I'd found a replacement for him. He's willin' to go at any time now, then we can have Dawson and his wife down and instal them in Crotchley's old quarters. No don't thank me for God's sake, it's little enough. Write it down to sheer thankfulness at havin' you back in one piece eh?'

'Alright,' said Henry lamely, 'but thanks just the same. Thanks awfully. By the way, what's happenin' about the Convalescent Home now that all the bods have gone?'

'Constance has a scheme,' Gyles told him.

They were crossing the car park, already considerably widened, where four men were throwing gravel. 'We are conferring with her in the mornin' also Jamieson and of course Uncle Charles. Come to that you might care to sit in. We go to Jamieson and in case we over-run I've arranged to take a hamper to ease Mrs Jamieson. Now that the women are headin' for fripperies in London we can get down to things; but for pity's sake say nothing to Grandmother. It might tempt her to stay behind and I particularly do not want that to happen.'

They had reached the twin fountains which they had found together in Italy. Here they stood for a moment for a man was testing and had switched them on. The plashing water took them back sharply to the Palazzo from whence they came. There were more men on the scaffold which netted the museum's frontage, applying fresh paint to the window frames, re-pointing the brickwork and below them in the gardens one of Sawbridge's offspring was dressing the rosebeds with manure from the tail of a dray drawn up at the foot of the low, white steps.

'Comin' on,' said Gyles approvingly. He stopped for a word with the men then they vanished inside. At which precise moment the two Brinkman boys and Gilbert Delahaye swept up the drive in Joe's Napier motor. They had been to a sale and were extremely pleased with themselves.

While it was comparatively easy for Gyles to cope with Henry's three disabled men, it seemed a far greater problem to find work for the people who had staffed the Convalescent Home. They were awkward material to place; six male nurses, all conscientious objectors, six ward maids, six nurses, two cooks and two storekeepers, all drawn from the ranks of militant suffragettes and about to be loosed on a market where the orthodox were filling the dole queues.

As usual Lady Constance produced a solution. The twelve nurses would form the nucleus of the Lady Constance Visiting Nurses Association which would have its headquarters at the Manor House. Jamieson would assume the extra-curricular position of Visiting Consultant both willing and able to travel at a moment's notice to any-one whom the staff were nursing. He concurred with alacrity. Furthermore, there was little doubt that these men and women would obtain regular employment since Constance had already received confirmation of assistance from the most eminent and suitable of patrons.

The five sat around the dining table in Doctor Jamieson's house listening as she explained, with her usual serenity, how she had bearded her patron in his Harley Street consulting room, he being none other than the distinguished gynaecologist who had performed the emergency caesarean section on Petula. She also pointed out that since he now held Royal Appointment his name would carry even greater weight. He expressed the view that it would be of considerable service to him to have a dozen skilled nursing staff at his disposition for his most eminent patients. She therefore proposed ordering elegant folders setting out the fees and their peripherals and bearing upon the outside the declaration 'under the distinguished patronage of Sir James Anstruther' followed by a long list of other names of power. Constance cited a few including their mutual friend the VAD Commandant, her redoubtable aunt, a couple of princesses, and therinafter as great a display of name-dropping as the somewhat bewildered Doctor Jamieson had ever heard.

Finally Constance closed her little notebook. Folding her hands quietly, she said, 'If and when the service becomes a *fait accompli* and, as I suspect may well happen with such powerful support, we come to need more nursing staff, Eustace's Mr Stone has volunteered to round up the ex-members of his Ambulance Unit and the thing will automatically spread from there. Of this I am confident. It all depends now upon your opinion.'

'She's a remarkable woman ain't she,' Charles mused contentedly. Constance was looking questioningly at Gyles.

He eyed her a trifle ruefully. 'I would say my dear that you have not only cut the Gordian knot for us but have in fact left us practically nothing to do except to acquiesce and congratulate.'

She flushed a little, murmured, 'Praise from Sir Hubert Stanley.' With a slightly quizzical expression, she asked, 'And what is the ground I have left uncovered by the "practically"?'

'The Castle,' said Gyles shortly. 'Surely it would be practical for us to leave that Convalescent Home wing as it stands. In a family like ours there are always contingencies and with your Unit operating as it were upon our own doorstep we should be doubly served by having all the facilities of a modern nursing home contained within the Castle. Jamieson,' Gyles turned slightly in his chair, 'how would Petula have fared if there had been no such facilities when, er . . . ?'

Henry looked startled. Dr Jamieson stroked his beard. At length he admitted, 'Well now, the circumstances *were* under the influence of that Convalescent Home you must remember. Had such facilities not been available I would have counselled Mrs Lorme's removal to a nursing home several days in advance of her anticipated labour, but I cannot deny that if the Castle's usual pattern continues, with so many employees, such a delightful superabundance of children, well, accidents do happen even in the, er, best regulated families and the facilities of our Cottage Hospital are not exactly lavish. To put not too fine a point upon it, it lacks a great many modern facilities. Between these four walls I confess there have been times with some of my patients in this vicinity when I should have been thankful to transfer them to the Castle and not to our gallant little hospital.'

'Then that settles it,' said Gyles. 'I have been most remiss. You are an ass Jamieson not to have come to me before.'

'And all those Relics,' exclaimed Henry suddenly, 'can make a special Queen Victoria Room in the museum. *Belle-mere* was only telling me yesterday she made the most extraordinary discoveries when it was all dismantled for the Home.'

'While that in turn will provide further pleasure and interest for both Mama and *Tante* Marguerite,' Gyles nodded. 'Splendid! Then the Home stays, that is to say the patients' rooms, staff room, dispensary, stores, theatre and recovery room. Our two old naughties can keep themselves out of mischief for some time to come planning and ordering your Queen Victoria's Room in the museum.'

Henry grinned, 'Look sir this is providential.' He turned to Constance who was watching the pair of them with some amusement. 'We were there only yesterday seein' how everythin' is progressin' at the museum. There are, also, two rooms for which no plans have yet been made. I suggested togs, you know, clothes from the past, Piers and Lucien could make marvellous figures to hang them on and there's a whacking great room aloft in the Castle bulgin' with rails and rails of clothes which that old girl from the village comes up every week to spray against moth and keep in good trim.'

Gyles had suddenly become abstracted and Henry noticed it. 'Is there anything wrong sir?' he asked quickly.

'No, nothing is wrong and I thoroughly approve but I am bound to tell you that my desire to retain the Home in some sort of working order has a rather deeper motive.'

'You make it sound ominous Gyles,' from Constance.

He did not deny this. Instead, 'Then let me ask you a question. What, in your opinion, will happen in the years ahead?'

The atmosphere of sudden unease intensified, but no one answered him so he continued, 'They're squabblin' already, the powers that be and the doubts are already growin', for few in their hearts believe that the League of Nations will really work. The Hun is busily whitewashin' his motives. He is already beginnin' to translate "war guilt" into somethin' very different from the culpability for startin' the war, and is now attemptin' to interpret it instead as *failure to win*. On the one hand you have Lloyd George exclaimin' "those insolent Germans!" and the old Tiger on the other replyin', "it is new to you and therefore it makes you angry. We are accustomed to their insolence. We have had to bear it for fifty years."

'As I see it the League will soon become the sole responsibility of France and Britain for, again, only as an opinion, I prophesy that America will soon withdraw from European affairs. Then what will happen? Germany is going to win the peace, I have little doubt of that. She is regaining her swagger already while her millions are walking the starvation line. I do not believe we have won a war at all. I think that at most we have won an uneasy respite and I for one am certain that in ten, twenty, maybe even thirty years it will all happen all over again, but next time it will be of such added intensity, with such an increase in lethal weapons, air strength, general and particular carnage, that everything we do and plan to do *from this moment* must be done with such an event in the forefronts of our minds. There will be another world war, probably within our lifetimes. Having said that let me particularise and thus come back to my initial query.'

'What of the Home itself?' Constance spoke very softly.

'Exactly m'y dear. The next war will be won or lost in the air. That I believe is obvious to us all. Cities will be wiped out; but there is just the possibility that rural areas may escape unharmed. It is not so strong a possibility that I would consider leaving anything we cherish within the Castle walls. So, in the intelligent anticipation of so awful an event should we not seek to retain our little Convalescent Home in such a way that it can be extended if needs be to absorb the entire Castle? In the light of what Constance intends doing I think we should use such funds as we can spare to improve and extend, as and when this is practical. There will also be times when members of your little nursing team are unemployed. There are bound to be. Let them sleep in the convalescents' rooms, free of charge, at such times. They would be little or no trouble to anyone and at the worst it would keep the rooms aired. Discount what I have been saying if you like. Consider my suggestions as a mere insurance. So long as we prepare, I do not mind whether you share my pessimistic views. Just let it be done, and let everythin' we do from now onwards be with an eye towards such an eventuality so that we may in our own small way be prepared for when it comes. I apologise for bein' such a Job's comforter, but it is a relief for me to say what I think to people like yourselves.'

The ticking of the mahogany clock on the sideboard sounded violent in the silence which followed. Behind the heavy wine-red curtains the village street lay drowsing. Somewhere amid the trees in the wall-sheltered garden rooks began to caw. An owl hooted. The sound was derisive. Finally with a curious touch of formality the Doctor spoke.

'I am honoured,' he said heavily, 'both in my guests and in your confidence, yet Lord Aynthorp I would have wished to be ennobled with some less horrible disclosure.'

Gyles frowned, 'Let us have done with Lord Aynthorp, James,' he said with a slightly wry smile. 'I owe you my wife, my daughter-in-law, and my grandson, I beg leave to remind you. Formality between us is ill-suited to such debts in my opinion.'

The Doctor was visibly moved. He made only a slight inclination of his head and murmured, 'So be it. And, er, thank you.'

Gyles smiled. Constance, watching him, thought again how like Henry he looked when he smiled, and how it stripped years from his autocratic face, making him young once more. 'Dear Gyles,' she too smiled, but sadly, 'we all know your words were not a revelation but, alas, a confirmation. It is in the very air we breathe. The unrest of the young derives from it. The furious pace, the refusal to think, eat, drink and be not merry but raucous. They dare not remember, those who have come back. They refuse to look at the future. What else could be the driving force for their hectic, artificial gaiety if it is not fear of what lies ahead?'

'I wonder if I shall live to see it,' mused Charles Davenant. 'It is a source of infinite consolation to me that if this armistice endures sufficiently my son will be too old ...'

Gyles rounded on him, temper suddenly flaming. 'False comfort,' he exclaimed. 'Think man, think. Next time we will all be in it. The modern warfare which is now being planned by Germany even in this her hour of defeat, will involve the old, the young, the civilian ...' he broke off. 'One cold comfort remains for me, *that we shall win*. Of that I have no doubt; but if you ask me what shall we win, then I am again confounded, as my friend Hamlet put it, "there's the rub" ... in an aftermath too terrible to contemplate.'

Constance gave him a very questioning glance. 'Are you being visionary or observer Gyles?'

'Neither m'dear. Put me down as a man able to make four from two and two. Fear y'see is the catalyst. The outcome will be muddled thinkin', false judgments, vainglorious deductions as lesser men rise to power, ill-equipped to cope – such bein' the natural outcome of this last war's decimations.'

'Can we do nothing?' Charles asked, 'you quoted the Bard so let me now do the same. What about "takin' arms against a sea of troubles, and by opposing end them"?'

'There's that of course,' Gyles agreed, *'but will it be enough?'*

Later, when the meeting broke up and they walked home together they spoke of other things. Gyles asked Constance if they were accepting the invitation for the twenty-ninth.

'We must,' she answered, 'if only to quell gossip. Besides, I need new clothes and if Lucy's were any criteria I believe I may find them in that little minx's salon.'

'Then come to luncheon and we will all go up together,' Gyles suggested, and on that note they parted.

Gilbert's talent for being unnoticed had never served him so well as when the Brinkmans came to stay. The trio came and went, their somewhat specious excuses accepted willingly, leaving them free to move about upon their highly questionable affairs without anyone paying the slightest attention. They were able to drive down to Dover on the morning of the war surplus sale, make their single five pound purchase, engage the services of a carter to bear their acquisitions to Upper Aynthorp village in three days' time, and return to the Castle without so much as a lifted eyebrow in their direction.

On the following morning the Castle cars were deployed to take the ladies up to London. The matter of finding suitable clothes in which to make an equally suitable entrance to Lucy and Lucien's salon took precedence over everything else. No one asked where the three boys had gone, indeed no one remarked their absence, so they were free to pursue the somewhat urgent matter of lodgement for their purchases. They went, in fact, to the village of Pluck Hollow some ten miles from the Castle and here sought that fount of all village information – the postwoman. This kindly old soul soon volunteered, 'Ef 'tis a barn you'm seeking fer there's a powerful big one empty on Farmer Tanner's land.' She rambled on for quite a while about the many years this had stood idle; but was eventually persuaded to give the trio the necessary directions. As they moved off she stood watching curiously.

They ran Farmer Tanner to earth on the edge of a field of mangel-wurzels where he leaned over a gate staring at them intently. They made themselves known by the names they had chosen then stated their business. After another fairly lengthy exchange the farmer cleaned the worst of the mud from his boots with a handful of torn grass, climbed in and proceeded to issue instructions as to the route – at full *fortissimo*, he being unaccustomed to motorised transport and scared bandy.

When the barn had been inspected and pronounced satisfactory or as its owner phrased it, 'Her's sound in wind and limb and as dry as one of Passon's sermons,' the deal was struck. Joseph handed over one golden sovereign for a three month's rental at five shillings a month, received his change and then, much to the stifled amusement of both Gilbert and Lionel, he proceeded to give a completely untruthful explanation of their intent. He told the man that a charitable exercise had been laid upon them by the headmaster of their school.

Then he went on to say mendaciously, 'I and my little cousins intend distributing certain charitable gifts to the needy. These will arrive by cart on the day after tomorrow so we shall be here to supervise their installation, lock the doors,' he held out one hand to receive the large iron key, 'and then keep this key.' Then with unerring timing Joe produced a further half sovereign, pressed it into an eager, horny hand, wrote down the farmer's full name and address in his diary, together with a tally of sums expended so far, and at length bade the man good day.

'Stage one completed,' said Lionel softly as he affixed his goggles in the back seat. 'Very nice.'

'Not if we don't sell,' said Gilbert gloomily. Joseph released the hand brake and they moved off. 'We'll sell,' he assured the others, 'don't forget there's one born every minute.' With which charitable comment he drove them back to the Castle, where Sawby let them in with the words, 'His Lordship your father has telephoned, Mr Joseph, he asks that you telephone him back, to Park Lane, he said you would understand. May I obtain the number for you, sir?'

Joseph nodded. 'Hang about you two,' he said to the others. 'I wonder what the old boy wants. No, on second thoughts, push off, I'll do better alone whatever it is. As soon as I've spoken to him I'll come to "In Transit".'

He joined them at length, rubbing his hands with pleasure, 'Talk of providence!' he exclaimed, remembering even in his obvious excitement to close the door very carefully. 'Father's going away Lionel. Now we don't have any problems. What a bit of transcendental, superlative luck, eh?'

'Well it might be,' said Lionel crossly, 'if we knew what the devil you were talking about.'

Joe sat himself down, 'Then listen,' said he. 'Father will not be in England for the next hols, so he wants us to go up to town and spend a day with him. That's what he rang about. He and mother leave for South Africa on the tenth of March and they won't be back until well on into the summer. Don't you see you dopey boy, he's leaving the town house open for us. I asked him if we could have Gilbert to stay. I said we'd had a splendid time here and it was only the decent thing to ask Gilbert back. He said of course.'

Lionel still looked blank. Gilbert merely watched like a cat at a mousehole.

'Oh don't be so stupid,' Joe chided, 'haven't we got one of the largest ballrooms in London? Don't the servants always do what we tell them because it suits us to turn a blind eye to the high jinks which go on in the Servants' Hall when the parents are out of the way? Well then . . . ?'

Gilbert caught on, 'Of course,' he said, 'it's perfect, we arrange for the stuff to be collected from the barn after March the tenth. Then when we get back for the Easter hols we can get stuck in *in your ballroom!*'

Joe nodded. 'What's more if all goes well I don't give a cuss what the servants think or try to say either because I'm going to tell father when it's all over. He'll be tickled pink, even if it does mean he'll have to pay me fifteen thou' for my part. What's more it will be easy enough to get an accommodation address in London and easy too to get cheap labour. In the meantime,' Joe lumbered to his feet, '*I think we should start right in now* and get as much done ourselves as we can before we go back to school. I've done my calculations and the more we do ourselves the less we shell out. If you're game then I am. It'll be a sweat but I think it's jolly well worth it.'

He ran on for some time, enlarging, explaining, planning aloud. Somewhere along the line Gilbert lost him and drifted off into a private speculation of his own. Suddenly he said, rather louder than he was wont to speak, 'What do I do with my share when I get it Joe?'

Joe looked at him shrewdly. 'I thought you might be getting round to that,' he approved. 'Tell you the truth I was rather surprised you hadn't said something before. Now that you have, let us examine the options. You cannot bank it, because you ain't got a banking account. I don't think you would want to keep it in your tuck box.'

Lionel giggled. Joe turned on him, 'The care of money,' he snapped, 'is not a laughing matter, now be quiet and let me think.'

Eventually he gave a little shrug which was entirely Jewish. 'There's nothing else for it, Gilbert, you'll have to let me invest it for you. We'll make it legal if you like. I'll sign a paper you can hold. I'll send you half yearly reports when I get the dividends. If I tried to welsh because I am still a minor,' he was reflecting aloud now, 'my father would be so mad he'd pay up anyway. I think that's the safest we can manage . . . until you get a banking account of your own.'

After this enigmatic conference the three fell into a routine pattern. They breakfasted early, took evasive action with the Napier and by adding a couple of miles to their journey managed to go round by the museum each morning and so drive over to the barn. Gilbert fabricated a story about bird-watching which he used to persuade Raikes to obtain a daily picnic basket from Mrs Parsons. Thus equipped they headed for the barn. In the remaining eighteen days of their holidays they spent seventeen in the barn, and one in London with Lord and Lady Brinkman. They also made some very large purchases which they offloaded at the barn before returning to the Castle. Then they went back to school.

CHAPTER 8

A Star Is Born

'I feel sick,' said Lucien, standing on the stage behind the pale apricot drapes. On the other side of them the buzz of conversation made it seem as if a thousand rooks were disputing a single crust.

'Well you can't be sick now,' said Piers sharply. 'In seven minutes time we're off my fine sir. So put down that glass like a good chap and let me inspect you.'

Obediently, but as clear evidence of his near-hysteria Lucien did so on the white baby grand piano which he would play throughout the display of the clothes he had created.

Piers, immaculate in grey with a most intricately folded stock pierced by a single black pearl walked round him slowly. 'Yes, you'll pass,' he said approvingly, 'have you an extra hanky for your hands?' Lucien held it out mutely.

'That's my good boy, but that tie is too tight, loosen it do, it looks like a piece of string.'

Lucien put up his hands, fumbled, despaired, exclaimed, 'You do it please, Piers, my hands are shaking. Where is Lucy? I want Lucy! I tell you Piers I feel frightful.'

Piers, busy with the offending tie, merely grunted, 'You'd be a codfish if you didn't. There that's better.'

He turned to see Lucy standing stricken in the entrance which the mannequins would take. 'Ah, there you are my little one, now let me inspect you too.'

Lucy raised huge, terrified blue eyes, 'Oh Pppppiers,' she stuttered, 'I ffeel sso ssick.'

'Oh my God, what a pair,' he exclaimed, *'you can't be sick now love*, it's almost time. Come and have one little peek through the hole I made specially for you. Then you can see that your family is here in full force and fig I may add.'

'Even after they accepted,' Lucy stammered, 'I nnnnever expected they would cccome.'

He drew her forward. 'Well, see for yourself – there. No look left, they're there alright. Your Uncle Gyles talking to the Begum, the adorable little Countess is with Lady Mendl, the Dowager, got them? I told you, and don't they look elegant? All the same I bet that coat of Mrs John's came from Busvine, *it's horsey*, but aren't you pleased?'

Lucy drew back. 'Amazed,' she said simply. At this moment Miss Poole thrust a beautifully coiffed head through the small screen behind which the mannequins were dressing.

'Lady Lucy could you come here a moment please,' she whispered.

'Only for a moment,' Piers warned.

Miss Poole nodded. Then as she held back the curtain for Lucy to pass through, 'How are you feeling?' Piers enquired.

'Sick,' replied Miss Poole succinctly.

Piers clasped his hands together. 'Oh my God,' he exclaimed, 'they can't all be in their second month of pregnancy!' Then he swung round, seeing out of the corner of one eye that Lucien was easing himself onto the piano stool.

'Good luck infant – don't forget to keep the soft pedal down and to turn your head occasionally so that they can see your irresistible profile, remember *this is your day*.' Very softly he added, 'Bosie,' but Lucien heard.

'That's the third time you've called me Bosie, why?'

'I'll tell you one day,' Piers sounded a trifle breathless suddenly, 'but not now.'

Lucien looked at him as he turned away. 'I don't know why,' he said childishly, 'but I am remembering the day we met. We've come a long way since then haven't we?'

Their eyes met. Piers thought he had himself well in hand but in that second something happened.

Lucien gave a little gasp as though he had touched a bare electric wire. Then Piers let go. 'You're so damnably beautiful,' the words were out before he could regain control.

As he said this Lucien's face became transfigured. 'I am so glad,' he told him, 'so very glad, dear Piers.' The lashes parted widely and their eyes held as a wave of indescribable sweetness engulfed them. They were as if frozen in the moment in a cold fire which made them tremble.

'I'm ... tingling,' Lucien whispered, 'Oh Piers ... oh what is ... it Piers?'

Piers shook his head, unable to answer.

'Oh Piers,' Lucien whispered again ... and then Lucy came sweeping back, very much in control of herself and her moment.

'It's time my darlings,' she said, 'it's time.'

Piers' hand went shakily to his stock. He hesitated, then swung round and walked unsteadily to his place – a little silver lectern with his notes arranged upon it. As the drapes swept back Lucien's fingers reached the keys while 'Darling Piers, oh darling Piers,' the words sang in his head leaving him with no knowledge of what he played.

There was a spatter of applause. Lucien rose, bowed, sat down again and continued playing. Lucy heard herself saying as from a long, long way off, 'My brother and I have the very greatest pleasure in welcoming you all here this afternoon. I thank your Royal Highnesses, your Graces, and you, my lords, ladies and gentlemen, for honouring our very first collection with your gracious presences. This is really a private showing of the clothes and accessories my brother has designed for this first season of restored peace, since the great and terrible war which made such things totally unimportant for over four long years; but now the future has opened up again for all of us with all its changes. These for my sex,' here the dimples came out evoking a little rustle of appreciation, 'include the clothes we wear today. Times have changed so greatly that it is necessary for fashions to change too and we hope very much to please you with the new clothes which my brother has created for us to wear with a totally new freedom of movement. Mr Piers Fournes,' she made a slight gesture in his direction, 'the distinguished portrait painter has honoured us too by painting our walls with the,' here she put all the charm she could muster into her following words, 'may I not say exquisite murals you now see?' she paused, demonstrating that extraordinary instinct which told her exactly how to conjure up applause. It broke out instantly.

'Now,' Lucy resumed, gaining confidence, 'Mr Fournes will share with me the descriptions of the models as they appear.' At this point she drew back to the right of their stage, the curtains parted behind her and the first mannequin sauntered towards them, moving down the narrow carpeted strip which ran half the length of the salon.

'Paula,' said Lucy, 'introduces our new colour "faun

beige", in a walking outfit which epitomises the easy line and slim elegance of our new fashions. Gone you see are those trailing skirts. Hems now swing clear of the wearer's ankles evincing a practicality in tune with the present scarcity of personal maids to attend us. This model is called *"L'Après midi d'un Faune"*, number four in your programmes. Paula's stole flung casually across her shoulders is, like her muff, made in faun beige fox, dyed specially and exclusively for this house. Note, too, how the muff conceals a modern, *pochette* handbag.'

Paula had almost completed her tour, and was back on the stage moving towards the exit. The second mannequin appeared and as she did so Piers picked up his cue and also the first sheet of his notes from his lectern and spoke. 'This is Monique, *petite* like our hostess, wearing what Lucien has called his "debutante day line". ' He glanced at his paper, 'I think I had better quote him here for the language of fashion is a trifle esoteric for a mere painter,' at which a ripple of laughter rose. Piers read, 'Nothing is prettier to the heart of man than the quick grace of a young girl when her movements are not constricted by the, er, more rigid dictates of fashion, and this ensemble, number two on your programmes, is called "Blue Skies", a day dress with matching cloak in this house's new soft wool crêpe with a charming hood to frame a pretty face with the softness of chinchilla ...'

Miss Poole had by this time slipped round to the back of the salon where she stood in the doorway beside a white and sweating 'Sissy'. On the farther side of him Elizabeth sat with her hands so tightly clasped together that the knuckles shone. In her lap Mr Silk slept tranquilly, his small head sunk between his paws and the bow which Lucien had made for him slid tipsily to one side.

Sissy saw Miss Poole and attempted to smile. 'It makes it sso vvery mmuch wworth wwhile,' he whispered.

She nodded back reassuringly. These children were holding them. It would do very well. Then the over-loud voice of one redoubtable dowager was heard confiding at the shout to an even more redoubtable 'ma'am', 'A beautiful trio of talented youth ma'am dontcher think?'

Miss Poole was now aware that the 'beautiful trio' had embarked upon the showing of their new redingotes. She waited long enough to hear the applause break out again, then patted Sissy's shoulder and hurried back to her post. Even Sissy ceased to sweat by the time Piers announced, 'Now we come to '*L'Heure de Thé Dansant*'', a comprehensive name for the next sequence of afternoon dresses all exemplifying the new Lucien signature, the "handkerchief line".'

There was not a woman over forty in that audience who did not experience a pang of wistfulness for her lost youth and thickening waistline now. Lucien had fulfilled his promise to his sister made when they were small children and in so doing he evinced such a sureness of touch with the gossamer materials of his choice; tulle, gauze, organza, chiffon and cobwebby lace, as might have come from a veteran dress designer. The applause intensified. Nor had he forgotten the golden strictures of the great Monsieur Paquin: 'In high fashion, little Lucien, it is the larger ladies, the more mature and *difficile* who always seem to have the very deepest purses. Create for them before all others.'

Lucien chose panne velvet and held to trains to lengthen the lines. He moulded the fabrics into sleeveless surcoats, massed the trains and opened surcoat fronts with rich embroideries; he moulded under-gowns of chiffon over de-lustred satins and draped small sleeves to cover upper arms which were no longer lovely. Then he became more opulent as the evening gowns were shown, banding soft apricot panne into a tiered spiral edged with sable. He caught gold and silver lamés in on the hip-line with large single buckles which sparkled as their wearers moved and then, growing gradually more youthful in his concepts, he flung petal-shaped cloaks of cobweb lace over fish-tail sheaths slashed and drawn upwards daringly in front, opening as the models walked; he made satin coats and three-quater length cloaks with huge collars and hems of pastel foxes; showed deeply fringed shawls, put fringe on cuffed gauntlet gloves to wear with sweeping Cavalier coats and looped chiffon scarves around the necks of his models in their floating chiffons. He made simple sheaths in *charmeuse* in such colours as pink jade, lapis lazuli and, most daring of all, styled, as Piers' commentary had it, 'for the ultra-sophisticate', tangerine frocks with tangerine beads looped twice and sometimes three times about the throats of the wearers of these his evening 'handkerchief line'. All were clothes which as Lucy stressed would float out gracefully when 'worn for dancing the tango and the two step'.

The applause became continuous until Lucien silenced it by rising from his piano and coming to centre stage. 'And now to close our little show,' he said shyly, 'May I please present you with my two bridal gowns.'

Paula and Monique came through, one on each side of Lucien. He led them down holding their hands and displaying them on the narrow line of carpeting as if he were showing Borzois.

'Paula is a very grand bride and Monique a very demure one,' he explained. Paula wore a pointed mediaeval headdress in white velvet, with a white chiffon wimple drawn close beneath her chin, and a close-moulded sheath in velvet which flowed out from her hips, embroidered richly at both hem and deep cuffs of the wide flaring sleeves which glistened with pearls and tiny bugle beads.

'There are five thousand pearls and ten thousand bugle beads in my embroidery and it took two girls six weeks to embroider,' he regarded the lifted faces of his guests artlessly, then added, 'So it is a very expensive dress to make.'

Amid the laughter he released Paula who turned to pace back displaying now the wide flow of the skirt, developing into its richly embroidered short train.

'While Monique, whose hand I still hold,' Lucien resumed, 'is dressed entirely in dotted Swiss with posies of white violets holding the skirt's cascades. Each one, as you can see, is tied up with narrow white ribbons – a Winterhalter bride, in fact, devised from the original which some of you may recall my sister wore at her coming out ball. Unfortunately I was far too young to attend – but I made it for her.'

Somewhere in that massed audience someone gasped. It was Christine who had sat, erect and lovely, already dumbfounded by what she was seeing. This was for her the *coup-de-foudre*, for as she realised immediately, Lucien had only been fourteen when he made that original dress which a King's eldest son had admired so greatly.

Her lapse made no impact. That gasp was lost in the now thunderous applause to which Lucien bent his fair head. Then turning, he ran lightly back to where Lucy and Piers stood waiting, took both their hands and the trio bowed again as the applause rolled up to them.

At length Piers made a slight signal which brought the drapes down gently to conceal them. Instantly he took control. 'Down to the salon now both of you,' he bade them, 'don't waste a moment, no wait Lucy, you have a tiny wisp of hair, Lucien are your hands dry?' The wisp was tucked in, Lucien merely nodded and then they went. Piers stood unmoving, a wry twist on his lips. Only when they had disappeared did he turn and follow slowly through the chattering covey of mannequins, through the press of scurrying dressers out of the staff door, past the lift, into the flower-massed foyer and so to the salon. As he moved so his thoughts ran, 'What now? How shall we come out of this? Indeed where do we go from here?'

The instant Paula reappeared in the dressing rooms, Miss Poole said hurriedly, 'None of you girls leave please until you have seen me.' Then she too plunged into the mêlée. Lucy and Lucien ran hand in hand, Lucy snatching up a notebook as she went.

A little later they spotted Miss Poole scribbling diligently in the midst of a group of excited women trying to make appointments and give orders. Lucy edged her way towards her, smiling, greeting friends, accepting a flood of congratulations. Lucien stationed himself at the entrance and let the flattery of each departing guest flow over him.

'I shall come tomorrow afternoon my dear ...'

'That nice Miss Poole has already taken my first little order.'

'Truly ravishing, dear boy, you really must do Polly's trousseau you clever, clever thing ...'

'Remember to keep a space for me, I am enchanted ...'

'You make me feel a frump, dear Lucien, you must re-dress me completely ...'

Thus the older women, while Lucien smiled and bowed and somehow made suitable replies. The young ones, reaching him, clutched his arms crying, 'Dar-ling, it was all too, too utterly divine and not a bogus note from first rustle to last shriek!'

'Heavenly bliss you clever one!'

'Perfectly deevy, I shall bring Mummie tomorrow ...' this last from a girl who came out with Lucy and the unfortunate Rosalind.

It was all exactly as they had dreamed it would be and it

went on and on until the Family who had held back came forward slowly with the Dowager in the van.

She said to Lucien, one veined hand holding his chin and tilting his face to her scrutiny, '*Maintenant c'est tous compris mon enfant.*' He kissed her impulsively. Then she announced in English, 'I intend comin' up with the family for Anne's overdue comin' out. Will you make your old *Belle-mère* a gown or two?'

Lucien hugged her, saying, 'Oh yes, *Belle-mère, avec grand plaisir.*' As he kissed her again he murmured, 'Darling, thank you for understanding.'

Eustace wandered after them, totally at sea. He had received congratulations from a dozen of his acquaintance. He had explained over and over again how much Gabrielle regretted she could not witness her children's triumph, had agreed again and again that his pair were exceedingly young, had accepted blandishments with suitable diffidence and an occasional, 'But nowadays ... so different you must appreciate ... freedom of choice ...' and so on until his head spun. All he wanted now was to escape from this hot and scented atmosphere into the tranquillity of his club for a large brandy and soda.

Christine and Gyles still lagged behind. Piers was in the doorway now, too, so they could hear and see very well what was passing. How Piers dealt with 'that precious pair' as if he were handling two precocious and over excited children and they were both thankful.

Primrose came next to have her say, then Marguerite who patted them smilingly and said gaily, 'You have your hands full Piers, make no mistake,' to which he answered in mock horror, 'I'll never hold them Countess, *les enfants terrible n'est pas,*' and she too was appeased. Then it was Claire's turn and Priscilla's, her arm linked with Sue-Ellen's who said in fairly passable accent, '*Epatant.* I shall be back again next week for you to make me new clothes for my trip.'

'What trip?' Lucy's eyes were beginning to glaze.

'I'm going to the States on a visit,' Sue-Ellen explained, 'hopefully, I shall take the in-laws with me.'

At the end Sinclair limped up with Henrietta who was of course tearful with praise and eager to be kind, and then Christine and Gyles were there. They had paused for a word with Miss Poole, with Gyles enquiring, 'Well Miss Poole, which is more arduous, runnin' a season for the Aynthorps or handlin' these two gifted children?'

'Oh this,' said Miss Poole at once, 'but it is so very rewarding Lord Aynthorp,' which again added to their growing tally of confidence.

Finally they were level with Lucy and Lucien. Christine just bent her head, kissed Lucy, murmured, 'I begin to understand a little,' and Lucy clung to her, managing to trifle incoherently, 'I am so glad, so very glad, dear Aunt Christine.'

It was triumph all the way, until they were almost dropping with combined excitement and fatigue. Miss Poole assumed command as the last of the Castle Rising contingent went down the steps. She banished the press. She pushed Lucy and Lucien into the lift. She urged them inside. She pressed the botton with unnecessary vigour saying only, 'Now you must rest, I will come to you in a few moments.' They went dazedly, not questioning her authority.

Once inside the first floor drawing room, Lucy kicked off her shoes and Lucien lay down on the floor and put his hands behind his head.

'Well?' asked Piers, standing above him, cigarette in one hand, drink in the other.

Lucien said dreamily, 'It hasn't happened; it's all just another dream.'

Piers looked down at him, 'Then my fine fellow you had better wake up and face reality. After this and until you close in the summer you will not have a moment to call your own. You will be inundated with press, drenched with invitations, flattered, written about, I wonder ... if you ... can ... possibly ... keep ... your ... head.'

Lucien sat bolt upright, 'It's what I wanted Piers. Can't you understand that? It is *my*, my, oh, what is the word I want?'

'Destiny?' Piers made it a question.

'Nno not quite, because you can make a mess of destiny, I can't make a mess of this by getting spoiled because it is the work that counts. It is my life, this kind of day only happens twice a year ...'

Piers pressed him. 'You are going to a party to-night? You want to go don't you?'

Lucien lay back again, 'Of course,' he said, a trifle defiantly.

'Can you go to parties every night and work all day?'

The boy hesitated, 'I think I can but if I can't then it's the parties that will have to wait.'

Piers' manservant Soles opened the door and walked in with a laden tray. Piers called him 'crêpe soles', because he could never hear him coming.

Soles put down his tray, straightened his black coat and gave tongue. 'Now sir, my lady,' he said, 'I know it is not my place to remonstrate; but you have eaten nothing all day, so here are sandwiches. I have also taken the liberty of bringing some hot coffee which I made myself and you will please to drink it. There is some brandy for you Mr Fournes, sir.'

Lucy giggled. 'There's always someone to bully us Lucien,' she exclaimed. 'You know Soles I think I am hungry.' She reached for a sandwich, bit it, mumbled, 'No I'm not, I'm starving ... come on Baby, eat and we'll talk later. No we will not. We'll talk and eat.' She was suddenly revitalised, 'Pour for us Soles will you? Piers, *how did you get on?*'

Piers sank into a chair, accepted a brandy from his man and sprawled, swirling the amber fluid in its balloon. 'I had five requests for murals,' he reported, 'including one from that grisly woman with the orange hair.'

'Piers,' Lucy shrieked, 'do you mean Elsie Mendl? She's terribly influential nowadays.'

'And rather exceptionally vulgar,' Piers retorted. 'Old Lady Singleton said she'd like me to paint her too and that I cannot do. Paintin' old women to look like girls is totally revoltin'.'

Lucien giggled, wolfing sandwiches as if he were a Great Dane.

'Who else?' Lucy demanded with her mouth full.

'Sue-Ellen,' Piers told her, 'that will be pure pleasure. She wants to get in some sittings before she goes off on this trip of hers to the States, so I have promised her she shall. I suppose you realise you will have to take on more staff? You took an immense amount of orders this afternoon and the bulk of the assorted bulges will be back tomorrow for their measures to be taken.'

'Wait till we get Pooley's report and I think we shall be *swamped*,' said Lucien gleefully.

'Oh no we shall not,' said Miss Poole from the doorway. 'Good afternoon Soles. Do you think you could prevail upon cook to make me a nice strong pot of tea?'

Thus she disposed of the manservant. She then permitted Piers to draw up a chair for her, sat down, produced her notebook and informed them, 'I have totalled up the orders to date, and made the necessary arrangements. We shall have to take on at least another six girls immediately, so I have arranged for what I think are suitable applicants to come for interviews tomorrow morning at fifteen minute intervals from nine-thirty am, therefore it behoves you all to make sure you have an early night.'

The trio exchanged guilty glances, knowing full well that they would be very late indeed.

'If we continue as we have begun,' Miss Poole went on, missing these glances, 'we shall have to take in more workrooms on the next floor. The interest shown by the lady journalists alone is enough to bring half London to your doors.'

'Goody,' said Lucien from the floor, 'then when the summer closing comes we can go to the South of France and charter a yacht,'

Lucy looked down at him fondly, 'If that's what you want my darling, of course. Just go on making clothes everyone wants to wear, and you can buy one of your own.'

'Have you any idea just how much it costs to buy a yacht?' Piers enquired, helping himself to a second brandy.

'How much?' Lucien sat up again, eyes bright.

'Well Lord Rothschild says that anyone who needs to know how much a yacht costs cannot possibly afford to buy one,' Piers yawned, 'so stop foolin' children. Good Gad, look at the time! It's nearly seven already. If we are hopin' to turn up at Olga's for dinner we had better begin to think about changin".' He turned to Miss Poole, 'What do we do about the mess downstairs Pooley?'

She clicked her tongue in disapproval, 'Pooley indeed! Pray remember your manners young man and the mess downstairs is being handled. The men are already collecting the chairs. There are two women sweeping the salon, another is dusting and two more are due from Moyses Stevens at seven o'clock to refresh all the flowers. Mr Sissingham is busy typing out the orders and his lady typewriter has kindly consented to stay on and enter these in the order book.'

'Sissy,' exclaimed Lucien contritely, 'we forgot all about poor Sissy.'

'He understands,' said Miss Poole, 'he told me that he would prefer to stay quietly in his office for a while and then I know he is going to have supper with that spotty friend of his. What I now wish to know is if you *are* going to Princess Olga's party, and pray remember I have had the organising of a great many of them, how do you imagine you will be in any shape for work to-morrow morning?'

Lucien jumped up, 'Vital and creative, Pooley darling, that's what we'll be, please love don't be cross. I want to go out, I'm all tangled up, I couldn't just sit about. It's all been too exciting.'

Lucy rose too. 'Miss Poole, I promise to keep an eye on both of them and bring them home well before the milkman,' she promised. 'I am going down now to have a word with Sissy, and while I'm about it I'd better see that the pressers are doing their job. Everything must be quite perfect for to-morrow. Who paid off the mannequins?'

'I did my dear,' Miss Poole was eyeing her quizzically, 'I also remembered to thank them on your behalf and I likewise engaged two of them to come again to-morrow. I assumed your ladies would prefer to see the clothes on them rather than on coat hangers.'

Piers gave her a brilliant smile, 'You are a marvel,' he told her very seriously. 'I tremble to think what would have happened today without your miraculous efficiency.'

A slight flush touched the woman's cheeks. All she said, a trifle brusquely was, 'As to that, Mr Fournes. I am merely fulfilling the duties of my post. However, I feel compelled to add my mite. Your clothes were beautiful Mr Lucien and the display was an unqualified success. Now we must just take care we do not lose our heads. They can so easily be turned by flattery.'

'Yes Miss Poole,' they chorused.

Still Miss Poole had the last word. 'Very well then, see that you do. Mark my words, it is one thing to show a single collection, another to fulfil the orders satisfactorily; but the crux will come when you show again. That is when you will establish your worth as a dress designer *and not a moment before*.'

When the Castle contingent were settled in their respective cars, Henry exclaimed, 'Lord I've left my coat! Hang on a minute Grantham.' He flung himself from the folding seat to which he had been relegated and disappeared through the still open front door of Number Two.

When he re-settled himself and the Royce slid away from the kerb he said breathlessly, 'Pretty efficient those infants. The salon is completely cleared already, there are two gels doin' fresh flowers and that precious pair were changin' for some party. Rum really, it only seems like yesterday they were both in the nursery.'

'It makes one wonder,' mused the Dowager, 'if they were ever nursery people in our meanin' of the term.'

'Devious and gifted,' Marguerite sounded rather cross, 'both then and now in my opinion. One has to admit this afternoon has been a staggerin' experience. The whole thing was so extraordinarily mature.'

'Christine?' the Dowager made her daughter-in-law's name into a question.

'Well now,' Christine spoke guardedly, 'what do you want me to say *Belle-mère*?'

'What you think my dear. What else?'

Christine hesitated, but eventually replied rather as if she were thinking aloud. 'I agree with *Tante* Meg. No one could gainsay their talent. Our own experiences have already taught us just how devious they both can be; yet in many ways I am reassured by this afternoon's experience. Yes I think that is exactly what I am. They are unusually close to one another but now Piers Fournes seems to have established himself as their mentor, while of course having Miss Poole, who is a nonpareil as we all know, makes the whole extraordinary business much . . .' again she hesitated, before concluding, 'much healthier.'

Petula remained silent. She was trying to clarify for herself her tremendous distaste for the 'goings on' as she thought of them, of the extraordinary 'new' hostesses who had mushroomed their way into café society . . . someone called 'Syrie' who like the hound of heaven seemed perpetually fleeing from something, for all her brittle chatter . . . and that Nancy one, smart enough but surely a trifle mad? Like the chirruping American who to Petula had simply bulldozed her way into her present status by weight of millions alone. These women were 'rather dreadful' she decided 'all jingling bracelets, dyed hair, and passionate addictions to bleached furniture'.

Once inside the Castle with Pearson waiting to take Christine's furs and muff, Palliser moving sniffily to do likewise for the Dowager and little Marguerite, and Christine's soft voice apologising to Sawby, 'Please give my regrets to chef for our tardiness. We will be ready to dine in fifteen minutes ...' Petula relaxed into her normal pattern dismissing 'them' as mushroom creatures with no sense of roots or faith in continuity. Then hand in hand she and Henry tore up the great staircase to say goodnight to their twins.

They dined without guests. Andrew brought Victoria, but she, as the foul-mouthed old Duke of Barton and Sale's orphaned niece was virtually family and even Sue-Ellen's visiting agent had absented himself, 'takin' a sabbatical' as Gyles reported, 'in order to inspect the Cinque Ports and explore Dover Castle', to which Gyles added, 'God alone knows why!'

The table talk concerned themselves and of course Petula's parents who dined with them. Indeed Constance chose this moment to say reluctantly, 'I thought this might be a propitious time dears for us to begin removing ourselves to the Manor House. There is such a very great deal to do.'

Gyles scowled at the entrée dish proffered by Wilkins, helped himself and gloomed, 'We shall miss you dreadfully m'dear. I must learn to accustom myself to bein' without Charles' invaluable assistance.'

'How would it be sir,' Andrew looked up, his colour rising, 'if I asked Sir Charles to break me in ... show me the ropes ... after all, sir, I'm home for good now and I don't want to cool my heels doing nothin'?'

Gyles looked astonished. Then he said abruptly, 'Frankly I never thought of it. I imagined you would want a bit of time to get used to civilian life again, find your feet and all that.'

'You imagined that with me sir,' Henry reminded him. 'It's only fair to let Andrew lend a hand, that is if he really wants to.'

'Good Gad,' said Gyles explosively, 'there's nothin' I should like better. Charles would you consent to break my young cub in before you leave and then keep an eye on him for the first few weeks?'

Sir Charles smiled at Andrew who was turning his head to and fro during this exchange with a mixture of eagerness and apprehension.

'If I could explain sir,' he said hopefully, 'I've given the matter some thought y'know. Town life doesn't attract me. I prefer it here. M'y father's responsibilities are increasin' all the time. Now there's the museum, the company, new staff, half a hundred different things. There's enough work here for a dozen of us and it's all very much to my taste. Of course I shall enjoy the shootin', fishin' and huntin' too,' he added hastily, 'but the work itself interests me, really sir I would like to have a shot at it.'

Gyles looked down the table to where Christine was sitting smiling at him. She just nodded. 'I knew this was coming,' she told him, 'I think it is an excellent plan. Anyway whatever keeps my sons about me after this terrible war is bound to be very much to my taste.'

Her husband turned to Henry, 'Will you school him a bit too then? If you could hand over some of your responsibilities it would leave you freer to help me more, you know.'

'Oh yes sir,' Henry replied equably, 'I'll school your cub for you alright. Between Charles and me might just lick him into shape.'

'Hey there, rein in,' Andrew retorted, 'I'm not havin' you come the big elder brother and don't forget it. I'm easy to ride and drive, and guaranteed good in double harness but I don't take kindly to a hard hand y'know.' The brothers settled to a mild wrangle. Across the table Gyles smiled at Sir Charles. When Christine rose and collected eyes the atmosphere had become much less oppressive.

Even so, when the door closed behind them, she began to wonder if there was anything brewing between her third son and Victoria and so thinking entered the White Drawing Room and picked up her embroidery. Marguerite had already taken her accustomed place behind the coffee tray. Spurling set the tray of *petit fours* on its usual table and Christine took up her needle with a contented sigh. It was the mixture as before again. The machinery had been set in motion; life was returning to its accustomed pattern. All this was very much to her taste and the thought that Andrew wished to stay quite banished Lucy and Lucien from her mind.

When the men joined them her sense of general felicity was in no way diminished. Gyles came over and settled himself beside her, accepted his coffee from his daughter and eyed her with approval. 'That is a very becomin' frock m'dear. Now I suppose your mother and I must discuss your come out and make the necessary arrangements.'

Anne smiled. 'Well Papa,' she reminded him, 'you did say you were going to ask your friend if the rumour was true that the *real* courts would be returning next year. If that is so I would much prefer to wait. It's fun enough for me being out of uniform, beginning to hunt again, helping Mama with your shooting parties.'

At this last Gyles exclaimed, 'Dear me, I had quite forgot. Christine, old Ritz has written a very civil letter askin' if we can increase the game supplies until the season closes and now that hostilities are ended. I wondered if you could face a small shootin' party next Tuesday? There's one thing to be said for the present wind of change, I can telephone these days and round up a sufficiency of guns I would imagine.'

Christine lifted a serene face. 'Give me until the morning,' she countered. 'Let me speak to André and then you can, I am sure, commence your, what did you call it, round up.'

Constance Danement chuckled. 'I want to do a more protracted round up,' she told them. 'Charles and I think we shall need about three months to put the Manor into order again. Then we thought, as we are taking up the reins for the first time together, we might celebrate the fact with a small dance – nothing like your balls, Christine, but just a gathering of the clans hereabouts. We would welcome your opinion.'

Sue-Ellen sat looking more and more disconsolate. 'I shall miss it all,' she wailed, 'a lovely English party in an old manor house, isn't it downright cruel?' Which made them all laugh.

'Bags I first dance with you Victoria,' said Andrew quickly.

'Andrew,' exclaimed Christine, scandalised, 'you haven't even been invited yet. Really your manners!'

'And bags I the second with you Lady Constance,' he retorted unabashed.

'I can see,' Gyles observed without rancour, 'that we shall

stand in need of all the schoolin' Sir Charles and Henry can impose upon you my boy, before we can loose you on even local society.'

It was almost four o'clock when Lucy, Lucien and Piers came somewhat unsteadily up the steps to Number Two, Halcombe Street. Lucy had been given her first cocktails, which she disliked, and a great deal of champagne which she infinitely preferred. She had been taken to her first night club into which Nada swept all her dinner guests after an all-tangerine dinner at a glass fish-tank of a table under a black ceiling where they were served by negroes with white gloves. Lucy was completely dazed. As she left the night club – somewhere called Murrays – she tried to find her hostess to deliver her duty thank you, only to be told by Piers, 'I shouldn't bother, she's probably petting in one of the cars.'

She let Piers put her into his car. She sat between the two of them for the short drive home through the silent streets; but when Piers had helped her out again, she stood on the steps of Number Two, Halcombe Street while Lucien fumbled for the key, raised wide eyes to Piers and asked, 'Darling what does "petting" mean?'

Piers took her arm. 'Never mind that now, I'll explain it to you in the morning baby,' he said persuasively, 'come along in.'

'But it *is* morning' Lucy protested, 'and, oh Piers, Miss Poole will I fear be dreadfully cross!'

The day after the collection had been shown was chaotic. Everyone wished to see Lucien and no one else. Photographers, journalists, clients and friends clamoured for him. Lucy did what she could but even so Lucien scarcely left the salon and it was the same on the following day.

She and Miss Poole then conferred and agreed upon a plan of action. When it all began again, 'I'm so sorry,' Lucy apologised again and again, as the day wore on, 'my brother is out of town today. Can I help you I wonder?' While Lucien worked away at sketches for trousseaux which had been ordered. When Lucy slipped in for a moment to see how he was doing, he wailed at her, 'Lucy-Lou I haven't started on Sue-Ellen's things yet and where's Piers, I haven't seen him all day?'

'Nor have I darling,' Lucy soothed him.

'Well where is he,' he repeated fretfully. 'Why isn't Piers here?'

Lucy perforce explained. Sue-Ellen had telephoned that morning from the Castle. When she was put through to Piers she told him that she would like him to begin on her portrait immediately. She asked him to drive down and see her and Piers agreed. Then late in the afternoon she telephoned again and when Lucy asked if Piers was still with her she was told that he was staying overnight. Sue-Ellen said, 'He has been working on some first sketches of me, he wants to finish them to-night. So Uncle Gyles asked if he would like to stay over, here he is, have a word with him yourself.'

Piers then spoke. 'Lucy-Lou, do try to make Lucien understand,' he urged. 'If I leave now it will never be any good. Tell him I will come straight to you tomorrow night and give him my love, baby.'

Lucy passed all this on to her brother ending, 'You must realise darling, Piers is a creative artist too. When the, er, whatever it is begins to flow it cannot be deflected.'

'Oh, pooh,' exclaimed Lucien, 'well then nor can mine. I shall just stay here until I have finished too. Even if it takes me all night.'

Wisely Lucy left him, only to find more people in the salon. She was kept busy until six o'clock when the last 'darling' was uttered and the last enthusiastic client friend waved to her car. But then as Miss Poole pointed out, 'You have become the fashion you two, and it would never do for any of them not to have ordered clothes from you. That is success. Shall we draw the curtains?'

They drew the apricot velvets across.

They went up to Sissy with whom they went through their order books. Then, orders in hand they entered the silent workrooms where they sought and pinned on scraps of the materials chosen. Only when all these were handed to Sissy was Lucy free to return to Lucien whom she found sprawled across his drawing board, sound asleep. She woke him gently, managing to persuade him to come and eat his dinner before returning to his sketches.

As dinner ended the telephone rang. It was Piers from

Castle Rising to say that he had begun Sue-Ellen's portrait, that it was going splendidly and that Lord and Lady Aynthorp had invited him to stay on until it was completed.

'Why can't you do it here?' Lucien asked sulkily.

'Because my infant, Mr Mobberly is here from the United States to confer with Sue-Ellen. He is only making a very brief visit and they need every moment together. Here she can sit for me and discuss her business affairs with Mobberly while I paint. Do be reasonable, this is going to be good, I know it is. Now listen to me quietly and I'll tell you what Sue-Ellen wants.'

Finally Lucien banged the receiver back on its hook and came back to the dinner table.

'Well darling is everything alright?' Lucy enquired solicitously.

'Oh, I suppose so,' Lucien answered grudgingly, 'Sue-Ellen wants me to send the sketches to her. Piers says he will undertake to make her choose and will see that the sketches come back so that I can get her first fittings ready. He says by that time Mr Mobb-something will have gone and she can come up because Piers will have finished with her portrait too.'

'Well I'm glad that's settled,' said Miss Poole briskly, 'now what about going to bed and getting a good night's sleep.'

Lucien stared at the tablecloth. 'I've a good mind,' he said, 'to take the sketches down myself.'

Lucy managed to persuade him otherwise and the trio, with Mr Sissingham, gradually settled to a quieter pattern. Lucien was brought out only for the most important clients and otherwise was left to sketch while the others ran the business. It resulted in some excellent designs, and another rush of orders.

Piers in the meantime was cheating. He feared the sudden recognition which had flared between himself and Lucien. He feared any contact for a while until he had regained his self control which he felt had slipped perilously.

He joined the guns on the following Tuesday, acquitted himself very well and returned with renewed enthusiasm to the portrait. Each evening he telephoned to 'Number Two' and had long talks with both Lucy and Lucien. All in all he was well content to stay on as long as possible.

CHAPTER 9

Caution – Landowners at Work

At length the Castle settled down again and in so doing its remaining inmates became sharply divided. As Petula reflected gloomily it was becoming like a tenants' party in the big barn, only now it was the family who, like their employees, placed themselves apart, the women on one side the men upon the other with no attempts by either to encroach upon opposing territory.

The Dowager and little Marguerite were busy: trotting about between two rooms, the one in which everything from Queen Victoria's Suite had been stored to make way for the Convalescent Home and the one in the museum. These two frail old persons effected their own transit from one to the other by dog cart. All the while the relevant corridors were being impeded by the two stout men provided by Pine, they hauled along buttoned chairs and over-stuffed conversation pieces covered in what the Dowager referred to with marked distaste as 'all that dreadful tartan'. Meanwhile the pair of them could be heard regretting *fortissimo* that the 'dear, late Queen had possessed quite execrable taste!'

This last little snippet was gleaned by Raikes and promptly relayed to her colleagues at the ensuing staff luncheon, whereupon Sawby intervened, finding herein an excellent opportunity for another of his familiar homilies on the general theme of 'people who never learn their places and therefore must be reminded of them'.

Sir Charles and his Constance moved back to the Manor House – a departure to across the Park and no more – with the full knowledge of all the Castle's inmates that they would be returning to dine with them a few hours later. But this evoked such crowding onto the steps, such hand waving, such gusty sighs and surreptitious eye-dabbings that anyone without knowledge of their destination might well have been excused for supposing they were embarking upon a journey across the world.

Once they drew up before their own front door, a five minute journey by a car containing a plethora of baggage Charles handed his wife out, kissed the top of her head somewhat absent-mindedly, and murmuring, 'So much to be done my love ... pray excuse me ...' and was off like a whippet, leaving Constance to her skeleton staff and the task of re-ordering her new home.

For many weeks thereafter she had the top of her head kissed at the breakfast table as her husband hurried away with his son. Then they were either seen no more until dinner or, at best, they came in, booted and apologetic, bolted luncheon while talking incessantly of repairs, renovations, innovations and expenditures and were off again with almost indecent haste. Constance told Petula amusedly, 'They gobble their food as if they were those new carpet cleaners, which at best is scarcely good for their digestion; yet they seem to thrive.'

Petula spent a great part of her time at her old home, which was undergoing such an orgy of cleaning, polishing and furniture moving that she was driven to confide in Henry at last, having barked her shins on an enormous tallboy which had been left amidships in a badly lit corridor, 'Anyone would think they were all pregnant and near their time. The whole distaff side is suffering from an overdose of spring fever.' This confidence was made as she snuggled down in their big bed, to which she added sleepily, 'And this is about the only place where I ever see you young man. Even when I do sleep I dream of hurrying down endless corridors all blocked by females and furniture in transit. Hi, Henry ... did you hear what I said?' Alas he did not, for he had fallen asleep already, exhausted by the pace set by his father and shared by his brother Andrew.

Andrew was having a rip-roaring time. Having studied his son with outward severity but inward pleasure, Gyles gave him the task of dealing with the new building which was to be the headquarters of their equally new company, Aynthorp Enterprises. Thus Andrew spent a long time studying the ground and elevation plans. When he had familiarised himself with them he marched off to make himself known to the foreman. From then onwards he spent from post-breakfast to pre-dinner time on the site as the building took shape, even hurrying away again after dinner to discuss any problems which had arisen with Henry and his father in the comfort of Gyles' old office. Here the trio lit pipes, created an enormous fug and enjoyed themselves hugely. The trio fell into a daily pattern. Gyles rode with his sons before breakfast. He then withdrew behind his copy of *The Times* while drinking several cups of coffee and eating a piece of toast, while the two younger sons ingested huge breakfasts. On a cue from their father they pushed back their chairs while 'the old man' kissed Christine perfunctorily and then hurried off in his wake, one or the other of them banging the breakfast room door behind them.

'And that,' as Christine murmured resigned, 'will be that for today.'

Sue-Ellen and her in-laws did not mind either. They were engrossed in plans for their departure to America. They were due to sail in a few days so were rushing about, making trips to London for Sue-Ellen and Henrietta's last fittings and for shopping sprees for which the girl insisted on picking up all the bills. She declared, 'This is your holiday. Call it my way of saying thank you for everything. These are your holiday clothes, hats, suits, valises, and they are part of that holiday!' Under this kind of domination Henrietta and Sinclair took on a new lease of life and Sinclair's stammer lessened even more.

When they left, with little Stephen hanging out over the car door waving excitedly, Christine, Claire, Petula, Anne and the two 'naughties' saw them off from the top of the steps and then settled in conclave over the elaborate plan which Gyles had approved for the launching of the extended museum. They would give a big party, invite the entire county. There were endless lists to be made, details to be agreed upon. At this juncture Petula was deputed to sound out Stephanie, to obtain her agreement to a very special merger which they all believed would add considerably to the day's success. They wanted her to try to persuade Stephanie to let them combine the opening with the post-war revival of their annual Fête and Flower Show, and thus, as Claire put it, 'Kill two horses with one brick.'

Christine was emphatic that it should be Harry and Stephanie's decision for it was their big benefit and, unless they agreed that the revenues from the Fête could easily be increased by so many guests coming anyway for the opening, none of them could proceed any further.

As they all knew, Christine was referring to the fact that

the revenues from the Fête had always in the past been shared between the incumbents of both Upper and Lower Aynthorp. This Christine and Gyles both wished to continue. If either the new Vicar, Stephanie's husband, or she thought that this was just another Aynthorp attempt to make life easier for this stubborn pair, they knew full well that the response would be 'thumbs down'.

Summing this up Petula mused, 'I shall have to ride 'em with a very loose rein indeed! Well I'm willing to do my best, but don't blame me if they scent patronage on the wind will you?'

All this time the two old 'Naughties' were happily engaged with their two current obsessions, the Clothes Room and the Queen Victoria Room, allowing scarcely more than a cursory trot round the temporary flower arrangers' quarters to examine the order book, and then to murmur, 'Yes well, you can manage that quite comfortably without our interference,' which drew startled glances from the girls who heretofore had been ruled by an iron, if bejewelled small white hand. Happily for all concerned there was a distinct diminution of orders in this pre-Easter period; even so the girls knew, very well, though the two old gentlewomen chose to ignore the fact, when the actual run up to Easter began they would be busier than at any other time in the year except just before Christmas. The truant pair turned a Nelsonian eye to this though it greatly concerned both Christine and Andrew.

As Christine remarked, strolling with her son towards the hive of activity which would one day become the permanent quarters for all the Aynthorp commercial activities, 'How anyone can expect them to cope in their present discomfort I simply do not know.' Andrew only made suitable comforting grunts as he began helping her over the unfinished floors, steering her through scaffolding and all the while talking at a great rate, at the shout.

'As you can see, here is Dispatch, Mama. It is almost completed, we shall hope to be clear within a week; but the new dairy will be many weeks I fear. I have asked father to postpone the launching of butter and cream sales until Whitsun at the earliest because Pet says it will take her all of that to teach the women. What a bit of luck it was she learned herself when she was squabbling with Henry in their salad days!' He hauled her across a pile of sawdust and through the entrance to the egg room and, over the sound of hammering roared, 'They'll do all pluckin' and singein' in here too, and I'm already thinkin' of ways to utilise the feathers.'

Christine put her hands over her ears and yelled back, 'Well if you do, make sure you destroy the fleas in them first. When your sister decided to copy Lucien's feather trimmings she brought in a bag of ducks' feathers and in five minutes we were all scratchin' like mangy dogs. Andrew, darling, pray leave the rest of your explanations until we get away from this noise.'

Abruptly the noise ceased, for Agnes appeared with a big basket covered with a white cloth from which she began dispensing tea and sandwiches among the men.

'That's better,' Andrew approved. 'Now where was I? Oh yes, Parkins and Titmuss are ready with their hen houses and runs. They've even got the feedin' troughs and all that. Next week we take delivery of two thousand head of Rhode Island Red pullets, but they're only six weeks old, so we shall have plenty of time. They won't come into lay until around September and even then the eggs'll be far too small to sell at first.'

'There will be game by then,' Christine reminded him. 'What are you doing about table birds?'

'They're on their way too but I've forgotten the breed,' he confessed.

'Light Sussex I expect,' she suggested.

'And I want to sell venison too, Mama,' he ran on. 'I haven't tackled the old man about that yet; but you know our deer have been breedin' undeterred through the war. We shall have to decimate, so why not turn that to a bit of extra profit as well?'

'Butchers?' Christine sounded dubious.

'That's alright, I had a word with André. He's waitin' to ask if he can train a lad or two. I understand he's fixed his sights on Appelby's son by her first marriage. He tells me the boy is leavin' school this term. Apparently André has discovered he's quite clever with his hands so it could be fortuitous. André just lends him to us to cut up our venison properly durin' the season and then employs and teaches him in the kitchens for the rest of the year.'

Christine still looked doubtful. 'Takin' on more staff is also a problem,' she warned. 'We are addin' so many already. Wages are soarin' yet none of them want to work the hours they did before the war.'

'Before the war, Mama,' Andrew whipped back, 'nothin' we did brought in any revenue.' And to her intense amusement he added, 'You can't break omelettes without makin' eggs.'

She corrected this with a twinkle and permitted herself to be led between two great piles of timber into the future flower quarters. Here she saw with dismay that all was still chaos, with men sawing, working with pipes at the future plumbing areas; but she could only nod and draw her son out hurriedly.

'I hate noise,' she confided, coming out into the fresh air thankfully. 'I once read the only quotation I ever liked about wealth. It said, "wealth is a high wall around a quiet garden, shutting out the cries of noisy people." I wonder who said it? I have quite forgotten.'

Andrew added, 'I cannot imagine anywhere in the world I would rather be than here. One way and another its, well, absolutely rippin'.'

Christine bided her time. After dinner she cornered the naughty pair who were sipping their coffee and chattering happily about their special rooms. Into a brief pause she managed, 'How is it all comin' along?' To which the Dowager said quickly, 'Most fortuitously, but we do need you to give us the benefit of your opinion on the final selection of *musée* clothes. Y'see Piers has been uncompromisingly firm about enlistin' Lucien's help with the models on which we must arrange them. I do see his point,' she conceded, 'but its tarsome. However, there it is.'

Christine looked fogged, so Marguerite explained, 'We wished Lucien to make the figures with Lucy and Piers' assistance; but it seems that Piers is engaged upon some portraits which he has been commissioned to paint and Lucien and Lucy are busy makin' clothes. Therefore we must see if Madame Tussaud's can help, but we cannot decide just how many models we need until we have made out final choice of clothes.'

'I see,' Christine took a deep breath. 'There was another matter on which I happen to need your urgent co-operation so, while I shall be delighted to help you with your final choice, I must beg of you to give me your attention first.'

The Dowager's face fell. 'Flowers, I suppose?'

'Yes my love, and with Easter comin', really the present conditions are deplorable.'

'I was hopin' our new quarters would be completed in time.' The Dowager confessed.

'But they will not *Belle-mère*.'

'Fatiguin',' the Dowager flicked open her fan and began fanning herself at a great rate, managing to achieve a sudden air of great fragility.

Inwardly chuckling, Christine grasped the advantage, 'Then let me help. I have a suggestion to make.'

With a show of resignation the two prepared to listen, aware that this time there was no escape.

'I do not see,' Christine began, 'why you could not be transferred immediately to Sawbridge's newly completed stove house. It would be warm, light and very pleasant to work in. You could use the staging for all your arrangements and the girls for the packing of flowers. There is ample access for vans too which could be drawn up outside the doors to make all easy.'

'Silly!' exclaimed the Dowager.

'I beg your pardon *Belle-mère*?'

'No, not you dear, silly of me not to have thought of it myself. But you will have to beard that old curmudgeon for us. He is becomin' *most* disagreeable with me. He actually grudges me flowers. Why he positively *sulked* the other day when I remarked that I should require a great many more freesias.'

Christine laughed. 'When have you ever known a gardener who was not grudging when it came to cutting flowers? I'll tackle him most certainly; but if I am successful you must promise me to take a day away from your present work to supervise the move. You really must have everything exactly where you wish it to be and no one else can possibly decide for you.'

'Meg could,' suggested the Dowager hopefully.

'Alicia,' Marguerite exclaimed, 'you know full well you would only change it all. It must be decided by you.'

They were behaving like the children they were in so many ways. Both were far too immersed in their new ploy to evince a flicker of interest in the old one. Happily Christine knew by long experience that this would all pass the very moment they were called upon to produce some new ideas.

In the meantime the museum game was clearly the only one they wished to play.

Again, like a child the Dowager bargained, 'If we do, will you *promise* to come and see the clothes with us?'

'I will do more,' she rose, 'I will come now. We can return here for tea, after which I will tackle Sawbridge in his potting sheds. Mrs Parsons always sends their tea out there which they do not have until five o'clock so we shall have finished ours by then. Come along *Belle-mère*, I am looking forward to this.'

There was a further delay. As they began climbing the staircase Claire ran down waving a letter. They met halfway.

'Splendid news,' she cried. 'It's Christian. He is being sent home at last. He says the All-High have decided he is well enough to travel. He expects to be in England within the next ten days. Isn't it marvellous? I think I shall go up to London and meet him there. We could stay the night which might tire him less.'

'Take the new Royce,' suggested Christine quickly, 'it really does glide like silk and let Grantham drive you she is so good and careful.'

'Oh, bless you,' Claire was radiant, then she apologised, 'I have interrupted you haven't I? Where were you going?'

'Into the Wardrobe Room, perhaps you would care to join us?' Christine invited her, so she about turned and remounted the stairs with them. The inspection was a protracted one.

They bade the woman good day at last and moved off with Christine musing as the door closed behind them, 'I am inclined to think we should show all the grandest ones, so that they can ooh and ah over them, link them together with something like 'Court Dresses worn by Aynthorps through the centuries'; and perhaps we should have cabinets in which we could arrange fans, swords, ruffs, stomachers. How would that be *Belle-mère*?'

She encountered the Dowager's gleaming eyes and cried out, 'Oh you two naughties you are laughing at me now. I will confess this sort of thing is most infectious.'

The aftermath included a fine display of petulance by Sawbridge with whom Christine elected to be very firm concerning the temporary appropriation of *his* new toy – the very latest thing in stove houses.

Gyles added his quota, grousing, 'I come in here weary

after a hard day grindin' about the estate, full of m'y news, wishin' to tell you all about our young pheasants, the poultry and old Charles' decision to start breedin' horses and none of you evince a flicker of interest. You just chatter on about moth-eaten old garments worn by long dead Lormes while live ones like me go to the wall. Its shockin'.'

They were all contrition; but although they listened with due attention and came in at the right places with the right queries, he knew and they knew he knew they were only waiting with as much patience as they could muster, an opportunity to get back to the 'moth-eaten old clothes'.

At least they persuaded Gyles to take them to the Sword Room for him to indicate the right dress swords for the various periods but he warned, 'Now you're not inveiglin' me into this affair. I'll show you swords but there the matter ends.'

Then Henry must needs upset the apple cart. 'I'd like to come with you when you return to the old Wardrobe Room. I haven't been up there since I hid from young Charles when we were both still in the nursery. Come to think of it old Stephen was with us...'

'Spare us the recollections dear boy,' his father begged, 'and permit me to remind you that your days are pledged to estate matters and me. Leave all this nonsense to our womenfolk.' He rose as he spoke, 'And now Christine, Mama, *Tante* Marguerite, Hetty, if you will pray excuse us I'll take m'y boys to m'office ... we have certain papers to deal with before we go to bed.'

It was all very dull Petula decided, so the following afternoon she set off down the drive on foot. She was bound for the Vicarage and had elected to walk. When she came to the newly-painted white gate she paused, seeing the Vicar was standing in his shirt sleeves, shovelling manure around some newly pruned young rose bushes.

'Good afternoon Harry.'

He straightened his back and came towards her exclaiming, 'How delighted I am to see you but pray do not touch me, I'm well laced with fruity old muck.'

He wiped one hand on his shirt sleeve, opened the gate for her and told her, 'Steph's in the kitchen making rock buns for tomorrow's WI. I expect it is she you want really.'

'No, I came to see you both but I do have something to

discuss with Steph. However as it concerns you both I wonder . . . ?' she looked up, 'could you take a break?' Harry laid down his shovel. 'Willingly,' he smiled.

'How are you settling to village life?' she asked, as they walked up the path together.

'As to that, my dear, you can quote me as saying that my way has fallen in very pleasant places. How is everyone at the Castle?'

'Galloping in all directions at once. My father has decided to breed horses, Andrew's going to sell venison, Claire is in transports because Christian is coming home at last, Constance is turning the Manor upside down and the two old naughties are hock deep in Victoriana and old clothes and Priscilla is, I think, restless. She will be off again one day soon I fancy.'

'And Henry?'

'Out all day, every day, stravanging over the estate with Gyles and Andrew. They're gone from breakfast to dressing gong. When dinner's over they either fall asleep in the drawing room while *Grandmère* nags, or else their conversation is all about pullets, plumbing and pig raising.'

'Pulling the old place together again eh? Come let me take you through.' Harry Devening slung his old tweed coat across one shoulder and ushered Petula into the big old kitchen. 'Stephanie, here's Petula to see you.' Stephanie put down the tray of buns she had just taken from the oven and rushed over for a good hug. While this was going on Harry abstracted a bun and began munching it with filthy fingers. Stephanie swung round. 'Just you put that down,' she ordered, 'your hands are disgusting Harry, go and wash do, and anyway those buns are not for you.'

'I know,' he agreed and turned to the sink, 'they're for the WI but there's one they won't get.'

Stephanie pushed Petula into an old rocker drawn close to the stove, 'I am glad to see you,' she confessed, characteristically catching an escaping wisp of hair and endeavouring to tuck it in.

Harry wiping his hands on a kitchen towel, observed resignedly, 'If my wife were suddenly called upon to confront the archangel Gabriel I am sure she would keep him waiting while she tucked in a wisp of hair.'

'Never mind that. Sit down and I'll pour out for you. I've made tea and we're lucky, Mrs Parsons sent George round this morning on his way to Mr Palfrey's with some of her "Pang der Piece".'

Her husband stared, 'Her what?'

Stephanie repeated Mrs Parsons' rendering of the French *Pain d'Epice*, explaining, 'It's the best she can do with the French but the result is delicious.'

During this exchange Petula looked round approvingly. The bright kitchen was fragrant with the warm smell of baking, the whole atmosphere redolent with harmony and content. She found herself marvelling at the miraculous way in which Stephanie had emerged from what had once been the cocoon of misery in which she languished.

They sipped their tea together companionably. They frittered away some small change of parochial chatter and then a significant glance was exchanged by the pair of them. With patently contrived lightness Stephanie said, 'My Mrs Johns has gone to market today.'

'Oh yes?' Petula waited.

'It's, er, fortunate really. I, er, we, that is, well, it would not be right to let this news of mine be bandied about too soon in the village.' Petula still waited, by now assured she knew what was coming.

'It's like this you see Pet,' Stephanie tried again, her face crimson with embarrassment, 'I'm, I'm going to have a baby. Perhaps you would like to tell them for me at the Castle?'

'Of course, love, but how marvellous. Oh I am glad for you, when is it?'

'Late October.' She took a huge bite of Mrs Parsons' *chef d'oeuvre* and her voice was muffled. So Harry got up and came round to sit on the arm of her chair. 'October,' he confirmed, 'my wife isn't much good at speaking with her mouth full.'

'But will you be up to coping with all those stalls you've planned for the Fête and Flower Show?'

'Oh yes,' Stephanie nodded vigorously, 'of course I will. We need the money. It's terribly important. Those kneeling pads in the church are in a dreadful state. I believe the boys deliberately make holes in them while they're supposed to be praying and then they work the sawdust filling out, the little fiends.'

'Well it's better than you reading *The Art of Bottling* in a plain brown paper cover during my sermon,' said Harry.

'I had read your sermon already darling and I was so short of time,' his wife protested quite unruffled.

Petula truncated this exchange, murmured her congratulations and went on to outline Gyles and Christine's proposals while accepting a second cup of tea. She was careful to emphasise that the choice was entirely theirs; but surprisingly she encountered no set-back. They both gave the plan a most enthusiastic reception, so much so that when at length she left them they were happily spending the anticipated extra revenue on new curtains for the vestry, new hymn books and speculating as to whether they would be justified in buying Harry a new surplice. Then, as Petula knew they would rush off, he to a Bible class and she to a WI committee meeting.

As Petula walked back darkness came down bringing with it the bright lights which sprang up at the old windows, whitening the gargoyles and laying a sheen upon the wide stone steps. She thought about the luxury and comfort to which she was returning and fell to wondering how it was that Stephanie could have rejected it all, indeed how it could be that she actively disliked the Lorme way of life even now; even to taking extreme measures in order to escape from it. Then she quickened her steps, remembering that for her it was almost bath time, Justin and Chantal's, which, to her, was the peak moment of every day.

Soon after this, news started coming from America. Sue-Ellen sent an extravagant cable first.

Arrived safely. In-laws flourishing. Stephen has decided to become a cowboy. We are having a party soon so that Henrietta and Sinclair can meet some of my dearest friends. We all miss you dreadfully and will write very soon. Cannot wait to return to the Castle. Have already made contact with a white hunter from whom I have learned much. Tell Richard and ask him to send me the list he promised of the white animals we want. Please give my love to everyone.

This was followed, a few days later by a letter, a joyous scribble clearly written in haste and anything but easy to decipher. However, the Family's combined efforts managed to elucidate from it that there was every chance the Delahayes would be home sooner than they had expected. Mr Mobberly's stewardship had been so excellent that there

was far less for Sue-Ellen to do than she had at first
expected. It was only a matter of determining future policies
and ratifying the plans submitted for the new aircraft
factories.

'Such a slip of a girl,' Christine sighed, 'yet with such an
extraordinary business head on those elegant shoulders.
Most remarkable. Not at all what one would fear an
emancipated woman would become.' She added, 'I miss
Sue-Ellen.'

'I miss her too,' Petula echoed, adding naughtily, 'and so I
am assured does my brother.'

This brought Gyles' head round his *Times* sharply. 'I
trust that by that remark you are not implyin' anythin'
untoward in the wind between young Charles and Sue-
Ellen.'

'No one's implyin' anythin' sir,' Henry protested, 'but it's
as plain as Palliser's face young Charles is potty about Sue-
Ellen.'

'How ... disastrous,' said Gyles austerely. He laid aside
his paper. 'I would remind you both that young Charles is
not up to it. Such immense wealth on one hand and such
limited means, if you will forgive my sayin' so Petula, on the
other is scarcely commensurate with happy married life.'

Gyles Aynthorp clearly considered the match as
hopelessly unsuitable as young Charles did himself. 'A
slight increase on the distaff side is one thing,' he confided in
his sister, 'but all those bloomin' millions! Abso-bally-lutely
impossible and I know it.' Even so, he was not immune to
dreaming that perhaps his father would breed another
Bendor from some unknown filly he would find at the
Dublin Horse Show, whither he and his wife were going at
the beginning of August. This pipe-dream changed when he
was in gloomy humour to, 'Probably come home with a ruck
of spavined horsemeat unloaded on them by some Irish
horsecoper.' Thus his mood flicked between 'wet and
windy' and 'set fair' as if he were an aneroid barometer.
'Anyway I'm not stuck at wet and windy,' he conceded
grudgingly before taking out his frustrations with a good
hard gallop over King's Ride.

Thus matters stood on the April afternoon when Petula
crossed from Lorme land into Danement territory, bound
for an afternoon with her step-mother whom she regarded
only slightly this side idolatry.

She walked Morning Star slowly across the famous field where Danement had fought with Lorme, and from which she remembered the great beam had been recovered recently. This was now safely inside a special, heated glass enclosure in the museum, displaying to all who cared to read, the ancient carved Latin inscription obligingly written in English also by Countess Marguerite for the benefit of the unlettered: 'Count Henri de Lorme won this field of Charles Edward Danement in fair combat. They became firm friends as the two families have remained ever since.'

She reined in at the spot from which the beam had been raised, revelling in the tremendous feeling of continuity which such recollections aroused in her. Admittedly times changed and perhaps in turn the pattern might change superficially; but she held firm to her belief that fundamentally all would remain the same for her son and his sons as yet unborn. The dark memory of the recent war cast a long shadow across such reflections so that young as she was she felt a chill of trepidation. If another war came then what would be the outcome? Already she knew her father's income had shrunk, by having such increased demands levied upon it as prices soared. She knew he was having to be very careful. So what of the Aynthorp revenues? Would new ventures, calculated by both her own father and Gyles Aynthorp to meet the situation, prove adequate. Or would the time come when they would both be forced to sell land? This was her greatest fear. She had already seen it happen with lesser landowners, people who were her lifelong friends. She knew of half a dozen who had solved their problems for the moment by selling off a farm or two; the purchasers invariably men who had profited by the war and who saw in the possession of land not a country way of life, but a sound commercial investment to lay against increasing taxes. They did the obvious things they were astute enough to know would give them a certain amount of entrée into the country: bought hunters, learned to handle guns, gave generously to local charities. But she held to the conviction that their motives were unsound – spurious was the word she found most fitting. She was beginning to see it all as an encroachment which as time went on could become disastrous.

The mare fidgeted, shaking her out of these desolate

anticipations, so she trotted on determining to put them out of her mind.

She came to her old home eventually at the fringes of the topiary gardens, trotted round to the stables, handed over the mare to a groom and continued on foot. She wanted a closer look at everything. When she obtained it she felt more secure. The topiary had lost all its ragged appearance and was again trimmed and clipped, as before the war, into the famous peacocks, gryphons, unicorns and other heraldic beasts. She climbed the low steps to the flagged terrace. It displayed itself once more as the beauty that it was – one of the finest examples of half-timbering in the county – built in the fifteenth century upon the site of the original Manor House which had been razed by fire.

She found Constance in the panelled hall arranging white hyacinths and early tulips in an old wine cooler. *Famille rose* bowls filled with pot-pourri added their fragrance to the flower-scented room. She curled up on a window seat to look around her appreciatively as Constance worked. Portraits of long dead Danements looked down at her and at the soft lemon and grey chintz which Constance had chosen as covering for the deep arm-chairs and sofas. Behind one of them, facing the chimney piece, a long low refectory had been drawn. Centred upon it was a twelfth-century T'ang bronze cooking vessel brimming with jonquils, while down each side ran rows of magazines and newspapers. Her eyes were caught by a very familiar livery cupboard which her step-mother had moved from its accustomed place.

'I like it better here,' Petula approved, 'and the Ducerceau dresser. You have a talent for placing furniture. It is all charming.'

She began wandering about, now stroking the carved gryphons and caryotids of a table at which she had played snakes and ladders with old Charles as a little girl. Then she sat down in the old ecclesiastical oak throne chair, laying her arms along the polished rests. 'I used to check how much I had grown,' she recalled, 'by seeing how far my legs reached towards the base bar.' Then she moved again, to run her fingers over the carving of a cupboard designed by Peter Flotner. 'I hid in there once,' she said suddenly, 'then something went wrong with the catch and I couldn't get out again. How I screamed! Until Daddy heard me and hauled me out,' another pause, then the exclamation, 'You've brought the armoire in here too. I am glad. It always seemed to be wasted on that rather dim landing.'

'I'm thankful,' said Constance softly, 'that you do not think I have spoilt your lovely home.'

'Our even lovelier home,' Petula corrected her, coming to rest at last on an old faldstool inside the great hearth.

Here they settled companionably while Constance rang for tea.

'Pet dear, I wanted to check my party list with you. It would be terrible if I overlooked any of your or your father's friends. Young Charles has already given me his special names.'

'Tell me first where you have decided to serve supper.'

'In the long gallery. It still has those beautiful old sconces. I thought if I put fat, white church candles in them and placed a table in each embrasure it might look rather lovely. It would also make it easy for us to move from table to table. I am proposing to lay an extra cover at each one. As supper progresses we can move around so that no one feels neglected, or indeed specially singled out for attention.'

'Lovely idea; but what about the Royals?'

'There are only two. *He* is bringing his brother George for whom I am to invite Miss Baring. They have expressed their wish for informality. *He* emphasised it the other night. *He* declared he was bored to extinction with ceremony. I must admit he does swallow a fearful lot of yawns, especially at levées so the men tell me.'

Petula nodded, 'He always has done. He was trying so hard to swallow some when he stood behind the throne for my post-marriage curtsey...' she broke off as an idea came to her. 'Darling are you asking Lucien and Lucy?'

'Why?'

'Well, it's quite a story. I wonder Daddy never mentioned it. There was a terrible rumpus over Lucy at her come-out ball.'

'I heard nothing of it,' Constance sounded surprised. 'Charles never said a word.'

'Then I will,' said Petula firmly. 'You do know the bit about Lucy *accidentally*' – she stressed the word – 'spilling wine over her dress at the pre-ball dinner party?'

'Yes I believe I did hear something.'

'It was all a put up job so that she could rush upstairs after dinner and change into a dress Lucien had secretly designed and made for her with, will you believe it, a little assistance from the village dressmaker.'

The light began to dawn for Constance. 'So that was what Lucien was referring to when he told us his bride's Winterhalter wedding dress was from an original design he made for Lucy.'

'Exactly so. Anyway when Christine saw what Lucy had done it was too late to do anything. Guests were already arriving. Then the Prince came. He asked Lucy to dance. They sat out together too for an unconscionably long time. He complimented her on the damned dress, so she promptly poured out the whole story to him.'

'Merciful heavens!'

'Oh yes, what is more Lucy told me the Prince was highly entertained. He told her the frock was delightful and if you please he advised her not to tell anyone else. He explained that in society some "dreary people" – his own words Lucy swore – might think less well of a frock which had been designed and made by a boy of fourteen. In the end he struck a bargain with her.'

'Wwwhat bbargain?' Constance managed.

'He pledged he would come to the salon that precious pair had planned already, to see their clothes, when the time came *if* Lucy would promise not to say another word. Oh I suppose it is very funny in retrospect,' Constance was laughing openly by now, 'but there was a fearful to-do at the time.'

Constance nodded. 'Then most certainly I shall invite the pair of them. Do you realise that *if* he promised and remembered and *did* put in an appearance in their salon they really would be made.'

'Well yes, but if you do invite them,' Petula hesitated, 'er, would you mind my suggesting a little personal note? Something to the effect that you hope they are both free because HRH is coming and you know he and Lucy get on famously together and it will be a chance for you to present Lucien.'

'Very subtle,' Constance approved, 'it shall be done.'

The date for the housewarming had been fixed for the last Thursday in May, while the combined museum and Fête affair was settled for the last Thursday in July. This, they calculated would ensure the presence of the majority of their friends after the season end and before the general exodus to Scotland for the shooting. Gyles and Christine had declared their intention of going to Clangowrie with Andrew who had begged an invitation for Victoria, but Henry and Petula were driving down to the French Riviera where, as they already knew, Lucy, Lucien, Piers and Nada would be on a chartered yacht.

The events which concerned them all more nearly were the return from Harrow of Richard for the Easter holidays and the imminent arrival of Christian. This would leave only one remaining gap in their closed post-war ranks, one which they all longed to have filled but feared would not happen for some time to come. They knew that the links which earned for the two cousins Ninian and James the soubriquet 'inseparables' were at once remarkable and, in the family's opinion, unique. Now that James had gone, Ninian it seemed, could not bring himself to return to the Castle where the pair had grown up together. Instead, when the war ended, he volunteered for garrison duty in the conquered Turkish territory of Mesopotamia, satirically known to both sides of the House as 'mess-up-at-home-here'. This caused great unease, for casualties were being reported frequently, yet as Gyles was at some pains to point out, 'What, pray can I do? I fancy my rule will not run with a twenty-five-year-old Colonel with Ninian's campaign record. He must be left to work out his own salvation.'

There was one other absentee for the Easter holidays; but no one paid any particular attention. When he was there, as they had all come to expect, Gilbert Delahaye, the be-spectacled fifteen-year-old academic was always more conspicuous by his absence than his presence; so it was with a certain sense of relief that the family accepted Eustace's decree that he should go to his friends the Brinkmans instead. At least then they would not have to endure his drifting into rooms silently, to sit prodding those spectacles of his, listening to adult conversation, nor drifting out again as silently as he had entered, usually with a copy of *The Financial Times* neatly folded and tucked under one arm. The Dowager actively disliked him and the general consensus of opinion was that he was a dreary little boy who held out little prospect of becoming other than a dreary young man.

★   ★   ★

Time and again the accusation of deviousness had been levelled at various Delahayes; yet none, as they would one day discover, were so devious as Gilbert who, at this moment, was sitting in one corner of a first class railway carriage speeding from Winchester to London and the Brinkmans' Park Lane house in company with the new peer's two sons Joseph and Lionel.

All three were reading and re-reading a small advertisement in the personal column of their copies of *The Times*, which each had ringed round in pencil. For three home-returning schoolboys for whom almost four weeks of freedom from school lay ahead their conversation was more than a little peculiar.

Joe said, 'We will tell Abrahams to drive us to that crummy little newsagent first. Three days should be enough to give us a pretty good idea of what we can expect. According to my very reliable information the usual pattern shows a steady rise from the third to the seventh day. On that basis there will be no fallback for us because the advertisement is repeated regularly.'

Gilbert moistened lips which had become unaccountably dry. 'So we should know one way or the other today?'

'I am absolutely certain we shall,' Joe stroked his waistcoat whose outward curve denoted even now a marked tendency towards corpulence. Lionel looked anxious from one to the other. He seemed to experience some difficulty in sitting still. He twiddled his fingers, crossed and uncrossed his thin legs, ran a finger between collar and neck until Joe swore at him. At length the train slowed and began snaking into Paddington station. All three jumped up, crowding round the door. Joe leaned out of the window waving frantically until he attracted the attention of a porter. Then they piled out, hurried to the guard's van and there identified their three trunks and tuck boxes. Eventually, with ill-concealed impatience they followed the plodding truck-pusher through the barrier.

'There's Abrahams with the car!' exclaimed Lionel, racing across, only to sit fidgeting inside the large and shining Daimler while the chauffeur saw to the luggage. The other two climbed in, Joe handed the porter his shilling, was thanked for it and at last the car slid away from the kerb into the flow of traffic.

'Last lap then,' said Gilbert through his teeth. Joe

grunted. The rest of the distance was covered in silence. When the car drew up outside a shabby little shop in a Paddington side street Joe jumped out, saying authoritatively, 'You two wait here, we don't want to draw unnecessary attention to ourselves.' Then, straightening his jacket, he sauntered across the pavement. The bell tinkled as he opened the door. Five minutes dragged by. Then, 'Gosh,' exclaimed Gilbert staring. Lionel expelled a long low whistle. Joseph appeared carrying a pile of bundled together envelopes which reached from his outstretched arms to his chin.

'Open the door you clot,' he shouted. This galvanised Gilbert. Joe reached in and let the bundles fall onto the carpet. Then he climbed in over them, pushed a few bundles with one foot and enquired triumphantly 'How's that for a start? ... Oh yes, Abrahams, home please.'

From the moment they reached the house until the evening before they were due to return to Winchester the three boys worked unceasingly.

That night, taking the shortest possible time over dinner they hurried to Brinkman *père's* study and there began ripping open envelopes, placing the contents into two neat piles. When these threatened to topple, Joe simply bundled them together with the rubber bands which had held the letters. The piles grew steadily until the big leather topped desk was covered with thick layers of them.

'Well that's it,' Joe sounded triumphant. 'Now let's count them.' He took a bundle of postal orders, moistened one finger with saliva and began to flick. The others copied. Each boy made pencilled notes. When the count was completed they checked each other's totals.

'Yes that's right,' said Gilbert on a note of triumph, 'two thousand two hundred and seventy postal orders.'

'Exactly,' Joe could not restrain a slight grin, 'and on a rising graph that will go well over what we need to get each day. So, we shall have to chuck some of the letters away. There's no point in wasting money on stamps or on writing regrets either is there? We just don't cash any over fifty thou.'

Behind them, in the Brinkman ballroom, one wall was piled high with the stacked cases which had been brought from the Essex barn the day after the senior Brinkmans sailed for South Africa. Also arrived, were what Isaacs the butler had termed 'other items which you ordered sir'.

This signified to them that all was ready. In the morning the two pound a week clerks would present themselves at nine o'clock by which time Abrahams would be on his way to the newsagent for the morning's collection. They had no qualms about the servants. As Joe repeated reassuringly, 'One step out of line by any one of them and they know I will not hesitate to tell my father about high jinks they get up to belowstairs when he and mother are away.'

On this consoling note the trio decided that they could do no more until the morning. Only when they turned their attention to the pile of smoked salmon sandwiches Isaacs had left for them did they look, for the first time since they had left the college, like the schoolboys they still were.

CHAPTER 10

'All that is within him does condemn Itself for being there...'

Miss Poole was wearing herself threadbare through her anxieties concerning the inevitable revelations which must come to Lucy. Miss Poole knew her to be totally innocent – but Lucy's innocence arose, not from purity but from incomprehension. Miss Poole also feared her own ability to present the reality, when this became imperative, in such a way that it would not deprive Lucy of her reason by driving her into a state of shock which might damage her mind permanently.

At this time Lucy first heard Piers calling her brother 'Bosie'. She also heard Lucien's petulant, 'When are you going to tell me what that means? You are always calling me "Bosie", why don't you tell me why?'

Because of this Lucy determined to discover for herself the significance of the name, if any. She waited until one day she and her great friend Nada were choosing hats together. As casually as she could, she then asked, seemingly much absorbed in the effectiveness of her reflection in the pier glass, 'Who was "Bosie"?'

Equally off-hand Nada answered, 'Lord Alfred Douglas of course, I thought everyone knew that.'

Lucy risked a quip, 'Oh but remember how dreadfully limited my education has been.' Then she pressed the girl until, with a sign of pure boredom, Nada pulled off a turban and recounted the scandal.

'There was a trial?' Lucy whispered, aghast.

'Oh yes, of course, darling. Don't you remember Wilde wrote his famous "Ballad of Reading Gaol" in prison?'

Lucy murmured, 'Oh of course,' having never heard of this either.

Subsequently she startled the assistant at Mudies by asking for the poem. Having read it she hurried off to Fleet

Street where she enquired as to how members of the public obtained permission to study back numbers of the august publication of her choice.

'What year?' asked a very bored young clerk.

'I do not know,' Lucy confessed, 'it is the Oscar Wilde trial I wish to read. Is that possible?'

The clerk looked at her curiously, then shrugged his shoulders. 'Sit down over there Miss,' he indicated a row of distant chairs, 'I'll have to ring down. Then I'll let you know when they're ready for you.' In due course the summons came.

When she had turned over the heavy volumes of bound back numbers, one word stayed in her mind above all else – *sodomite.*

On returning home she consulted her dictionary which defined this as 'unnatural form of sexual intercourse, especially that of one male with another'.

This made her very watchful. It also increased her protectiveness towards Lucien; but in no way did it otherwise disturb her. If *that* was what Lucien wanted it must be right for him and, of course, what he wanted he must have; including absolute protection from any danger which could arise therefrom. She just watched very carefully and thus matters might have continued indefinitely if it had not been that Piers developed an increasingly troublesome cough.

Lucy noticed that he was smoking a great many cigarettes these days, of the kind which their friends called 'Turks'. He was seldom without one and, understandably, his cough worsened. Off she trotted again, this time to a nearby chemist. On his advice she returned with a large bottle of J. Collis Browne's Chlorodyne, a world renowned specific so the chemist assured her. She dosed Piers regularly with it, despite which he continued to cough ... and paint.

He was in great demand and working for long hours at his easel. They were all working very hard, for the first spate of orders had been more than sustained. It had soon become fashionable for both old and young 'society' women to drop into the salon in the afternoons between three and five o'clock. While they sat about on the buttoned conversation pieces sharing the latest scandal, Lucy sent in her two resident models Paula and Monique to sway among them displaying Lucien's latest creations for which the gossips broke off, placed orders and returned to nibble at their ripe plums of scandal.

The order books were kept filled and there was no diminution of labour for anyone until the very last day in July when the work-room girls, pressers and packers stayed with their seniors until almost midnight and then were themselves packed into taxi-cabs and sent home; but this was only when the very last stitch had been put into the very last shiny white box with the house name sprawled across it in gold lettering. As these were tied, Sissy grabbed them and completed the final deliveries in Lucy's grey Royce.

Two days later Lucien and Lucy left for the Côte d'Azur in Piers' six cylinder Straker Squire. In Lucy's dressing case were two more large bottles of cough mixture and a giant-sized bottle of Formamint tablets for Piers to suck during the journey. He was still coughing. Increasingly Lucy worried over this, particularly since he had become so very thin.

Often, during gay and noisy parties aboard their chartered yacht, when they danced after breakfast, before and after luncheon and far into the night to the music from either a gramophone or ukeleles and banjos played by their new acquaintances, she watched him anxiously, noting how two bright spots of colour burned on his cheeks as the champagne went down and also how the thin hand which held the glass was seldom without a cigarette as well.

The next time she was ashore she went to the British pharmacy for a large bottle of Owbridge's Lung Tonic. Armed with this and a teaspoon she pursued him round the deck, dosing him every time he coughed.

'Dam' stuff ruins the taste of my champagne,' he complained; but he submitted to these dosings docilely enough, teasing her because she was so small she always had to stand on tiptoe to administer them.

They cruised very little, content to drop anchor each morning in the 'roads' between the two islands of Ste Marguerite and St Honoré. Here they amused themselves endlessly, diving into the crystal-clear, blue water, trying but always failing to capture the cruising *langoustes* which they could see so clearly lumbering over the sandy bottom.

To their immense frustration one of their Monegasque crew would come up on deck, stand watching, then plunge overboard and come up holding one of the struggling creatures across its saddle, so that its great claws waved ineffectually.

Then they would all crowd round while Piers gravely inspected the creature's behind. If this were pointed and narrow back would go the *langouste*; but if it were broad and rounded he would hand it to one or other of the *matelots* with instructions to take it instantly to chef.

When they clamoured for an explanation, on the first occasion of this small pantomime Piers grinned wickedly and informed them, it was a '*cause du sexe, mesdemoiselles,*' adding, 'males have narrow *derrières* like Lucien, David and me. Females have fat little rounded ones like you my darlings. Only the females have eggs, as you might suppose. These are called the "coral". Connoisseurs always reject the males' – here he caught Lucien's eyes and amended hastily, 'in either lobster or crawfish. We are all connoisseurs here, as are our humble *matelots* so *no male langoustes.*'

Every day Piers and Lucien swam ashore. They waded out onto the springy beds of dried seaweed and grasses which were washed up onto the fringes of St Honoré in order to take their daily stroll. They then followed the path which encircled both the island and the monastery where Piers explained, 'The monks live a dreary life, eating salt fish and flagellating'.

Lucien wrinkled his nose the first time he heard this and commended naively, 'Then I do not think I would ever want to be a monk.'

Piers reminded him, 'There are compensations my little one, as you might suppose. They also made a perfectly revolting liqueur called *Izarra*, a cross between paregoric and *Aguardiente* but I don't suppose you have ever heard of that either.' Then they would stroll on between the white-flowered myrtle bushes and the distorted pines which the winter winds had bent into travesties of bent old men with long beards.

The rest swam ashore too; but they were content to lie like basking sharks on the springy sea vegetation, one or other of them flopping like seals into the warm water from time to time, drowsy with heat and talking little until a series of hoots from the yacht's siren roused them. With cries of 'Cocktails!' and 'Race you to the yacht!' they then pelted back into the water while, as often as not, the signal was picked up by other craft moored in the roads, and young men and girls would tumble into small boats and come chugging across with their outboard motors buzzing like hornets, to climb aboard amid the rattle of ice in shakers.

They would congregate in the stern under the bright blue and white striped awning; among them Piers' friends, painters, writers, dilettante poets, and an occasional dancer from the Monte Carlo Ballet. Nada drew intense young Russians and sophisticated girls with whom she had made her 'come out'. Lucy's contribution usually consisted of fugitives from their parents' 'bogus' great yachts, girls with whom she had 'finished', or been at school, while Lucien acted as magnet to any number of rich young men who showed a marked inclination towards bangles.

L'heure du cocktail was duly celebrated from noon until two o'clock, when the tooting of irascible-sounding sirens from other craft would summon a greater part of the guests to parental luncheon tables while the rest sat about on palliasses devouring *langoustes*, or *assiettes des fruits de mer*, and drinking 'bubbly'. The mixed sea food platters invariably included pink-tongued *oursins*. These, once the flesh was scooped out, would be left on deck by the careless, so seldom a day passed without one of their number treading on one. Then up went eldritch howls as *matelots* came running armed with large darning needles with which to excavate the brittle prickles. If left these were prone to cause sepsis in the intense heat. When the operations were completed and brandy – in lieu of antiseptic – splashed onto the sufferer's feet they would devour *glaces portatif* bought in their cork containers from the shop in the rue d'Antibes and eventually, one by one, they would sleep the rest of the afternoon away. When they woke, stretched, yawned, and at length rose to stand leaning against the taffrail the sun had begun to sink. Finally one would dive in, the rest would follow, swimming, treading water or just floating until it was time to think of the evening's ploys.

While they dressed, the yacht would up anchor and they would glide very slowly round the head of St Honoré to Monte Carlo or to tiny Villefranche where the leathery-footed fisher folk squatted along the quay mending their nets.

When they had dined they either went to the little casino at Beaulieu, or else, if *en grande tenue* the yacht would nose

very slowly into harbour below the *Principauté* and the toy
Palace of Grimaldi. They, spilling noisily onto the cobbles,
would pile into musty old *fiacres* with fringed canopies and
be trotted aloft to the gaming rooms for 'a flutter'.

Piers and Nada played high. They had struck a lucky vein;
but even there, in the very warm room, heavy with cigar
smoke and French scents, Lucy noticed that Piers kept
himself supplied with glasses of iced water, clearly to avoid
causing irritation to other gamblers by his cough. She took
to carrying Formalin in her bag and would often slip him
one as he played. He would murmur, 'Thank you pretty
baby,' and smile a little, putting out his over-thin hands to
draw in yet another pile of winning plaques pushed towards
him by the croupier.

One morning they cruised west, anchoring off quiet little
Juan-les-Pins where they lunched in a minute shack. The
stout and beaming *patron* brought them platters piled high
with *petits fritures* and dishes of baby *pulpi* in pungent *sauce
niçoise* which they wiped up with crusts of French bread. He
laid before them boards of goat cheeses, baskets of figs and
peaches and when they had done gave them slightly bitter
coffee in amusing ceramic jugs. These intrigued them so
they asked where they could be obtained. The patron came
out again to explain that they were made in a small Italian
village called Vietri-sur-Mare and that little steamers plied
from there to the next bay Golfe Juan, which he dismissed as
'*de rien*' save that it was the source of their supply of special
clay. He added, 'There are potters there too, but the better
ones work in the villages in the hills. It might please you to
visit, there are always motor cars to hire.'

They cruised on further west, passing Golfe Juan – a mere
stretch of empty sands with a crude and solitary fishermen's
hut standing on the sands. They had decided to spend the
night in yet another tranquil little place called St Tropez
to which they came at sunset.

They roamed about the tiny cobbled streets where by day
a handful of painters set up their easels and as Piers said,
'Blobbed away manfully.' Lucien and Lucy were charmed
but Piers, dismissing it as *vieux jeu* slipped away to drink
alone in a sawdust-floored bistro where he speedily made
friends with the local fishermen. One old rascal drew his
attention with his ragged beard, an even more ragged blouse
and his skin resembling brown, cracked parchment; there

was, too, a gleam in his rheumy old eyes which attracted Piers who plied him with absinthe until he agreed, for a consideration, to sit for him the next morning.

When he came rolling on bandy legs along the little quay Piers had already set up his easel, a chair, table, a bottle of absinthe and two glasses. As a final concession he laid a pack of Gauloise by the bottle and a box of French matches which only a Frenchman could ignite.

The rest took to the hills for an exploration of the nearer Saracen villages. They went in an ancient hired Ford which coughed nearly as badly as Piers according to Lucy. Somehow, it managed to work its way like an ancient tortoise up winding lanes crowded in by cork trees and Arbutus bushes just setting their first strawberry-like fruits. They returned late in the afternoon sated with *paté des Grives* and spit-roasted baby *gigot aux aromates* which last caused a vulgar spate of burping. They had eaten the lamb with their fingers at a minute inn with the grandiloquent name of L'Auberge de la Grande Duchesse Anne-Marie. A table was set out for them under the shade of a Mirabelle tree. The branches hung low under their burdens of ripening fruits, laying gouts of apricot, rose and coral colouring against the green leaves.

Lucy, dimples well in evidence then set about enslaving a curly-haired youth with ardent eyes. She was determined to find the source of those coffee pots as well as some olive bowls and cork platters on which she intended arranging fruits and vegetables as decorations for her table when she gave post-theatre parties in her kitchen.

After luncheon she and Lucien set out with the bewildered youth who seemed like a chameleon on a plaid pillow as he vacillated between admiration of both Lucy and Lucien, glancing, under absurdly long lashes, first at one and then at the other. Of this the brother and sister were completely unaware; but they found what they sought. An old man in a dark workshop produced his and his son's handiwork and after they had bought excessively he volunteered to lend them his own *brouette* in which to trundle their purchases back to the *auberge*.

Altogether Lucy had a halcyon day with her brother who was by now tanned to the colour of wild honey. His hair was bleached too by the strong sun. Lucy whispered to Nada, 'He really does look . . . well . . . rather beautiful doesn't he?'

Nada who was biting off mouthfuls of grapes from a bunch which she held, dangling, just nodded with her mouthful, ingested and then agreed, gulping. 'Like a young god; he should have been a girl though it's so wasted on a man. Darling do have some grapes, this is the *only* way to eat them properly.'

When they returned to St Tropez, spilling themselves in their bright clothes like confetti over the twilit quay Piers was dismantling his easel. His sitter was perilously lurched on the rickety bistro chair. He was sound asleep and snoring.

Piers nodded at him. 'He's steeped in absinthe and very happy,' he said, rising and holding his nose between thumb and first finger as he bent over to tuck some notes into the ragged blouse. 'Lord how he stinks,' he exclaimed, 'come on, let's go now.' He took Lucy's hand. 'Come on little one and tell me, have you had a good day?'

'Terrific,' she replied rather absently, seeing that the cobblestones were littered with cigarette ends.

'Please Piers,' she wheedled, 'may I see what you have painted?'

'No my love,' he refused her smilingly. 'I may add, Lucy, that you look ravishingly pretty. I must paint you again exactly as you are now, with your poppy-garlanded hat in one hand; but you may not see my portrait until it is completed. However it is absolutely essential that you keep that hat for me. By the way, where's Lucien?'

'Putting our shopping on board. Oh Piers, we have had such fun, have you?'

'Me? Oh no, I have had a lost day. All I can claim for it is an unfinished painting which just *may* be rather good. You see child, when I paint *I am not*. I am the brushes, the gobs of paint on my palette. Today I was also the shadow on a dirty old sinner's face; the blue of an old man's veins on the backs of his even dirtier hands, the breeze blowing his white hair into shards, but now I am me again.' He stopped dead in his tracks suddenly as they drew level with the gangplank and Lucien appeared on deck. The sun was almost over the horizon now. Lucien stood in its path.

'God ... that ... child ...!' Piers exclaimed in a strangled kind of voice.

'That's what I think,' Lucy agreed serenely. 'He *is* beautiful ... but then so I think are you with your searchlight eyes and your white hair ...' Piers recovered.

'How nice darling,' he approved, striving for a flippant note, 'there is nothing so delicious as being admired. Come along now little Mees, no more dawdling, the others are waiting and those rascals of crew are champing to draw in the gangplank.'

Once aboard Lucy wandered to the stern and lay down on one of the candy-striped palliasses. The yacht drew away from the quayside. She lifted her arms and linked fingers behind her head, looking up at the darkening sky. She was very busy now with what proved as time progressed to be her final conclusions concerning her brother and the man whom she always referred to now as 'my brother's friend'. Constructed as these conclusions were upon so much misleading half knowledge; based upon a premise which to many would seem shocking; Lucy lay with the swishing of the bows through water sounding in her ears as the engine cut through the silver sea. She was shaping her own destiny with all the headlong foolishness of a little lemming.

They never did encounter Henry and Petula on this holiday. They left a trail of messages from St Tropez to San Remo and notes too . . . at the Hotel de Paris . . . at the tennis club . . . where Lucy made her curtsey to the immensely tall King of Sweden and learned that the young Lormes had been there the day before. They picked up their trail again at the Carlton in Cannes . . . and at the Archery Club . . . only to lose it just after Nada met Prosper Merrimé and pronounced him, 'Tedious, he has too much *flégme Brittanique* that one for my taste.'

They were hot on the Lormes' heels when they went gambling for the last time, but while Le Broq examined Lucien dubiously at the casino and politely requested his passport because he looked so young, their informant drifted off and was lost in the crush.

Towards the end of the holiday Lucien began thinking about his forthcoming collection which was due to be shown on the first Wednesday and Thursday in October as had been settled before they closed for August. Miss Poole had at the same time strongly recommended that this time they show for two days. She pointed out that this would lessen considerably both the crush and the rush by distributing the load. No one had disputed her reasoning.

It was Lucy who planted the first seeds of her intention by observing very casually, 'What a pity it is that Lucien and

Sissy have to work at Number Two with so many interruptions. I think it would be much nicer for both of you darling if you could sketch without being disturbed by anything. I do wish we could think of a really nice place!'

'Without either you or Piers!' Lucien exclaimed indignantly.

'Piers is off to Yorkshire the moment we get back. He has to paint those Sysonby children remember. Anyway I could come and visit you from Fridays to Mondays couldn't I?'

'I need you *all* the time.' Lucien's mouth set in the familiar stubborn, downward curve. 'I hate having to be with only myself.'

'But you'll have Sissy darling. Now that he helps you with your sketches it would be simply perfect for you both.'

'Oh pooh,' he sounded very cross, 'anyway I couldn't think of anywhere to go.' He sat up and scowled at the shimmering sea. 'Why I might just as well stay here only Sissy isn't here and I just *will not work alone*, so there.'

Lucy grasped at this straw. 'What a perfectly splendid idea. Clever you and poor, dear Sissy would so love to come out here.'

'Where could we go?' Lucien's voice indicated that he was suddenly rather taken with the idea.

Before Lucy could reply Nada interrupted them, looking up from an embattled game of Mah Jong. 'That's no problem darlings. You can have Mummy's villa. It's always empty until the end of September. Mummy finds the heat too utterly grisly. If you like I'll cable her but I know she will say yes and then you can cable Sissy to come out at once.'

'Do you know I think that's not at all a bad idea. It just might work,' Lucien began warming up. 'After all I've chosen all my fabrics. Sissy could bring out the swatches and my colour charts. I could always post my embroidery designs to you so that you can do the orders for beads and crystals and the rest.' He suddenly appeared revitalised. 'I want to work with lots and lots of crystal beads in loops, instead of silk fringes so that they look like pastel icicles. I also intend scattering them on tulle, like stardust. Lucy-Lou did I tell you I have decided to change all the colour names?'

Lucy sighed thankfully. She knew now that she was winning. He never called her Lucy-Lou when he was being a cross-patch.

All she said was, 'And think love, the faster you work out

here the sooner you will be able to come home and in the meantime we get all the dull work done for you. We could tell the lady journalists what you are doing. Being lent a villa by a Russian Princess is very chic – to them. They would lap it up. It will stir up a lot of interest in you beforehand which is exactly what should be done.'

'Umm. I'd have to see the villa though. Nada when could we go? I must *know* where I am going, you do see that don't you? Then we shall need a car and someone nice to drive us. Oh what a lot we must plan before you all go tearing off home leaving poor me behind!' He pulled down the corners of his mouth again, like a child about to burst into tears. At the same time he managed to look both neglected and pathetic. So, they all rallied round him making consoling assurances and Nada helped by telling him that there was her mama's car and a chauffeur who was doing 'positively nothing pet except flirt with the maids and receive a vast salary'.

When Piers re-joined them Lucien rushed to tell him. He was pulled up short, however, by Piers' enthusiastic cry, 'What a perfectly splendid idea! Whose brain-wave was it?' This raised another drama. Lucien told them angrily they were all a rotten lot and just longing to get back without him. Again they flung themselves into a fervour of reassurances until he was made to feel important and precious once more. After which he went ashore with Nada and Piers for the cable-sending session while Lucy hurried to her cabin and wrote a long, explanatory letter to Miss Poole.

They spent the last night at Princess Maria Alexandra's villa, having said the goodbyes to both the yacht and her crew and pledged to return next year. Then they had an extremely gay dinner with about twenty guests. As it was to be a moonlit night the dinner was set in the garden. The Italian couple who ran the villa would wait on them assisted by a wide-eyed cousin who evinced a slight tendency towards hip-wiggling and eyelash fluttering at Piers, who was not amused and chose to ignore the pantomime.

The two gardeners produced strings of fairy lights which they wound with consummate artistry between the trees, from olive to oleander, cypress to palm and magnolia to eucalyptus. They sank tendrils of Aristolochia into water butts to drown the ants who consider the trumpet flowers to be their natural habitat and then they intermingled them with bunches of green grapes in a long central panel down the tables. Meantime the one intimidating member of the staff – a disheartening mountain of perspiring flesh with black beady eyes which were sharp and hard and calculating – proved her talents at an *al fresco* luncheon by turning out to be an inspired cook. The rest of the staff called her 'Mama' and she was presumably deaf for the villa rang with shrieks of 'Mama' at all hours. Happily Mama seldom left her kitchen where she laboured like a large and spiteful spider; but the food which emerged therefrom was exquisite.

Sissy, arrived that afternoon, resplendent in white flannels, monogrammed silk shirt and a pair of shoes which they told him were called 'co-respondents'. She was completely dazed by it all to begin with; by the chatter, the drinking, the *noise*; for the whole staff, including Juan the chauffeur considered themselves embryo Carusos so tended to burst into '*O Sole Mio*' or snatches from *Traviata* at the most inauspicious moments.

Under the benevolent influence of a great many glasses of beautifully chilled *Belley rosé* Sissy soon relaxed to the point of snatching up a silk shawl and dancing round a fountain; but this last happened far into the night and after the performance Sissy abruptly lost interest and concertina-ed to the ground.

Someone got up and examined the corpse without rancour, merely observing, 'Plastered to the eyebrows, I just hope you got plenty of Bass and aspirin for his breakfast.'

For Lucy there was one significant moment. They were all still at table under a fairy-light-spangled canopy of vines. The stars were out and pitting a navy blue sky as if a company of angels had strewn it with jewels. The moon rose slowly, soaring to full height and shafting a path of polished pewter across the still sea. The cicadas rattled their transparent wings in applause at this bacchanal of youth and the air lay like a warm caress on their faces, arms and the bared backs of the girls.

Philipe the nephew came down the grey stone steps carrying his guitar. He drew up a stool, rested one bare, brown foot on its cross bar and began to play. That was when Piers quoted very softly to a young painter with a beard and pink sandals whom he called Torquemada, 'Sea without fish, Flowers without scent, Men without shame, and Women without honour.'

'That's supposed to have been said of Nice,' someone called out of the darkness.

Piers shrugged, 'But it can be said of the entire coast can it not?'

Torquemada merely grunted. His eyes were on Lucien who sat with chin tilted upwards gazing at the panoply of stars.

'Piers,' whispered Torquemada, *'est qu'il de nous?'*

Piers turned in his chair slightly to meet his curious eyes, *'N'importe,'* he answered curtly, *'il est fruit défendu pour tai, n'oubliez jamais mon vieux.'*

The other laughed and called across, 'Lucien a penny for your dreams.'

Lucien started, 'Oh er, I was just designing a dress that's all. I think I must call it "Stardust". Lucy-Lou do you like that name?'

She nodded smiling at him with great tenderness, *but she had heard every word*, so she began to wonder just how many of *them* there were and how she could learn to recognise them.

During the return journey Piers complained several times of her silence. She countered hurriedly that if he expected her to conduct conversation at the *shout* above the rushing wind and the engine's *cross snarling* he was very much mistaken. Then she went back to her thinking. She worked through every member of her family until she came to these two cousins of hers, Damien and Robert, her uncle Alaric's middle-aged sons who had vanished to America at the outbreak of war and had not been seen since. Out of the past came her Uncle Gyles' distasteful dismissal of 'that precious pair' as 'nothing more than a couple of demmed old pussies in trousers!'

So that was it. Damien and Robert were the same and it had happened before in the Lorme family.

Motoring home, the four days were her own for speculating and conjecturing; at night she was careful to keep up a steady flow of chatter.

Piers had telegraphed ahead to the Hotel St James and Albany reserving rooms for the three of them in Paris. He said nothing to either girl but simply drove them there. Thereafter, as he acknowledged inwardly, he had only himself to blame for what he described as 'a flamin' route march' up the rue Royale to the Madelaine, around this august edifice and back again in order that Nada and Lucy could peer into every shop window. They then dragged him into the Faubourg St Honoré which he declared had suddenly become seven miles long. However he bought them gigantic bottles of the latest scent, Coco Chanel's *Numereau Cinque*, and very nearly bought a cigarette case for Lucien in a small antique shop almost facing the gates of the Elysée Palace. It was by Fabergé, but just in time he realised that Lucien hated smoking.

Recovering from this jaunt in a steaming bath, Piers did a little more telephoning with the result that when he ushered his two beauties into Voisin's for dinner an elegant young man rose and came towards them. Piers greeted, then presented him as, 'My friend Comte Bourbon-Lucinge whom I dare swear would prefer that you called him Jean-Marie.'

As they settled at an excellent table Piers explained to Lucy and Nada that they were in the ultimate *temple des gourmets* of all Paris. He then settled to his '*conférence*' with the *grande-maître*, after apologising to this august personage for not having done so that morning. Having listened, twirled his moustache and bowed, the man gave a little Gallic shrug and murmured, '*Faute de mieux M'sieu nous ferons de notre possible.*'

A long time afterwards Piers found the dinner menu, which had been slipped inside his folded bill, as was the custom. It had slid down behind a pocket of his dressing case. He read it again.

Crème de Germiny
Carpe Froide de Ris-de-veau Carignan
Fonds d'Artichauds Richemonde
Les Becquefigues au Sarment des Vignes Richelieu
Le Fois Gras aux Raisins Oporto Voisin
Bombe Maréchale de Saxe
Les Amuses Geules de la Jeunesse

Piers recalled, staring at this, that they had drunk nothing with their soup, of course; a *Château Coutet* with the carp; nothing again with the artichokes since there was a soupçon of wine vinegar in their sauce; an *Haut Brion* with the little vinepeckers and the *foie gras* and *Dom Perignon* with the *bombe*.

He stared out over the snow-capped mountains somewhat

wryly as he remembered Lucy's delighted exclamation when the *amuses geules* were placed on the table. The exquisite little hearts, stars, roses and lovers' knots nestled in the backs of two love birds made in spun sugar. They sat, beak to beak on a gold platter. Piers seemed to hear again Lucy's enchanted cry, 'Oh Piers, even Chef André has never done anything so ravishingly pretty!'

At the end of dinner he and Jean-Marie sat at ease cradling their small balloons of 1878 *armagnac*. The *maître sommelier* brought up his humidor for them to select their cigars. Lucy suddenly leaned across and whispered, 'Would you not like a cigarette first dear Piers? You have been so very good.' This too he remembered smiling ruefully amid those snow-capped Swiss mountains.

That lovely night in Paris had then been extended, by Jean-Marie who proposed a visit to a *boîte de nuit* which he assured the girls was, '*Assez propre, mais aussi tres courante.*' He then confirmed how *courante* by telling them that they would have the incomparable experience of seeing the great Mistinguette whose legs were insured for millions of francs.

When the night was very old they all piled back into Piers' car. He drove them to *Les Halles*, berthed the car opposite the *Veau Noir*, apologising that the little dog was not on his chair at this hour, then led them across the road to wander down the aisles of fruit and vegetables until a wave of assorted scents combining moist peat, damp moss and the aroma from a thousand different flowers confirmed the imminence of their objective. They bartered with the old women, exchanged a few obligatory, bawdy quips, were complimented on the beauty of their charges and left with the girls' arms filled with tuberoses.

Piers remembered it all. He could even see Lucy now as she had been then, a tiny figure in draped white silks, her hair dressed '*à la Grecque*' with artifice and despite '*le bobbing*', her mother's diamond spray pinned to one shoulder and quivering as she moved. The other creamy shoulder was bare. He remembered carrying her bag, fan and gloves and following her through the market where they in turn were followed by some fruity comments in accents mercifully difficult for the girls to understand.

At dawn Lucy draped an ermine shawl across her shoulders. He quickened his pace, slipped his free hand through her arm and bending down said, 'You look so lovely little Lucy. I have worn you on my arm tonight with outrageous complacence. I have been followed by envious glances which have flattered my distorted ego. I hope you do not mind.'

She lifted those big blue eyes and she murmured, 'I do not mind. I do not understand, but I do at least know ... now.' As she spoke she was thinking compassionately how dreadfully worn he looked in the pale light of morning.

When they met again for luncheon he appeared more rested; but he ate little, smoked continuously and after the luncheon he drove them up to Calais.

They crossed the next morning. Piers went off immediately to his own chambers in Albany, for he was due in Yorkshire that night to paint those children. When he left he was coughing and when he returned, just before the showings of their second collection, he still coughed although he seemed very gay.

The three worked feverishly together on that last night until very late indeed so Lucy persuaded Piers to stay with them and send for his man in the morning. She was almost dropping with exhaustion by the time she closed her bedroom door. When half an hour had elapsed Piers came out of his room in a dressing gown, walked softly along the corridor, opened Lucien's door with infinite slowness, went in and closed it again behind him.

There was a maharanee among the glittering assembly who packed the Salon for the first day's showing. She was seen to slip away as the last of the mannequins vanished back stage and none of them had the chance of talking to her; but she returned the next afternoon with her maharajah, by which time the fashionable world knew that Lucien, only now rising twenty, had 'arrived' as a couturier.

There were, predictably, a few predatory fashionables who had sharpened their little buffered claws in the pleasurable anticipation of an opportunity to rend this golden boy who had stormed the bastions of high fashion so precociously; but the claws were sheathed hastily when it became plain that Lucien had 'done it again'.

The assembly gave him a standing ovation after that first day's showing. When the five woke early, staggered into Lucy's boudoir and fell upon the morning newspapers, only Lucy and Lucien were sleepily un-surprised; but then they had known their own destiny since they were very small. However when pressed they agreed that it was 'nice'.

Miss Poole found it all rather frightening. Piers chose to take a partly flippant, partly fatherly attitude towards them; while Sissy stammered himself into such total incoherence that they were led to believe he too was satisfied. The new 'star' merely lay on a rug in cream silk pyjamas with enormous silk frogs on them and spread butter lavishly on hot croissants with which he then stuffed himself.

When he was replete, he belched, giggled, and went off barefoot to congratulate the workroom girls and the mannequins, snatching up a bolt of *duchesse* satin in which to envelop himself before facing his staff.

Then into the Salon on that second afternoon, came the beautiful maharanee again, but this time with the small, not unduly dark-skinned husband who was quite superbly turned out by the combined efforts of Messrs Anderson and Sheppard, Sulka, Lobb and Locke. When the show ended the maharanee gave Miss Poole an order which even made her blink, while the owner of an Indian province which was slightly larger than England strolled round the Salon examining Piers' murals.

When he rejoined his wife he observed casually, 'I believe Lady Lucy that I was at School with your Uncle Gyles. Is he not the Gyles Aynthorp who captained us at Lords in seventy eight?'

After this Lucy invited them to take a quiet glass of champagne with her in her private quarters. She then rushed through her duties, led them to the lift and when they entered her drawing room three people rose from their chairs, Miss Poole, Piers and Lucien.

Lucy presented them, Miss Poole excused herself gracefully, the champagne was broached and the maharajah came straight to the point.

'Mr Fournes,' said he smilingly, 'we dined last night with Elvira Martingale so we were able to admire your portrait of her. Quite remarkable! Now, alas, my wife and I return to India in a few weeks. It would give us both very great pleasure if we could persuade you to accompany us. I would of course want you to paint my wife and, if I can further persuade you to spend some time studying some of our Indian murals ... well, maybe you only do such work for

very old friends, but there is a room in my palace at
Bahawanepur which I would greatly like you to decorate. If
you consented I think we can also promise you some
entertainment. You shoot?'

Piers nodded, a little taken aback.

'Then we can offer you tiger if that would attract you. As
to the paintings, well perhaps if you agree in principle we
could discuss the, er, details later.'

Lucien made a small, involuntary movement but
managed to remain silent. Lucy exclaimed, 'Oh Piers, what
an enchanting invitation!'

Piers smiled then. 'What an irresistible invitation,' he
corrected her. Turning to the maharanee he told her, 'I saw
you in the audience Highness. I thought then how I would
love to paint you, particularly,' he hesitated, 'well, if I can be
sure it would not displease you, I thought, in a sari and not
western dress.'

'I would like both,' corrected the maharajah calmly, 'I
thought that white jewelled gown you designed Mr Lorme
and the coat of course, would be superb and then also the
dress of my country.'

At this juncture Lucy elected to be artless. Clasping her
hands together she exclaimed, 'Oh Piers, it would be simply
wonderful for you. You would be away from this dreadful
winter climate, oh dear! That does sound farouche Princess,
but, you see, Mr Fournes has such a dreadful cough....'

They laughed as she had hoped they might.

'Then assuredly Lady Lucy that absolutely settles it. The
climate is delightful in the north until well into April so you
see I could have my portraits and murals while Mr Fournes
could leave his cough behind with us. Just what the doctor
ordered. Absolutely top-hole in fact.'

Soon after this they left, by which time Piers had
undertaken to call on them at Claridges at eleven o'clock the
next morning. With a nod from Lucy he followed them to
the lift, raising a hand to the pair he left and saying, 'Forgive
me infants but I simply must tear myself away. I will be back
in the morning. There are several things arising out of today
which we simply must discuss.' Then he was gone.

As the lift descended Lucien flew into a tantrum. 'Damn
Piers!' he shouted, stamping his foot. 'Oh damn, damn,
damn. What right has he to go away and leave us? He's a

stinking, rotten beast that's what he is. I jolly well hate him Lucy, and I just shan't speak to him – ever – again.'

As it transpired he did not have the opportunity for quite a long time.

CHAPTER II

The Day an Elephant Came to Castle Rising

Alicia Aynthorp and Marguerite de Tessedre were sipping *tisanes* in the latter's private sitting room. This had been denuded of almost every plant, bulb and indoor tree in recent weeks. Since they were moved lock, stock and the last strand of florists' wire to Sawbridge's precious new stove house, that worthy had made it his business to urge the foreman with every persuasion he could exert – and a considerable quantity of his own home brewed beer in stone flagons – to expedite the completion of the permanent flower headquarters so that he could, 'See the last of them dratted flower girls and those two old madams with 'em.'

The foreman, an old friend of the head gardener, had so exerted himself that even Andrew was astonished at the celerity with which this department reached completion. Then, as the season loomed ahead, and soon after the final removal was effected, orders flowed in at such an unprecedented rate that the little Countess was forced to relinquish her own floral treasures from her sitting room in order to fulfil them. Even her special pride and joy, a standard white bougainvillaea, had been hauled down by a footman and pushed into the delivery van. These deprivations continued until there was nothing left.

Now, sitting together with their small feet up, wrapped in filmy tea gowns and feeling as the Dowager remarked with some asperity, 'Somewhat as Gaius Marius must have felt standin' among the ruins of Carthage,' they were indulging in a little retrospective complacency.

Marguerite launched them by observing as she scrutinised her flowerless room, 'One way and another we have taken pretty well to trade Alicia, considerin' our advanced age. Now I feel justified in takin' a Sabbatical which I own I desire greatly.'

The Dowager nodded approvingly, 'We can safely leave the gels to handle things now. After all August is a dead month and September not much better. There are only the hotels and restaurants to supply and the gels are now well able to manage those.' Thus she excused them both.

Palliser was already lining trunks with layers of tissue paper, preparatory to packing for the visit the two old naughties had arranged to their old cousins at Cheyne Abbot in Somerset, from whence it was their declared intention to pay frequent visits to Bath to partake of the remedial waters.

'Gyles has done well too,' the Dowager reflected. 'Fancy sellin' butter! Or cream either. Who would ever have imagined it? But really one has to admit it has been very well done. Were we not by nature rather curious, we could live here without ever suspectin' what was goin' on.'

'That also applies to the museum,' Marguerite reminded her, rising to replenish her cup as she spoke. 'With its own road nicely concealed, just as Gyles and Christine had planned it, one might not ever guess that hordes come gawpin' every day, with their tea drinkin' and all that carry on. I understand from Henry that Gyles is well satisfied.'

The Dowager chuckled. 'It's really rather like livin' over the shop now,' she mused. 'But the flower stall must wait until the autumn. I fancy that if we specialise in small pot plants which can be carried away easily it will go very well just outside the museum where everyone can look on their way in and buy on their way out. Stephanie was ecstatic over the money we made from the Fête too. That affair went extremely well. People were most flatterin'.'

'For my part,' the little Countess put her head on one side like a small bird, 'I think of all our diversions this summer I enjoyed Constance and Charles' housewarming party more than anything else.' After a pause she added, '*He* is a downright charmer don't you think?'

'My dear, of course, and Constance told me *he* spent quite a long time with Lucy which I own I did not notice. She says *he* has promised to drop in and see their clothes with, one presumes, one of his lady loves.'

'And *he* seems to have taken to Lucien,' Marguerite reflected. 'Lucien was bubblin' over with excitement. He is to be summoned to a levée.'

'What a world!' The Dowager shrugged. 'Fancy in *our* day, a King's son askin' a dressmaker to Court. Who would ever have imagined it!' Adding with total irrelevance, 'And now our hens have come into lay.' She giggled mischievously, 'Lucien had better take a basket to Court with him.'

This attitude was more or less constant with them all. They had taken what Gyles called 'a calculated risk', which seemed wholly justified by the results so far. Gyles spent a great deal of money not only on the 'Enterprises' but, as he had warned Henry, he had laid out considerable sums for his tenant farmers as well, in order to make it possible for them to revert from arable to dairy farming without his imposing on them repayment rates which would dishearten and possibly cripple them.

It was early days yet, as he was at some pains to remind himself; but with a reasonable amount of luck things seemed as though they would 'come round nicely', despite the now iniquitous taxes.

In this general atmosphere of felicity the Nursery made its resumed, annual departure to the holiday house in Bognor with Nanny Rose in complete charge and old Nanny – now very frail and inclined to wander – left in the care of Mason and Pearson who undertook to cope with her 'turn and turn about my lady' as they explained to Christine.

Then, just one week before the family were due to leave, Pearson climbed to the nursery wing with old Nanny's tea and some of her favourite black plum cake cut into fat fingers. The old woman was, as usual, sitting in her even older rocking chair around and about which dozens of what Plum called 'liddle Lormes' had clambered and played. She seemed to be sleeping. Her button-booted feet were resting firmly on the cross bar like a pair of particularly knobbly, black Jerusalem artichokes. Her work-shabby hands lay idle in her lap.

'Wake up Nanny, here's your tea and I've cut your plum cake just the way you like it,' said Pearson cheerfully.

The figure in the chair remained quite still. Pearson set down the tray and touched Nanny gently on one shoulder. The body just slumped forward and then slid down, a crumpled pile of greeny black into which the face sank.

'Oh my Gawd!' whispered Pearson. She stood for a moment looking down at the pathetic heap which Nanny had left behind. Then realising that Nanny would not be needing tea any more, 'You pore old soul,' she regretted, ''aving to go all alone!'

The despot of the nursery for almost forty years, who

had ruled her 'liddle Lormes' in the great Victorian tradition, caused only the gentlest of ripples by her departure. There was sadness on the part of the many whose ears had stung to her hard slaps and whose behinds had burned after her canings. Christine remembered poignantly Nanny's unerring predictions and her clairvoyant corns which had acted as prophet to her interpretations for so many years. Sitting at dinner they recalled her with an affection which is indigenous to Nanny-ruled families; quoted her favourite dictum 'never pick blackberries below dog-leg lifting height' and Gyles Aynthorp concluded while they sat on at the candlelit table, 'She was one of the last of her kind y'know. *We* were her life which she lived vicariously through us, for us and because of us.' Then abruptly he stood up, lifted his port glass and said, 'Come children, let us drink a toast to Nanny and wish her many more children to bully on whatever astral plane she now inhabits.'

Below stairs Mrs Parsons – her old arch-enemy – said after the simple funeral which was, of course, attended by the entire household, 'Oo'd 'ave expected 'er ter go so quiet like after all them scenes?' But no one answered her.

Despite Nanny's passing, the general atmosphere of content had spread, even to the Servants' Hall. They were fulfilling their duties in the pleasurable anticipation of a quiet time ahead. Appelby, always the prime belowstairs diplomatist, had managed to heal her breach with Cook, who loud and often had declared her antipathy to what she deemed 'a wolf in sheeps's clothin' wot learns all she can git and then forsakes her teacher for a fancy French chef'.

So, these things forgotten for the moment, the cook and the French chef's pupil conspired together over the agreeable little supper and tea parties which would be given to their cronies after their employers' departure. To make all doubly comfortable Chef André was off to France for his first holiday in five years.

Into this general atmosphere of felicity came a cable. Gyles took it from the proffered tray during tea, when all the adults were assembled for the last time before they set off.

Gyles ripped it open and read the contents aloud.

Returning immediately. Fear we may just miss you all.

Have a lovely time. Request permission to proceed with zoo in your absence. Have obtained some splendid animals. Also bringing two excellent keepers with me. Please let Richard remain as I know he will otherwise be fearfully disappointed. He is never any trouble to me and is marvellous with little Stephen. Sinclair and Henrietta are flourishing. Sinclair is a new man and very actively interested in the Zoo. Much love Sue-Ellen.

He looked up with a distinct gleam in his eyes. 'How anyone can willingly undertake that son of mine beats comprehension,' he observed drily, 'however, if you approve my love?' He looked directly at his wife.

'Oh I think so, dear, Sue-Ellen does seem to have a way with him and then of course with the animals ...'

'So be it,' Gyles nodded. 'Will you telephone to Nanny Rose tonight, explain to her and ask her to send him back? No wait, I think it would be better if Perkins collected him in the car, *after we have left.*'

'Anyone would think you didn't love your son Gyles,' Christine exclaimed indignantly.

'Love him!' Gyles riposted, 'he's a thorn in m'y side. Loosin' hornets from matchboxes in m'y dressin' room. Think of his crime sheet for a moment.' He broke off and smiled, 'He's what Plum calls "a proper varmin".' but the smile belied his words.

The Dowager sounded the first note of protest. 'That gel seems to have besotted you,' she exclaimed. 'Are you seriously suggestin' lettin' her have the run of the place while we're away?' It was unaccountably and extraordinarily out of character, besides badly said. Everyone else realised this instantly, for it was the one thing calculated to sway Gyles in Sue-Ellen's favour, Gyles having been crossed so often by his redoubtable mama.

'Oh, I think so, dear Mama,' he replied thoughtfully 'Havin' just endured all the alarums and excursions concomitant with the completion of the new office buildin' about which,' he appended hastily, 'you, Andrew, have been gratifyin'ly splendid; to say nothin' about the highly successful but fatiguin' re-opening of the museum with all its hubble-bubble of re-preparation; and takin' into account that the staff will now have absolutely nothin' to do while we are all away and they on board wages, I consider that it will be infinitely preferable for us to allow Sue-Ellen to build her cages, take delivery of her wild beasts and get them satisfactorily housed and her staff run in during our absence. After all Mama, the matter was agreed upon and settled some time ago.' He paused again, removed his monocle, polished it, re-affixed it and gave his redoubtable parent the full benefit of a very glinting stare, 'I see nothin' against it and shall implement exactly what Sue-Ellen requests forthwith.'

He held his stare a second after he finished speaking and for once the Dowager retreated. She laughed lightly as if the matter were of no vital import either way, said, 'Well she's a nice gel, pretty too, and seemingly quick-witted enough to run these extraordinary factories of hers so perhaps no ill will come of it. And now my dear, if you will excuse me . . . packing. . . .' But it was a retreat nevertheless.

After she had gone Gyles added to Christine, 'I think, my dear, we agree there is little pleasure in the prospect of lions, tigers and rhinoceros all over our lawns and herbacious borders. If there are to be – er – crises, let us avoid 'em. Sue-Ellen has a very sound head on those pretty shoulders and I believe she will encompass the worst while we are comfortably out of the way.'

Henry then lent his support. 'I agree sir, besides that will ensure Charles lends a hand. Which is a great deal better than havin' his moonin' about like a love sick calf all over the Riviera and spoilin' everythin' for us.' He added cheerfully, 'Anyway Sir Charles and Constance will be around should somethin' awful happen.'

'Lucky old Danements,' murmured Petula.

'Well they're not goin' away,' Henry retorted. 'It's demmed tempting one must admit. It would almost be worth givin' up the Riviera to see Mrs Parsons bein' run up the behind by a dirty great white rhino.'

These last words were spoken at the precise moment that Sawby walked in. He heard, of course. The resultant scene belowstairs was epic.

'Wot!' screamed Mrs Parsons, turning from her stove with a tray of meringues and letting them slide straight down into the cinders. 'Naow jest look wot you've gorne and made me do! Albert Sawby you're 'orrible. No never mind Agnes, leave them be they're ruined anyways. Stop scrabbling girl and get back to them veg.' She then swung round on Sawby. 'Are them wild beasts coming 'ere while our lot's orf on 'olidays?'

'As far as I can deduce,' Sawby confirmed. 'I may be wrong but it seems his lordship has agreed. Mr Henry's very words were "I can imagine Mrs Parsons and Plum at their first sight of a dirty great rhino ..." then he laughed. The little Countess laughed too, and then they were all at it, the Dowager mopping her eyes and even his lordship shaking with laughter. When he saw me he pulled himself together, coughed, they all turned, saw me and shut up.'

'I'll give 'em shut up,' Mrs Parsons snarled, 'wot they think they're doin' then? Are your footmen supposed to be animal minders now? Oh it's more'n flesh and blood can stand! Jest when we was looking forward to a bit er peace an' quiet too. I could cry, that I could.'

Appelby rushed into the breach. 'Now don't do that dear,' she urged, 'though it's pretty dreadful I will admit.'

George heaped fuel to the fire. 'It'll be nice,' he said, 'imagine coming in 'ere and findin' a roaring lion in the 'earth, or a nice wiggling snake sliding up your skirts Mrs Parsons.'

Mrs Parsons loosed an eldritch shriek. 'I'll pack me bags, that's wot I'll do. I'll not endure it.'

Sawby attempted to quell the rising hysteria. 'That is enough George, frightening women. You ought to be ashamed of yourself.'

Edward assumed an attitude of boredom, 'Wot's wild animals after the trenches. They'll just bring a little colour into our dull lives.'

By this time the kitchenmaids were huddled in the scullery doorway round-eyed, mouths open, gawping.

'Oh wot's happenin'? Mr Sawby carn't you find out? I'm that scared even of mice. . . .' Agnes wailed. This finished the footmen, George leaped onto a chair, shouting, 'Look out then there's a mouse now!' and the kitchenmaids fled incontinently while into the resultant bedlam the drawing room bell tolled dolorously.

Mrs Parsons elected to have a protracted attack of the sulks. This meant she had made up her mind to get a rest somehow, if only before the advent of the contingent from America and the dreaded animals. She dragged around complaining of her rheumatism, her corns, her lumbago, her head, and left Appelby to do the best she could unaided.

By the time Grantham returned from driving the Dowager and her sister-in-law to Somerset, to snatch a hurried meal before setting off again for Bognor for the fourteen-year-old future white hunter, a further cable arrived. It was addressed to Sawby who opened and read it, and only then disclosed its contents to the rest of them. 'Arriving 4.45 p.m. at Lower Aynthorp Station. Please send two cars to collect us and at least one van for the luggage. Delahaye.'

'That's torn it,' said Grantham, looking contradictorily thankful. 'Now Master Richard must wait till the morning or there won't be enough cars.' So Sawby must needs telephone to Nanny Rose, explain what had happened and undertake to send Grantham down the next day.

Mason and Pearson fled from the table to make a final check of the Delahaye rooms. Mrs Parsons unaccountably rallied and began planning dinner with Appelby who, when this was settled, rose saying, 'Be back in a tick Mrs P but I must do some flowers for their rooms.'

'Why carn't them flower girls do 'em?' she asked fretfully, 'there've time on their 'ands which is more'n you and me 'ave?' Sawby came in to support this proposal so the flower girls were telephoned.

When at length the two cars and the van returned from the station, Spurling, standing on the top step with Sawby, George and Edward, so far forgot herself as to exclaim as they drew up, 'We're used to luggage but this really beats the band!' which won her an Awful Look from Sawby and a warning cough as they opened the door, saying, 'Welcome home madam.'

Sue-Ellen stepped out, saying, 'You go right up to your rooms darlings. I'll stay a while and direct the luggage. We don't want it all upstairs.'

The piles of baggage accumulated. Then came some very large crates, which Sue-Ellen directed to, 'The Parcels Room please, George?' at which moment, galloping like a stag young Charles appeared from the general direction of the stables. He was whooping as he ran. Behind him at a somewhat leisurely pace came his father and stepmother to welcome the travellers.

On her way in, having disposed of the baggage problems, Sue-Ellen said to Sawby, 'There will be three extra for dinner if you please Sawby,' smiled and then asked, 'and how is your wife? Well, I hope?' thereby gaining his instant allegiance. Then, still holding firmly onto young Stephen's hand, she went into the Drawing Room. Stephen had grown as Sawby noticed at once, thinking how very like his father the boy was, and so preoccupied was he with this that he only realised when he eventually went belowstairs again that Mr Delahaye had walked in without a stick.

In the end the staff caught the infectious atmosphere which Sue-Ellen brought with her and became deeply absorbed in every stage of the future zoo's construction.

As the days went by without the slightest indication of any wild animals arriving their fears abated too.

Sue-Ellen was off the next morning with Grantham. When they returned the chauffeuse reported that she had driven Mrs Delahaye to the little market town of Bishop's Stortford where she had been directed to seek out the employment centre. Here madam had spent some considerable time. After this she went to the local ironmongers and there spent even longer. Finally a timber merchant was visited, and all Grantham could say was that Madam had emerged into the yard with the owner with whom she had inspected timber at great length, only then directing the chauffeuse, 'Back to the Castle please Grantham, I'm sorry to have kept you waiting so long.'

The results of this expediton were soon evident. In the meantime Richard was collected, and the following morning sharp on 9 a.m. a truck appeared containing twenty-four workmen and a great number of spades, picks and shovels. After which surreptitious peeps by the staff from the Long Gallery's west windows revealed young Mr Charles with posts and ropes carried by the new arrivals, making their way in company with Sue-Ellen and Richard to beyond the pleasure gardens, and on over to the other side of the river across the lane which wound down to the West Gates and the unoccupied West Lodge which had been struck by lightning and was at present uninhabitable.

'That's where they'll 'ave it,' predicted Mrs Parsons. 'Well it's a nice long way orf which is summink. I must say that Mrs Delahaye 'as a nice enough manner. Come down 'ere she did and spoke to me ever so nice. Said she 'oped she would cause no inconvenience while the fambly was away. Then broke it gently like there'd be twenty-four labourers to feed every day. Mid-morning tea, mid-day dinner and ale wot she 'as ordered speshull and not to be tapped from 'is lordship's supplies, no 'ow. She does it all so nice she makes you feel you're doin' 'er a favour.'

This amiable reaction was further encouraged by Sue-Ellen's next move. She rang for Sawby after dinner on the following evening. She began by asking if it would not be possible for her to dine with Mr and Mrs Delahaye and Mr Charles Danement in the Morning Room. 'I have asked them both,' she explained, 'and they would welcome it. If we could just have the round table laid in the window, for six, as Master Richard and Master Stephen will stay up for dinner while we are alone, we all feel it would make the work much easier for you.' This conversation was conducted in 'In Transit', which she had taken over as her office.

When Sawby had thanked her she waved a pencil at a large pile of boxes resting on the window seat saying, 'And those I would like one of your footmen to collect and distribute among your staff. There are boxes of American chocolates for all your womenfolk and cigars for the men. As you are I believe something of a connoisseur your special box has your name on it. Just a small token of my appreciation of your services.'

When they had gone she and young Charles and Richard spread out their plans and worked on them. It was the same every night. In the daytime they worked in close harmony with their labourers, until gradually paths took shape, and white posts were inserted bearing in black lettering, 'Hippo Pool', 'White Aviary', and many more. At the end of the first week the working team was split. Six men were given the task of excavating the hippo pool. Then vans began to appear thick and fast, off-loading on site mountains of sand, while bags of cement were stacked on a temporary floor and covered by a huge tarpaulin. A cement mixer was then delivered. After it came the first cages. Some were huge affairs delivered in sections and fastened together on site. Soon the whole area was dotted with huts, concrete cages with iron bars sunk deep into them and huge iron gates with strong bolts and bars.

The staff took to strolling in the warmth of the August evenings to see what more had happened during each day. Plum was a frequent visitor too. He ambled up on his bandy old legs at all hours, questioning, peering about, ordering Richard away to tend his own 'hanimals, wot is in a fair way to becoming neglected if it weren't for me. So 'op it young feller me lad and git them 'orses mucked out.' To which he added, rounding on Sue-Ellen, 'And wot 'appens to them with all these new 'omes for new beasties?'

Sue-Ellen invited him to join her on a pile of freshly delivered timber. When they were both seated she told him, 'They're going Plum; but I do not wish Master Richard to know ... yet. There is a home for handicapped children not far from here.'

'I knows,' Plum nodded.

'Well then, I saw the people who run it just before I went to the States, er, to America. I put a proposition to them, I said, take the animals and make a little zoo for your children, almost all have disabilities, like your children. If you will do this and teach the children to take care of the animals I will defray both the initial costs and the costs of maintaining them thereafter and my delighful, schoolboy cousin Richard, who rescued them in the first place, will come over and show everyone exactly how they should be treated. They were delighted Plum. But I want this Zoo's animals here before Master Richard learns what I have planned. This way he can work with me without having a conscience over his strays so please Plum don't jump the gun for me.'

Plum scratched his pate vigorously. 'I'll lay a shade of odds that set yer back a pretty penny,' he observed sagely. 'Don't bother tellin' me I'm berginning ter know yer. Allus at it like a dog scratching fleas, now don't get me wrong,' he added hurriedly as he saw her expression at his unlovely simile, 'howsomever, it's a danged good idea both for the children and the hanimals so I'll say nuffin' ter no one, except that you've got a sound head on yer shoulders and no mistake.' Saying which he touched his disreputable cap and lumbered off to get in the way of the labourers.

One of them paused, leaned on his spade and looked across to where Sue-Ellen was picking her way. He watched her in her simple cotton frock, her fair hair down, tied back with a ribbon but blowing out in the light breeze.

'She'm a bit of orlright she is,' he observed, sucking his teeth in mingled approbation and frustration. 'Yankee ain't she?'

'Best not say so to 'er,' Plum warned. 'She'm proper sold

on us she is, Gawd knows why. Plans to live 'ere fer the rest of 'er life. Shockin' rich she is too. Makes hairyplanes she does.'

'Go on,' said the other incredulously, 'well I never,' and then bent hastily to his spade as the subject under discussion turned and came towards him.

The third week in August saw the completion of the first series of Plum's ''omes for wild beasties'. This title stuck until Sue-Ellen wearied of explaining to astonished callers, so put a stop to it.

The day the elephant came to Castle Riding was a red letter one in the Castle's history. The animal was off-loaded by crane from the ship which brought her from Africa to the London Docks. Her companion came ashore on his own two feet after supervising this operation. He was English and had a long circus history behind him. The other trainer had long since been despatched to India to assume responsibility for the white tiger bred by a maharajah who amused himself by specialising in these superb creatures. Cables then flowed in reporting on the progress of both men and beasts until Sue-Ellen was able to murmur to Sawby in mild, conversational tone, 'Oh Sawby, there is one other thing?'

'Yes madam,' he turned from the sideboard where he was slicing ham, a thing he had never been known to do before; but now did for Sue-Ellen.

'There will be a tiger arriving some time today and an elephant. Each will be accompanied by the man who will take care of them. Will you be so kind as to ask Mrs Peace to arrange for the men to be given rooms in the old Convalescent Home? I have already spoken to Lady Constance. She tells me that numbers seven and eleven will not be required by her nurses for some time to come.'

It said much for Sawby that he replied without a tremor, 'Where will they eat madam, I mean the, er, animal escorts?'

Suppressing a wild desire to laugh Sue-Ellen said, 'Below stairs with you, if you please, just until I can make the necessary future arrangements.'

When he had gone she let go, as did the rest of them.

'Did you see his face?' she gurgled. 'Oh my, that was hilarious! I only wish I could be belowstairs this very minute.'

'He'll take it out on the rest of them,' said Sinclair without the trace of a stammer.

'You're a wicked girl you know,' Henrietta told her. 'Where are they at the moment?'

Sue-Ellen showed every sign of going off again.

'At Bishop's Stortford. I rented a barn. Frank telephoned me to say he expected to be here about two o'clock. He says the crowds which have followed him are simply enormous. Mick, he's Irish, is coming straight down in a circus cage with the tiger. What will happen when they reach the village ...' she broke down and collapsed with laughter.

'Can I go and meet them?' demanded Richard. 'Oh do say yes. I promise to be good, honest I do.'

'You couldn't be good if you tried,' Sue-Ellen told him cheerfully, 'but you can go. There's a flower van going in at one o'clock to catch the London train at one-thirty. Run and ask Venetia at the flower Depot if she will let you both hitch a ride.'

Henrietta coughed. 'Dearest,' she said diffidently, 'not "hitch a ride", it, er, is not quite suitable; "if you may go with her" would be just a little prettier.'

Sue-Ellen nodded. 'Thank you,' she said simply. 'I will remember.' She rose from the table murmuring, 'If you can go with her, if you can ...'

The two Delahayes smiled at each other. They had never been so happy. Nor had they ever seemed so relaxed.

With breakfast over the couple went off to prepare for the day. This consisted of acquiring rugs and wraps, putting on comfortable out-door shoes and collecting a couple of very large green parasols. Thus armed they went down the steps, where Sinclair climbed into his waiting wheel chair which he was needing less and less. The two boys then wrangled over whom should push but eventually the cortège moved off with an invisible Sinclair totally obscured by impediments, submerged and quite contented. Half an hour later, arriving on site, Sinclair disentangled himself, Henrietta opened up her folding stool, set up her easel and began painting, looking under the huge green umbrella not unlike the Parsee under the palm tree especially when she accepted a bun from the ever stodging Richard.

It was all done by numbers – daily. Henrietta settled and dabbing away serenely at her water colours – which always ended up looking as though she had wept over them on completion – while Sinclair went off to collect the plans from his daughter-in-law. Thereafter he assumed the office of overseer, moving from one working group to the next checking, supervising the taking of measurements by the boys and generally making himself genuinely useful. He was at last a contented man; but this was a very special day and while routine was pursued by the zoo teams the boys were extremely restless until Sue-Ellen gave them a shilling each and shooed them off, saying resignedly as she returned to her interrupted luncheon, 'It's just hopeless expecting them to stay here and eat. Don't worry Mama, they had a very good breakfast and will probably compensate at tea time.'

The villagers of Lower Aynthorp were never to forget that day either. The first intimation of what was in store came when the two boys erupted into Mr Palfrey's shop demanding, 'Jelly babies please, two liquorice sticks and if one shillin' each is enough a whipped cream walnut each as well.'

The addressee promptly vanished to inform Mr Palfrey that 'Castle folk's come in sir' – thus the stout and red-cheeked Boy as he was still called although he was now rising twenty. Mr Palfrey came in bustling and hand-rubbing unctuously in anticipation of a new, larger order. His face fell when he learned that the ceiling tally was to be two shillings. However, it was Castle folk if only small ones so he assured them, 'young gents you can 'ave some brandy balls too if so be you've a mind'. To which a delighted Richard promptly agreed then volunteered, 'If you happen to look out of your window any time now you will see a white elephant walking down the street.'

'Ha ha,' said Mr Palfrey, well versed in the ways of small boys, 'and pink mice too I dare suppose?'

'No,' replied Stephen gravely, 'but you will see a white tiger with black stripes as well. It's come all the way from India from a maharajah.'

'Go on with you Master Stephen. Tigers ain't white for a start. Whose leg are you trying to pull, eh?'

'Oh yes they are white,' Richard corrected him hotly, 'they are for our White Zoo. We aren't having anything but white animals so there!'

This rattled the little grocer but he still found it hard to credit, though it caused him to wonder a little for he had already heard zoo talk in the village.

When Widow Tremlow popped in from across the street for a block of salt, he repeated this conversation to her. 'Go on,' she exclaimed, 'well I never! They do say as how the Castle is having a zoo. I know there are men working at it up there because my son Timmy is walking out with a girl from Bishop's Stortford and her dad's one of the labourers.'

She counted out her tuppence hurriedly and went off to spread the tale. Thus for no apparent reason except that they wished quite suddenly to take the air, every man, woman and child hurried out from their little houses onto the pavement where they stood about in groups, turning their heads this way and that, peering up and down, while nothing more untoward than Mr Tink's grandson appeared to divert them by leading down a large pig tethered to a length of tattered rope.

Outside the Palfrey shop Richard and Stephen sucked, chewed and loitered. Then they parked their remaining sweets on Mr Palfrey's window sill and attempted to climb the lamppost until Richard tore his trousers on the bus notice board which was fastened to the column by a piece of wire. So they gave that up and began trying to see who could spit the farthest until George, sent on an errand from the Castle, walked by saying, 'Mrs Delahaye will fetch you 'ome if you do that.' So they desisted, blew the footman two loud raspberries and began casting about for a new mischief. Then suddenly a great shout went up. Down the road marched Timpling the village policeman waving his arms portentously and shouting, 'Keep off the road there's hellyfunt approaching,' to which the crowd answered with a rousing cheer.

It was true. Mr Timpling, being a cautious man with no experience of elephant behaviour, quickened his speed to ensure maintaining a good distance between his portly person and the even more portly animal which could at last be seen. It was not really white at all but a pale pinky grey and was being led along at a lumbering plod by a small wiry man in a cloth cap who chewed on a wisp of hay.

Mr Palfrey had been bobbing about at his window for some time. Now he was heard to ejaculate, 'By gum it's true!' ... then 'Mother!' he shouted, ''ere Mother ... Boy come quick.' After which he dashed out into the roadway, hotly pursued by the fat Boy and the stringy little Mrs Palfrey with her hair tied up in curling rags.

As the keeper and the elephant came level with the second window of the Palfrey shop, the elephant fired from her broad behind a thunderous and prolonged fart, paused for a moment to eject an enormous dollop and then sauntered on.

Richard and Stephen dashed across the road with Richard shouting, 'Hello there, we're from the Castle, I'm Richard Lorme and this is my cousin Stephen Delahaye. What's your name? What's the elephant's name? Oh gosh, isn't she marvellous!'

Behind them a small village child could be heard exclaiming in awe, 'Look at that Mum! It's the biggest shitty pat in all the world, look Ma at that gurt shitty pat,' only to be soundly cuffed by his mother and hauled back onto the pavement by his ear.

'I'm Frank,' the unruffled custodian informed the Castle pair, 'her's not got a name, leastways so far as I know.'

This brief exchange was conducted to a background of shrieks and comments, with small boys dashing out to have a closer look and adults forming a solid wodge on either side until a fearful hooting and tooting sounded in the rear of this unlovely procession. This became so persistent that even Frank turned his head. Behind the last stragglers, chauffeur at the wheel, Richard and Stephen, turning with the rest, recognised the ancient Royce belonging to the choleric old Duke of Barton and Sale. As if to dispel any lingering doubts as to what personage this vehicle contained, the old Duke's crimson face appeared over one window and a stream of abuse poured out with dreadful clarity.

Frank glanced in his direction, murmured 'Ornery old codger,' and resumed his plodding, as did the elephant. At the same moment, up the street came another village woman carrying an enormous armful of freshly baked loaves from the little Aynthorp bakery. They were hot. The elephant picked up their warm sweet whiff on the light breeze, swerved slightly, stretched out her trunk and calmly abstracted one of the topmost loaves which she proceeded to curl upwards and inwards into her pink mouth. The woman let out a yell, dropped the remainder and scuttled like a frightened rabbit into the crowd. The loaves scattered in all directions. The elephant, well pleased with such bounty, swung out her trunk and tucked a second cottage loaf into her mouth . . . and then another. Frank tugged unavailingly; the villagers, entranced, flowed into the road completely thwarting the Duke's chauffeur in his attempts to obey the Duke's bawled order, 'Mount the pavement man, damme don't dither, I'm in a hurry, mount you damn fool, mount!'

Conversely, the elephant saw no need for haste. In leisurely fashion her trunk curled outwards and scooped up a fourth loaf. The Duke's invective was now becoming frightful. So Frank exerted all his strength on the halter's reins which up to now he had held quite negligently and the young elephant, bothered by the increasing uproar, suddenly became uncertain and confused. Rather petulantly, backing as she did so, she curled her trunk around the tugging Frank, scooped him up as if he were a slightly larger loaf of bread and deposited him upon her back, quite unharmed.

'Nah look wot yer's done!' he shouted, from this unexpected vantage position. 'Why carn't yer all shut up. Proper upset she is, it's a shame!'

By now the persistent tooting of the Royce's horn was becoming an increased irritant. The press of village folk was growing, one woman was pushed perilously close to that now swinging trunk which nearly caught her as she fell forward, dementedly scrabbling on her hands and knees into the protective sea of human legs where she collapsed in screaming hysterics.

The hooting stopped abruptly. Instead the Duke's voice could be heard shouting, 'Turn the bloody car round you demented idiot. I've had enough of this tomfoolery. We'll cut through Lorme land by their West Gate. The lane comes out on the same road only higher up.'

The elephant had halted. Straddle-legged in front of her, Richard was paying hot fresh loaves into her trunk. Seizing this opportunity Frank slid down, ran forward and began making soothing noises into one huge ear. The crowd watched entranced. The Royce executed her reversing exercise only to find, as the chauffeur brought her round, that she was face to face with a vast lorry which in turn was surmounted by a large iron cage containing a pacing, snarling, tail-lashing white tiger. In the driving seat sat

Mick the Irish custodian. He wore a scarlet fisher-cap, pulled down over his ears and not for nothing was he known to his cronies as Mick-the-lug for his ears stuck out at right angles.

The Duke was by now out of the car, still screaming invective and waving his arms. Mick pushed his red cap back a couple of inches, applied his brakes and leaned down. 'Whisht,' he yelled back, 'God blast yer for a foul mouthed old spalpeen, 'tis yerself that is dirtyin' the lane with yer black word bi'God. Have done with yer blasphemin' and get that auld jaunty car of yers out of the way. This tiger's for his Lordship at the Castle. I've a moind to loose her on yer and then see yer run. Glory be to God if I don't ...'

The Duke was speechless at last. That he had lived to hear his car called an 'auld jaunty car' by a rogue and vagabond in a red bonnet paralysed him momently. Mick seizing the advantage, bawled, 'Out of the bleedin' way my bhoy,' and began inching the truck forward. The chauffeur, backed in panic; the Duke gave tongue again, screaming to the man to, 'Stay where you are, I tell you!' While the elephant, soothed by Frank's crooning, plodded forward once more and the crowd scattered as the great vehicle with its enraged, caged inmate atop swerved, mounted the pavement and was through, with Mick jeering as he went by, 'Get ye to a sink my foine fellow and wash yer auld mouth out wi' a bar of carbolic soap.'

The villagers had never witnessed such a delirious scene. Mick drove on, bumped off the pavement onto the road ahead of the plodding elephant, leaned down again to shout, 'Top of the morning to ye Frank. Who'm yon auld blabber mouth?'

The small boys shot forward. 'Can we come up with you,' shouted Richard reaching for the truck door handle. 'We can show you the way, we're from the Castle.' The last the Duke saw as he hopped and howled was of Richard and Stephen clambering in beside the lunatic who had referred to him as 'auld blabber-mouth'.

With a final valedictory, 'You'll pay for this my man,' the Duke wrenched open the Royce's door and dived inside; but not before Mick shot one hand out over the driving door and stuck two derisive fingers into the air.

'That ould bastard needs a dip in the village trough an'

oive a moind to give it him,' he observed to his two passengers.

'I shouldn't if I were you,' said Richard sobering, 'that's the Duke of Barton and Sale.'

When the repercussions of this affair had eventually subsided it began to impinge upon Sue-Ellen that there was more to starting a zoo than just building the correct homes and obtaining men to staff them. Concurrently she had a rough passage with Richard who had automatically assumed that he and his American cousin would run the entire affair themselves. Never very far from the outer edges of aggression he faced her, straddle-legged as usual, his colour high, and his mouth mutinous.

'Bbbut it's *our* zoo,' he insisted.

Sue-Ellen sat down on some newly-laid turf. 'Now listen honey,' she still reverted to Americanese when thoroughly bayed, which always made her crosser. 'You still have three years to do at Harrow. *If* I don't get someone else who loves and knows animals how am I to cope in term time? Be reasonable Rikki, *I'm* only learning – no, beginning to learn – just how much *is* involved. Your job, during term, is as vital as any we can do here because you've got to learn and learn. Do they teach you wild life dietetics in your house?'

'Don't be daft,' he scoffed, apologising immediately afterwards. 'Of course they don't, it's all Latin and Greek and silly stinks which don't help.'

Sue-Ellen frowned at the turf layer who immediately became disconsolate. 'You have to know,' she said desperately, 'how about if I get a top man to do me a series of papers and send them will you sweat on them?'

'Of course.'

'Then there's the business of photographs. If I get you the right cameras will you sweat up photography too?'

Richard nodded, frustration and anger giving place to eagerness. 'What sort of pictures?'

'Absolutely realistic ones. It doesn't matter if it's the Head scratching himself, or Matron being sick or a cat walking along a wall. Now *listen*. Stop that glaring at me and I'll explain.'

Andrew, searching for her some moments later, saw the golden head and the copper one close together, in what he still judged in the schoolboy term 'deep confabulation', smiled gently and strolled on.

Richard now sat cross-legged, dirtying one already grubby finger by tracing the outline of a camel in the sand between the turf pads. Sue-Ellen then explained what she had in mind.

'I think it is essential that we have pictures of the animals against the front of their homes' – she fought shy of the word cages because of its imprisoning implication – 'because then if the animal is sleeping, hibernating, or just hiding, at least the public can see what the creature looks like. In addition we must have the Latin names, the country of origin, a précis of the creature's habits, diet ... you see?'

Richard nodded, attention riveted and temper fled.

'Those old stick-in-the-muds wouldn't release me to spend a day at the zoo on Sundays,' he said. 'It's just not on, out of bounds and all that stuff; but if you could come down on a Tuesday, Thursday or Saturday – pass days you see – and could bring a few snakes, or small mammals with you I could take pictures like mad. Come to that,' he cocked a doubtful, questioning eyes in her direction, 'you could just send Irish Mick, him and me get along fine.'

'Him and *who*?' shrieked Sue-Ellen, appalled. Richard adjusted his grammar obligingly and they talked on. By the time they had done he was her man again, so they strolled off companionably to 'Irish' as the rest of the staff called the foul-mouthed little keeper.

The money began to fly again when the trio set off for London to confer with a Fellow of the London Zoo, to buy the most modern and costly of camera equipment that ever a small boy took back to any school with him, and to acquire from the Fellow much information as to what they should do generally.

Sue-Ellen, sitting back as Grantham drove them home to the Castle, observed a trifle ruefully, 'This is going to prove almost as costly as building a new aircraft factory!' So Richard, removing a huge humbug from one cheek, asked anxiously, 'Can you afford it?' He was rewarded by a light laugh, a reassuring pat and the comforting, 'Of course, don't give it another thought.'

The end product of all this was the introduction of a specialist architect who produced a small sea of plans, after which work began apace on the erection of a central building. This would house the Diet Department, the Photographic Department, each with a large filing area for instant reference, and the Clinic with its own skilled staff who would deal with all ailing creatures in the most modern conditions available.

Dramas were naturally frequent. These reached their climax when the white tiger went off his feed. Mick, Andrew and Sue-Ellen conferred, walked together to the great beast's cage and stopped short, frozen in their tracks at the sight which confronted them. It was Richard, inside the cage, squatting on the straw with one arm around the tiger's neck, feeding him shards of raw meat with the other hand while the embracing arm's fingers scratched at the immense poll. They stared appalled. The tiger turned his head, blinked at them sleepily and yawned, so Richard popped in another shard of meat and the trio began signalling frantically for him to come out. He nodded. The tiger moved, rolled over and Richard promptly began tickling the immense belly. The tiger made a deep purring sound, Richard eased his arm away, still tickling and talking softly. 'Clever boy,' said he approvingly, 'move over a scrap you're on my leg.'

The trio remained in frozen stillness. Richard shoved the main hunk of meat nearer to himself with the now released foot, picked it up and offered it to the zizzing tiger who was rumbling like a swarm of bees. Slowly, slowly he stood up. As he did so the tiger's golden topaz eyes rested on him thoughtfully for a moment. The great body moved and Mick's hand slid to the catch on his rifle. The tiger dropped his eyes and put out a paw ... to the bone.

'That's a good boy,' said Richard soothingly. Back went one leg, a single pace ... then another ... until he slid one hand behind his back talking on soothingly while the tiger began to devour the flesh. Mick muttered under his breath 'Jesus, Mary and Joseph!' Richard's back-stretched hand found the unlatched gate, slid round it, shot back the bolt, stepped out and slid the bolt back. Sue-Ellen promptly burst into tears. Not so Mick. He dropped his rifle, caught the boy by his shoulders and shook him like a rat, 'You black, sinful spalpeen you!' he roared. 'You evil Protestant! May God have mercy on your soul ...'

Andrew was mopping Sue-Ellen and making similar soothing noises in his throat to the tiger who was now savaging the hunk of bone and meat. 'Don't be a clot!' shouted Richard, between rattlings, 'Stop it Mick. I'm alright and the tiger is too. *You* couldn't get him to eat, but *I* did, I knew I could and I did.'

Mick's hands loosed him and he used them to cover his face. It should have been his mouth, for the blasphemies which emerged were bone-chilling.

Then Andrew, still white to the gills, took a hand, speaking very quietly. 'If you ever do that again,' he told him with shaking lips, 'I shall tell father and you will never again be allowed to come within a hundred yards of this Zoo. *Is that clear?*'

Andrew used to say, many years later, when his small brother had become a famous figure, that it was the one and only time he ever saw fear in Richard's eyes.

'You wouldn't?' he breathed.

'You just try me you young sod and then you'll know.'

Richard nodded slowly. 'Yes ... you ... would,' he admitted reluctantly. 'Alright, Andy, I promise.'

Andrew underlined the occasion. He made his small brother shake hands on it. He called Mick to witness and when this was done he turned and strode off without another word.

'Blimey,' said Richard, staring after him. 'That's torn it!'

But within minutes he was busily engaged upon another ploy with the elephant plodding after him.

'More like a dawg than a hellyfunt,' mumbled Plum who had come up to see what was going on. 'I know 'im, ee's gotter kind er magic 'ee 'as.' But Mick was too exhausted and shocked to tell him just how far Richard's 'magic' had gone.

Later in the day when he and Sue-Ellen were standing together watching the shepherding of the first consignment of white deer into their newly completed paddock, Christian came limping towards them, a tall man at his side.

Sue-Ellen stopped and stared.

'Hi there Richard!' shouted Christian. 'Look who I've brought to see you!'

'Another Lorme,' her mind registered, 'but *which one is it?*'

Richard let out a shriek of delight and flung himself against the long legs, crying, 'Oh gosh, Nin, how perfectly splendid. We thought you were never coming home. Oh what a super surprise!'

Over the tumult Christian attempted an introduction.

'Colonel Lorme, Mrs Delahaye, otherwise Ninian – and our Sue-Ellen.' He added swiftly, 'Ninian's only on a flying visit, more's the pity.'

Sue-Ellen proffered a distinctly grubby hand. She smiled up at a pair of what she registered immediately as very hard blue eyes, saw a sudden flash in them which puzzled her and heard him saying, 'I was recalled unexpectedly you see so I thought it was high time I came home.'

Then she realised who this man was. The other one of that pair of cousins the Family used to call the 'Inseparables'. James had been killed in 1915, leaving behind an embittered and lonely Ninian who had thereafter shown such indifference to his own fate that his courage, no more than a by-blow of despair, had brought him through the war unscathed because he no longer cared whether he lived or died.

She rallied quickly enough, murmured a formal, 'How delightful. Would you like to be shown round the beginnings of our White Zoo and be told what it is all about or go straight in to tea?'

'Tea later,' Ninian smiled suddenly. 'Christian has given me the bare bones but I would love to see for myself if you can spare the time.'

Hannibelle had come up behind them, unnoticed. Now, as they moved off, she just fell in at the rear and plodded sedately in their wake. Ninian found himself laughing involuntarily as he glanced back over his shoulder. 'Are we being followed with sinister intent or is our fat appendage of good behaviour?' he enquired.

'Who? Oh, I see. No that's Hannibelle, Richard's boon companion; but she has learned that she may not come in to the Castle – at last.'

For the first time in years Ninian began to enjoy himself.

'The Dowager,' Sue-Ellen continued, 'now recites a little poem when she sees the pair, "I have a little shadow that goes in and out with me, though what can be the use of it I really cannot see", but you should have been here the day she arrived, it was, er, something of an epic.'

'I can imagine,' Ninian agreed, finding himself very much at his ease with this unusual girl.

Richard cut in, 'You should have been here to see Sawby's face when I went up the main steps with her. She tried to follow me in.' The rather splendid looking Ninian grinned appreciatively. 'What did you do Rikki?'

'Ticked it off.'

'Who, Sawby?'

'No, Hannibelle. You see Sawby opened the door and said, very stately, "Master Richard you are being followed by an elephant and it is more than my place is worth to admit you both so can you please dismiss the animal."'

Ninian's shoulders shook.

'So I told her to push off and she turned herself round and went down again; come on Nin I'm starving,' Richard concluded breathlessly.

This time it was Ninian and Richard, hanging on his arm, who mounted the steps together. Sawby on opening the door was for an instant bereft of anything with which his training had invested him. He grabbed Ninian's outstretched hand saying, 'Oh, sir, Mr Ninian, Colonel sir, this is the day we have been waiting for. Oh Master Ninian it is so very good to have you back,' which, as Sue-Ellen observed from the shadowy interior, made Ninian's cold eyes very warm indeed.

Curiously, she took particular pains with her toilet that night and came down at last, almost late, in one of the dinner frocks Lucien had designed for her trip. Ninian was in the hall and as he looked up she saw again that gleam for a moment in his generally sombre eyes and was extraordinarily absent-minded during dinner.

The next day the Dowager and the little Countess returned to make much of the prodigal, who left the Drawing Room with them after luncheon to spend the afternoon in the Dowager's boudoir under the famous and beloved portrait of Justin, his grandfather. Here he dutifully sipped a *tisane* which penance also warmed him curiously as he sat answering innumerable questions about the war.

Having already said that this was to be a mere, flying visit, it came as something of a surprise to them all when he asked, with elaborate casualness during dinner, 'Anyone mind if I hang about a bit, just for a few days?' Adding quickly, 'I haven't seen your *musée* yet *Belle-mère*, at least not the new extensions. I want to look over your offices, Andy, and, well, there are so many things to see. Young Charles when does your splendid papa return?'

Young Charles, who by now had made himself a fixture, jerked himself away from watching Sue-Ellen to reply. 'They haven't been anywhere, just stayin' overnight with the Playdons for a prance, they'll be back again in the morning.' And found himself wondering if he really wanted 'old Ninian' to stay, which was rum, he thought.

Later Ninian learned that Henry and Petula were expected in forty-eight hours and his parents were due down on the night train from Scotland the evening after, so of course he agreed with his informant, the Dowager, that it would be unthinkable for him to leave before they arrived.

Sue-Ellen soon noticed that Ninian had a trick of lapsing into silences from which he would start when spoken to, and for a moment look blankly at the speaker before picking up the thread again. As they all knew why, they handled him with great gentleness.

After they had left the luncheon table she felt in need of fresh air so went off down the terrace steps to wander through the gardens. As she came to the lake she saw Ninian sitting on a seat watching the cleaning activities of the two black swans who were combining their grooming with keeping a sharp eye on their latest brood of cygnets. On impulse she slid onto the seat beside him and for a long while they sat without speaking. Presently he said, 'The last time I sat here James and I came down to see old Ulysses before we went ... er ... to France.'

'You were very close weren't you?' Sue-Ellen said softly.

'We thought alike,' he said simply. 'Did everything together, and although it's been over three years since he went, well it's not much different. He's everywhere only I just can't see the beggar.'

She bit her lip. 'Then why not welcome him instead of grieving for him?' she asked gravely. 'Perhaps he *is* here and if he were,' the words began tumbling out, 'surely he'd be glad if *you* were glad instead of sorry? Perhaps there is a kind of sharing, even now. It is not as if you were lovers,' she giggled almost hysterically. He turned to stare at her.

'What I mean is that when this happens between a husband and wife there's the physical bit which makes the not seeing part so much more dreadful. *I know* that one, you see; but between two men who have been very close I cannot suppose that the physical side was ever more than a huge nudge, or a sudden scuffle?'

She made this last a question. He continued to stare. 'Of course,' he said thoughtfully, 'it depends whether or not you think *they* come back.'

She flung up a small plea that she should give him the answers he needed. 'Well now,' she spoke hesitantly, 'I do and I don't.'

'Can you explain?'

'I think so. At first the hardest part about going dead suddenly is coming to terms with the fact that you *are* dead. Or rather as I like to think of it, on the other side of life. So you, the one to whom it has happened, must be the lonely one really. Therefore until you become acclimatised of course you turn to whatever was most familiar, whoever was most loved; but as you begin to understand, then I think the visiting becomes less and less until it only happens when someone you cared about deeply sends up a special message of trouble or loneliness.'

'Could that kind of special message be wrong?'

She caught her breath a bit on that one, but sensing his need struggled on. 'It ... could ... be ... if we believe that they've got their own lives to live on that other side of life. Let me put it another way. If you were desperately busy, like I am with my son, the Zoo and my rather big commitments in the States, and someone you cared about very deeply was always ringing you up and keeping you for hours on the telephone....' she trailed into silence, then tried again. 'I haven't said it right, of course you'd be glad to hear from whoever it was but if you just had to get on ... think of it as if your longing for your cousin James was like a blinding light to him obscuring what he had to do ...'

They sat on beside the lake. The little flotilla of cygnets took to the water. Ulysses waddled down, swam in, with the pen following and the cygnets in a line astern behind.

Suddenly Sue-Ellen said, 'I think you have needed to talk about your twin. Oh, I know he's not your proper twin, but there are people who are twins without being so in fact, if you can understand what I mean. Wherever James is, he'll always keep an eye on you. He couldn't do otherwise; but I think he should be allowed to do so in his own time. Remember he's wiser than you are now. He'll always know when you need him. He doesn't even need telling.'

'He wasn't all that bright,' said Ninian dubiously. 'We were just two chaps who liked the same things and liked to do them together. Why, I remember ...'

She had him now and she knew it. She sat very still as he talked himself back into their shared past, from toddlers to schoolboys to young men, through 'In Transit' and their companionable evenings with their form books, cricket scores, and copies of the 'Pink 'Un', on through Sandhurst and to France, as the light faded and the evening star came out. Still he talked on right through to the moment when James 'bought it', dying instantly, then she just took him by the hand and led him back over the dew-heavy grass, as the dressing gong sounded in the distance. He walked beside her, his hand lying passively in hers and suddenly he seemed to her, for all his rather splendid appearance, just a lost little boy: an habitually rather inarticulate one, who was bewildered by the burden of his own life and needed solace which it was beyond his powers to ask of anyone.

CHAPTER 12

The Sleeveless Errand

On a fine spring morning in 1920, Christine sat curled up on what she called 'my thinking seat', a window one which commanded a view of which she never tired.

As she looked down she could see the balustrade which framed the terrace and the steps which cleft it, descending to the long narrow lawn which always resembled for her a long, green arrow piercing the big herbacious borders and ending at the ornamental arch. This framed the entrance to the Urn Garden beyond. Through the charcoal lacework of the wrought iron gates she could see the urns crowned with the swaying heads of narcissi and daffodils. These would presently give place to the blue of climbing lobelia which would cascade from them all summer. Only memory gave her the still farther picture of the Sunken Garden beyond; but intermittently the breeze-tossed water from the dancing fountains became visible as the sun caught the drops and silvered them. Then if she just turned her head, she could see on either side the twin wings of the Rose Gardens, each of which were framed by long crescents of pillared pergolas about which the entwining roses would soon burst into first flowers. Even farther off from where she sat lay the dark smoothness of the Topiary with, curving round it, the gleam of polished pewter which declared the river curling its way round like a mailed arm.

Christine was fifty today. The years and her circumstances had conspired to deal very generously with her appearance. The errant sun slipping from behind a scudding cloud caught the undimmed lights in her chestnut hair which she still wore piled high, refusing to bob it as fashion now decreed and as her daughter-in-law Petula had done already. Save for a few fine lines traced at the corners of her eyes, and for that inescapable look of maturity which no amount of preservation can gainsay, she was still as much a beauty as she had been when Gyles Aynthorp saw her for the first time and murmured ruefully to himself on the instant, '*Hélas, mon partie est pris!*'

She had given him six children, the last the tempestuous Rupert whose birth had so nearly brought her life to an end; though fate had relented when it had seemed certain she would go.

Now, on this glorious birthday morning her brood were all safely inside the castle once again; joyously safe after the years of fear for Henry, Ninian and Andrew. The rest's names slid through her mind serenely enough until she baulked again at her youngest's. Sometimes she felt such fear for little Rupert, such a coldness of spirit that even thinking of him made her shiver. She did so now, for twin with such thoughts was always the *damnosa hereditas* of those other Lormes who had ploughed such courses of destruction through the centuries.

It had to be Rupert, she thought wearily. He was the most beautiful of all her children, possessed of such frightening charm and such a startling facility for whatever caught his interest that this too multiplied her fears. He was totally without fear. He rode better than any other of her sons, taking fences like an Irish horse-coper, which only served to draw the comment from old Plum, 'He'm another hell-fer-leather warmint wot'll break his neck if he ain't curbed, an' whose to school such a liddle divil I dursn't think!'

Rupert used his charm with consummate guile even in babyhood, notably with his formidable papa; hammering his small fists on Papa's knee until he was hauled up and given sips of Papa's wine which he took with ceremony demanding thereafter 'Name please Papa?'. Then, when he had repeated the name, as it were, paying it into his memory bank it remained there forever, he would further demand, 'Year please Papa', never forgetting either.

When he shouted, shooting like a comet from calm to fury, 'Why should I learn to read?' at his 'Bemmer', the Dowager, she gave him back, 'Because my love, books are our windows over the world and the knowledge contained therein is a very precious treasure. All man's knowledge down the ages can be found stored between the pages of great books.' She went on, 'You have the gift from God of a very good memory, therefore remember two names and when you are older and have prepared yourself come back to me and I will give you their writings.'

'Names?' Rupert said briefly.

'Matthew Paris and William Shakespeare. Remember them my fine fellow and understand that you must learn to read or the precious doors of wisdom will remain closed to you.'

He nodded. 'Useful,' he agreed and commenced the struggle. Then came the questions, 'But why Mama? ... Bemmer? ... Papa? ...' gaining answers which appeared to satisfy him until his luckless great aunt Primrose gave him the deadly one by saying, 'You will understand when you are grown up dear, but that is not a question a little boy should ask.'

Christine shivered again as she remembered the ensuing scene. 'Not an answer!' he spluttered, crimsoning with fury on the instant. 'Not an answer!' he shrieked again hammering at Primrose with clenched fists.

Then he silenced, looked around him, seized a small Ming teapot and flung it into the chimney piece. Shards flew in all directions. Flowers and water spilled and as the startled Primrose flung out a restraining hand Rupert's paw closed upon a jade paper weight. 'Hate you!' he screamed, and flung with unerring aim at her face. Primrose's face poured blood. Dr Jamieson was summoned to stitch the ugly gash. 'That boy needs purging,' he said grimly as he worked. 'He even came from his mother's womb in a towering rage, I suggest he requires very careful watching.'

'But how?' Christine wondered, 'and what in the world will happen to him when he goes to school!'

Gyles whipped him when Rupert threw his mug of scalding milk into Nanny Rose's face. The punishment administered, Rupert slid from his father's knee, enquired, 'Finished?' and stalked off with swaggering indifference.

He climbed, too, shinning up Scottish pines like a monkey, then hanging and jeering from the topmost boughs at his shouting older brothers who stood exhorting him to come down.

'Come and get me – if you can,' was all the encouragement they received.

On one awful occasion when Richard refused to take him into the bear pit Rupert just said, 'Right, see if I care,' and marched off to draw all the bolts of the monkey cage. As the curious, slightly timorous little animals peeked round the opened door and began swinging down Rupert pelted them with gouts of cement scooped from a nearby mixer. One landed smack across a small white face, blinding the creature. As if this were not enough and in a final burst of fury Rupert gave the demented little animal a flying kick up his behind. He had to be destroyed.

'Worst of all,' mused his mother on her window seat, 'Plum will have none of him and of all my little son's list of crimes at five years old this is what I fear most.'

Ridiculous as it might seem to anyone outside the family, bandy-legged Plumstead, head coachman extraordinary, had become their Oracle. Such phrases as, 'Well if Plum says so...', or 'If Plum approves...' were used to dismiss any doubts concerning anyone on whom the old man could be persuaded to comment. Thus 'Her's orlright' as his pronouncement on Sue-Ellen confirmed unanimous Lorme opinion. His, 'He'll do', served to assure them of the manifold virtues of Stephanie's Harry. When he un-burdened himself concerning Piers Fournes after the young convalescent was found collapsed in the home park by Gyles and old Charles, Plum confided to Pearson, 'I'm not as you might say took wiv' 'im some'ow. I know 'ee's a great faverit wiv' 'er old Leddyship but still I'm nowise comfortable alonger 'im,' he told her, scratching his old poll in token of his unease. Pearson, as usual, bided her time and then repeated Plum's words during one of her confidential hair-brushing sessions with Christine. In due course Christine told Gyles. He commented, 'Shrewd feller, Plum. I'm like a weathercock m'yself over young Fournes; sometimes deuced uneasy and at other times reproachin' m'yself for bein' like a carpin' hen.'

Of late, Plum had his eyes on Anne. Again it was Pearson who reported to her mistress his, 'Her'm all wilty with love and mooning. Took bad if you arst me. I'll lay as it's young Mr Charles too wot's got no eyes for anyone but little Mrs Stephen!'

Christine felt sure that if Plum was so sure, then her daughter was in love with Charles Danement's only son whom she needed no one, not even Plum, to tell her was hopelessly in Sue-Ellen's thrall.

She had already seen Anne from her thinking seat as she wandered rather aimlessly towards the box garden where she stood looking down at what her Great Aunt Marguerite had insisted were *reticulatas* and not early dwarf iris saying,

'Gentlewomen my dear never use English names in horticulture.'

Anne stared at a beetle struggling up a stem. 'Just about as fruitless,' she told herself, 'as me trying to attract young Charles who simply doesn't see me but only watches Sue-Ellen like a hungry puppy and it's worse since Nin came home.'

Of course, Ninian had only stayed a few days but anyone with half an eye could see that Sue-Ellen drew his attention.

'She's got them both,' thought Anne despairingly.

Her mother began thinking about Ninian too and how he had vanished the day after their return from Scotland, only to reappear a couple of weeks later, to announce, 'I thought I would look round for a small place of m'y own where I can base, 'tanyrate durin' the huntin' season.'

Gyles failed to conceal his total astonishment so Ninian added, 'I've changed m'y mind sir. Thought I might give civvie street a go after all.'

A fleeting smile lightened this remembrance, for like a flash the Dowager enquired tartly, 'And what pray is "civvie street" might I be enlightened? Kindly show some respect for the language of our adoption, Ninian.'

Even so Christine was puzzled, as was Gyles. Neither of course entertained any thought of asking their second son what had changed him so abruptly from a determined absentee wedded to his regiment, into a civilian enigma. Christine secretly sought the cause, not daring to enquire, so merely remained bewildered if very thankful. Had she realised it, it would have helped little to enquire of Ninian as to his motive for he did not know himself. Then her thoughts turned to Andrew, 'my uncomplicated son' as she called him. He warmed her with a sudden glow of contentment. He too was back from the dreadful war, unharmed and settled into Castle life, thoroughly content to work with Aynthorp Enterprises, to ride, shoot, fish, race up to London in his snarling little motor for a dance or regimental dinner. He also left no room for doubt in any of their minds that in due course he would propose to Victoria whom they had already decided would fit in perfectly and become another member of the Family without a single drama. Christine made a mental note to see if Plum could be drawn on this subject for if he too thought the scandalous old duke of Barton and Sale's delightful niece were 'up to the mark' that would be the absolute end to conjecture concerning her suitability. At least she had no doubts as to Plum's opinion of Victoria's uncle having heard him telling a stable boy, 'Seat like a sack er taties but allus up at the kill! 'Ee cusses somethink 'orrible but minds 'is lands and beasteses, looks to 'is tenants and all in all 'ee's a proper squire wot anyone can respec', cussin' or no cussin'.'

Christine had always indulged in these periodic thinking sessions, finding in them a means whereby she could determine what she must do thereafter. As usual, Gilbert Delahaye the inconspicuous one had slipped through her net of speculation. She progressed until she found herself hovering once more upon the brink of vexatious territory. While Gilbert's father and mother at last had come to represent no further anxieties, as a result, she acknowledged, of the arrival, behaviour and gentleness of Sue-Ellen, the same could not be said of poor Eustace Bartonbury. Christine had developed a tremendous personal admiration for him since his war-time metamorphosis; but still she was moved to great sympathy towards him not only because of his wife, but also his two problem children, Lucy and Lucien, whom he had handled with such tolerance and compassion. Now, despite all this, not only was Gabrielle heading for what she, Christine, saw as sheer disaster; but 'those two' were always about something which set the tongues wagging, the press reporting and the gossips extending and embroidering.

Christine sighed. She and indeed all the family thought that the deliberate string-pulling in which Gabrielle had indulged immediately after the Armistice had been in order that she might reunite with Eustace and they had been immensely relieved. Instead of which, once safely installed in Paris, as gradually became known to them all, Gabrielle had flung herself into a set of frivolous, extravagant, pleasure-seeking friends and French relations and swiftly become one of the most gossiped about 'fashionable', 'daring' figures in post-war Parisian society; always being featured in the French glossy magazines, photographed, commented upon for her daring adoption of extreme fashion; as she darted about, her hair cut extremely short, her skirts cropped alarmingly, invariably smoking cigarettes through over-long jade or amber holders all in such company as was clearly calculated to displease and alienate her anglicised relations. Eustace remained silent. They did hear that Gabrielle had paid a flying visit to Eustace's Yorkshire estates where the still convalescing Ralph and her were engaged in 'pulling things round again as best they could' a general exercise for their kind.

No one had even an inkling of just how near disaster lay. Still on St John territory, Christine was forced to acknowledge to herself that all seemed well with Lucy and Lucien at the moment. She also thought it providential that Piers had accepted that invitation to India and would be out of the way for at least six months. She who had for so many years fought to keep brother and sister apart, had now come round to believing that it was best for them to be together without any third appendage – whether his intentions ... here she baulked and let her mind skip on to dwell in gratitude and admiration upon the rock of strength which was Miss Poole. Miss Poole seemed to be holding the two in double harness by her beneficial influence. This was also true of an entirely different person, the quiet, scarred Elizabeth who had begun her association with Lucy as her chauffeuse and was now installed, with Mr Sissingham, Lucien's erstwhile tutor, in a joint office in Halcombe Street where they ran the business side of *Lucy et Lucien* under Miss Poole's supervision.

Christine admitted to herself that 'that pair's' names were constantly appearing in print, either at a ball, or presenting a charity display of their undeniably lovely clothes; or attending a first night; or 'seen at Brooklands ... Ascot ... Goodwood ... Hurlingham ...'.

They were very gay, she decided tolerantly, very clever and very much in demand. With all the work they did, it should do well enough; but still her mind nagged, not reassured sufficiently to dispel the constant sense of unease which beset her when ever she thought of them.

At this point Christine resolved to ask Gyles if they could visit one of the night clubs they visited so frequently. Then she could see for herself what were the 'goings on' therein. She had already gone so far as to ask Piers, just before he left. He had hesitated and then had replied, rather vaguely, 'Oh just a sort of a Nautch.' When she had asked him to explain what in the world he meant he had shrugged his shoulders and said, 'Just a sort of illicit union in the half-dark between a bottle and a saxophone,' which had not assuaged her qualms at all.

Petula and Henry often rushed away after dinner with a vague explanation, 'Just goin' on the town for a spot of bright lights, fun, see you at breakfast.' Then they would vanish in a snarl of noisy engine and a stench of exhaust fumes. Sometimes she woke to hear the returning growl of the Bugatti as dawn was sliding through the curtains. Frequently, Andrew and Victoria would crowd in with them and sometimes young Charles would persuade Sue-Ellen, who would then slide down onto the base of her spine in Charles' uncomfortable small motor and home returning would bring down to breakfast some huge and fluffy animal which Andrew said he had 'won' for her at Skee-Ball or Tombola. Once she heard them speaking of something they called 'a raid' after which it was made known to her by Pine that 'Mr Henry has a great rent in the seat of his new dress trousers.' It was all very confusing. And now Petula had 'won' a Felix over which Justin and Chantal fought in the nursery. These young were really quite extraordinary!

She tackled Gyles who smiled reminiscently for he was blessed with the ability to remember his own escapades in dealing with his brood of sons.

'Order some more trousers,' he requested. 'But please see Pine sends those up so that they may be copied accurately and for pity's sake enquire first whether Henry wears one, two or three braid stripes on 'em now. I cannot keep abreast of these constant vacillations.'

On the next occasion when all six had absented themselves on a foray Gyles enquired of his eldest son during dinner. 'Did Pine ask you about the braid for your dress trousers?'

Henry had the grace to flush. 'Yessir.'

'How did you manage to tear 'em?' Gyles prepared to enjoy himself.

Henry exchanged glances across the table with Andrew and grinned a trifle ruefully. 'Er, Bag of Nails sir.'

'A whole bag?'

'Nno sir, that's the name of the, er, night club.'

'Ah.' Gyles cut a small wedge from the Stilton on his plate, broke a crust of bread, laid the cheese upon it and ate. The table waited. At length, 'Raided one supposes?'

'Yessir.'

'How did you get away?'

'Out into the yard and over the wall.'

'Were the gels with you?.

'Yessir.'

'Commendably agile! Costly on frocks though. Be careful there's a good chap. We don't want a scandal.'

By this time the Dowager was all agog. 'Please my dears,' the glint in her fine old eyes belied the mildness of her speech, 'what is Bag of Nails; I have always prided myself on being *au courant.*'

Henry choked. The three girls laughed openly. 'A nightclub *Belle-mère*. It's called The Bag of Nails. Now don't start pesterin' to go there. It just ain't suitable.'

Her pecker was now well and truly up. 'On what grounds may I enquire can you advance such a claim when you take your wife, your sister and Sue-Ellen too?'

'Yes,' Henry mumbled stretching out his long legs beneath the table in a vain attempt to jab her into silence.

'Then pray explain. I am all attention.'

'OmiGawd,' he muttered.

Petula came to his rescue. 'Darling,' she said to her wicked grandmother, 'it is very much for our age group, all in a stuffy room, with a great crush and very late at night. The band is noisy, the room dense with cigarette smoke and it's all illegal. It's just not suitable.'

'Pshaw,' snapped she. 'Give me a more sensible reason.'

Petula flushed. 'Would you like to read in one of the newspapers, Dowager Lady Aynthorp of Castle Rising, one of Britain's most famous stately homes, taken in Black Maria to Bow Street after last night's raid on the Bag of Nails.'

'Yes,' said she defiantly. 'It sounds a great deal of fun and that is what I feel myself lacking at the moment. So does *Tante* Marguerite.'

'Indeed I do,' said the little Countess warmly, 'it sounds most excitin', though,' she paused, head tipped like a bird, 'I doubt my capacity to scale walls, however, doubtless the boys would give me a leg up.'

Gyles intervened. 'Tell me Mama,' he asked turning a baleful eye upon his redoubtable parent, 'would you be prepared to go unattended? For I assure you I would not take you.'

Christine bit her lip vexatiously. 'That's put the fox

among the hens,' she murmured to Primrose softly, 'why *will* Gyles provoke her?'

The Dowager retorted, eyes now glinting ominously, 'I am confident that if you decide to be so unchivalrous I can prevail upon my grandsons to escort me, dear Gyles, so pray do not contemplate incommoding yourself.'

Henry turned to his father. 'You know, sir, all the best people go an' we'd look after 'em if they're dead set on it. It might be rather a lark.'

Which settled how the Dowager and the little Countess were presently escorted by a posse of young men who followed them as they made a head-turning progress towards their reserved table at the Bag of Nails, both wearing Lucien et Lucy gowns and some quite startlingly beautiful jewellery. They had already been entertained by the two dress designers at Ciro's beforehand; but it did not come about without what Henry described as 'a bang up family blow up'.

On the morning after the escapade, when the two elderly delinquents were said to be taking their breakfast in bed, Gyles ripped open an envelope containing a letter from Eustace Bartonbury. It ran,

My dear Gyles, it is with the greatest regret that I write to tell you that I have agreed to give Gabrielle grounds for divorce. As it is quite unthinkable that I should be a contributory cause to any further distress to the family, I have agreed to supply her with the necessary evidence. All will be done as quietly as possible, which will, I fear, still not be quiet enough for any of our tastes. Gabrielle and I have, as you know, been drifting apart for some years.

Matters have come to a head now because she wishes to marry someone else. She also intends to live in France, in fact she returned to Paris this morning.

I have already conferred with old Truslove. He has undertaken to put me in touch with what he describes as 'a specialist in such matters but otherwise a man of the utmost probity' which might serve to make you smile. Our dear old Pelican is looking very frail and means to retire shortly as doubtless you know already. I will, if you concur, as I am sure you will, keep well clear of you all until this is over. I have told the children who have been most kind and understanding.

Gyles skimmed through the ending, then looked up. The young had left the table, the older members of the family were alone, the servants had withdrawn. He sighed, then he told them, and immediately afterwards left the room, strode to his office with Diana following, sat down and wrote out a telegram. 'Message received and understood. Insist you return here as usual. See Proverbs 21 Verse 19. Aynthorp.'

It gave nothing to the village postwoman who rushed for her Bible and therein read, 'It is better to dwell in the wilderness than with a contentious and angry woman.'

In Halcombe Street, when Piers tossed the casual words back over his shoulder as he followed the maharanee and her spouse to the lift, 'I'll be round again in the morning,' he knew that nothing was farther from the truth.

In the brief interlude provided by the two 'charmin' Indians' Piers had made a decision, though he knew perfectly well that a more honest definition would be a postponement.

He was, as any Lorme would have recognised, 'in all his states', surging with excitement over the forthcoming trip to India and on the other tortured by his own surrender to what had been a kind of painful ecstasy. He was now sure that only one course was open to him; to get right away from this deadly pair and to try and think things through. As for the Indians, they merely represented the means and the opportunity so to do.

He was tempted to regard their invitation as the hand of fate; had he not always considered such to be sheer clap-trap nonsense. Instead he forced himself away from the undistinguished realms of superstition to an acceptance of what he saw as fact – that man made his own destiny.

The following morning he telephoned to Halcombe Street. He was careful not to ask for Lucien but spoke instead to Elizabeth. He explained that his mother was far from well and that he was compelled to visit her immediately. Thereafter he used the telephone to convey specious excuses while he prepared for the trip. In the end he left without seeing either of them again.

Lucien alternately stormed and sulked. This made the women's tasks extremely trying.

There then followed a transitional period in which Lucien

changed to the 'see if I care' attitude which proved an even greater strain upon poor Sissy as well as Miss Payne, Elizabeth and Lucy.

On board ship, Piers wrote Lucien innumerable letters which he then tore up until at length he hit upon the only obvious explanation for his seemingly extraordinary behaviour. He posted this in Port Said where the ship put in for coaling. In it he 'confessed' that he had been rather ill himself but preferred not to worry his two darlings with such trivia. He sent his love, assured them he was feeling better already and filled pages with descriptions of the trip and his patrons, whom he genuinely liked. He added promises of exciting 'loot' which he would bring home with him and feeling this was the best he could achieve tried to put it out of his mind. This was a sleeveless errand.

He was to have many long weary days ahead in which he would be forced to face the truth – that he might just as well not have run away for all the good it did – for as it turned out he did not leave his cough in India. He saw much which delighted him, lived splendidly, was magnificently entertained and was also provided with superb quarters and a group of servants to wait upon him. To crown all he was given an excellent studio in which to work. It overlooked an English rose garden which, at whatever daylight hour he looked out, it was invariably spattered with gardeners crouching on their hunkers, their bare, brown feet gripping the soil and their black heads bared to the sun. His suite and studio were sited in the oldest part of the huge palace high above the red stone tracery of a great courtyard. Adjacent to it was the maharajah's own private viewing balcony from which his ancestors had once looked down upon games of human chess which they played between visiting rulers and themselves. They used the ladies of their two harems as the pawns, knights, kings and bishops. These 'pieces' were set upon squares marked out when the courtyard was laid during the beginning of the great Moghul Empire. When these games were played thereon the winner merely took all, thereby doubling his harem.

In explaining all this to Piers in the voice of one who had learned his English at Harrow and Oxford the maharajah was quick to stress that he had elected to take only one wife, as his father had done before him. When the tale was done he concluded, 'Alas I am no Shah Jehan, though I wish I could outdo him in another respect by raising a tomb to my wife which would achieve the impossible by being even more beautiful than the Taj Mahal.'

All this was very much to Piers' taste, as was also the big game shooting at which he acquitted himself very favourably. He raised shouts of approval from mahouts, beaters, bearers and guests alike when he bagged his first tiger and was duly photographed with one foot on the dead beast and his host standing beside him.

Before he left, with the paintings completed, and a huge cheque brought to him in an ivory casket which also contained a fire opal for Lucy, his host drove him through endless villages towards Agra. By the red dust roadside, bullock stood hock-deep in weed-encrusted water pools on whose red-gold sand banks women in brilliantly coloured saris washed clothes by beating them against the boulders, while egrets and cranes picked in the shallows.

The fleet of white Daimlers led by the maharajah's white Rolls Royce sped past cane fields, past fakirs with their begging bowls and past swaying women with great brass pots balanced effortlessly upon their heads; and on again through more villages where pigs and goats clustered about the entrance to ragged shelters in whose apertures old crones squatted, tending tiny fires; and all the while, high in the dazzling blue above them the vultures curved and wheeled.

Then for a very long while Piers stood among the plumed cypresses which stood sentinel against the water-course leading to the dream in marble which towered above him – the incomparable Taj. Piers climbed the steps to stand enraptured in turn before each of the four sides. He gazed up at the onion skin domes. He ran his hands over the carved lotus flowers, feeling dazed by the symmetry of those four exactly matching sides which soared above him.

That night, after dinner, they went *en suite* in the cars to see the Taj by moonlight. Then the mists from the Jumna river rose like ectoplasm from the valley below, swirling about the Taj's base so that it seemed to float. The words drifted through Piers' mind as he stood . . . 'clothed in white samite . . . mystic . . . wonderful' but he could find no words of his own with which to describe it afterwards.

When at length in the April of 1921, he left his hosts they delivered him to some cousins of his with whom he then spent a few days playing tennis, polo and dancing with the daughters of the 'fishing fleet'. Finally his uncle and aunt despatched him in the care of his cousin David to Bombay where the pair stayed at the pride of India – the Taj Mahal hotel – where Piers lay under a recently installed, giant white fan, linked his hands behind his head *and thought about Lucien.*

The following morning a little fat Parsee was ushered in, accompanied by what at first appeared to be a pair of small brown feet, for the rest was obscured by an enormous bundle. The bundle was then lowered so that the feet became revealed as a small very bony boy who, with his master had been summoned to show the young men some saris.

Sitting cross-legged on the bed Piers watched as the boy spread the Parsee's wares over the chairs, the tables, even over the bed. Thus David found him.

'Here's glorious loot!' Piers greeted him. 'This stuff is fantastic. Lucy will be in transports and as for Lucien...' He shook out a tiny bundle which fell into clouds of white chiffon studded with tiny emeralds.

'Or if the sahib prefers,' intoned the fat little man, flinging out another studded with ruby stones ... and a third with sapphires.

'No, not rubies,' Piers drew the sapphire studded one aside and flung the emerald one on top. 'These two, now what about embroidered ones?'

The Parsee paused, drew from his person a florid card. 'Mr Baharaiwalla.' He bowed as best he could over his belly, proffering the card murmuring, 'At your service sahibs,' then turning he snapped at the boy in Hindustani, who rushed to the pile and began turning the room into a lesser Sargasso Sea of dazzling draperies.

This went on for more than an hour while the two sahibs sipped limes and sodas and Piers bought lavishly. Eventually Mr Baharaiwalla was in such an ecstasy of unctuous palm-rubbing gratitude that both young men were reduced to helpless laughter.

At length Piers handed over what seemed to him an absurd sum for such a haul while the boy scuttled about like a scorpion re-folding the rejects and once more vanishing behind the completed bale until he was only feet again.

They bowed themselves out with ludicrous elation and the door closed.

'Rum beggars ain't they?' said David. 'What now? How about luncheon at the Sporting Club? There is no need to go aboard before eight tonight. We've got time to see a bit of polo too.'

'Oh no, we haven't,' said Piers suddenly galvanised to action. 'I have to find the finest white opal in the world for a very pretty lady and I want a complete maharajah's outfit for her brother who is curly haired and very slim. Y'know the sort of thing, tight satin pants gripping the ankles, gold embroidered slippers, a bejewelled tunic and a turban with an aigrette and a jewel to hold it ... actually I've got that already.'

They travelled by rickshaw. Piers removed his topee a couple of times to mop the sweat from his forehead. He also flung annas at the hordes of beggars who pursued them, despite David's disapproval, as they were threaded through a morass of bullock, camels, scuttling women, aimless goats and mangy dogs with always this press of maimed and scabby or crippled beggar-children.

'They're a bloody nuisance,' David complained, 'the only thing to do is ignore them.' Piers could not, however.

When at last he boarded the ship which was to take him back to England he did so a trifle unsteadily after their belated visit to the Sporting Club. They were followed up the gangway by a string of porters carrying Piers' luggage and what he called his 'princely loot', which included the skins of the two tigers he had shot, a case of peacock fans, another of ancient Indian weapons and Lucien's maharajah outfit for the next Chelsea Arts Ball.

In the days which followed Piers lay stretched out in a rattan chair on deck, well shaded. All he thought about was Lucien. When he slept he dreamed about him and once he had a nightmare in which a curtain of blood came down between Lucien and himself through which he fought and struggled until he awoke, soaked with sweat and trembling.

When they docked he went by two cabs, one filled with the 'loot', directly to Halcombe Street, arriving at a little after seven o'clock in the evening. He found both the salon and the workroom were closed and empty, though he suspected the cleaning women would still be there, so directed his cabby round to the back entrance in the mews. Here he leaped out and tried the door himself. It was still open so, shouting back to the cabbies to 'Hang on a moment', he dashed to the lifts just as the private one was coming down. The door slid back, Lucien stepped out and halted in his tracks. 'Oh Piers,' he said.

Piers tried to say something but found he couldn't speak. 'Oh Piers,' said Lucien again, and this time he flung himself against Piers uncaringly.

'Excuse me young gents,' wheezed a voice behind them, 'do we bring the luggage in 'ere?'

They sprang apart. 'No, yes, well?' Piers stared questioningly at Lucien. The cabby, intent on his burdens, saw nothing amiss.

'Lucy's gone out to dinner,' Lucien stammered, 'I was just going up to dress ... I'm supposed to join her but I shan't go now. There's no one here but me – actually.'

Piers' head was hammering now. He began to cough. 'Leave everything here,' he managed to the cabby, 'we'll have 'em collected later. I don't live here you see, I'm just off a ship.'

Lucien seemed to rally. 'You stay *here* tonight,' he said rather shrilly, 'don't you Piers?'

Piers coughed again, leaned against the side of the lift and just nodded. 'Just leave the bags then cabby,' said Lucien. 'Is this the lot – yes, well then thank you very much' – he extended money, the cabby touched his cap and hurried to share Lucien's bounty with his mate.

Once the two were in the lift, Piers said rather shakily, 'But this doesn't mean ...' he met Lucien's excited eyes, turned his head away and said as the lift came to a standstill, 'I haven't spent all these months away, trying to forget you just to –' he stepped out and completed his sentence, 'just to wreck my resolutions the moment I come back. Given a bit of luck they'll hold until I get away again.'

'Oh pooh,' said Lucien childishly, 'let's split a bottle of fizz and then you can tell me all about the trip. Go on into the parlour while I raid the refrigerator, we've changed the curtains and I want your opinion.'

He pushed Piers gently inside and ran off to the kitchen. Piers just stood looking around him with intense pleasure, noting the changes and additions, approving the curtains, the Marie Laurencin, the marble and gilt pedestal with a lavish arrangement of all-white flowers. His mind clicked, 'Syrie Maugham one supposes, like the new curtains.' Then Lucien was back carrying an ice bucket. 'Look,' he said it out proudly, 'isn't that better? Lucy-Lou suggested it rather crossly because she insisted her second glass from a magnum was always too cold...'

Piers laughed, 'I know I've heard her. And the first glass is not cold enough because no ice bucket is made to immerse all but the actual neck of the bottle. Who produced this?'

Lucien was busying himself with the foil so his head was bent. 'Oh a rather gifted chap, you'll meet later on, he had it made for us. It's much better but I don't want you to say a word about it to Uncle Gyles. I have ordered some for him for his birthday.'

He held out a fizzing glass; then took it away again, pushed Piers into a deep chair, settled him with the glass beside him and took his own filled glass onto the hearthrug where he sank down cross-legged.

'You look offensively young,' Piers said staring.

'Oh never mind me! Tell me all about it and them and any thems I don't know about. Oh and what prezzies have you brought for me?'

'None,' said Piers, 'you've got too much already.' Then, seeing the crestfallen look this produced, he relented after a second glass of champagne, but he flatly refused to fetch the 'prezzies' and instead made an attempt at explanation. He began, 'I had plenty of time for thinking on the boat going out; all the time in fact when I wasn't actually painting.'

Lucien nodded, 'Piers what colour is my maharjah's outfit?'

Piers sighed. 'Please will you listen to me and what I am saying, it is vital to us both. Your outfit's white as a matter of fact, *now listen*. The first thing you must think about is our ages. I am nearly thirty-four.'

'So what's that got to do with anything? I'm nearly twenty-one!'

'It is not just a matter of age but of experience. I went away to try and clear my mind of remorse or self-reproach after what was tantamount to your seduction my beautiful young man. I tried to expiate some of my guilt by resolving to stay away from you forever...' he broke off in desperation. 'Lucien you do not understand a word of this do you?'

Lucien hung his head. 'Well, no,' he mumbled, 'I only know I was so very glad to see you and so excited inside me and, well that quivering thing began again and now you are trying to spoil it all with this silly talk. I simply don't see why we have to go on about all that but just do it all again and enjoy every moment.'

Piers lifted one thin hand to his prematurely white hair, '*You*,' he emphasised, 'have just not had time in your short life to know *what* you are! This is a phase which you might easily have gone through at school if you'd ever been to one. It need not be a fundamental thing. Can you at least grasp that? Thousands of boys have love affairs at school, sometimes with older boys, sometimes with the masters and then when they leave and the unnatural years of segregation are over they automatically gravitate to girls. Except as a rather shaming memory of what they once did at school it is then *over*.'

'Not with me,' Lucien's mouth was down. He spoke stubbornly.

'Not necessarily,' Piers strove to be patient, as with a child which clearly this one was still. 'You see *my* knowledge brings to me one great over-riding fear.'

'Bogeys,' snapped Lucien, 'silly bogeys.'

'Not bogeys, child, just plain, stark facts. I have had time to know what I am. I have even come through the stage of doubting not only to certainty but alas to the acceptance but you are so much younger, and sexually such an infant you haven't begun to know *anything* yet.'

'Who says not?'

'I do. Oh I suppose you have been fondled by a few youngsters while I've been away. That means nothing except that presently if I am right you will be very sexual indeed my darling Lucien.'

'Oh hell!' Lucien scuffed the rug with his heels, 'I just do not want to listen to any of this stuff. I don't know what's come over you. You sound so prosy and if you are trying to tell me I might like going to bed with soft, squidgy girls you must be off your head so there!'

'I am trying to tell you,' Piers felt himself struggling more and more ineffectually, 'that this is what has made me so remorseful. That I *may* have destroyed in you the capacity for what the world calls "normal relationships" just as Diaghileff destroyed Nijinsky.'

Lucien frowned. 'That fat man who is afraid of daylight and even travels by night and that divine ballet dancer?'

Piers nodded. 'That fat man seduced Nijinsky. Oh,

admittedly he was younger than you at the time; but that is not the vital thing. What bays me is that in Nijinsky's case he *did* experience an inner desire for a heterosexual relationship. Indeed he went off and married in order to escape from Diaghileff; but he found it was too late, he could not *because of what had gone before*. Do you know where Nijinsky is now?'

'I don't, and I know that I don't care. It all sounds rather horrid. Besides I can't see what these people have to do with us.'

'Then I will tell you.' Piers controlled himself with an effort. 'Nijinsky was a very gifted little boy...'

'Like me?' Lucien flicked his eyelashes, sounding rather pleased.

'Yes. Just like you only his gift was for the ballet. He was a pupil in the Imperial Russian Ballet – before the revolution. Diaghileff found him there when he was a man very old in experience and especially homosexual experience. He seduced him as I have already said.'

'Like me?' again Lucien asked the same question.

'As I seduced you,' Piers agreed grimly. 'Later Nijinsky went off and got married; but the pull was too strong and in the end he went back to Diaghileff and it was *all* too much for him. He went mad. Stark, raving mad. Do you know where he is now?'

'Oh hell,' exclaimed Lucien, thoroughly bored and irritated, 'no I don't and I can't see that it matters.'

Piers thrust on, ignoring him. 'He is in a lunatic asylum in Switzerland where he spends his time drawing huge spiders. All of them have Diaghileff's face.'

'Why spiders?' Lucien stared, 'and what a perfectly beastly story.'

'Oh forget it,' Piers said wearily, 'you know I might just as well be talking Urdu. Tell me just one thing. Have you ever slept with a girl?'

'You know I haven't' – indignantly – 'what a question, from you!'

'It's a perfectly normal question to a young man of nearly twenty-one. Your cousin Stephen seduced one when he was fourteen *and* she had a baby!'

Lucien started up. 'I think you've gone mad. Are you suggesting I should try to start a baby with some beastly girl?'

'In a sense yes,' Piers' voice was harsh, 'at least no, not a baby, but just that you find out by having sexual relations with a girl before ... well before you do anything else,' he finished lamely.

'But I don't want to.'

'How do you know if you haven't tried?'

'I don't get erections from girls but I do from boys,' Lucien said sounding very cross. 'Piers we have drunk all the champagne, shall I open another bottle? Are we going to sit here all night talking about you not wanting to make love to me any more because I suppose you've fallen for some stinking black Indian princeling.'

'Christ! Is that what you think?'

'Well, nnno, bbut oh do shut up and let's go out to dinner and have fun as we always do together. Don't let's go on spoiling everything with nasty bug-a-boo stories, I shan't go bats I promise you.' He rattled on while Piers stared at him. 'I've had another perfectly splendid season and London simply adores me and my clothes ... and I've found a rather brilliant young man to help me,' he giggled. 'I suppose I had better keep him away from you though ...'

Piers just shook his head as if someone had struck him. Then he flung out his hands in a gesture of defeat. All the time Lucien watched him under those absurd eyelashes.

'Dinner together?' he wheedled.

Piers gave up. 'Dinner together,' he repeated obediently.

'The Ritz?'

'Caviar?'

'Yes, all the things you like best you disgusting little pig. Then I'll damn well add to your education by taking you on to meet Rosa. We might as well begin with her.' His eyes were incredulous as he stared at the boy on the rug. 'Not one single fraction of what I have tried to make you understand has even penetrated. I don't know whether you are just being mulish as you used to do when you put on your little acts for the Dowager, or whether you are just plain daft already; but how can you be to have got where you are already?'

Lucien's eyes were fixed on him. 'I wouldn't be where I was now if it wasn't for Lucy,' he said simply. 'Surely you know all that. Lucy irons out all the crumples for me ... in everything. She always will.'

Piers shrugged. 'Am I to suppose,' he enquired drily,

'that the role in life you have selected for me is to put the crumples in?'

In lieu of reply Lucien giggled. 'Ritz,' he urged, 'come on, you can always go on talking and I'm so hungry...'

They came out into Duke's Street just before midnight. Piers had been coughing dreadfully in the Cavendish until at length Rosa, hands on hips, stood eyeing him severely. She bent and plucked the half-smoked cigarette from his fingers. 'Better push off 'ome young feller me lad,' she ordered. 'No more smokes, at least not in 'ere; an' you better do summink about that cough pronto. You're too thin by half. If I was you I should go and see a doctor in the morning. I don't suppose all that racketting in India 'as done you no good, no more'n this room. It might do you good though to remember that bloody cigars took off the best man wot ever wore shoeleather and then to stop it before you go the same way you silly twit. Lucien, you walk 'im 'ome. It's only a step from 'ere. *No*, put that back in your pocket, you don't pay nothin here tonight. It's already on the Duke's bill. Now vamoose orf the pair of yer.'

They strolled into Piccadilly, crossed by the Berkeley and went slowly towards Grosvenor Square. An occasional sports car zizzed by. One ancient hansom came clippety clop alongside to disgorge a bewhiskered old man in tails, a white silk muffler and velvet collared overcoat who handed himself down like a parrot over the side of a cage.

Two tarts dripping with monkey fur stepped from a doorway, made their sad propositions; then were dealt with, drew back again cupping cigarettes in their palms like soldiers.

'What a bloody life,' Piers regretted.

'Very nasty,' Lucien shuddered.

They made their leisurely progress, Piers talking of his loot, the saris, Lucy's white opal, then as they turned into Halcombe Street Piers said, 'If we go in through the mews door I can collect my overnight case.'

'Why bother,' Lucien protested, 'I can lend you what you need though I fear my pyjamas will *hang* on you. Truly you are *terribly* thin. Ugh, it's chilly now.'

'Funny,' Piers said thoughtfully, 'I don't seem to feel the cold these days, I wonder why?'

They drifted in and up. They inspected the principal

guest room and found it already prepared, even the bed turned down. Lucien said, 'Hang on, I'll get you some things.' He ran off to collect them and Piers went to the windows. He drew back the curtains and stood looking out over the silent street. Then Lucien came back saying, 'Lucy-Lou's door is open, she's still out. I'm just going to have a bath.'

Half an hour later Piers came out into the corridor in Lucien's pyjamas and dressing gown. He passed Lucy's opened door, paused, went in to gentle Mr Silk who greeted him with great enthusiasm. Then he went out again, opened Lucien's door, went in and closed it quietly behind him.

CHAPTER 13

'Toujours à Trois'

Muffled by distance from the huge four poster where Constance slept with her Charles, the sound of knocking just penetrated; but she was too deep away to do more than move her head restlessly on the big, square pillows. This disarranged her long, fair hair which Charles had spread out so tenderly before he slept.

The knocking continued, drawing her back through the long corridors of sleep. Charles Danement grunted, 'Who the deuce...?' Then he sat up, calling out irritably, 'Come in, whoever you are.'

His butler, in a dressing gown, displayed himself nervously, his hair sadly reminiscent of forked lightning. 'Begging your pardon sir, my lady, but Lady Lucy St John is on the telephone. She says to please hurry for it is very, very urgent.'

Charles swung his legs over the side throwing back the bedclothes. 'It's her ladyship sir, as Lady Lucy wants, she asked particularly,' the man's voice was uncertain, troubled.

Constance was fully awake now, swinging back her hair, reaching for a ribbon with which to tie it. 'Tell Lady Lucy I'm on my way. Make sure she is telephoning from the mews or ask for whatever other number she is speaking from in case we are cut off ... hurry please Jennings, I will be with you immediately.'

Charles helped her into her wrapper, warning, 'Slippers now, no running down these draughty corridors in bare feet! I expect it is only a storm in a teacup.' But his rider, 'Anyway I am coming with you,' was delivered to the empty room. Constance was away, flying down the corridor, heading for the old, wide, staircase up which an excelling runt, Rupert de Lorme had once ridden 'Star Lady', his famous mare, as he had also done at Castle Riding.

The hall below had the disturbed atmosphere common to rooms whose night-time privacy is invaded. Constance took the receiver from the butler's hand with a hasty, 'That will be all Jennings thank you,' and into the mouthpiece, standing on tip-toe as usual she said, 'Lucy darling it is I, Constance. I'm so sorry to have been such a long time. What is it child?'

Lucy's voice came in little gasps which even in transmission suggested she had passed beyond terror into some dreadful abyss. It was indescribably chilling.

'Do you know about haemorrhages?'

'Of course I do, but what kind of haemorrhage? Try to tell me more.'

'Mouth ... bright red and rather bubbly, each time enough to fill a teacup ... what do I do until you get here? Constance it must be you and absolutely no one else, you will understand when you know.'

'Lucy, wait ... you must tell me whom. Is it you?'

The sound which followed was half way between a choke and a rasping laugh. 'No, but before I tell you will you swear not to tell anyone else?'

'Only Uncle Charles, child. He will drive me and if you wish it he can wait outside in the car when we get there.'

'Then ... it is Piers.'

She connected instantly, remembering the cough, his case history when he was in the Convalescent Home. All she said was, 'I see,' while her mind demanded, 'Is it a wild party? Or what does Piers in the middle of the night in their house?' Then, to Lucy, 'Before I explain what you must do will you please get rid of everyone immediately.'

Lucy's now wooden voice answered, 'There is no one here ... except Lucien. Miss Poole and the rest are sleeping on the top floor *and they must not be awakened.*' Hysteria sounded very near. 'Constance listen to me. This is vital. Will Piers die if I move him from one room to another. If Lucien and I carry him?'

'No he will not; but prepare the bed to which he goes. Lay him fairly flat with just one pillow and turn his head to one side. Making him understand he must keep it so, to stop more blood getting into his lungs. Have *you* understood that?'

Lucy repeated her instructions. Constance thought she could be speaking to a zombie.

'Right,' she tried to sound brisk and calm but her mind was racing. 'Have you any ice in the house?'

'Did you say ice?'

'Yes.'

'We have ice.'

'Then fill a large flannel bag with it, a thick one, and place it on his chest. Keep it there until I come. Pack each side of him with towels to catch the melting water, have another bucket of ice to hand for replenishing. No matter what Piers says or does, see that you do exactly as I say.'

Abruptly the voice dropped into childish loneliness, 'Constance will you be long?'

She glanced across at the old grandfather clock. 'It is now three fifteen,' she told the mouthpiece. 'Say fifteen minutes to dress and reach the motor and then at this hour we will drive as fast as we can. We could be with you by four thirty. Go and do what I have told you as quickly as possible. Then telephone the night line to where the porter sleeps in the Home. Tell him to awaken the male nurse Hansen. Have him telephone Paddington 001093, ask for a Mr Tonks, and tell him I say he is to proceed at once to you, and have him wait downstairs in the salon until I come.'

She wrapped a long scarf around her head, slid down under the car rugs and surrendered to useless speculation and conjecture. Questions sprouted like mushrooms. 'What had brought on this sudden haemorrhage? Was it some violent scene? Or had he been drinking and carousing with "that silly crowd of children" at some night club?' She dismissed such questions knowing that none could engender the fear or the absolutely terrifying ruthlessness she had detected in Lucy's voice. What then was there which could cause it? She thought back to the time when Piers had defected from the Home, when Gyles and Charles had searched for him in the darkness and sheeting rain. How they had found him at last collapsed in the Home Park and brought him back delirious. She thought too of those muttered revelations which had kept her protectively beside him through the night lest any other ears than hers heard what came through those dry and burning lips.

The car sped on, the engine running joyously as is the way with cars in darkness; but even so the distance seemed an endless one, as if she were experiencing one of those nightmare dream journeys in which like mirages destination is never reached, but always remains ahead.

Lucy had returned after her rather dull dinner party hoping to find her brother in the drawing room; but there was no one there. Only an upturned magnum of Dom Perignon in an ice bucket and two empty champagne glasses bearing testimony to the fact that Lucien had celebrated something in there with someone. She stood in the middle of the room, for some reason touched by uncertainty. Then Elizabeth came in quietly, 'I have put the car away Lady Lucy, is there anything I can do for you?'

'No thank you,' Lucy answered absently, 'go to bed Elizabeth.'

The woman hesitated. 'Should I not bring up the luggage from the staff corridors? I can do so easily, I did just wonder if someone coming in through the staff entrance might not switch on the light and so could stumble.'

'What luggage?'

Elizabeth smiled. 'I think, as the initials on the leather valises are "PF" they must belong to Mr Fournes. It will be nice to have him back won't it? We have all missed him.'

Lucy looked startled. 'But what are they doing in the staff corridor?'

'I should imagine that Mr Fournes' taxicab brought him through the mews. Then he had the luggage put there temporarily, Mr Lucien heard him and they both went off somewhere. I expect they will be in later.'

Lucy's face cleared. 'Oh, of course, how silly. That's what must have happened. Well I don't think we will wait up for them. If those two haven't seen each other for months they may not be in till all hours. They might even go back to Albany to Mr Fournes' chambers, Soles is there isn't he?'

'Oh yes. He called here yesterday so Mr Sissingham told me. He said Mr Fournes was on his way home.'

'Well, that's the solution then. If you could just go down again in the lift and switch that corridor light on, then there would be no danger of anyone tripping. The luggage can be returned in a taxicab or in Mr Fournes' car, in the morning. It would be silly to bring it all upstairs. I imagine there is quite a lot?'

Elizabeth smiled again. 'A small mountain,' she

confirmed. 'Well then, I will say goodnight, if you are sure there is nothing else?'

When she was alone again Lucy went to the little escritoire which was her special treasure. It was small, French and with elegantly carved legs. It had charmed her when, with Piers, she had been taken to see it. She could almost hear his voice now saying, 'Six different woods, look Lucy, this is basically bur walnut cross-banded in satin and box wood and' – folding the front down – 'look at this, the inside is fitted with bird's-eye maple, king wood, box wood, satin wood and tulip wood – come here and look at the back which, yes, I thought so, is rosewood.'

She opened it now, smiling to herself as she scribbled a note in her round, still rather childish hand. She propped it up on the mantelshelf so that her pair would see it when they came in. Then, gathering up bag, gloves, fan, she left the light burning and went through to her own rooms.

Her bed looked particularly lovely in the shaded lamp light with the silk sheets folded back. Sunk into the eiderdown, almost embedded in billows of white maribou Mr Silk leapt up, fan-tail weaving frantically as she came in. She sat down on the big bed and fondled him, telling him how they thought that Piers was back and eventually carrying him with her into her bathroom. He adored running round the sunken bath fussing over her, so far lacking the nerve to plop into the steaming, scented water; but even after her bath Lucy felt cold so she pulled a Florence Nightingale from between the lavender bagged layers of lingerie, snuggled into it, caught Mr Silk up again, climbed into bed and turned out the light.

She awoke very suddenly. Mr Silk was barking in a positive frenzy, off her bed and up against the door, scrabbling with both paws.

'Whatever is the matter sweetheart?' she asked sleepily. Then she heard it. A keening sound, shattering the quiet house, a demented sobbing sound of hysteria into which her name came repeated, 'Lucy-Lou, oh God, Lucy-Lou, help me...'

Barefoot, in only a gossamer nightdress through which her pubic hair made a shadow, she ran to wrench the door open. Across the corridor, through the open door of Lucien's room she stopped short, hand to throat, staring, blanching, beginning to tremble.

Lucien lay across Piers' body screaming, sobbing, both were spattered with blood which trickled from Piers' mouth as he lay. For one frozen instant of horror and terror Lucy thought Lucien had murdered him; but then his head moved slightly, one hand came up, caught at the corner of the bloodstained sheet and wiped the red foaming stuff away. It came again and as it did so, 'Stop it!' screamed Lucien, 'Stop it, stop it, stop it!' and ran, still screaming, from the room. Lucy hesitated for a second then went after him, into her bedroom, closed the door, remembering her war-time training, and slapped him hard, first one one pallid blood streaked cheek and then on the other.

He stared at her, halted at mid-scream, then flung himself face downwards onto the exquisite bed.

'Now you listen to me Lucien and you do not dare speak until I have done,' she ordered, her love for him dredging up authority somehow. 'You stand in peril, dreadful peril. It depends on me to save you. *Do you* understand? Nothing else matters now. I do not understand what you have done but I know *about* it and *it is criminal*. You can go to prison for what you and Piers have done.' The hunched shoulders jerked but he lay silent. 'Only you and I can save *you*. So I do not care what it costs you, or how you manage to find the strength but if *I can*, then you can for we are twin in everything but birth. You have told me often that you can always use your strength when it is needed so *use it now*. You and I are going into your room so get up now off my bed, immediately, there is no time to lose. We are going to carry Piers in here. Only then I will telephone to Lady Constance and ask for her to help me with him.'

This brought him bolt upright, terror writ large again on his tear-stained face.

'Lucy-Lou, you can't! No one must know.'

'No one will know, *if* Piers is found in my bed.'

'Oh no,' his hands went up to his face, 'Lucy you cannot.'

'There is no such word, now get up off ... that ... bed Lucien, we do not want Piers to bleed to death do we?'

He came reluctantly. She went from the room without even looking back for she knew fear would make him follow, as it did.

Piers lay where they had left him, but he had haemorrhaged again and pity made her run into the bathroom for a damp sponge to wipe his mouth and face clean.

As she did this she began talking quietly.

'Don't speak, save your strength and just listen. We are going to lift you into my bed.'

His eyes blazed with shock.

'That is the only way. Never fear Piers, I understand and I know enough not to let any living person find you here. I want you to wait while I telephone the one person I can trust. Will you promise me not to move in any way until I return?'

'Who?' his lips framed the word.

'Lady Constance Danement. I think she knows anyway.'

Again she caught his whispered, 'I have suspected it for some time.'

'Stop talking. You must understand though that whatever she says you have to be moved from here.'

The words she then spoke remained with him for the rest of his life. She bent over him to whisper in his ear, one little pointed breast almost brushing his shoulder through the flimsy nightdress,

'You must marry me Piers as soon as you are able. There is no other way to protect you both.'

Then she was gone, passing Lucien at the door.

'Sit beside him,' she ordered, 'and do not let him talk.' After which she went into the drawing room, lifted the receiver and asked for the Manor House number.

She returned to them carrying a bucket of fresh ice, a pair of scissors and a blanket.

Lucien sat slumped in the chair, helpless tears trickling down his stained cheeks. His hands seemed to have developed a life of their own, for they twitched, tangled and plaited unceasingly.

Lucy reported, 'Lady Constance is on her way. She will tell no one. Piers turn your head to one side, it will help you not to cough. Lucien take the other ends of this blanket, I have to cut a piece off to make a container for ice.' She sawed through the thick, fluffy fabric, tipped in the ice, folded it into a parcel and ordered,

'Now unfasten Piers' pyjama jacket, he must have this on his chest to help stop the bleeding.'

Clumsily, with shaking fingers Lucien obeyed. Lucy laid

the improvised pack in position, re-fastened the jacket, stripped back the dreadful bedclothes.

'Now Piers you must try *not* to help us. Just stay quite still, like that. No not your arms down, fold them across the pack to keep it in position. That's right. Now I am going to ease the pillow away from under your head.'

The struggle began. Lucien was strong enough, although unused to such labour and Lucy pantingly made it as far as the doorway and then gasped, 'I shall have to put him down, just for a moment.'

Her burden relinquished she stumbled to her own bed, pulled the clothes back, threw all but one pillow onto the carpet and whipped away the maribou and laces. Mr Silk, bewildered, bored, feeling neglected, promptly trotted over and curled up on the untidy heap. Back ran Lucy.

'Now,' she said, through clenched teeth, 'one big effort please Lucien.'

Somehow they managed it. Somehow they eased Piers onto the bed and then even before they could cover him Lucy shook her head defeated and clung to one wing, with her breath whistling.

All the time Piers fixed his eyes on her, those headlamps, dimmed now but still unaccountably brilliant. When she had regained her breath Lucien was lying on the floor collapsed and sobbing. She said harshly, 'Get up, go to the other side and let us cover him.'

'Can ... I have ... a drink ... of ... water?' Piers whispered.

'I don't know,' she told him distressfully. 'I forgot to ask. If I give you a piece of ice to suck will that do?'

His head moved fractionally in assent, so she gave him a piece, and taking his head in her hands she turned it again to one side.

'Like that Piers. Please, Lady Constance says. Are you in a comfortable position?'

He lifted one hand and stuck his thumb up in assent.

'Well then Lucien must go now and have a bath.' She glanced at the little bedside clock. 'It is just past four o'clock. He must be back in a quarter of an hour.' She turned to her brother. 'Take off those things, roll them into a bundle *and bring them back with you*. Then put on a clean pair of pyjamas and a dressing gown, remember I am supposed to have woken you when this happened. When Lady Constance comes you must try to say as little as possible. In the meantime I will hide all the sheets and pillow slips from your bed and re-make it. If I leave both doors open you can watch Piers in case he has another haemorrhage.'

She bent over him. 'Take the handle of this little bell, try now to see if you can shake it, but do it softly.'

The little bell tinkled. 'That's all right. Lucien will you go at once please, it is vital you are not seen in that state. Change and come back very clean and tidy.'

Lucien went draggingly away while she ran soft footed down the corridor to the linen room.

There was blood on the sheets, blood on the pillows, blood on the blankets. She dragged all off, carried the rough bundle into her bedroom and stuffed all but one blanket into a wall cupboard then she locked it. She made the bed, untidied it, made a single dent in the freshly covered pillows, then remembered hers and came back to make another dent with two fresh pillows on her side of her bed in which Piers lay. Then she laid the blood-stained blanket over him and tucked the top under the silk sheet. Finally she stood over him and said very quietly, 'Shut your eyes and keep them shut, I am going to do something beastly.'

Once more he obeyed her, though his thoughts were chaotic and her figure seemed strangely blurred.

She held the coagulating blood in the tumbler beside Lucien's bed for which Piers had groped in the first uprush of blood to his mouth. This she now splashed onto her bed pillows, her nightdress, and went through to her bedroom to wash the glass. 'Blood', she thought watching the flowing tap, 'takes a lot of getting rid of. I had never realised.' Only then did she catch up her foamy negligée and put it on over the shameful nightdress, making sure that this still showed. Finally she scraped her polished nails into an encrustation on a hidden sheet, unlocking and re-locking the cupboard to do so.

She stood in the centre of the room looking round her. She tried to think of everything. Then she returned to the bathroom soaked a hand towel under the cold tap, twisted out the surplus water and laid it on her throbbing forehead. All the time Piers watched her under his half-closed eyes.

Finally she came back to the little French chair beside her bed and sat down.

The devil then entered into Piers. By some ill-chance Lucy had turned his head so that the jade heart he had given her was immediately in front of him. Long ago, it seemed to him experiencing the sensation of almost floating as he lay rigid and still, fearful himself now of another haemorrhage, that long ago almost in another life he had fallen in love with beautiful little Lucy. Then he had met her younger brother and he had joined battle with himself. Had Lucy been compliant, he thought now, he might have saved himself by marrying her. But she soon showed him that she too was, in a totally different way, outside the herd as much as he was himself, creature of a half-world, a freak, not in love with her younger brother but loving him to the total exclusion of any other consideration. There was no room in Lucy's life for anyone else, and yet still she drew him, not of course as Lucien did, but with an immense attraction and, his dazed mind groped for the word and eventually finding it – *compatibility*.

This night had shown him just how completely ruthless she could be when she thought Lucien was in danger. Not for an instant, even in this bemused state did he imagine that any of this *frenzy* was for the danger of *his* being found out. It was all for Lucien. He wondered fleetingly how such a girl, brought up as she had been, sheltered, protected, kept from any carnal knowledge of any kind, could have found out what she must know to have acted as she had done. She had, of course, heard much and seen much in the short time she and Lucien had lived in London; but even so he remembered how in the sheer blind innocence which stems from ignorance, she had asked childishly, 'What's petting Piers?' So of whom had she asked, 'What's sodomy?' And what reply had she been given?

This led his drifting mind to Oscar, and then he had his answers. Someone must have told her enough to arouse her curiosity. Some light remark, made perhaps at a party, must have led her towards discovery. It was that which caused her now to compromise herself deliberately, to throw her reputation, without a thought, onto the dung heap and inform him that they would be married! She had worried it all out for herself. How Oscar had been married and to the outside world was safe enough while he shared his wife's home, sired a son. . . . She had drawn such conclusions as she could from what scant knowledge she had gleaned. Thus she

had become convinced that while they were married, Lucien
would be safe. Then did she, he speculated, condone
them – merely conspiring like this to make their way easy . . .
secure . . . or so she thought?

She sat so still now beside him. What were *her* thoughts?
And this in his mind crystallised into the one devilish
remark, whispered from the deliberately bloodied bed like a
silver galleon.

'Lucy,' he whispered, 'will you marry me?'

The words once uttered lay between them like a sword.
She lifted her head of curls all ruffled and disarrayed, she
showed her blue white face to him and she nodded.

'That is the only way to make . . . you and Lucien safe. Yes
Piers, I will marry you. I insist upon it, and when we are
married I will be the one wife from whom you will never get
away.'

'How?' the whisper came.

'I am working that out now,' she told him. 'We must put
an announcement in *The Times*, that will be best. That a
marriage has been arranged and will take place very quietly
between us, and then something about your being ill. We
have been seen together so much, no one will question a
hurried marriage, or a quiet one either after that and also if
you are said to be rather more ill than you are, you see that
don't you?'

He let the question pass, instead after a long pause the
whisper came, 'I . . . may . . . be . . . dying.'

She shook her head. 'I do not think so,' she stated. 'Nor, if
you are truthful, do you. So Piers I accept your proposal of
marriage knowing that there will be no conflict between us
about . . .' here he saw even she flinched and in a sudden
surge of pity he gave her the ironic word, 'Intimacy, my
dear?'

She bent her head in acknowledgement. As she did so she
caught the face of the clock in that downward glance and saw
that it was nearly half past four. Then Lucien walked into
the room, curls brushed into order, a blue silk scarf knotted
at his throat, a long white, spotted dark blue dressing gown
tied around his narrow waist.

'Very pretty,' whispered Piers.

Lucien looked as if he had had a very rough night.

'Listen darling to what I have to say,' said Lucy hurriedly,
'for I must go downstairs and wait to let Constance in. You

came in late from a party. You saw my door closed and no light showing so you decided not to disturb me to say good-night as usual. You just went to bed and the next thing you knew was *me* hammering at *your* door, calling to you to wake up ... you came in here and found Piers with me in my bed. Say nothing else, no matter what happens. Remember that everything depends on it.'

She caught up her chinchilla coat and thrust her feet into some mules, saying as she did so, 'Now don't leave Piers and as soon as Constance comes, run away as if you could not bear to stay. If you can manage somewhere to moan "Oh Lucy, how could you!" and "Piers my best friend?" it would help.'

She went through the silent foyer, pulled back the bolts softly, unfastened the chain and looked out. The cold air struck her cheeks. The street was empty. It flashed through her mind that it looked lonely. Only a black cat stalked, tail erect, from one side to the other.

She left the door open, wandered into the shrouded salon and sat down on a buttoned kissing chair, got up again and then heard a car's brakes. She met Constance coming up the steps with a small Gladstone bag in one hand and a hard little pillow in the other. There was no longer any need for control. She put out her hands, gropingly, blinded at last by the tears which rained down making pale rivulets in the bloodstains. She cried, 'Oh Constance, I am so sorry!' acting her part even then.

She was quite unaware that Charles Danement, cap tipped forward over his nose, sat watching behind the wheel of his car; or that ever after he would see her with the eyes of memory as she stood now, chinchilla thrown back, disclos-ing the blood-stained nightdress; tear-stained, tiny, holding out quivering hands to his wife. Inevitably, and as yet knowing nothing of the night's events the words came to him 'All the perfumes of Arabia will not sweeten this little hand!' Fleetingly he wondered if he should have allowed his wife to go in alone but at that moment he saw her put protective arms around the dreadful little figure, to draw her back inside. Then the door closed.

Constance stood with the small body held closely letting the storm of weeping abate. Then, as the tremors subsided, she spoke firmly, 'Lucy love, which is Piers' room? You must understand I have to go to him now.'

Lucy drew herself away. She met Constance's gentle eyes and crossed this bridge for ever by saying defiantly,

'*My* room Constance, we were sleeping together when . . . when it happened.'

The older woman caught her breath; quickly steadied and went on into the lift carrying that bag and pillow, struggling to assimilate what had been said. *Lucy! In bed with a man?* Part of her startled senses cried out that it was simply not believable, while the sophisticated part reminded her cynically, 'One never really knows', and yet, while Lucy pressed the button and the lift rose she remembered Piers' delirious mutterings and their import. This time one *did* know, unless . . . unless . . . like all her sex, even the most level-headed, she was incapable of resisting an instant conclusion. Piers was not interested in women; Lucy had never shown by as much as a fluttering eyelash that she cared a whit for any man, though God knows the child had had offers. This simply could *not* be and yet it had happened . . . or had it? With this query baying her she followed Lucy along the deep carpet on which no footfall sounded.

'In there,' Lucy pointed, 'but please Constance when you have seen him will you promise to tell me if he is going to die? Because we want,' she broke off, 'no, we *must* be married first.'

'Here,' prodded Constance's mind as she walked to the bed, 'is no tender girl dreading the loss of her lover!'

On a combined wave of revulsion and incredulity Constance bent over Piers. He opened his eyes and to her horror she saw in them a flash of pure mockery. Lucien rose from his chair and rushing past her fled into Lucy's outstretched arms.

'There, there, my darling,' she soothed, 'Piers will be all right . . . everything will be all right.'

They were still there when Constance turned, only now they were standing hand in hand as she had seen them that first time when they were children running across the lawn under the windows of her bedroom at Castle Rising.

'Hh-how is he?' Lucy stammered.

'Ill,' Constance spoke curtly. 'Where can I telephone please? And while you show me Lucy you, Lucien, must oblige me by going downstairs to the front door. I am expecting a male nurse called Tonks. In fact he should be here by now. Please bring him up as soon as he arrives and at the same time ask Uncle Charles who is sitting in the car, to go round to number 427 Harley Street and await Mr Gervaise Sanderbury, whom I am about to telephone. Ask Uncle Charles to bring him here please, then suggest he goes to his club and has some breakfast.'

Lucien stared at her vaguely. 'Now come along Lucien, pull yourself together,' she said sharply, 'do as I ask dear it is very urgent.'

He reacted to the authoritative tone and went, reluctantly. As he did so he heard Constance saying to Lucy, 'Go and take off those terrible clothes child, in your dressing room. Make yourself presentable. Soon now your staff will be awakening, and Miss Poole ... I imagine you will not wish them to see you as you are now. But before you go let me make one thing clear, I shall tell Mr Sanderbury, the specialist whom I am summoning, that Piers had his first haemorrhage in the drawing room shortly after he arrived back from dining with you and Lucien. That you and your brother chose to put him in here because it was the nearest room. Do you understand? Well, then lock your brother's door, we can say that it is a storeroom if he enquires, though there is no reason whatever why he should – one more thing, make a pot of strong tea, put milk into it and at least three lumps of sugar to each cup, then give one to Lucien, and see he drinks it. Drink the other yourself.'

'We don't like sugar in tea,' Lucy protested.

'Nor do I dear, nevertheless you will please drink one cup each. Thank you.'

When Constance and the man Tonks had done all that they could for Piers, she sat down to wait beside him and Tonks went down to keep an eye on the front door and await the arrival of the specialist.

Now that the first impact of Lucy's appalling statement had penetrated, Constance's instinct began to stir. From it grew the conviction that all was not anyway what she was required to believe. The more she thought and remembered, the more she doubted the truth of Lucy's admission. There was a very false note to it. She and Piers could not have been in bed together while Lucien slept across the corridor. It could not be so. There had to be lies in it somewhere. She knew what Piers was by his own delirious revelations. In the light of such knowledge was it really possible that in the past she had been completely wrong? She doubted it.

There was nothing to indicate any passionate emotion between them; only the disturbing mockery in those penetrating blue eyes which Lucy called Piers' 'headlamps'.

She looked at him again, startled to find the 'headlamps' directed fully upon her.

'Am I about to die Lady Constance?' he asked, 'even before I have time to lead my bride to the altar.'

He shocked her, although she pitied him. Even so, 'I think not,' she replied calmly enough, 'but I believe if you two wish to be married immediately it will have to be from your bed. We must, of course, wait until we have heard what Mr Gervaise has to say. I have sent for him and he promises to be here shortly. My husband has gone to fetch him in our car.'

'I am much more interested in what you have to say,' Piers told her.

'Then stop trying to talk and I will tell you. I think you have ill-used yourself shamefully, both physically and emotionally. You smoke too much, probably drink too much, rampage in fact. I believe you are very ill. If it was my decision I should keep you in bed for a month and then take you to a man in Switzerland.'

She saw a flicker of interest in those over-brilliant eyes, so continued, 'He is a genius whose name is Spahlinger. A tiny little man with an enormous brain and a great sense of humour. You would enjoy him. He has done wonderful work with lung cases already. Indeed the world is beginning to recognise him as the foremost man in this field. Since we are alone, and I am a trained nurse I believe I should tell you that your marriage must be one in name only for some time to come, that you must give up smoking, and never again drink to excess. Given these undertakings from you I believe you may still live to a ripe old age.'

The whisper came again, ruefully, 'No wine, women or smokes!'

'Exactly – a small price to pay for living I would say.'

Silence lay between them for several minutes. She thought he was deliberating what she had told him. Instead he spoke two words, making them a question. 'You know?'

Despite her self-control the unwelcome colour flooded to her cheeks. 'I am afraid so,' she spoke quietly, 'but why this?'

'One wonders, does one not?' he mused. Then as they

both heard voices outside he added, 'I cannot help wondering, if you are wrong and I do die, if she will marry the next
one as well.'

The verdict was exactly as Lady Constance had predicted.
The great man came, pronounced, departed. Constance
telephoned to Eustace whom she knew was at his club, told
him what she thought he should know and required of him a
private ambulance within an hour. It came in twenty
minutes with Eustace Bartonbury inside it. Frank Stone
drove, two ambulance men lifted Piers into a slope-backed
wheel chair, conveyed him to the lift and down into the hall.
They then laid him on a stretcher, carried him out into the
street and were away so speedily that no crowd collected. As
the ambulance vanished round the corner into Bond Street
the sunburst clock in the salon registered eight am.

As Piers went out of the front door, so two cleaning
women rang the staff bell at the mews entrance. They stood
gossiping while they waited for the door to be unlocked; by
which time Lucien lay sound asleep on his own bed with the
door locked on the inside, at Lucy's instructions, a notice
hanging from the doorhandle stating *do not disturb!*

Constance had also gone with Piers in the ambulance.
Presently, as she explained to Lucy, she would return to
make several telephone calls. In the meantime would Lucy
please telephone Piers' parents, give them the name of the
nursing home, break the news as gently as she could and ask
them to come round to the mews house as soon as they
could.

'Then, my dear, you can tell them yourself that you and
Piers intend marrying as soon as possible.'

Lucy steeled herself to meet the onslaughts of this terrible
day. She had no qualms whatever at what she had chosen to
do. She merely awaited a holocaust only to find that she was
not only enmeshed in love and sympathy, warmth and, of
course, total misunderstanding; but through these misin-
terpretations of her intention to marry Piers she was shocked
to discover herself being regarded as an heroic figure. She
found it much harder to endure than all the rest.

Miss Poole felt as if the ground upon which she stood was
falling away beneath her feet when she learned that Piers had
been taken seriously ill during the night and that he and
Lucy were to be married just as soon as his medical advisers
would allow the ceremony to take place. She became in

turn, bewildered, dreadfully uneasy and finally convinced that she faced only two alternatives. Either she must accept that all her anxieties had been groundless, erroneously based on what she imagined she had read into Lucien's behaviour, first with Piers and then, later, during Piers' absence in India with 'that Simon', as she thought of him. Otherwise she would have to accept that her instincts had not been at fault and there was something dreadful which they were all at pains to conceal under the cloak of this marriage and that no tender and compassionate love had ever existed between the pair of them. She was torn between those old fears of quite a different kind of shock lying in wait for little Lucy one day which was painful enough; or else she must acknowledge that all her previous conclusions had been imaginary. This she found even harder to accept. Finally she sought refuge in what she felt would be the conventional attitude to be most acceptable from her in the position she held in this unusual household.

She went to Lucy and in her normal, briskly efficient, matter of fact way said, 'Now Lady Lucy, the first thing we must all do is to see that you get as much rest as possible. First let me say though that I firmly believe that dear, brilliant young man will recover completely. So, may I wish you both many years of happiness together once Mr Fournes has been restored to health.' That night when she lay in her bed the fact of Annanias sounded loud and clear.   Lucy sat dumbly while the kind words flowed over her. It had never touched her thoughts that everyone around her would invest what she had chosen to do with an aura of great romance and tenderness.

The next was Eustace, who came hurrying round to take her in his arms and tell her, 'My dearest child how cruel it is that you two should have found each other in this way only to have Piers stricken with a terrible illness. You must let me do everything in my power to help. We will make sure Piers has the finest attention in the world and then put our trust in the Almighty that he will be benevolent to you both. Such a gallant, brilliant young man. I shall be proud to call him my son-in-law.'

Lucy with her head on her father's shoulder and her cheeks burning only wanted to shriek out the truth, to do anything, but anything, to stop these awful condolences, this dreadful kindness. Only fear held her back and the one sustaining thought that came from all these kind people's immediate and unquestioning acceptance of the situation. It was exactly as she had intended they should react to make Lucien safe.

She choked back emotion. She stifled her conscience. She forced herself to go on; but it took its toll. In that first twenty-four hours she shed the last of her girlhood like a chrysalis, while remaining externally as youthful as when she first met Piers.

Sissy came to her, tears raining unashamedly, to stammer, 'Bbless you, ffor your ccompassion. It wwwill be all right, I know it will. So I only want to wish yyou eevery happiness when Mr Piers is well aagain.'

The Catholic staff burned candles for him. The Protestants went in their lunch hour to St Martin-in-the Fields to pray for him. The evening papers carried the news in the early edition: 'Famous painter gravely ill on eve of engagement' and 'Lady Lucy St John will wed famous painter Mr Piers Fournes at his bedside.'

Lady Lucy had told them nothing; but this suited very well. Miss Poole then stationed herself at the telephone switchboard and coped with the press. Eustace Barton-bury stood by the door, handling the representatives who swarmed outside. Clients came, with flowers, until there was no room for more so Elizabeth filled the Royce with them and took them to various hospitals.

Mr and Mrs Fournes rubbed salt into Lucy's wounds when they came after their consultation with the specialist. He expressed the view that the proposed marriage could only do good by giving his patient added incentive towards recovery. He confirmed that he was writing immediately to the great Dr Spahlinger to whose clinic he hoped to send their son in approximately one month.

They were tender to Lucy and manifestly delighted.

'We had so hoped my dear; but at times we feared you did not care sufficiently for our son. Now you have shown us that you care so very much.' They gave her the album of photographs which they had kept since Piers was born, 'To keep you in reminder of him during this sad separation.'

Piers' father drew a slim box from his pocket, opened it and insisted on clasping the pearls inside it around her throat himself.

Her eyes became larger, her face more pointed as the

hours went by until Constance, who knew too much and as ever was condemned to keep her own counsel, insisted she take a sedative in order to get some sleep.

Before this, however, Gyles and Christine were ushered into the drawing room with only just enough warning for Constance to conceal herself which she felt compelled to do, lest they question her presence and Lucy's reasons for sending for her.

From time to time, while the staff worked on downstairs, Lucy unlocked Lucien's door and went in locking it again behind her with her duplicate key. He slept throughout the day; but when she went in after the staff had gone, he woke up, put his arms out to her. She drew him close, cuddling him like a child.

'It's all right my darling,' she soothed him. 'Piers is safely in a nursing home. No one knows anything. You are perfectly safe.'

He nestled even closer, 'But Lucy,' he said, 'what about you?'

She stroked his untidy curls. 'Well what about me? I shall marry Piers in a few days. There are some complications about a licence I believe; but then he will go to Switzerland to get well again and we shall be together exactly as before.'

Lucien pulled back, eyes clouded, 'But when he comes back again Lucy-Lou?'

'We shall take a separate house near here. Because of safeguarding Piers' health, which we must always do, I shall have my own rooms, and you will, of course, live with us. We will always be together, that I can promise you.'

He looked at her searchingly, then suddenly his head went down, 'Lucy-Lou?'

'Yes my love.'

'Lucy-Lou I'm sorry,' he said, 'I suppose it must be the nature of myself. Are you sure you don't mind terribly?'

Lucy drew him back into the shelter of her arms.

'Just remember darling that what makes you happy always makes me happy too. Hasn't it always been like that?'

'Yyes, I suppose so,' he was still doubtful, and for the first time ashamed. 'This is a bit different though isn't it?'

'I made it so,' she reminded him.

'Well then that's all right isn't it, if you say so? We can go on being the same for ever and ever.'

'For ever and ever,' she repeated and suddenly she was no

longer ravaged by it all though it did seem a pity that Piers had chosen such a time to have a haemorrhage.

The verdict of the great world, their fashionable one, was expressed by little dabs with wispy handkerchieves and exclamations of 'So sad' ... 'such a beautiful, gifted couple!' ... and 'it only shows one cannot have everything in this life', which satisfied Lucy. In the ensuing days before the wedding she not only worked as hard as ever but she worked when her day in the salon and workrooms was over, rehearsing herself ... for the wedding.

Piers found the clergyman, a young man, recently in holy orders whom he knew very well; a fashionable young man who only had to appear in his West End pulpit for every society woman to crowd his church, swelling the offertory bags because he was so very charming.

Lucien knew him and Lucy too. Piers sent him a note. He then went round to the nursing home and because he was astute enough to assume his dog collar, although he rarely wore it socially, he was admitted with the strict injunctions from the matron, 'Five minutes only please, my patient is not allowed to receive any visitors at present.'

Piers managed in the time to give him a further duty to execute for which he handed over a signed, blank cheque and a drawing. When the matron reappeared the Reverend Desmond McCarthy had stashed both cheque and sketch into the slim case he carried. These he then took to Asprey's where he ordered Lucy's engagement ring. Three sapphires of the very first quality, held by a knot of platinum to a narrow platinum band. He also required the frock-coated individual who attended him as if he were the Primate, to send round to Piers a selection of platinum wedding rings.

'Could they,' he asked earnestly, 'send someone that afternoon and would it then be possible when Mr Fournes had made his selection to have three words engraved inside very speedily?'

All this was both promised and done. So Piers chose Lucy's wedding ring and handed over a paper with the three words written upon it which were to be engraved inside. *Toujours à trois.*

Propped up by pillows and wearing a very splendid dressing jacket Piers took Lucy to be his wedded wife from his bed in the nursing home. Sinclair gave the bride away.

Lucien was the best man. Mrs Fournes wept copiously throughout the ceremony. Both Eustace and Edward Fournes blew noses vehemently when all was done and it was not until the couple were left alone for half an hour that Lucy said to her husband, 'I'm glad you chose this engagement ring. It symbolises what our marriage means to us doesn't it?'

He smiled at her, brilliantly, 'Exactly, and now may I hope that our *à trois* relationship will be full of the fun, laughter and understanding that we have shared together for so long now.'

He picked up her left hand, kissed it gently and added, 'You know, don't you, Lucy that I fell in love with you the moment you came into the Rest Room all those years ago. You wore a blue velvet dress, with a sash around your waist and I thought you were the most beautiful thing I had ever seen.'

'I was afraid of that later on,' she admitted.

'I still love you Lucy in my own way, but the other happens to be stronger. Can you understand?'

Lucy hesitated. 'I do and I don't,' she admitted. 'Piers, promise me something and it will all have been worth while.' The words came suddenly in a rush. He sensed the urgency and just gripped the hand he still held and waited.

'Be good to Lucien always, promise me that and I will be very happy.'

'I promise,' he said gravely, 'what a strange marriage this is little one! Tell me will you come to see me when I go to Switzerland?'

She widened her eyes. 'Of course I will, and I will write you a long letter every week with all the gossip in and what everyone has said and done; but I cannot promise to bring Lucien. You do understand don't you?' She tilted her head in the way she had which he had always found so endearing.

'It's just that ... well *they* say, particularly Constance, that to get well quickly you must not be excited and while I know I cannot excite you, I am not so sure that Lucien would not, and we both so want you to get well.'

He looked at her strangely, as she reminded herself later, with those headlamps blazing and she was astonished to see slow tears slipping down his sunken face.

'Oh Lucy,' he said, 'if only it could have been different!'

She stared at him – her wide blue eyes blank and uncomprehending. She opened her pochette, took out a wisp of handkerchief and bent over him to wipe the tears away; but no way could she find a single thing to say. Providentially the nurse rustled in to 'take my lovely little bride from her groom so that dear Mr Fournes may rest a little'.

She was tender, solicitous, but as uncomprehending in her romantic sympathy as Lucy was in her bewilderment. However, she followed the nurse thankfully, just pressing Piers' hand as she left. Her mind was chaotic, 'How could it be different,' she thought, 'when he is what he is and even if he weren't I would still be what I am', and even this query lightened the moment for her as now *her Lucien would be safe* and therefore whatever else happened this would always be what mattered to her most.

For Piers there was one more interview before he was taken away from them all into the isolation of his treatment. Lucien of course stayed away as he always did from anything which was not made easy and amusing for him. Illness terrified him, indeed sickness in any form was anathema; so all he saw now was that *he* was safe and that Lucy had done again what she had always been relied upon to do.

Not for a single moment did it occur to him at what dreadful price would be paid by his sister for what she had brought about. He just ran down the steps of the nursing home when the simple ceremony was complete, hailed a taxi and told the cabbie to take him to the theatre where his latest 'friend' was resting after his matinée. He, characteristically, as Lucien stared into his dressing-room, demanded rather shrilly, 'Does this mean that the Piers piece is off to Switzerland? Because I warn you, Lucien, I will not be second fiddle to anyone any more, so you may as well face the fact it's me or nothing from now on.'

Lucien pouted, 'Then you, darling,' he answered, rearranging a curl and simultaneously admiring his own reflection in the actor's looking-glass. 'Where are you taking me to supper after the show tonight?'

Henry was waiting to see Piers. Christine and Gyles had sent him under duress, and as a matter of form, plus what Gyles dismissed as 'common courtesy'. Gyles added as a rider, since by this time Christine had left them, and he was at his most majesterial, 'And any distasteful possibilities we may have discussed in the past must now be expunged from our memories with ignominy since from now onwards Piers is your cousin Lucy's husband. I trust, Henry, that you fully understand me?'

'Yessir' said Henry mournfully, making chaos of his hair as usual. 'I – er – quite understand, sir.'

Thus it was that he walked into the clinical room with its widely opened windows, outwardly presenting the picture of an elegant man about town from double-breasted jacket to wide trousers with the turn-ups which had invoked from his Monarch, King George the Fifth, the immortal query, when he had seen the like for the first time on the legs of his sons David and George, 'Dear me, is it raining? I had no idea.'

Outwardly, too, Henry was suitably quiet and suitably languid as he set down his bowler, gloves and stick. Inwardly he felt faintly sick and only just able to control his rising anger and disgust at what he would not in any way condone nor understand either.

'Hallo, old boy,' he managed, 'rotten show – come to commiserate, and of course to congratulate.' His voice trailed away.

Piers focussed on him with an effort. The room was beginning to blur and he was poised on a razor's edge of exhaustion.

'How very kind, Henry,' he dragged the words out. 'Lucy is a darling and I am unbelievably fortunate, I am sure you will agree?'

It was at this moment that Henry's scarcely leashed control snapped. 'Well now,' he drawled, hitting at the crease in his trousers. 'There are extentuating circumstances' and at this the red rage of the Lorme temper veiled for him the heinousness of what he then said. 'After all, old boy,' the drawl was now deadly, 'If I am right on my current information you did fall in love with my cousin Lucy *first*, did you not?'